The 13 Crimes
of Science Fiction

The 13 Crimes of Science Fiction

EDITED BY ISAAC ASIMOV,
MARTIN HARRY GREENBERG,
AND CHARLES G. WAUGH

1979
DOUBLEDAY & COMPANY, INC.
GARDEN CITY, NEW YORK

All of the characters in this book are fictitious,
and any resemblance to actual persons,
living or dead,
is purely coincidental.

Library of Congress Cataloging in Publication Data
Main entry under title:
The 13 crimes of science fiction.
CONTENTS: Asimov, I. The universe of science
fiction.—Reamy, T. The Detweiler boy.—Garrett, R.
The Ipswich phial. [etc.]
1. Science fiction, American. 2. Detective
and mystery stories, American. I. Asimov, Isaac,
1920-   II. Greenberg, Martin Harry. III. Waugh, Charles.
PZ1.T3445   [PS648.S3]   813'.0876
ISBN: 0-385-15220-5
Library of Congress Catalog Card Number 78-22762

ACKNOWLEDGMENT

Many thanks to Frank D. McSherry, Jr., for his several suggestions.

"The Detweiler Boy" by Tom Reamy, copyright © 1977 by Mercury Press,
Inc. Reprinted from *The Magazine of Fantasy and Science Fiction* by per-
mission of Virginia Kidd, agent for the author's estate.
"The Ipswich Phial" by Randall Garrett, copyright © 1976 by Condé Nast
Publications, Inc. Reprinted by permission of the author and the author's
agent, Scott Meredith Literary Agency, Inc., 845 Third Avenue, New York,
NY 10022.
"Second Game" by Charles V. De Vet and Katherine MacLean, copyright ©
1958 by Street and Smith Publications. Reprinted by permission of the
authors.
"The Ceaseless Stone" by Avram Davidson, copyright © 1975 by Avram David-
son. Reprinted by permission of the author and the author's agent, Mc-
Cauley, Blassingame and Wood.
"Coup de Grace" by Jack Vance, copyright © 1958 by Headline Publications,
Inc. Originally titled "Worlds of Origin." Reprinted by permission of the
author and the author's agent, Scott Meredith Literary Agency, Inc., 845
Third Avenue, New York, NY 10022.
"The Green Car" by William F. Temple, copyright © 1957 by Nova Publica-
tions, Ltd. Reprinted by permission of the author's agent, Forrest J. Acker-
man, 2495 Glendower Avenue, Hollywood, CA 90027.

Contents

The Universe of Science Fiction

ISAAC ASIMOV

Science fiction is a literary universe of no mean size, because science fiction is what it is, not through its content, but through its background. Let me explain the difference that makes.

A "sports story" must have, as part of its content, some competitive activity, generally of an athletic nature. A "Western story" must have, as part of its content, the nomadic life of the cowboy of the American West in the latter half of the nineteenth century. The "jungle story" must have, as part of its content, the dangers implicit in a forested tropical wilderness.

Take the content of any of these and place it against a background that involves a society significantly different from our own and you have not changed the nature of the story—you have merely added to it.

A story may involve, not the clash of baseball and bat, or of hockey stick and puck, but of gas gun and sphere in an atmosphere enclosed on a space station under zero gravity. It is still a sports story by the strictest definition you care to make, but it is science fiction *also*.

In place of the nomadic life of a cowboy and his horse, herding cattle, you might have the nomadic life of a fishboy and his dolphin, herding his schools of mackerel and cod. It could still have the essence of a Western story, and be science fiction *also*.

In place of the Matto Grosso, you can have the jungle on a distant planet, different in key factors of the environment, with exotic dangers in atmosphere, in vegetation, in planetary characteristics never encountered on Earth. It would still be a jungle story, and be science fiction *also*.

For that matter, you needn't confine yourself to category fiction. Take the deepest novel you can imagine, one that most amply plumbs the secret recesses of the soul and that holds up a picture that illuminates nature and the human condition, and place it in a society in which interplanetary travel is common, and give it a plot that involves such travel, and it is not only great literature—it is science fiction *also*.

John W. Campbell, the late great science fiction editor, used to say that science fiction took as its domain all conceivable societies, past and future, probable or improbable, realistic or fantastic, and dealt with all events and complications that were possible in all those societies. As for "mainstream fiction," which deals with the here and now and introduces only the small novelty of make-believe events and characters, that forms only an inconsiderable fraction of the whole.

And I agree with him.

In only one respect did John retreat from this grand vision of the limitless boundaries of science fiction. In a moment of failure of nerve, he maintained that it was impossible to write a science fiction mystery. The opportunities in science fiction were so broad, he said, that the strict rules that made the classical mystery story fair to the reader could not be upheld.

I imagine that what he expected was the sudden change of rules without warning in the midst of the story. Something like this, I suppose—

"Ah, Watson, what that scoundrel did not count on was that with this pocket-frannistan which I have in my pocket-frannistan container I can see through the lead lining and tell what is inside the casket."

"Amazing, Holmes, but how does it work?"

"By the use of Q-rays, a little discovery of my own which I have never revealed to the world."

Naturally, there is the temptation to do this. Even in the classical mystery story that is not science fiction there is the temptation to give the detective extraordinary abilities in order to advance the plot. Sherlock Holmes' ability to distinguish, at sight, the ashes of hundreds of different kinds of tobacco, while not perhaps in the same class as the invention of a Q-ray at a moment's notice, is certainly a step in the direction of the unfair.

Then, too, there is nothing to prevent even the strictest of strict mystery writers from using actual science, even from using the latest available findings of science, which the reader may not have heard of. That is still considered fair.

There are dangers to that, however, since many mystery writers know no science and cannot prevent themselves from making bloopers. John Dickson Carr in one book revealed that he didn't know the difference between the element antimony and the compound antimony potassium tartrate. That was only irritating, but in another book, he demonstrated that he couldn't tell the difference between carbon monoxide and carbon dioxide, and reduced the plot to a shambles. One of Dorothy Sayers' more grisly short stories involved the effect of thyroid hormones, and, though she had the right idea, she made the effects impossibly rapid and extreme.

Writing a scientific mystery, then, has its extraordinary pitfalls and difficulties; how much more so the writing of a science fiction mystery. In science fiction, you not only must know your science, but you must also have a rational notion as to how to modify or extrapolate that science.

That, however, only means that writing a science fiction mystery is difficult; it does *not* mean that it is conceptually impossible as John Campbell thought.

After all, it is as perfectly possible to cling to the rules of the game in science fiction mysteries as in ordinary ones.

The science fiction mystery may be set in the future and in the midst of a society far different from ours, one in which human beings have developed telepathy, for instance, or in which light-speed mass transport is possible, or in which all human knowledge is computerized for instant retrieval—but the rules still hold.

The writer must carefully explain to the reader all the boundary conditions of the imaginary society. It must be perfectly clear what can be done and what can't be done, and with those boundaries fixed, the reader must then see and hear everything the investigator sees and hears, and he must be aware of every clue the investigator comes across.

There may be misdirection and red herrings to obscure and confuse, but it must remain possible for the reader to out-deduce the investigator, however outré the society.

Can it be done? You bet! Modestly, I refer you to my own science fiction mysteries, *The Caves of Steel* and *The Naked Sun*, which I wrote, back in the 1950s, in order to show John that he was being too modest about science fiction.

If, however, you don't care to rush out and buy those books at this moment, why not consider the book you actually have in your hand. Read through it and see how every type of mystery—and not merely the classical puzzle—can be found within the universe of science fiction.

If you like science fiction, or if you like mystery, and especially if you like both—read and enjoy.

Hard-Boiled
Detective

The 1920s brought new vitality to the detective story. Pulp magazines such as *Black Mask* and writers such as Carroll John Daly and Dashiell Hammett developed the concept of the hard-boiled detective. He was usually found in the mean streets rather than the country manor, his crimes typically involved the underbelly of society, and his solutions normally depended more on provocation and legwork than analysis.

Since forceful, active protagonists characterize the mainstream of science fiction, it would seem to provide a natural home for hard-boiled detectives, and yet it does not. There are several delightful parodies skewering Mickey Spillane, several stories by Keith Laumer, and then virtually nothing. Talented Tom Reamy might have filled this void with his propensity for crime stories and his Chandler-like skill with analogy and description. But we shall never know, for he was one of our field's most tragic losses, struck down by a heart attack after completing only a handful of stories.

The Detweiler Boy

TOM REAMY

The room had been cleaned with pine oil disinfectant and smelled like a public toilet. Harry Spinner was on the floor behind the bed, scrunched down between it and the wall. The almost colorless chenille bedspread had been pulled askew exposing part of the clean, but dingy, sheet. All I could see of Harry was one leg poking over the edge of the bed. He wasn't wearing a shoe, only a faded brown and tan argyle sock with a hole in it. The sock, long bereft of any elasticity, was crumpled around his thin rusty ankle.

I closed the door quietly behind me and walked around the end of the bed so I could see all of him. He was huddled on his back with his elbows propped up by the wall and the bed. His throat had been cut. The blood hadn't spread very far. Most of it had been soaked up by the threadbare carpet under the bed. I looked around the grubby little room but didn't find anything. There were no signs of a struggle, no signs of forced entry—but then, my Bank-Americard hadn't left any signs either. The window was open, letting in the muffled roar of traffic on the Boulevard. I stuck my head out and looked, but it was three stories straight down to the neon-lit marquee of the movie house.

It had been nearly two hours since Harry called me. "Bertram, my boy, I've run across something very peculiar. I don't really know what to make of it."

I had put away the report I was writing on Lucas McGowan's hyperactive wife. (She had a definite predilection for gas-pump jockeys, car-wash boys, and parking-lot attendants. I guess it had something to do with the Age of the Automobile.) I propped my feet on my desk and leaned back until the old swivel chair groaned a protest.

"What did you find this time, Harry? A nest of international spies or an invasion from Mars?" I guess Harry Spinner wasn't much use to anyone, not even himself, but I liked him. He'd helped me in a couple of cases, nosing around in places only the Harry Spinners of the world can nose around in unnoticed. I was beginning to get the idea he was trying to play Doctor Watson to my Sherlock Holmes.

"Don't tease me, Bertram. There's a boy here in the hotel. I saw something I don't think he wanted me to see. It's extremely odd."

Harry was also the only person in the world, except my mother, who called me Bertram. "What did you see?"

"I'd rather not talk about it over the phone. Can you come over?"

Harry saw too many old private-eye movies on the late show. "It'll be a while. I've got a client coming in in a few minutes to pick up the poop on his wandering wife."

"Bertram, you shouldn't waste your time and talent on divorce cases."

"It pays the bills, Harry. Besides, there aren't enough Maltese falcons to go around."

By the time I filled Lucas McGowan in on all the details (I got the impression he was less concerned with his wife's infidelity than with her taste; that it wouldn't have been so bad if she'd been shacking up with movie stars or international playboys), collected my fee, and grabbed a Thursday special at Colonel Sanders, almost two hours had passed. Harry hadn't answered my knock, and so I let myself in with a credit card.

Birdie Pawlowicz was a fat, slovenly old broad somewhere between forty and two hundred. She was blind in her right eye and wore a black felt patch over it. She claimed she had lost the eye in a fight with a Creole whore over a riverboat gambler. I believed her. She ran the Brewster Hotel the way Florence Nightingale must have run that stinking army hospital in the Crimea. Her tenants were the losers habitating that rotting section of the Boulevard east of the Hollywood Freeway. She bossed them, cursed them, loved them, and took care of them. And they loved her back. (Once, a couple of years ago, a young black buck thought an old fat lady with one eye would be easy pickings. The cops found him three days later, two blocks away, under some rubbish in an alley where he'd hidden. He had a broken arm, two cracked ribs, a busted nose, a few missing teeth, and was stone-dead from internal hemorrhaging.)

The Brewster ran heavily in the red, but Birdie didn't mind. She had quite a bit of property in Westwood which ran very, very heavily in the black. She gave me an obscene leer as I approached the desk, but her good eye twinkled.

"Hello, lover!" she brayed in a voice like a cracked boiler. "I've lowered my price to a quarter. Are you interested?" She saw my face and her expression shifted from lewd to wary. "What's wrong, Bert?"

"Harry Spinner. You'd better get the cops, Birdie. Somebody killed him."

She looked at me, not saying anything, her face slowly collapsing into an infinitely weary resignation. Then she turned and telephoned the police.

Because it was just Harry Spinner at the Brewster Hotel on the wrong end of Hollywood Boulevard, the cops took over half an hour to get there. While we waited I told Birdie everything I knew, about the phone call and what I'd found.

"He must have been talking about the Detweiler boy," she said, frowning. "Harry's been kinda friendly with him, felt sorry for him, I guess."

"What's his room? I'd like to talk to him."

"He checked out."

"When?"

"Just before you came down."

"Damn!"

She bit her lip. "I don't think the Detweiler boy killed him."

"Why?"

"I just don't think he could. He's such a gentle boy."

"Oh, Birdie," I groaned, "you know there's no such thing as a killer type. Almost anyone will kill with a good enough reason."

"I know," she sighed, "but I still can't believe it." She tapped her scarlet fingernails on the dulled Formica desk top. "How long had Harry been dead?"

He had phoned me about ten after five. I had found the body at seven. "A while," I said. "The blood was mostly dry."

"Before six-thirty?"

"Probably."

She sighed again, but this time with relief. "The Detweiler boy was down here with me until six thirty. He'd been here since about four fifteen. We were playing gin. He was having one of his spells and wanted company."

"What kind of spell? Tell me about him, Birdie."

"But he couldn't have killed Harry," she protested.

"Okay," I said, but I wasn't entirely convinced. Why would anyone deliberately and brutally murder inoffensive, invisible Harry Spinner right after he told me he had discovered something "peculiar" about the Detweiler boy? Except the Detweiler boy?

"Tell me anyway. If he and Harry were friendly, he might know something. Why do you keep calling him a boy; how old is he?"

She nodded and leaned her bulk on the registration desk. "Early twenties, twenty-two, twenty-three, maybe. Not very tall, about five five or six. Slim, dark curly hair, a real good-looking boy. Looks like a movie star except for his back."

"His back?"

"He has a hump. He's a hunchback."

That stopped me for a minute, but I'm not sure why. I must've had a mental picture of Charles Laughton riding those bells or Igor stealing that brain from the laboratory. "He's good-looking and he's a hunchback?"

"Sure." She raised her eyebrows. The one over the patch didn't go up as high as the other. "If you see him from the front, you can't even tell."

"What's his first name?"

"Andrew."

"How long has he been living here?"

She consulted a file card. "He checked in last Friday night. The 22nd. Six days."

"What's this spell he was having?"

"I don't know for sure. It was the second one he'd had. He would get pale and nervous. I think he was in a lot of pain. It would get worse and worse all day; then he'd be fine, all rosy and healthy-looking."

"Sounds to me like he was hurtin' for a fix."

"I thought so at first, but I changed my mind. I've seen enough of that and it wasn't the same. Take my word. He was real bad this evening. He came down about four fifteen, like I said. He didn't complain, but I could tell he was wantin' company to take his mind off it. We played gin until six thirty. Then he went back upstairs.

About twenty minutes later he came down with his old suitcase and checked out. He looked fine, all over his spell."

"Did he have a doctor?"

"I'm pretty sure he didn't. I asked him about it. He said there was nothing to worry about, it would pass. And it did."

"Did he say why he was leaving or where he was going?"

"No, just said he was restless and wanted to be movin' on. Sure hated to see him leave. A real nice kid."

When the cops finally got there, I told them all I knew—except I didn't mention the Detweiler boy. I hung around until I found out that Harry almost certainly wasn't killed after six thirty. They set the time somewhere between five ten, when he called me, and six. It looked like Andrew Detweiler was innocent, but what "peculiar" thing had Harry noticed about him, and why had he moved out right after Harry was killed? Birdie let me take a look at his room, but I didn't find a thing, not even an abandoned paperclip.

Friday morning I sat at my desk trying to put the pieces together. Trouble was, I only had two pieces and *they* didn't fit. The sun was coming in off the Boulevard, shining through the window, projecting the chipping letters painted on the glass against the wall in front of me. BERT MALLORY Confidential Investigations. I got up and looked out. This section of the Boulevard wasn't rotting yet, but it wouldn't be long.

There's one sure gauge for judging a part of town: the movie theaters. It never fails. For instance, a new picture hadn't opened in downtown L.A. in a long, long time. The action ten years ago was on the Boulevard. Now it's in Westwood. The grand old Pantages, east of Vine and too near the freeway, used to be the site of the most glittering premieres. They even had the Oscar ceremonies there for a while. Now it shows exploitation and double-feature horror films. Only Grauman's Chinese and the once Paramount, once Loew's, now Downtown Cinema (or something) at the west end got good openings. The Nu-View, across the street and down, was showing an X-rated double feature. It was too depressing. So I closed the blind.

Miss Tremaine looked up from her typing at the rattle and frowned. Her desk was out in the small reception area, but I had arranged both desks so we could see each other and talk in normal voices when the door was open. It stayed open most of the time except when I had a client who felt secretaries shouldn't know his troubles. She had been transcribing the Lucas McGowan report for half an hour, *humphing* and *tsk-tsking* at thirty-second intervals. She was having a marvelous time. Miss Tremaine was about forty-five, looked like a constipated librarian, and was the best secretary I'd ever had. She'd been with me seven years. I'd tried a few young and sexy ones, but it hadn't worked out. Either they wouldn't play at all, or they wanted to play all the time. Both kinds were a pain in the ass to face first thing in the morning, every morning.

"Miss Tremaine, will you get Gus Verdugo on the phone, please?"

"Yes, Mr. Mallory." She dialed the phone nimbly, sitting as if she were wearing a back brace.

Gus Verdugo worked in R&I. I had done him a favor once, and he insisted on returning it tenfold. I gave him everything I had on Andrew Detweiler and asked him if he'd mind running it through the computer. He wouldn't mind. He called back in fifteen minutes. The computer had never heard of Andrew Detweiler and had only seven hunchbacks, none of them fitting Detweiler's description.

I was sitting there, wondering how in hell I would find him, when the phone rang again. Miss Tremaine stopped typing and lifted the receiver without breaking rhythm. "Mr. Mallory's office," she said crisply, really letting the caller know he'd hooked onto an efficient organization. She put her hand over the mouthpiece and looked at me. "It's for you—an obscene phone call." She didn't bat an eyelash or twitch a muscle.

"Thanks," I said and winked at her. She dropped the receiver back on the cradle from a height of three inches and went back to typing. Grinning, I picked up my phone. "Hello, Janice," I said.

"Just a minute till my ear stops ringing," the husky voice tickled my ear.

"What are you doing up this early?" I asked. Janice Fenwick was an exotic dancer at a club on the Strip nights and was working on her master's in oceanography at UCLA in the afternoons. In the year I'd known her I'd seldom seen her stick her nose into the sunlight before eleven.

"I had to catch you before you started following that tiresome woman with the car."

"I've finished that. She's picked up her last parking-lot attendant —at least with this husband," I chuckled.

"I'm glad to hear it."

"What's up?"

"I haven't had an indecent proposition from you in days. So I thought I'd make one of my own."

"I'm all ears."

"We're doing some diving off Catalina tomorrow. Want to come along?"

"Not much we can do in a wetsuit."

"The wetsuit comes off about four; then we'll have Saturday night and all of Sunday."

"Best indecent proposition I've had all week."

Miss Tremaine *humphed*. It might have been over something in the report, but I don't think it was.

I picked up Janice at her apartment in Westwood early Saturday morning. She was waiting for me and came striding out to the car all legs and healthy golden flesh. She was wearing white shorts, sneakers, and that damned Dallas Cowboys jersey. It was authentic. The name and number on it were quite well-known—even to non-football fans. She wouldn't tell me how she got it, just smirked and looked smug. She tossed her suitcase in the back seat and slid up against me. She smelled like sunshine.

We flew over and spent most of the day *glubbing* around in the Pacific with a bunch of kids fifteen years younger than I and five years younger than Janice. I'd been on these jaunts with Janice before and enjoyed them so much I'd bought my own wetsuit. But I didn't enjoy it nearly as much as I did Saturday night and all of Sunday.

I got back to my apartment on Beachwood fairly late Sunday night and barely had time to get something to eat at the Mexican restaurant around the corner on Melrose. They have marvelous carne asada. I live right across the street from Paramount, right across from the door people go in to see them tape *The Odd Couple*. Every Friday night when I see them lining up out there, I think I might go someday, but I never seem to get around to it. (You might think I'd see a few movie stars living where I do, but I haven't. I did see Seymour occasionally when he worked at Channel 9, before he went to work for Gene Autry at Channel 5.)

I was so pleasantly pooped I completely forgot about Andrew Detweiler. Until Monday morning when I was sitting at my desk reading the *Times*.

It was a small story on page three, not very exciting or newsworthy. Last night a man named Maurice Milian, age 51, had fallen through the plate-glass doors leading onto the terrace of the high rise where he lived. He had been discovered about midnight when the people living below him had noticed dried blood on *their* terrace. The only thing to connect the deaths of Harry Spinner and Maurice Milian was a lot of blood flowing around. If Milian had been murdered, there *might* be a link, however tenuous. But Milian's death was accidental—a dumb, stupid accident. It niggled around in my brain for an hour before I gave in. There was only one way to get it out of my head.

"Miss Tremaine, I'll be back in an hour or so. If any slinky blondes come in wanting me to find their kid sisters, tell 'em to wait."

She *humphed* again and ignored me.

The Almsbury was half a dozen blocks away on Yucca. So I walked. It was a rectangular monolith about eight stories tall, not real new, not too old, but expensive-looking. The small terraces protruded in neat, orderly rows. The long, narrow grounds were immaculate with a lot of succulents that looked like they might have been imported from Mars. There were also the inevitable palm trees and clumps of bird of paradise. A small, discrete, polished placard dangled in a wrought-iron frame proclaiming, ever so softly, NO VACANCY.

Two willowy young men gave me appraising glances in the carpeted lobby as they exited into the sunlight like exotic jungle birds. It's one of those, I thought. My suspicions were confirmed when I looked over the tenant directory. All the names seemed to be male, but none of them was Andrew Detweiler.

Maurice Milian was still listed as 407. I took the elevator to four and rang the bell of 409. The bell played a few notes of Bach, or maybe Vivaldi or Telemann. All those old Baroques sound alike to me. The vision of loveliness who opened the door was about forty, almost as slim as Twiggy, but as tall as I. He wore a flowered silk shirt open to the waist, exposing his bony hairless chest, and tight white pants that might as well have been made of Saran Wrap. He didn't say anything, just let his eyebrows rise inquiringly as his eyes flicked down, then up.

"Good morning," I said and showed him my ID. He blanched. His eyes became marbles brimming with terror. He was about to panic, tensing to slam the door. I smiled my friendly, disarming smile and went on as if I hadn't noticed. "I'm inquiring about a man named Andrew Detweiler." The terror trickled from his eyes, and I could see his thin chest throbbing. He gave me a blank look that meant he'd never heard the name.

"He's about twenty-two," I continued, "dark, curly hair, very good-looking."

He grinned wryly, calming down, trying to cover his panic. "Aren't they all?" he said.

"Detweiler is a hunchback."

His smile contracted suddenly. His eyebrows shot up. "Oh," he said. "Him."

Bingo!

Mallory, you've led a clean, wholesome life and it's paying off.

"Does he live in the building?" I swallowed to get my heart back in place and blinked a couple of times to clear away the skyrockets.

"No. He was . . . visiting."

"May I come in and talk to you about him?"

He was holding the door three quarters shut, and so I couldn't see anything in the room but an expensive-looking color TV. He glanced over his shoulder nervously at something behind him. The inner ends of his eyebrows drooped in a frown. He looked back at me and started to say something, then, with a small defiance, shrugged his eyebrows. "Sure, but there's not much I can tell you."

He pushed the door all the way open and stepped back. It was a good-sized living room come to life from the pages of a decorator magazine. A kitchen behind a half wall was on my right. A hallway led somewhere on my left. Directly in front of me were double sliding glass doors leading to the terrace. On the terrace was a bronzed hunk of beef stretched out nude trying to get bronzer. The hunk opened his eyes and looked at me. He apparently decided I wasn't competition and closed them again. Tall and lanky indicated one of two identical orange- and brown-striped couches facing each other across a football-field-size marble and glass cocktail table. He sat on the other one, took a cigarette from an alabaster box and lit it with an alabaster lighter. As an afterthought, he offered me one.

"Who was Detweiler visiting?" I asked as I lit the cigarette. The lighter felt cool and expensive in my hand.

"Maurice—next door," he inclined his head slightly toward 407.

"Isn't he the one who was killed in an accident last night?"

He blew a stream of smoke from pursed lips and tapped his cigarette on an alabaster ashtray. "Yes," he said.

"How long had Maurice and Detweiler known each other?"

"Not long."

"How long?"

He snuffed his cigarette out on pure-white alabaster and sat so prim and pristine I would have bet his feces came out wrapped in cellophane. He shrugged his eyebrows again. "Maurice picked him up somewhere the other night."

"Which night?"

He thought a moment. "Thursday, I think. Yes, Thursday."

"Was Detweiler a hustler?"

He crossed his legs like a Forties pin-up and dangled his Roman sandal. His lips twitched scornfully. "If he was, he would've starved. He was de-*formed!*"

"Maurice didn't seem to mind." He sniffed and lit another cigarette. "When did Detweiler leave?"

He shrugged. "I saw him yesterday afternoon. I was out last night . . . until quite late."

"How did they get along? Did they quarrel or fight?"

"I have no idea. I only saw them in the hall a couple of times. Maurice and I were . . . not close." He stood, fidgety. "There's really not anything I can tell you. Why don't you ask David and Murray. They and Maurice are . . . were thick as thieves."

"David and Murray?"

"Across the hall. 408."

I stood up. "I'll do that. Thank you very much." I looked at the plate-glass doors. I guess it would be pretty easy to walk through one of them if you thought it was open. "Are all the apartments alike? Those terrace doors?"

He nodded. "Ticky-tacky."

"Thanks again."

"Don't mention it." He opened the door for me and then closed it behind me. I sighed and walked across to 408. I rang the bell. It didn't play anything, just went *bing-bong.*

David (or Murray) was about twenty-five, red-headed, and freckled. He had a slim, muscular body which was also freckled. I could tell because he was wearing only a pair of jeans, cut off very short, and split up the sides to the waistband. He was barefooted and had a smudge of green paint on his nose. He had an open, friendly face and gave me a neutral smile-for-a-stranger. "Yes?" he asked.

I showed him my ID. Instead of going pale he only looked interested. "I was told by the man in 409 you might be able to tell me something about Andrew Detweiler."

"Andy?" He frowned slightly. "Come on in. I'm David Fowler." He held out his hand.

I shook it. "Bert Mallory." The apartment couldn't have been more different from the one across the hall. It was comfortable and cluttered, and dominated by a drafting table surrounded by jars of brushes and boxes of paint tubes. Architecturally, however, it was almost identical. The terrace was covered with potted plants rather than naked muscles. David Fowler sat on the stool at the drafting table and began cleaning brushes. When he sat, the split in his shorts opened and exposed half his butt, which was also freckled. But I got the impression he wasn't exhibiting himself; he was just completely indifferent.

"What do you want to know about Andy?"

"Everything."

He laughed. "That lets me out. Sit down. Move the stuff."

I cleared a space on the couch and sat. "How did Detweiler and Maurice get along?"

He gave me a knowing look. "Fine. As far as I know. Maurice liked to pick up stray puppies. Andy was a stray puppy."

"Was Detweiler a hustler?"

He laughed again. "No. I doubt if he knew what the word meant."

"Was he gay?"

"No."

"How do you know?"

He grinned. "Haven't you heard? We can spot each other a mile away. Would you like some coffee?"

"Yes, I would. Thank you."

He went to the half wall separating the kitchen and poured two cups from a pot that looked like it was kept hot and full all the time. "It's hard to describe Andy. There was something very littleboyish about him. A real innocent. Delighted with everything new. It's sad about his back. Real sad." He handed me the cup and returned to the stool. "There was something very secretive about him. Not about his feelings; he was very open about things like that."

"Did he and Maurice have sex together?"

"No. I told you it was a stray puppy relationship. I wish Murray were here. He's much better with words than I am. I'm visually oriented."

"Where is he?"

"At work. He's a lawyer."

"Do you think Detweiler could have killed Maurice?"

"No."

"Why?"

"He was here with us all evening. We had dinner and played Scrabble. I think he was real sick, but he tried to pretend he wasn't. Even if he hadn't been here I would not think so."

"When was the last time you saw him?"

"He left about half an hour before they found Maurice. I imagine he went over there, saw Maurice dead, and decided to disappear. Can't say as I blame him. The police might've gotten some funny ideas. We didn't mention him."

"Why not?"

"There was no point in getting him involved. It was just an accident."

"He couldn't have killed Maurice after he left here?"

"No. They said he'd been dead over an hour. What did Desmond tell you?"

"Desmond?"

"Across the hall. The one who looks like he smells something bad."

"How did you know I talked to him and not the side of beef?"

He laughed and almost dropped his coffee cup. "I don't think Roy *can* talk."

"He didn't know nothin' about nothin'." I found myself laughing also. I got up and walked to the glass doors. I slid them open and then shut again. "Did you ever think one of these was open when it was really shut?"

"No. But I've heard of it happening."

I sighed. "So have I." I turned and looked at what he was working on at the drafting table. It was a small painting of a boy and girl, she in a soft white dress, and he in jeans and tee shirt. They looked about fifteen. They were embracing, about to kiss. It was

quite obviously the first time for both of them. It was good. I told
him so.

He grinned with pleasure. "Thanks. It's for a paperback cover."

"Whose idea was it that Detweiler have dinner and spend the
evening with you?"

He thought for a moment. "Maurice." He looked up at me and
grinned. "Do you know stamps?"

It took me a second to realize what he meant. "You mean stamp
collecting? Not much."

"Maurice was a philatelist. He specialized in postwar Germany—
locals and zones, things like that. He'd gotten a kilo of buildings
and wanted to sort them undisturbed."

I shook my head. "You've lost me. A kilo of buildings?"

He laughed. "It's a set of twenty-eight stamps issued in the
American Zone in 1948 showing famous German buildings. Conditions in Germany were still pretty chaotic at the time, and the
stamps were printed under fairly makeshift circumstances. Conse-
quently, there's an enormous variety of different perforations, wa-
termarks, and engravings. Hundreds as a matter of fact. Maurice
could spend hours and hours poring over them."

"Are they valuable?"

"No. Very common. Some of the varieties are hard to find, but
they're not valuable." He gave me a knowing look. "Nothing was
missing from Maurice's apartment."

I shrugged. "It had occurred to me to wonder where Detweiler
got his money."

"I don't know. The subject never came up." He wasn't being defensive.

"You liked him, didn't you?"

There was a weary sadness in his eyes. "Yes," he said.

That afternoon I picked up Birdie Pawlowicz at the Brewster
Hotel and took her to Harry Spinner's funeral. I told her about
Maurice Milian and Andrew Detweiler. We talked it around and
around. The Detweiler boy obviously couldn't have killed Harry *or*
Milian, but it was stretching coincidence a little bit far.

After the funeral I went to the Los Angeles Public Library and
started checking back issues of the *Times*. I'd only made it back
three weeks when the library closed. The LA *Times* is *thick*, and
unless the death is sensational or the dead prominent, the story
might be tucked in anywhere except the classifieds.

Last Tuesday, the 26th, a girl had cut her wrists with a razor blade in North Hollywood.

The day before, Monday, the 25th, a girl had miscarried and hemorrhaged. She had bled to death because she and her boy friend were stoned out of their heads. They lived a block off Western—very near the Brewster—and Detweiler was at the Brewster Monday.

Sunday, the 24th, a wino had been knifed in MacArthur Park.

Saturday, the 23rd, I had three. A knifing in a bar on Pico, a shooting in a rooming house on Irolo, and a rape and knifing in an alley off La Brea. Only the gunshot victim had bled to death, but there had been a lot of blood in all three.

Friday, the 22nd, the same day Detweiler checked in the Brewster, a two-year-old boy had fallen on an upturned rake in his backyard on Larchemont—only eight or ten blocks from where I lived on Beachwood. And a couple of Chicano kids had had a knife fight behind Hollywood High. One was dead and the other was in jail. Ah, *machismo!*

The list went on and on, all the way back to Thursday, the 7th. On that day was another slashed-wrist suicide near Western and Wilshire.

The next morning, Tuesday, the 3rd, I called Miss Tremaine and told her I'd be late getting in but would check in every couple of hours to find out if the slinky blonde looking for her kid sister had shown up. She *humphed.*

Larchemont is a middle-class neighborhood huddled in between the old wealth around the country club and the blight spreading down Melrose from Western Avenue. It tries to give the impression of suburbia—and does a pretty good job of it—rather than just another nearly downtown shopping center. The area isn't big on apartments or rooming houses, but there are a few. I found the Detweiler boy at the third one I checked. It was a block and a half from where the little kid fell on the rake.

According to the landlord, at the time of the kid's death Detweiler was playing bridge with him and a couple of elderly old-maid sisters in number twelve. He hadn't been feeling well and had moved out later that evening—to catch a bus to San Diego, to visit his ailing mother. The landlord had felt sorry for him, so sorry he'd broken a steadfast rule and refunded most of the month's rent Detweiler had paid in advance. After all, he'd only been there three days. So sad about his back. Such a nice, gentle boy—a writer, you know.

No, I didn't know, but it explained how he could move around so much without seeming to work.

I called David Fowler: "Yes, Andy had a portable typewriter, but he hadn't mentioned being a writer."

And Birdie Pawlowicz: "Yeah, he typed a lot in his room."

I found the Detweiler boy again on the 16th and the 19th. He'd moved into a rooming house near Silver Lake Park on the night of the 13th and moved out again on the 19th. The landlady hadn't refunded his money, but she gave him an alibi for the knifing of an old man in the park on the 16th and the suicide of a girl in the same rooming house on the 19th. He'd been in the pink of health when he moved in, sick on the 16th, healthy the 17th, and sick again the 19th.

It was like a rerun. He lived a block away from where a man was mugged, knifed, and robbed in an alley on the 13th—though the details of the murder didn't seem to fit the pattern. But he was sick, had an alibi, and moved to Silver Lake.

Rerun it on the 10th: a woman slipped in the bathtub and fell through the glass shower doors, cutting herself to ribbons. Sick, alibi, moved.

It may be because I was always rotten in math, but it wasn't until right then that I figured out Detweiler's timetable. Milian died the 1st, Harry Spinner the 28th, the miscarriage was on the 25th, the little kid on the 22nd, Silver Lake on the 16th and 19th, etc., etc., etc.

A bloody death occurred in Detweiler's general vicinity every third day.

But I couldn't figure out a pattern for the victims: male, female, little kids, old aunties, married, unmarried, rich, poor, young, old. No pattern of any kind, and there's *always* a pattern. I even checked to see if the names were in alphabetical order.

I got back to my office at six. Miss Tremaine sat primly at her desk, cleared of everything but her purse and a notepad. She reminded me quite a lot of Desmond. "What are you still doing here, Miss Tremaine? You should've left an hour ago." I sat at my desk, leaned back until the swivel chair groaned twice, and propped my feet up.

She picked up the pad. "I wanted to give you your calls."

"Can't they wait? I've been sleuthing all day and I'm bushed."

"No one is paying you to find this Detweiler person, are they?"

"No."

"Your bank statement came today."

"What's that supposed to mean?"

"Nothing. A good secretary keeps her employer informed. I was informing you."

"Okay. Who called?"

She consulted the pad, but I'd bet my last gumshoe she knew every word on it by heart. "A Mrs. Carmichael called. Her French poodle has been kidnaped. She wants you to find her."

"Ye Gods! Why doesn't she go to the police?"

"Because she's positive her ex-husband is the kidnaper. She doesn't want to get him in any trouble; she just wants Gwendolyn back."

"Gwendolyn?"

"Gwendolyn. A Mrs. Bushyager came by. She wants you to find her little sister."

I sat up so fast I almost fell out of the chair. I gave her a long, hard stare, but her neutral expression didn't flicker. "You're kidding." Her eyebrows rose a millimeter. "Was she a slinky blonde?"

"No. She was a dumpy brunette."

I settled back in the chair, trying not to laugh. "Why does Mrs. Bushyager want me to find her little sister?" I sputtered.

"Because Mrs. Bushyager thinks she's shacked up somewhere with *Mr.* Bushyager. She'd like you to call her tonight."

"Tomorrow. I've got a date with Janice tonight." She reached in her desk drawer and pulled out my bank statement. She dropped it on the desk with a papery plop. "Don't worry," I assured her, "I won't spend much money. Just a little spaghetti and wine tonight and ham and eggs in the morning." She *humphed.* My point. "Anything else?"

"A Mr. Bloomfeld called. He wants you to get the goods on Mrs. Bloomfeld so he can sue for divorce."

I sighed. Miss Tremaine closed the pad. "Okay. No to Mrs. Carmichael and make appointments for Bushyager and Bloomfeld." She lowered her eyelids at me. I spread my hands. "Would Sam Spade go looking for a French poodle named Gwendolyn?"

"He might if he had your bank statement. Mr. Bloomfeld will be in at two, Mrs. Bushyager at three."

"Miss Tremaine, you'd make somebody a wonderful mother."
She didn't even *humph;* she just picked up her purse and stalked
out. I swiveled the chair around and looked at the calendar. Tomorrow was the 4th.

Somebody would die tomorrow and Andrew Detweiler would be
close by.

I scooted up in bed and leaned against the headboard. Janice
snorted into the pillow and opened one eye, pinning me with it. "I
didn't mean to wake you," I said.

"What's the matter," she muttered, "too much spaghetti?"

"No. Too much Andrew Detweiler."

She scooted up beside me, keeping the sheet over her breasts,
and turned on the light. She rummaged around on the nightstand
for a cigarette. "Who wants to divorce him?"

"That's mean, Janice," I groaned.

"You want a cigarette?"

"Yeah."

She put two cigarettes in her mouth and lit them both. She
handed me one. "You don't look a bit like Paul Henreid," I said.

She grinned. "That's funny. You look like Bette Davis. Who's
Andrew Detweiler?"

So I told her.

"It's elementary, my dear Sherlock," she said. "Andrew Detweiler is a vampire." I frowned at her. "Of course, he's a *clever*
vampire. Vampires are usually stupid. They always give themselves
away by leaving those two little teeth marks on people's jugulars."

"Darling, even vampires have to be at the scene of the crime."

"He always has an alibi, huh?"

I got out of bed and headed for the bathroom. "That's suspicious
in itself."

When I came out she said, "Why?"

"Innocent people usually don't have alibis, especially not one
every three days."

"Which is probably why innocent people get put in jail so often."
I chuckled and sat on the edge of the bed. "You may be right."

"Bert, do that again."

I looked at her over my shoulder. "Do what?"

"Go to the bathroom."

"I don't think I can. My bladder holds only so much."

"I don't mean that. Walk over to the bathroom door."

I gave her a suspicious frown, got up, and walked over to the bathroom door. I turned around, crossed my arms, and leaned against the door frame. "Well?"

She grinned. "You've got a cute rear end. Almost as cute as Burt Reynolds'. Maybe he's twins."

"What?" I practically screamed.

"Maybe Andrew Detweiler is twins. One of them commits the murders and the other establishes the alibis."

"Twin vampires?"

She frowned. "That is a bit much, isn't it? Had they discovered blood groups in Bram Stoker's day?"

I got back in bed and pulled the sheet up to my waist, leaning beside her against the headboard. "I haven't the foggiest idea."

"That's another way vampires are stupid. They never check the victim's blood group. The wrong blood group can kill you."

"Vampires don't exactly get transfusions."

"It all amounts to the same thing, doesn't it?" I shrugged. "Oh, well," she sighed, "vampires are stupid." She reached over and plucked at the hair on my chest. "I haven't had an indecent proposition in hours," she grinned.

So I made one.

Wednesday morning I made a dozen phone calls. Of the nine victims I knew about, I was able to find the information on six.

All six had the same blood group.

I lit a cigarette and leaned back in the swivel chair. The whole thing was spinning around in my head. I'd found *a* pattern for the victims, but I didn't know if it was *the* pattern. It just didn't make sense. Maybe Detweiler *was* a vampire.

"Mallory," I said out loud, "you're cracking up."

Miss Tremaine glanced up. "If I were you, I'd listen to you," she said poker-faced.

The next morning I staggered out of bed at six a.m. I took a cold shower, shaved, dressed, and put Murine in my eyes. They still felt like I'd washed them in rubber cement. Mrs. Bloomfeld had kept me up until two the night before, doing all the night spots in Santa Monica with some dude I hadn't identified yet. When they checked into a motel, I went home and went to bed.

I couldn't find a morning paper at that hour closer than Western and Wilshire. The story was on page seven. Fortunately they found the body in time for the early edition. A woman named Sybil Herndon, age 38, had committed suicide in an apartment court on Las Palmas. (Detweiler hadn't gone very far. The address was just around the corner from the Almsbury.) She had cut her wrists on a piece of broken mirror. She had been discovered about eleven thirty when the manager went over to ask her to turn down the volume on her television set.

It was too early to drop around, and so I ate breakfast, hoping this was one of the times Detweiler stuck around for more than three days. Not for a minute did I doubt he would be living at the apartment court on Las Palmas, or not far away.

The owner-manager of the court was one of those creatures peculiar to Hollywood. She must have been a starlet in the Twenties or Thirties, but success had eluded her. So she had tried to freeze herself in time. She still expected, at any moment, a call from The Studio. But her flesh hadn't cooperated. Her hair was the color of tarnished copper, and the fire-engine-red lipstick was painted far past her thin lips. Her watery eyes peered at me through a Lone Ranger mask of Maybelline on a plaster-white face. Her dress had obviously been copied from the wardrobe of Norma Shearer.

"Yes?" She had a breathy voice. Her eyes quickly traveled the length of my body. That happens often enough to keep me feeling good, but this time it gave me a queasy sensation, like I was being measured for a mummy case. I showed her my ID and asked if I could speak to her about one of the tenants.

"Of course. Come on in. I'm Lorraine Nesbitt." Was there a flicker of disappointment that I hadn't recognized the name? She stepped back holding the door for me. I could tell that detectives, private or otherwise, asking about her tenants wasn't a new thing. I walked into the doilied room, and she looked at me from a hundred directions. The faded photographs covered every level surface and clung to the walls like leeches. She had been quite a dish—forty years ago. She saw me looking at the photos and smiled. The make-up around her mouth cracked.

"Which one do you want to ask me about?" The smile vanished and the cracks closed.

"Andrew Detweiler." She looked blank. "Young, good-looking, with a hunchback."

The cracks opened. "Oh, yes. He's only been here a few days. The name had slipped my mind."

"He's still here?"

"Oh, yes." She sighed. "It's so unfair for such a beautiful young man to have a physical impairment."

"What can you tell me about him?"

"Not much. He's only been here since Sunday night. He's very handsome, like an angel, a dark angel. But it wasn't his handsomeness that attracted me." She smiled. "I've seen many handsome men in my day, you know. It's difficult to verbalize. He has such an incredible innocence. A lost, doomed look that Byron must have had. A vulnerability that makes you want to shield and protect him. I don't know for sure what it is, but it struck a chord in my soul. Soul," she mused. "Maybe that's it. He wears his soul on his face." She nodded, as if to herself. "A dangerous thing to do." She looked back up at me. "If that quality, whatever it is, would photograph, he would become a star overnight, whether he could act or not. Except—of course—for his infirmity."

Lorraine Nesbitt, I decided, was as nutty as a fruitcake.

Someone entered the room. He stood leaning against the door frame, looking at me with sleepy eyes. He was about twenty-five, wearing tight chinos without underwear and a tee shirt. His hair was tousled and cut unfashionably short. He had a good looking Kansas face. The haircut made me think he was new in town, but the eyes said he wasn't. I guess the old broad liked his hair that way.

She simpered. "Oh, Johnny! Come on in. This detective was asking about Andrew Detweiler in number seven." She turned back to me. "This is my protege, Johnny Peacock—a very talented young man. I'm arranging for a screen test as soon as Mr. Goldwyn returns my calls." She lowered her eyelids demurely. "I was a Goldwyn Girl, you know."

Funny, I thought Goldwyn was dead. Maybe he wasn't.

Johnny took the news of his impending stardom with total unconcern. He moved to the couch and sat down, yawning. "Detweiler? Don't think I ever laid eyes on the man. What'd he do?"

"Nothing. Just routine." Obviously he thought I was a police detective. No point in changing his mind. "Where was he last night when the Herndon woman died?"

"In his room, I think. I heard his typewriter. He wasn't feeling well," Lorraine Nesbitt said. Then she sucked air through her teeth and clamped her fingers to her scarlet lips. "Do you think he had something to do with *that?*"

Detweiler had broken his pattern. He didn't have an alibi. I couldn't believe it.

"Oh, Lorraine," Johnny grumbled.

I turned to him. "Do you know where Detweiler was?"

He shrugged. "No idea."

"Then why are you so sure he had nothing to do with it?"

"She committed suicide."

"How do you know for sure?"

"The door was bolted from the inside. They had to break it down to get in."

"What about the window? Was it locked too?"

"No. The window was open. But it has bars on it. No way anybody could get in."

"When I couldn't get her to answer my knock last night, I went around to the window and looked in. She was lying there with blood all over." She began to sniffle. Johnny got up and put his arms around her. He looked at me, grinned, and shrugged.

"Do you have a vacancy?" I asked, getting a whiz-bang idea.

"Yes," she said, the sniffles disappearing instantly. "I have two. Actually three, but I can't rent Miss Herndon's room for a few days —until someone claims her things."

"I'd like to rent the one closest to number seven," I said.

I wasn't lucky enough to get number six or eight, but I did get five. Lorraine Nesbitt's nameless, dingy apartment court was a fleabag. Number five was one room with a closet, a tiny kitchen, and a tiny bath—identical with the other nine units she assured me. With a good deal of tugging and grunting the couch turned into a lumpy bed. The refrigerator looked as if someone had spilled a bottle of Br'er Rabbit back in 1938 and hadn't cleaned it up yet. The stove looked like a lube rack. Well, I sighed, it was only for three days. I had to pay a month's rent in advance anyway, but I put it down as a bribe to keep Lorraine's and Johnny's mouths shut about my being a detective.

I moved in enough clothes for three days, some sheets and pillows, took another look at the kitchen and decided to eat out. I took a jug of Lysol to the bathroom and crossed my fingers. Miss Tremaine brought up the bank statement and *humphed* a few times.

Number five had one door and four windows—identical to the

other nine Lorraine assured me. The door had a heavy-duty bolt
that couldn't be fastened or unfastened from the outside. The window beside the door didn't open at all and wasn't intended to. The
bathroom and kitchen windows cranked out and were tall and
skinny, about twenty-four by six. The other living room window,
opposite the door, slid upward. The iron bars bolted to the frame
were so rusted I doubted if they could be removed without rip-
ping out the whole window. It appeared Andrew Detweiler had another perfect alibi after all—along with the rest of the world.

I stood outside number seven suddenly feeling like a teen-ager
about to pick up his first date. I could hear Detweiler's typewriter
tickety-ticking away inside. Okay, Mallory, this is what you've been
breaking your neck on for a week.

I knocked on the door.

I heard the typewriter stop ticking and the scrape of a chair
being scooted back. I didn't hear anything else for fifteen or twenty
seconds, and I wondered what he was doing. Then the bolt was
drawn and the door opened.

He was buttoning his shirt. That must have been the delay: he
wouldn't want anyone to see him with his shirt off. Everything I'd
been told about him was true. He wasn't very tall; the top of his
head came to my nose. He was dark, though not as dark as I'd expected. I couldn't place his ancestry. It certainly wasn't Latin-
American and I didn't think it was Slavic. His features were soft
without the angularity usually found in the Mediterranean races.
His hair wasn't quite black. It wasn't exactly long and it wasn't exactly short. His clothes were nondescript. Everything about him
was neutral—except his face. It was just about the way Lorraine
Nesbitt had described it. If you called central casting and asked for
a male angel, you'd get Andrew Detweiler in a blond wig. His body
was slim and well-formed—from where I was standing I couldn't
see the hump and you'd never know there was one. I had a glimpse
of his bare chest as he buttoned the shirt. It wasn't muscular but it
was very well made. He was very healthy-looking—pink and flushed
with health, though slightly pale as if he didn't get out in the sun
much. His dark eyes were astounding. If you blocked out the rest
of the face, leaving nothing but the eyes, you'd swear he was no
more than four years old. You've seen little kids with those big,
guileless, unguarded, inquiring eyes, haven't you?

"Yes?" he asked.

I smiled. "Hello, I'm Bert Mallory. I just moved in to number five. Miss Nesbitt tells me you like to play gin."

"Yes," he grinned. "Come on in."

He turned to move out of my way and I saw the hump. I don't know how to describe what I felt. I suddenly had a hurting in my gut. I felt the same unfairness and sadness the others had, the way you would feel about any beautiful thing with one overwhelming flaw.

"I'm not disturbing you, am I? I heard the typewriter." The room was indeed identical to mine, though it looked a hundred per cent more livable. I couldn't put my finger on what he had done to it to make it that way. Maybe it was just the semidarkness. He had the curtains tightly closed and one lamp lit beside the typewriter.

"Yeah, I was working on a story, but I'd rather play gin." He grinned, open and artless. "If I could make money playing gin, I wouldn't write."

"Lots of people make money playing gin."

"Oh, I couldn't. I'm too unlucky."

He certainly had a right to say that, but there was no self-pity, just an observation. Then he looked at me with slightly distressed eyes. "You . . . ah . . . didn't want to play for money, did you?"

"Not at all," I said and his eyes cleared. "What kind of stories do you write?"

"Oh, all kinds." He shrugged. "Fantasy mostly."

"Do you sell them?"

"Most of 'em."

"I don't recall seeing your name anywhere. Miss Nesbitt said it was Andrew Detweiler?"

He nodded. "I use another name. You probably wouldn't know it either. It's not exactly a household word." His eyes said he'd really rather not tell me what it was. He had a slight accent, a sort of soft slowness, not exactly a drawl and not exactly Deep South. He shoved the typewriter over and pulled out a deck of cards.

"Where're you from?" I asked. "I don't place the accent."

He grinned and shuffled the cards. "North Carolina. Back in the Blue Ridge."

We cut and I dealt. "How long have you been in Hollywood?"

"About two months."

"How do you like it?"

He grinned his beguiling grin and picked up my discard. "It's very . . . unusual. Have you lived here long, Mr. Mallory?"

"Bert. All my life. I was born in Inglewood. My mother still lives there."

"It must be . . . unusual . . . to live in the same place all your life."

"You move around a lot?"

"Yeah. Gin."

I laughed. "I thought you were unlucky."

"If we were playing for money, I wouldn't be able to do anything right."

We played gin the rest of the afternoon and talked—talked a lot. Detweiler seemed eager to talk or, at least, eager to have someone to talk with. He never told me anything that would connect him to nine deaths, mostly about where he'd been, things he'd read. He read a lot, just about anything he could get his hands on. I got the impression he hadn't really *lived* life so much as he'd *read* it, that all the things he knew about had never physically affected him. He was like an insulated island. Life flowed around him but never touched him. I wondered if the hump on his back made that much difference, if it made him such a green monkey he'd had to retreat into his insular existence. Practically everyone I had talked to liked him, mixed with varying portions of pity, to be sure, but liking nevertheless. Harry Spinner liked him, but had discovered something "peculiar" about him. Birdie Pawlowicz, Maurice Milian, David Fowler, Lorraine Nesbitt, they all liked him.

And, God damn it, I liked him too.

At midnight I was still awake, sitting in number five in my jockey shorts with the light out and the door open. I listened to the ticking of the Detweiler boy's typewriter and the muffled roar of Los Angeles. And thought, and thought and thought. And got nowhere.

Someone walked by the door, quietly and carefully. I leaned my head out. It was Johnny Peacock. He moved down the line of bungalows silent as a shadow. He turned south when he reached the sidewalk. Going to Selma or the Boulevard to turn a trick and make a few extra bucks. Lorraine must keep tight purse strings. Better watch it, kid. If she finds out, you'll be back on the streets again. And you haven't got too many years left where you can make good money by just gettin' it up.

I dropped in at the office for a while Friday morning and

checked the first-of-the-month bills. Miss Tremaine had a list of new prospective clients. "Tell everyone I can't get to anything till Monday."

She nodded in disapproval. "Mr. Bloomfeld called."

"Did he get my report?"

"Yes. He was very pleased, but he wants the man's name."

"Tell him I'll get back on it Monday."

"Mrs. Bushyager called. Her sister and Mr. Bushyager are still missing."

"Tell her I'll get on it Monday." She opened her mouth. "If you say anything about my bank account, I'll put Spanish fly in your Ovaltine." She didn't *humph*, she giggled. I wonder how many points *that* is?

That afternoon I played gin with the Detweiler boy. He was genuinely glad to see me, like a friendly puppy. I was beginning to feel like a son of a bitch.

He hadn't mentioned North Carolina except that once the day before, and I was extremely interested in all subjects he wanted to avoid. "What's it like in the Blue Ridge? Coon huntin' and moonshine?"

He grinned and blitzed me. "Yeah, I guess. Most of the things you read about it are pretty nearly true. It's really a different world back in there, with almost no contact with the outside."

"How far in did you live?"

"About as far as you can get without comin' out the other side. Did you know most of the people never heard of television or movies and some of 'em don't even know the name of the President? Most of 'em never been more than thirty miles from the place they were born, never saw an electric light? You wouldn't believe it. But it's more than just *things* that're different. People are different, think different—like a foreign country." He shrugged. "I guess it'll all be gone before too long though. Things keep creepin' closer and closer. Did you know I never went to school?" he said grinning. "Not a day of my life. I didn't wear shoes till I was ten. You wouldn't believe it." He shook his head, remembering. "Always kinda wished I coulda gone to school," he murmured softly.

"Why did you leave?"

"No reason to stay. When I was eight, my parents were killed in a fire. Our house burned down. I was taken in by a balmy old woman who lived not far away. I had some kin, but they didn't want me."

He looked at me, trusting me. "They're pretty superstitious back in there, you know. Thought I was . . . marked. Anyway, the old woman took me in. She was a midwife, but she fancied herself a witch or something. Always making me drink some mess she'd brewed up. She fed me, clothed me, educated me, after a fashion, tried to teach me all her conjures, but I never could take 'em seriously." He grinned sheepishly. "I did chores for her and eventually became a sort of assistant, I guess. I helped her birth babies . . . I mean, deliver babies a couple of times, but that didn't last long. The parents were afraid me bein' around might mark the baby. She taught me to read and I couldn't stop. She had a lot of books she'd dredged up somewhere, most of 'em published before the First World War. I read a complete set of encyclopedias—published in 1911."

I laughed.

His eyes clouded. "Then she . . . died. I was fifteen, so I left. I did odd jobs and kept reading. Then I wrote a story and sent it to a magazine. They bought it; paid me fifty dollars. Thought I was rich, so I wrote another one. Since then I've been traveling around and writing. I've got an agent who takes care of everything, and so all I do is just write."

Detweiler's flush of health was wearing off that afternoon. He wasn't ill, just beginning to feel like the rest of us mortals. And I was feeling my resolve begin to crumble. It was hard to believe this beguiling kid could possibly be involved in a string of bloody deaths. Maybe it was just a series of unbelievable coincidences. Yeah, "unbelievable" was the key word. He *had* to be involved unless the laws of probability had broken down completely. Yet I could swear Detweiler wasn't putting on an act. His guileless innocence was real, damn it, *real*.

Saturday morning, the third day since Miss Herndon died, I had a talk with Lorraine and Johnny. If Detweiler wanted to play cards or something that night, I wanted them to agree and suggest I be a fourth. If he didn't bring it up, I would, but I had a feeling he would want his usual alibi this time.

Detweiler left his room that afternoon for the first time since I'd been there. He went north on Las Palmas, dropped a large manila envelope in the mailbox (the story he'd been working on, I guess), and bought groceries at the supermarket on Highland. Did that mean he wasn't planning to move? I had a sudden pang in my belly. What if he was staying because of his friendship with *me?* I felt more like a son of a bitch every minute.

Johnny Peacock came by an hour later acting very conspiratorial. Detweiler had suggested a bridge game that night, but Johnny didn't play bridge, and so they settled on Scrabble.

I dropped by number seven. The typewriter had been put away, but the cards and score pad were still on the table. His suitcase was on the floor by the couch. It was riveted cowhide of a vintage I hadn't seen since I was a kid. Though it wore a mellow patina of age, it had been preserved with neat's-foot oil and loving care. I may have been mistaken about his not moving.

Detweiler wasn't feeling well at all. He was pale and drawn and fidgety. His eyelids were heavy and his speech was faintly slurred. I'm sure he was in pain, but he tried to act as if nothing were wrong.

"Are you sure you feel like playing Scrabble tonight?" I asked.

He gave me a cheerful, if slightly strained, smile. "Oh, sure. I'm all right. I'll be fine in the morning."

"Do you think you ought to play?"

"Yeah, it . . . takes my mind off my . . . ah . . . headache. Don't worry about it. I have these spells all the time. They always go away."

"How long have you had them?"

"Since . . . I was a kid." He grinned. "You think it was one of those brews the old witch-woman gave me caused it? Maybe I could sue for malpractice."

"Have you seen a doctor? A real one?"

"Once."

"What did he tell you?"

He shrugged. "Oh, nothing much. Take two aspirin, drink lots of liquids, get plenty of rest, that sort of thing." He didn't want to talk about it. "It always goes away."

"What if one time it doesn't?"

He looked at me with an expression I'd never seen before, and I knew why Lorraine said he had a lost, doomed look. "Well, we can't live forever, can we? Are you ready to go?"

The game started out like a Marx Brothers routine. Lorraine and Johnny acted like two canaries playing Scrabble with the cat, but Detweiler was so normal and unconcerned they soon settled down. Conversation was tense and ragged at first until Lorraine got off on her "career" and kept us entertained and laughing. She had known a lot of famous people and was a fountain of anecdotes, most of them funny and libelous. Detweiler proved quickly to be the best player, but Johnny, to my surprise, was no slouch. Lorraine played dismally but she didn't seem to mind.

I would have enjoyed the evening thoroughly if I hadn't known someone nearby was dead or dying.

After about two hours, in which Detweiler grew progressively more ill, I excused myself to go to the bathroom. While I was away from the table, I palmed Lorraine's master key.

In another half hour I said I had to call it a night. I had to get up early the next morning. I always spent Sunday with my mother in Inglewood. My mother was touring Yucatán at the time, but that was neither here nor there. I looked at Johnny. He nodded. He was to make sure Detweiler stayed at least another twenty minutes and then follow him when he did leave. If he went anywhere but his apartment, he was to come and let me know, quick.

I let myself into number seven with the master key. The drapes were closed, and so I took a chance and turned on the bathroom light. Detweiler's possessions were meager. Eight shirts, six pairs of pants, and a light jacket hung in the closet. The shirts and jacket had been altered to allow for the hump. Except for that, the closet was bare. The bathroom contained nothing out of the ordinary—just about the same as mine. The kitchen had one plastic plate, one plastic cup, one plastic glass, one plastic bowl, one small folding skillet, one small folding sauce pan, one metal spoon, one metal fork, and a medium-sized kitchen knife. All of it together would barely fill a shoebox.

The suitcase, still beside the couch, hadn't been unpacked—except for the clothes hanging in the closet and the kitchen utensils. There was underwear, socks, an extra pair of shoes, an unopened ream of paper, a bunch of other stuff necessary for his writing, and a dozen or so paperbacks. The books were rubber-stamped with the name of a used-book store on Santa Monica Boulevard. They were a mixture: science fiction, mysteries, biographies, philosophy, several by Colin Wilson.

There was also a carbon copy of the story he'd just finished. The return address on the first page was a box number at the Hollywood post office. The title of the story was "Deathsong." I wish I'd had time to read it.

All in all, I didn't find anything. Except for the books and the deck of cards there was nothing of Andrew Detweiler personally in the whole apartment. I hadn't thought it possible for anyone to lead such a turnip existence.

I looked around to make sure I hadn't disturbed anything, turned off the bathroom light, and got in the closet, leaving the door open a crack. It was the only possible place to hide. I sincerely hoped Detweiler wouldn't need anything out of it before I found out what was going on. If he did, the only thing I could do was confront him with what I'd found out. And then what, Mallory, a big guilty confession? With what you've found out he could laugh in your face and have you arrested for illegal entry.

And what about this, Mallory. What if someone died nearby tonight while you were with Detweiler; what if he comes straight to his apartment and goes to bed; what if he wakes up in the morning feeling fine; what if nothing is going on, you son of a bitch?

It was so dark in there with the curtains drawn that I couldn't see a thing. I left the closet and opened them a little on the front window. It didn't let in a lot of light, but it was enough. Maybe Detweiler wouldn't notice. I went back to the closet and waited.

Half an hour later the curtains over the barred open window moved. I had squatted down in the closet and wasn't looking in that direction, but the movement caught my eye. Something hopped in the window and scooted across the floor and went behind the couch. I only got a glimpse of it, but it might have been a cat. It was probably a stray looking for food or hiding from a dog. Okay, cat, you don't bother me and I won't bother you. I kept my eye on the couch, but it didn't show itself again.

Detweiler didn't show for another hour. By that time I was sitting flat on the floor trying to keep my legs from cramping. My position wasn't too graceful if he happened to look in the closet, but it was too late to get up.

He came in quickly and bolted the door behind him. He didn't notice the open curtain. He glanced around, clicking his tongue softly. His eyes caught on something at the end of the couch. He smiled. At the *cat*? He began unfastening his shirt, fumbling at the buttons in his haste. He slipped off the shirt and tossed it on the back of a chair.

There were straps across his chest.

He turned toward the suitcase, his back to me. The hump was

artificial, made of something like foam rubber. He unhooked the
straps, opened the suitcase, and tossed the hump in. He said something, too soft for me to catch, and lay face down on the couch with
his feet toward me. The light from the opened curtain fell on him.
His back was scarred, little white lines like scratches grouped
around a hole.

He had a hole in his back, between his shoulder blades, an un-
healed wound big enough to stick your finger in.

Something came around the end of the couch. It wasn't a cat. I
thought it was a monkey, and then a frog, but it was neither. It was
human. It waddled on all fours like an enormous toad.

Then it stood erect. It was about the size of a cat. It was pink
and moist and hairless and naked. Its very human hands and feet
and male genitals were too large for its tiny body. Its belly was
swollen, turgid and distended like an obscene tick. Its head was
flat. Its jaw protruded like an ape's. It too had a scar, a big, white,
puckered scar between its shoulder blades, at the top of its jutting
backbone.

It reached its too-large hand up and caught hold of Detweiler's
belt. It pulled its bloated body up with the nimbleness of a monkey
and crawled onto the boy's back. Detweiler was breathing heavily,
clasping and unclasping his fingers on the arm of the couch.

The thing crouched on Detweiler's back and placed its lips
against the wound.

I felt my throat burning and my stomach turning over, but I
watched in petrified fascination.

Detweiler's breathing grew slower and quieter, more relaxed. He
lay with his eyes closed and an expression of almost sexual pleasure
on his face. The thing's body got smaller and smaller, the skin on its
belly growing wrinkled and flaccid. A trickle of blood crawled from
the wound, making an erratic line across the Detweiler boy's back.
The thing reached out its hand and wiped the drop back with a
finger.

It took about ten minutes. The thing raised its mouth and
crawled over beside the boy's face. It sat on the arm of the couch
like a little gnome and smiled. It ran its fingers down the side of
Detweiler's cheek and pushed his damp hair back out of his eyes.
Detweiler's expression was euphoric. He sighed softly and opened
his eyes sleepily. After a while he sat up.

He was flushed with health, rosy and clear and shining.

He stood up and went in the bathroom. The light came on and I heard water running. The thing sat in the same place watching him. Detweiler came out of the bathroom and sat back on the couch. The thing climbed onto his back, huddling between his shoulder blades, its hands on his shoulders. Detweiler stood up, the thing hanging onto him, retrieved the shirt, and put it on. He wrapped the straps neatly around the artificial hump and stowed it in the suitcase. He closed the lid and locked it.

I had seen enough, more than enough. I opened the door and stepped out of the closet.

Detweiler whirled, his eyes bulging. A groan rattled in his throat. He raised his hands as if fending me off. The groan rose in pitch, becoming an hysterical keening. The expression on his face was too horrible to watch. He stepped backward and tripped over the suitcase.

He lost his balance and toppled over. His arms flailed for equilibrium, but never found it. He struck the edge of the table. It caught him square across the hump on his back. He bounced and fell forward on his hands. He stood up agonizingly, like a slow motion movie, arching his spine backward, his face contorted in pain.

There were shrill, staccato shrieks of mindless torment, but they didn't come from Detweiler.

He fell again, forward onto the couch, blacking out from pain. The back of his shirt was churning. The scream continued, hurting my ears. Rips appeared in the shirt and a small misshapen arm poked out briefly. I could only stare, frozen. The shirt was ripped to shreds. Two arms, a head, a torso came through. The whole thing ripped its way out and fell onto the couch beside the boy. Its face was twisted, tortured, and its mouth kept opening and closing with the screams. Its eyes looked uncomprehendingly about. It pulled itself along with its arms, dragging its useless legs, its spine obviously broken. It fell off the couch and flailed about on the floor.

Detweiler moaned and came to. He rose from the couch, still groggy. He saw the thing, and a look of absolute grief appeared on his face.

The thing's eyes focused for a moment on Detweiler. It looked at him, beseeching, held out one hand, pleading. Its screams continued, that one monotonous, hopeless note repeated over and over. It lowered its arm and kept crawling about mindlessly, growing weaker.

Detweiler stepped toward it, ignoring me, tears pouring down his face. The thing's struggles grew weaker, the scream became a breathless rasping. I couldn't stand it any longer. I picked up a chair and smashed it down on the thing. I dropped the chair and leaned against the wall and heaved.

I heard the door open. I turned and saw Detweiler run out.

I charged after him. My legs felt rubbery but I caught him at the street. He didn't struggle. He just stood there, his eyes vacant, trembling. I saw people sticking their heads out of doors and Johnny Peacock coming toward me. My car was right there. I pushed Detweiler into it and drove away. He sat hunched in the seat, his hands hanging limply, staring into space. He was trembling uncontrollably and his teeth chattered.

I drove, not paying any attention to where I was going, almost as deeply in shock as he was. I finally started looking at the street signs. I was on Mullholland. I kept going west for a long time, crossed the San Diego Freeway, into the Santa Monica Mountains. The pavement ends a couple of miles past the freeway, and there's ten or fifteen miles of dirt road before the pavement picks up again nearly to Topanga. The road isn't traveled much, there are no houses on it, and people don't like to get their cars dusty. I was about in the middle of the unpaved section when Detweiler seemed to calm down. I pulled over to the side of the road and cut the engine. The San Fernando Valley was spread like a carpet of lights below us. The ocean was on the other side of the mountains.

I sat and watched Detweiler. The trembling had stopped. He was asleep or unconscious. I reached over and touched his arm. He stirred and clutched at my hand. I looked at his sleeping face and didn't have the heart to pull my hand away.

The sun was poking over the mountains when he woke up. He roused and was momentarily unaware of where he was; then memory flooded back. He turned to me. The pain and hysteria were gone from his eyes. They were oddly peaceful.

"Did you hear him?" he said softly. "Did you hear him die?"

"Are you feeling better?"

"Yes. It's all over."

"Do you want to talk about it?"

His eyes dropped and he was silent for a moment. "I want to tell you. But I don't know how without you thinking I'm a monster."

I didn't say anything.

"He . . . was my brother. We were twins. Siamese twins. All those people died so I could stay alive." There was no emotion in his voice. He was detached, talking about someone else. "He kept me alive. I'll die without him." His eyes met mine again. "He was insane, I think. I thought at first I'd go mad too, but I didn't. I think I didn't. I never knew what he was going to do, who he would kill. I didn't want to know. He was very clever. He always made it look like an accident or suicide when he could. I didn't interfere. I didn't want to die. We had to have blood. He always did it so there was lots of blood, so no one would miss what he took." His eyes were going empty again.

"Why did you need the blood?"

"We were never suspected before."

"Why did you need the blood?" I repeated.

"When we were born," he said, and his eyes focused again, "we were joined at the back. But I grew and he didn't. He stayed little bitty, like a baby riding around on my back. People didn't like me . . . us. They were afraid. My father and mother too. The old witch-woman I told you about, she birthed us. She seemed always to be hanging around. When I was eight, my parents died in a fire. I think the witch-woman did it. After that I lived with her. She was demented, but she knew medicine and healing. When we were fifteen she decided to separate us. I don't know why. I think she wanted him without me. I'm sure she thought he was an imp from hell. I almost died. I'm not sure what was wrong. Apart, we weren't whole. I wasn't whole. He had something I didn't have, something we'd been sharing. She would've let me die, but he knew and got blood for me. Hers." He sat staring at me blankly, his mind living the past.

"Why didn't you go to a hospital or something?" I asked, feeling enormous pity for the wretched boy.

He smiled faintly. "I didn't know much about anything then. Too many people were already dead. If I'd gone to a hospital, they'd have wanted to know how I'd stayed alive so far. Sometimes I'm glad it's over, and, then, the next minute I'm terrified of dying."

"How long?"

"I'm not sure. I've never been more than three days. I can't stand it any longer than that. He knew. He always knew when I had to have it. And he got it for me. I never helped him."

"Can you stay alive if you get regular transfusions?"

He looked at me sharply, fear creeping back. "Please. No!"

"But you'll stay alive."

"In a cage! Like a freak! I don't want to be a freak anymore. It's over. I want it to be over. Please."

"What do you want me to do?"

"I don't know. I don't want you to get in trouble."

I looked at him, at his face, at his eyes, at his soul. "There's a gun in the glove compartment," I said.

He sat for a moment, then solemnly held out his hand. I took it. He shook my hand, then opened the glove compartment. He removed the gun and slipped out of the car. He went down the hill into the brush.

I waited and waited and never did hear a shot.

Psychic Detective

Usually involved with the supernatural, modern psychic detectives can perhaps best be said to start with Sheridan Le Fanu's Dr. Martin Hesselius (1872). In the two major varieties of such tales, the most common detective is the normal man, such as William Hope Hodgson's Carnacki, who investigates strange occurrences. But there are also several "gifted" sleuths, such as Sax Rohmer's Morris Klaw, who use paranormal powers to investigate mundane matters. Though less well known than other varieties of sleuth, these practitioners have a more difficult task, since they, unlike Sherlock Holmes, cannot simply discard the impossible as a means of finding the truth.

Most psychic detective tales are clearly fantasy, but many have appeared in science fiction magazines, and some have presented such cleverly rational explanations for their improbable happenings that they should, at least, be considered science fantasy. Prolific Randall Garrett, for example, has written a series of short stories, and a novel, about a parallel world in which the Plantagenets still rule England and magic has undergone an "industrial" revolution.

The Ipswich Phial

RANDALL GARRETT

The pair-drawn brougham moved briskly along the Old Shore Road, moving westward a few miles from the little village of St.-Matthew's-Church, in the direction of Cherbourg.

The driver, a stocky man with a sleepy smile on his broad face, was well bundled up in a gray driving cloak, and the hood of his cowl was pulled up over his head and covered with a wide-brimmed slouch hat. Even in early June, on a sunshiny day, the Normandy coast can be chilly in the early morning, especially with a stiff wind blowing.

"Stop here, Danglars," said a voice behind him. "This looks like a good place for a walk along the beach."

"Yus, mistress." He reined in the horses, bringing the brougham to an easy stop. "You sure it's safe down there, Mistress Jizelle?" he asked, looking to his right, where the Channel stretched across to the north, toward England.

"The tide is out, is it not?" she asked briskly.

Danglars looked at his wristwatch. "Yus. Just at the ebb now."

"Very well. Wait for me here. I may return here, or I may walk on. If I go far, I will signal you from down the road."

"Yus, mistress."

She nodded once, sharply, then strode off toward the beach.

She was a tall, not unhandsome woman, who appeared to be in late middle age. Her gray-silver hair was cut rather shorter than the usual, but was beautifully arranged. Her costume was that of an upper-middle-class Anglo-French woman on a walking tour, but it was more in the British style than the Norman: well-burnished knee-high boots; a Scottish woolen skirt, the hem of which just brushed the boot-tops; a matching jacket; and a soft sweater of white wool that covered her from waist to chin. She wore no hat. She carried herself with the brisk, no-nonsense air of a woman who knows what she is and who she is, and will brook no argument from anyone about it.

Mistress Jizelle de Ville found a pathway down to the beach. There was a low cliff, varying from fifteen to twenty feet high, which separated the upper downs from the beach itself, but there were slopes and washes here and there which could be maneuvered. The cliff itself was the ultimate high-tide mark, but only during great storms did the sea ever come up that high; the normal high tide never came within fifteen yards of the base of the cliff, and the intervening space was covered with soft, dry sand which was difficult to walk in. Mistress Jizelle crossed the dry sand to the damper, more solidly packed area, and began walking westward.

It was a beautiful morning, in spite of the slight chill; just the sort of morning one would choose for a brisk, healthful walk along a pleasant beach. Mistress Jizelle was a woman who liked exercise and long walks, and she was a great admirer of scenic beauty. To her right, the rushing wind made scudding whitecaps of the ebbing tide and brought the "smell of the sea"—an odor never found on the open expanse of the sea itself, for it is composed of the aroma of the sea things which dwell in the tidal basins and the shallow coastal waters and the faint smell of the decomposition of dead and dying things beached by the rhythmic ebb and flow of tide and wave.

Overhead, the floating gulls gave their plaintive, almost catlike cries as they soared in search of the rich sustenance that the sea and shore gave them.

Not until she had walked nearly a hundred yards along the beach did Mistress Jizelle see anything out of the ordinary. When she did, she stopped and looked at it carefully. Ahead and to her left, some eight or nine yards from the base of the cliff, a man lay sprawled in the dry sand, twenty feet or so above the high-tide line.

After a moment, she walked toward the man, carefully and cautiously. He was certainly not dressed for bathing; he was wearing the evening dress of a gentleman. She walked up to the edge of the damp sand and stopped again, looking at the man carefully.

Then she saw something that made the hairs on the back of her neck rise.

Danglars was sitting placidly in the driver's seat of the brougham, smoking his clay pipe, when he saw the approaching trio. He eyed them carefully as they came toward the carriage. Two

young men and an older one, all dressed in the work clothes typical
of a Norman farmer. The eldest waved a hand and said something
Danglars couldn't hear over the sound of the waves and the wind.
Then they came close enough to be audible, and the eldest said:
"Allo! Got dee any trouble here?"

Danglars shook his head. "Nup."

The farmer ignored that. "Me an' m'boys saw dee stop up here,
an' thought mayap we could help. Name's Champtier. Samel
Champtier. Dese two a my tads, Evrit an' Lorin. If dou hass need a
aid, we do what we can."

Danglars nodded slowly, then took his pipe from his mouth.
"Good o' ya, Goodman Samel. Grace to ya. But I got no problem.
Mistress wanted to walk along the beach. Likes that sort of thing.
We head on pretty soon."

Samel cleared his throat. "Hass dou broke dy fast, dou an' d'
miss-lady? Wife fixin' breakfast now. Mayap we bring du somewhat?"

Danglars took another puff and sighed. Norman farmers were
good, kindly folk, but sometimes they overdid it. "Broke fast, Goodman Samel. Grace to ya. Mistress comes back, we got to be gettin'
on. Again, grace to ya."

"Caffe, then," Samel said decisively. He turned to the elder son,
"Evrit! Go tell dy mama for a pot a caffe an' two mugs! Run it,
now!"

Evrit took off like a turpentined ostrich.

Danglars cast his eyes toward heaven.

Mistress Jizelle swallowed and again looked closely at the dead
man. There was a pistol in his right hand and an ugly hole in his
right temple. There was blood all over the sand around his head.
And there was no question about his being dead.

She looked up and down the beach while she rather dazedly
brushed at her skirt with the palms of her hands. Then, bracing her
shoulders, Mistress Jizelle turned herself about and walked back
the way she had come, paralleling her own footprints. There were
no others on the beach.

Three men were talking to Danglars, and Danglars did not seem
to be agitated about it. Determinedly, she strode onward.

Not until she was within fifteen feet of the brougham did Danglars deign to notice her. Then he tugged his forelock and smiled

his sleepy smile. "Greeting, mistress. Have a nice walk?" He had a mug of caffe in one hand. He gestured with the other. "Goodman Samel and his boys, mistress, from the near farm. Brought a pot o' caffe."

The three farmers were tugging at their forelocks, too.

"I appreciate that," she said. "Very much. But I fear we have an emergency to attend to. Come with me, all of you."

Danglars widened his eyes. "Emergency, mistress?"

"That's what I said, wasn't it? Now, all of you follow me, and I shall show you what I mean."

"But, mistress—" Danglars began.

"Follow me," she said imperatively.

Danglars got down from the brougham. He had no choice but to follow with the others.

Mistress Jizelle led them across the sparse grass to the edge of the cliff that overlooked the place where the dead man lay.

"Now look down there. There is a dead man down there. He has, I think, been shot to death. I am not much acquainted with such things, but that is what it looks like to me."

The four knelt and looked at the body below. There was silence for a moment, then Samel said, rather formally: "Dou be right, mistress. Dead he be."

"Who is he, goodman?" she asked.

Samel stood up slowly and brushed his trousers with calloused hands. "Don't rightly know, mistress." He looked at his two sons, who were still staring down with fascination. "Who be he, tads?"

They stood up, brushing their trousers as their father had. Evrit, the elder, spoke. "Don't know, papa. Ee not from hereabout." He nudged his younger brother with an elbow. "Lorin?"

Lorin shook his head, looking at his father.

"Well, that does not matter for the moment," Mistress Jizelle said firmly. "There is Imperial Law to follow in such cases as this, and we must do so. Danglars, get in the brougham and return to—"

"But, Mistress Jizelle," Danglars cut in, "I can't—"

"You must do exactly as I tell you, Danglars," she said forcefully. "It is most important. Go back to St.-Matthew's-Church and notify the Rector. Then go on to Caen and notify the Armsmen. Goodman Samel and his boys will wait here with me and make sure nobody disturbs anything. Do you understand?"

"Yus, mistress. Perfec'ly." And off he went.

She turned to Samel. "Goodman, can you spare some time? I am sure you have work to do, but I shouldn't like to be left here alone."

Samel smiled. "Mornin' chores all done, mistress. Eldest tad, Orval, can take care of all for a couple hours. Don't fret." He looked at the younger boy. "Lorin, go dou an' tell dy mama an' dy brother what happen, but nobody else. An' say dey tell nobody. Hear?"

Lorin nodded and ran.

"And bring dou back somewat ta eat!" Evrit yelled after him.

Samel looked worried. "Mistress?"

"Yes, Goodman Samel?"

"Hass dou noticed somewat funny about d' man dere?"

"Funny?" She raised an eyebrow.

"Yea, mistress." He pointed down. "All round him, sand. Smooth. No footprints but dine own, an' dey come nowhere near him. Fresh dead, but—how he get dere?"

Five days later, Sir James le Lien, Special Agent of His Majesty's Secret Service, was seated in a comfortable chair in the studylike office of Lord Darcy, Chief Investigator for His Royal Highness, Richard, Duke of Normandy.

"And I still don't know where the Ipswich Phial is, Darcy," he was saying with some exasperation. "And neither do they."

Outside the open window, sounds of street traffic—the susurration of rubber-tired wheels on pavement, the clopping of horses' hooves, the footsteps and voices of a thousand people, and the myriad of other small noises that make up the song of a city—were wafted up from six floors below.

Lord Darcy leaned back in the chair behind his broad desk and held up a hand.

"Hold it, Sir James. You're leaping far ahead of yourself. I presume that by 'they' you mean the *Serka*—the Polish Secret Service. But what is this Phial, anyway?"

"I can't tell you for two reasons. First, you have no need to know. Second, neither do I, so I couldn't tell you if I wanted. Physically, it's a golden cylinder the size of your thumb, stoppered at one end with a golden stopper, which is sealed over with soft gold. Other than that, I know nothing but the code name: The Ipswich Phial."

Sean O Lochlainn, Master Sorcerer, who had been sitting quietly in another chair with his hands folded over his stomach, his eyes half closed, and his ears wide open, said: "I'd give a pretty to know who assigned that code name; sure and I'd have him sacked for incompetence."

"Oh?" said Sir James. "Why?"

Master Sean opened his eyes fully. "If the Poles don't know that the Ipswich Laboratories in Suffolk, under Master Sir Greer Davidson, is devoted to secret research in magic, then they are so incredibly stupid that we need not worry about them at all. With a name like 'Ipswich Phial' on it, the *Serka* would *have* to investigate, if they heard about it."

"Maybe it's just a red herring designed to attract their attention while something else is going on," said Lord Darcy.

"Maybe," Master Sean admitted, "but if so, me lord, it's rather dear. What Sir James has just described is an auric-stabilized psychic shield. What would you put in such a container? Some Khemic concoction, like an explosive or a poison? Or a secret message? That'd be incompetence compounded, like writing your grocery list on vellum in gold. Conspicuous consumption."

"I see," said Lord Darcy. He looked at Sir James. "What makes you think the *Serka* hasn't got it already?"

"If they had it," Sir James said, "they'd have cut and run. And they haven't; they're still swarming all over the place. There must be a dozen agents there."

"I presume that your own men are all over the place, too?"

"We're trying to keep them covered," Sir James said.

"Then they know you don't have the Phial, either."

"Probably."

Lord Darcy sighed and began filling his silver-chased porcelain pipe. "You say the dead man is Noel Standish." He tapped a sheaf of papers with his pipestem. "These say he was identified as a man named Bourke. You say it was murder. These say that the court of His Majesty's Coroner was ready to call it suicide until you put pressure on to keep the decision open. I have the vague feeling, James, that I am being used. I should like to point out that I am Chief Criminal Investigator for the Duke of Normandy, not— repeat: *not*—an agent of His Majesty's Secret Service."

"A crime has been committed," Sir James pointed out. "It is your duty to investigate it."

Lord Darcy calmly puffed his pipe alight. "James, James." His lean, handsome face was utterly impassive as he blew out a long plume of smoke. "You know perfectly well I am not obliged to in-vestigate every homicide in the Duchy. Neither Standish nor Bourke was a member of the aristocracy. I don't *have* to investigate this mess unless and until I get a direct order from either His Highness the Duke or His Majesty the King. Come on, James—con-vince me."

Master Sean did not smile, although it was somewhat of a strain to keep his face straight. The stout little Irish sorcerer knew per-fectly well that his lordship was bluffing. Lord Darcy could no more resist a case like this than a bee can resist clover blossoms. But Sir James did not know that. He did know that by bringing the case before his superiors, he could eventually get an order from the King, but by then the whole thing would likely be over.

"What do you want, Darcy?" the King's agent asked.

"Information," his lordship said flatly. "You want me to go down to St.-Matthew's-Church and create a diversion while you and your men do your work. Fine. But I will not play the part of a dupe. I damn well want to know what's going on. I want the whole story."

Sir James thought it over for ten or fifteen seconds, then said: "All right, my lord. I'll give it to you straight."

For centuries, the Kings of Poland had been expanding, in an ebb-and-flow fashion, the borders of their territories, primarily to-ward the east and south. In the south, they had been stopped by the Osmanlis. In the east, the last bite had been taken in the early 1930s, when the Ukraine was swallowed. King Casimir IX came to the throne in 1937 at the age of twenty, and two years later had plunged his country into a highly unsuccessful war with the Em-pire and her Scandinavian allies, and any further thought of expan-sion to the east was stopped by the threat of the unification of the Russian States.

Poland was now, quite literally, surrounded by enemies who hated her and neighbors who feared her. Casimir should have taken a few years to consolidate and conciliate, but it was apparent that the memory of his father and his own self-image as a con-queror were too strong for him. Knowing that any attempt to march his armies into the German buffer states that lay between his own western border and the eastern border of the Empire would be sui-cidal as things stood, Casimir decided to use his strongest non-mili-tary weapon: the *Serka*.

The nickname comes from a phrase meaning roughly: "The King's Right Arm." For financial purposes, it is listed in the books as the Ministry of Security Control, making it sound as if it were a division of the King's Government. It is not; none of His Slavonic Majesty's ministers or advisors know anything about, or have any control over, its operation. It is composed of fanatically loyal men and women who have taken a solemn vow of obedience to the King himself, *not* to the Government. The *Serka* is responsible to no one but the King's Person.

It is composed of two main branches: The Secret Police (domestic), and the Secret Service (foreign). This separation, however, is far from rigid. An agent of one branch may at any time be assigned to the other.

The *Serka* is probably the most powerful, most ruthless instrument of government on the face of the Earth today. Its agents, many of them Talented sorcerers, infest every country in Europe, most especially the Anglo-French Empire.

Now, it is a historical fact that Plantagenet Kings do not take kindly to invasion of their domain by foreign sovereigns; for eight centuries they have successfully resisted such intrusive impudence.

There is a saying in Europe: "He who borrows from a Plantagenet may repay without interest; he who steals from a Plantagenet will repay at ruinous rates."

His present Majesty, John IV—by the Grace of God, King of England, Ireland, Scotland, and France; Emperor of the Romans and Germans; Premier Chief of the Moqtessumid Clan; Son of the Sun; Count of Anjou and Maine; Prince Donator of the Sovereign Order of St. John of Jerusalem; Sovereign of the Most Ancient Order of the Round Table, of the Order of the Leopard, of the Order of the Lily, of the Order of the Three Crowns, and of the Order of St. Andrew; Lord and Protector of the Western Continents of New England and New France; Defender of the Faith—was no exception to that rule.

Unlike his medieval predecessors, however, King John had no desire to increase Imperial holdings in Europe. The last Plantagenet to add to the Imperial domain in Europe was Harold I, who signed the original Treaty of København in 1420. The Empire was essentially frozen within its boundaries for more than a century until, during the reign of John III, the discovery of the continents of the Western Hemisphere opened a whole new world for Anglo-French explorers.

John IV no longer thought of European expansion, but he deeply resented the invasion of his realm by Polish *Serka* agents. Therefore, the theft of a small golden phial from the Ipswich Laboratories had provoked instant reaction from the King and from His Majesty's Secret Service.

"The man who actually stole it," Sir James explained, "is irrelevant. He was merely a shrewd biscuit who accidentally had a chance to get his hands on the Phial. Just how is immaterial, but rest assured that that hole has been plugged. The man saw an opportunity and grabbed it. He wasn't a Polish agent, but he knew how to get hold of one, and a deal was made."

"How much time did it take him to deal, after the Phial was stolen?" Lord Darcy asked.

"Three days, my lord. Sir Greer found it was missing within two hours of its being stolen, and notified us straight away. It was patently obvious who had taken it, but it took us three days to trace him down. As I said, he was a shrewd biscuit.

"By the time we'd found him, he'd made his deal and had the money. We were less than half an hour too late. A *Serka* agent already had the Phial and was gone.

"Fortunately, the thief was just that—a thief, not a real *Serka* agent. When he'd been caught, he freely told us everything he knew. That, plus other information received, convinced us our quarry was on a train for Portsmouth. We got hold of Noel Standish at the Portsmouth office by teleson, but . . ."

The plans of men do not necessarily coincide with those of the Universe. A three-minute delay in a traffic jam had ended with Noel Standish at the slip, watching the Cherbourg boat sliding out toward the Channel, with forty feet between himself and the vessel.

Two hours later, he was standing at the bow of H.I.M.S. *Dart*, staring southward into the darkness, listening to the rushing of the Channel waters against the hull of the fast cutter. Standish was not in a good mood.

In the first place, the teleson message had caught him just as he was about to go out to dine with friends at the Bellefontaine, and he had had no chance to change; he felt silly as hell standing on the deck of a Navy cutter in full evening dress. Further, it had taken better than an hour to convince the Commanding Admiral at the Portsmouth Naval Docks that the use of a cutter was imperative— and then only at the cost of a teleson connection to London.

There was but one gem in these otherwise bleak surroundings: Standish had a firm psychic lock on his quarry.

He had already had a verbal description from London. *Young man, early to middle twenties. Five feet nine. Slender, but well-muscled. Thick, dark brown hair. Smooth shaven. Brown eyes. Well formed brows. Face handsome, almost pretty. Well-dressed. Conservative dark green coat, puce waistcoat, gold-brown trousers. Carrying a dark olive attaché case.*

And he had clearly seen the quarry standing on the deck of the cross-Channel boat as it had pulled out of Portsmouth, heading for Cherbourg.

Standish had a touch of the Talent. His own name for a rather specialized ability was "the Game of Hide and Seek," wherein Standish did both the hiding and the seeking. Once he got a lock on someone he could follow him anywhere. Further, Standish became psychically invisible to his quarry; even a Master Sorcerer would never notice him as long as Standish took care not to be located visually. Detection range, however, was only a matter of miles, and the man in the puce waistcoat, Standish knew, was at the limit of that range.

Someone tapped Standish on the shoulder. "Excuse me, sir—"

Standish jerked round nervously. "*What? What?*"

The young officer lifted his eyebrows, taken aback by the sudden reaction. This Standish fellow seemed to have every nerve on edge. "Begging your pardon, sir, but the Captain would have a word with you. Follow me, please."

Senior Lieutenant Malloix, commanding H.I.M.S. *Dart,* wearing his royal blue uniform, was waiting in his cabin with a glass of brandy in each hand. He gave one to Standish while the junior officer quietly disappeared. "Come in, Standish. Sit and relax. You've been staring off the starboard bow ever since we cast off, and that's no good. Won't get us there any the faster, you know."

Standish took the glass and forced a smile. "I know, Captain. Thanks." He sipped. "Still, do you think we'll make it?"

The captain frowned, sat down, and waved Standish to a chair while he said: "Hard to say, frankly. We're using all the power we have, but the sea and the wind don't always do what we'd like 'em to. There's not a damn thing we can do about it, so breathe deep and see what comes, eh?"

"Right you are, Captain." He took another swallow of brandy. "How good a bearing do we have on her?"

S/Lt Malloix patted the air with a hand. "Not to worry. Lieutenant Seamus Mac Lean, our navigator, has a Journeyman's rating in the Sorcerer's Guild, and this sort of thing is his speciality. The packet boat is two degrees off to starboard and, at our present speed, forty-one minutes ahead of us. That's the good news."

"And the bad news?"

Malloix shrugged. "Wind variation. We haven't gained on her in fifteen minutes. Cheer up. Pour yourself another brandy."

Standish cheered up and drank more brandy, but it availed him nothing. The *Dart* pulled into the dock at Cherbourg one minute late, in spite of all she could do.

Nevertheless, Goodman Puce-Weskit was less than a hundred yards away as Standish ran down the gangplank of the *Dart,* and the distance rapidly closed as he walked briskly toward his quarry, following his psychic compass that pointed unerringly toward Puce-Weskit.

He was hoping that Puce-Weskit was still carrying the Phial; if he wasn't, if he had passed it on to some unknown person aboard the packet, the whole thing was blown. The thing would be in Krakowa before the month was out.

He tried not to think about that.

The only thing to do was follow his quarry until there came a chance to waylay and search him.

He had already given a letter to the captain of the *Dart,* to be delivered as soon as possible to a certain address on the Rue Queen Brigid, explaining to the agent in charge of the Cherbourg office what was going on. The trouble was, Standish was not carrying a tracer attuned to the Cherbourg office; there was no way to get in touch with them, and he didn't dare leave Puce-Weskit. He couldn't even set up a rendezvous, since he had no idea where Puce-Weskit would lead him.

And, naturally, when one needed an Armsman, there wasn't one in sight.

Twenty minutes later, Puce-Weskit turned on to the Rue Queen Brigid.

Don't tell me he's headed for the Service office, Standish thought. *My dear Puce-Weskit, surely you jest.*

No fear. A dozen squares from the Secret Service office, Goodman Puce-Weskit turned and went into a caffe-house called the Aden. There, he stopped.

Standish had been following on the opposite side of the street, so there was less chance of his being spotted. Dodging the early morning traffic, narrowly avoiding the lead horse of a beer lorry, he crossed the Rue Queen Brigid to the Aden.

Puce-Weskit was some forty feet away, toward the rear of the caffe-house. Could he be passing the Phial on to some confederate?

Standish was considering what to do next when the decision was made for him. He straightened up with a snap as his quarry suddenly began to move southward at a relatively high rate of speed.

He ran into the Aden. And saw his mistake.

The rear wall was only thirty feet away; Puce-Weskit had gone through the rear door, and had been standing *behind* the Aden!

He went right on through the large room, out the back door. There was a small alleyway there, but the man standing a few feet away was most certainly not his quarry.

"Quick!" Standish said breathlessly. "The man in the puce waistcoat! Where did he go?"

The man looked a little flustered. "Why—uh—I don't know, sir. As soon as his horse was brought—"

"Horse? Where did he get a horse?"

"Why, he left it in the proprietor's charge three or four days ago. Four days ago. Paid in advance for the keeping of it. He asked it to be fetched, then he went. I don't know where."

"Where can I rent a horse?" Standish snapped.

"The proprietor—"

"Take me to him immediately!"

"And that," said Sir James le Lien, "is the last trace we were able to uncover until he reported in at Caen two days later. We wouldn't even know that much if one of our men hadn't been having breakfast at the Aden. He recognized Standish, of course, but didn't say anything to him, for obvious reasons."

Lord Darcy nodded. "And he turns up dead the following morning near St.-Matthew's-Church. Any conjecture on what he may have been doing during those two days?"

"It seems fairly clear. The proprietor of the Aden told us that our quarry—call him Bourke—had his saddlebags packed with food packets in protective-spell wrappers, enough for a three, maybe four-day trip. You know the Old Shore Road that runs southeast from Cherbourg to the Vire, crosses the river, then goes westward, over the Orne, and loops around to Harfleur?"

"Of course," Lord Darcy said.

"Well, then, you know it's mostly farming country, with only a few scattered villages, and no teleson connections. We think Bourke took that road, and that Standish followed him. We think Bourke was headed for Caen."

Master Sean lifted an eyebrow. "Then why not take the train? 'Twould be a great deal easier and faster, Sir James."

Sir James smiled. "It would be. But not safer. The trouble with public transportation is that you're essentially trapped on it. When you're fleeing, you want as much freedom of choice as possible. Once you're aboard a public conveyance, you're pretty much constrained to stay on it until it stops, and that isn't under your control."

"Aye, that's clear," said Master Sean. He looked thoughtful. "This psychic lock-on you mentioned—you're sure Standish used it on Bourke?"

"Not absolutely certain, of course," Sir James admitted. "But he certainly had that Talent; he was tested by a board of Masters from your own Guild. Whether he used it or not at that particular time, I can only conjecture, but I think it's a pretty solid assumption."

Lord Darcy carefully watched a column of pipesmoke rise toward the ceiling and said nothing.

"I'll agree with you," Master Sean said. "There's no doubt in me mind he did just that, and I'll not say he was wrong to do so. *De mortuis non disputandum est*. I just wonder if he knew how to handle it."

"How do you mean?" Sir James asked.

"Well, let's suppose a man could make himself perfectly transparent—'invisible', in other words. The poor lad would have to be very careful, eh? In soft ground or in snow, he'll leave footprints; in a crowd, he may brush up against someone. Can you imagine what it would be like if you grabbed such a man? There you've got an armful of air that feels fleshy, smells sweaty, sounds excited, and would taste salty if you cared to try the experiment. You'll admit that such an object would be suspect?"

"Well, yes," Sir James admitted, "but—"

"Sir James," Master Sean continued, "you have no idea how conspicuous a psychically invisible person can be in the wrong circumstances. There he stands, visible to the eye, sensible to the touch, audible to the ear, and all the rest—*but there's nobody home!*

"The point I'm making, Sir James, is this: How competent was Noel Standish at handling his ability?"

Sir James opened his mouth, shut it, and frowned. After a second, he said: "When you put it that way, Master Sean, I must admit I don't know. But he handled it successfully for twelve years."

"And failed once," said Master Sean. "Fatally."

"Now hold, my dear Sean," Lord Darcy said suddenly. "We have no evidence that he failed in that way. That he allowed himself to be killed is a matter of cold fact; that he did so in that way is pure conjecture. Let's not leap to totally unwarranted conclusions."

"Aye, me lord. Sorry."

Lord Darcy focused his gray eyes on Sir James. "Then I have not been called in merely to create a diversion, eh?"

Sir James blinked. "I beg your pardon, my lord?"

"I mean," said his lordship patiently, "that you actually want me to solve the problem of 'who killed Noel Standish?'"

"Of course! Didn't I make that clear?"

"Not very." Lord Darcy picked up the papers again. "Now let's get a few things straight. How did the body come to be identified as Bourke, and where is the real Bourke? Or whoever he was."

"The man Standish was following checked into the Green Seagull Inn under that name," Sir James said. "He'd used the same name in England. He was a great deal like Standish in height, weight, and coloring. He disappeared that night, and we've found no trace of him since."

Lord Darcy nodded thoughtfully. "It figures. Young gentleman arrives at village inn. Body of young gentleman found next morning. Since there is only one young gentleman in plain sight, they are the same young gentleman. Identifying a total stranger is a chancy thing at best."

"Exactly. That's why I held up my own identification."

"I understand. Now, exactly how did you happen to be in St.-Matthew's-Church that night?" Lord Darcy asked.

"Well, as soon as Standish was fairly certain that his quarry had settled down at the Green Seagull, he rode for Caen and sent a message to my office, here in Rouen. I took the first train, but by the time I got there, they were both missing."

"Yes." Lord Darcy sighed. "Well, I suppose we'd best be getting down there. I'll have to ask His Royal Highness to order me to, so you may as well come along with me and explain the whole thing all over again to Duke Richard."

Sir James looked pained. "I suppose so. We want to get there as soon as possible, or the whole situation will become impossible. Their silly Midsummer Fair starts the day after tomorrow, and there are strangers showing up already."

Lord Darcy closed his eyes. "That's all we need. Complications."

Master Sean went to the door of the office. "I'll have Ciardi pack our bags, me lord. Looks like a long stay."

The little village of St.-Matthew's-Church was transforming itself. The Fair proper was to be held in a huge field outside of town, and the tents were already collecting on the meadow. There was, of course, no room in the village itself for people to stay; certainly the little Green Seagull couldn't hold a hundredth of them. But a respectable tent-city had been erected in another big field, and there was plenty of parking space for horse-wagons and the like.

In the village, the storefronts were draped with bright bunting, and the shopkeepers were busy marking up all the prices. Both pubs had been stocking up on extra potables for weeks. For nine days, the village would be full of strangers going about their hectic business, disrupting the peace of the local inhabitants, bringing with them a strange sort of excitement. Then they would go, leaving behind acres of ugly rubbish and bushels of beautiful cash.

In the meanwhile, a glorious time would be had by all.

Lord Darcy cantered his horse along the River Road up from Caen and entered St.-Matthew's-Church at noon on that bright sunshiny day, dressed in the sort of riding clothes a well-to-do merchant might wear. He wasn't exactly incognito, but he didn't want to attract attention, either. Casually, he made his way through the already gathering throngs toward the huge old church dedicated to St. Matthew, which had given the village its name. He guided his mount over to the local muffin square, where the array of hitching posts stood, tethered his horse, and walked over to the church.

The Reverend Father Arthur Lyon, Rector of the Church of St.-Matthew, and, *ipso facto*, Rector of St.-Matthew's-Church, was a broad-shouldered man in his fifties who stood a good two inches taller than six feet. His bald head was fringed with silvery hair, and his authoritative, pleasant face was usually smiling. He was sitting behind his desk in his office.

There came a rap at his office door. A middle-aged woman came in quickly and said: "Sorry to bodder dee, Fahder, but dere's a Lord Darcy to see dee."

"Show him in, Goodwife Anna."

Lord Darcy entered Father Art's office to find the priest waiting with outstretched hand. "It's been some time, my lord," he said with a broad smile. "Good to see you again."

"I may say the same. How have you been, old friend?"

"Not bad. Pray, sit down. May I offer you a drink?"

"Not just now, Father." He took the proffered seat. "I understand you have a bit of a problem here."

Father Art leaned back in his chair and folded his hands behind his head. "Ahh, yes. The so-called suicide. Bourke." He chuckled. "I thought higher authority would be in on that, sooner or later."

"Why do you say 'so-called suicide', Father?"

"Because I know people, my lord. If a man's going to shoot himself, he doesn't go out to a lonely beach for it. If he goes to a beach, it's to drown himself. A walk into the sea. I don't say a man has never shot himself by the seaside, but it's so rare that when it happens I get suspicious."

"I agree," Lord Darcy said. He had known Arthur Lyon for some years, and knew that the man was an absolutely dedicated servant of his God and his King. His career had been unusual. During the '39 war, he had risen to the rank of Sergeant-Major in the Eighteenth Infantry. Afterwards, he had become an Officer of the King's Peace, and had retired as a Chief Master-at-Arms before taking up his vocation as a priest. He had shown himself to be not only a top-grade priest, but also a man with the Talent as a brilliant Healer, and had been admitted, with honors, to the Order of St. Luke.

"Old friend," Lord Darcy said, "I need your help. What I am about to tell you is most confidential; I will have to ask you to disclose none of it without official permission."

Father Art took his hands from behind his head and leaned forward with a gleam in his eyes. "As if it were under the Seal of the Confessional, my lord. Go ahead."

It took better than half an hour for Lord Darcy to give the good father the whole story as he knew it. Father Art had leaned back in his chair again with his hands locked behind his head, smiling seraphically at the ceiling. "Ah, yes, my lord. Utterly fascinating. I remember Friday, sixth June, very well. Yes, very well indeed." He continued to smile at the ceiling.

Lord Darcy closed his right eye and cocked his left eyebrow. "I trust you intend to tell me what incident stamped that day so indelibly on your mind."

"Certainly, my lord. I was just reveling in having made a deduction. When I tell my story, I dare say you'll make the same deduction." He brought his gaze down from the ceiling and his hands from behind his head. "You might say it began late Thursday night. Because of a sick call which had kept me up most of the previous night, I went to bed quite early Thursday evening. And, naturally, I woke up a little before midnight and couldn't get back to sleep. I decided I might as well make use of the time, so I did some paper work for a while and then went into the church to say the morning office before the altar. Then I decided to take a walk in the churchyard. I often do that; it's a pleasant place to meditate.

"There was no moon that night," the priest continued, "but the sky was cloudless and clear. It was about two hours before dawn. It was quite dark, naturally, but I know my way about those tombstones pretty well by now. I'd been out there perhaps a quarter of an hour when the stars went out."

Lord Darcy seemed to freeze for a full second. "When the *what?*"

"When the stars went out," Father Art repeated. "One moment, there they were, in their accustomed constellations—I was looking at Cygnus in particular—and the next moment the sky was black all over. Everywhere. All at once."

"I see," said Lord Darcy.

"Well, *I* couldn't," the priest said, flashing a smile. "It was black as the Pit. For a second or two, I confess, I was almost panicky. It's a weird feeling when the stars go out."

"I dare say," Lord Darcy murmured.

"But," the Father continued, "as a Sensitive, I knew that there was no threat close by, and, after a minute, I got my bearings again. I could have come back to the church, but I decided to wait for a while, just to find out what would happen next. I don't know how long I stood there. It seemed like an hour, but it was probably less than fifteen minutes. Then the stars came back on the same way they'd gone out—all at once, all over the sky."

"No dimming out?" Lord Darcy asked. "No slow brightening back on?"

"None, my lord. *Blink:* off. *Blink:* on."

"Not a sea fog, then."

"Impossible. No sea fog could move that fast."

Lord Darcy focused his eyes on a foot-high statue of St. Matthew that stood in a niche in the wall and stared at the Apostle without actually seeing him.

After a minute, Lord Darcy said: "I left Master Sean in Caen to make a final check of the body. He should be here within the hour. I'll talk to him, but . . ." His voice trailed off.

Father Art nodded. "Our speculation certainly needs to be confirmed, my lord, but I think we're on the right track. Now, how else can I help?"

"Oh, yes. That." Lord Darcy grinned. "Your revelation of the extinguished stars almost made me forget why I came to talk to you in the first place. What I'd like you to do, Father, is talk to the people that were at the Green Seagull on the afternoon and late evening of the fifth. I'm a stranger, and I probably wouldn't get much out of them—certainly not as much as you can. I want to know the whole pattern of comings and goings. I don't have to tell an old Armsman like yourself what to look for. Will you do it?"

Father Art's smile came back. "With pleasure, my lord."

"There's one other thing. Can you put up Master Sean and myself for a few days? There is, alas, no room at the inn."

Father Art's peal of laughter seemed to rock the bell tower.

Master Sean O Lochlainn had always been partial to mules. "The mule," he was fond of saying, "is as much smarter than a horse as a raven is smarter than a falcon. Neither a raven nor a mule will go charging into combat just because some human tells him to." Thus it was that the sorcerer came riding toward St.-Matthew's-Church, clad in plain brown, seated in a rather worn saddle, on the back of a very fine mule. He looked quite pleased with himself.

The River Road had plenty of traffic on it; half the population of the Duchy seemed to be converging on the little coastal village of St.-Matthew's-Church. So Master Sean was mildly surprised to see someone headed toward him, but that feeling vanished when he saw that the approaching horseman was Lord Darcy.

"Not headed back to Caen, are you, me lord?" he asked when Lord Darcy came within speaking distance.

"Not at all, my dear Sean; I rode out to meet you. Let's take the cutoff road to the west; it's a shortcut that bypasses the village and takes us to the Old Shore Road, near where the body was found." He wheeled his horse around and rode beside Master Sean's mule. Together, they cantered briskly toward the Old Shore Road.

"Now," Lord Darcy said, "what did you find out at Caen?"

"Conflicting evidence, me lord; conflicting evidence. At least as far as the suicide theory is concerned. There was evidence at the cliff edge that he had fallen or been pushed over and tumbled down along the face of the cliff. But he was found twenty-five feet from the base of the cliff. He had two broken ribs and a badly sprained right wrist—to say nothing of several bad bruises. All of these had been inflicted some hours before death."

Lord Darcy gave a rather bitter chuckle. "Which leaves us with two possibilities. *Primus:* Goodman Standish stands on the edge of the cliff, shoots himself through the head, tumbles to the sand below, crawls twenty-five feet, and takes some hours to die of a wound that was obviously instantly fatal. Or, *secundus:* He falls off the cliff, crawls the twenty-five feet, does nothing for a few hours, then decides to shoot himself. I find the second hypothesis only slightly more likely than the first. That his right wrist was sprained badly is a fact that tops it all off. Not suicide; no, not suicide." Lord Darcy grinned. "That leaves accident or murder. Which hypothesis do you prefer, my dear Sean?"

Master Sean frowned deeply, as if he were in the awful throes of concentration. Then his face brightened as if revelation had come. "I have it, me lord! He was accidentally murdered!"

Lord Darcy laughed. "Excellent! Now, having cleared that up, there is further evidence that I have not given you yet."

He told Master Sean about Father Art's singular experience with the vanishing stars.

When he had finished, the two rode in silence for a minute or two. Then Master Sean said softly: "So *that's* what it is."

There was an Armsman standing off the road at the site of the death, and another seated, who stood up as Lord Darcy and Master

Sean approached. The two riders dismounted and walked their mounts up to where the Armsmen were standing.

"I am sorry, gentlemen," said the first Armsman with an air of authority, "but this area is off bounds, by order of His Royal Highness the Duke of Normandy."

"Very good; I am happy to hear it," said his lordship, taking out his identification. "I am Lord Darcy; this is Master Sorcerer Sean O Lochlainn."

"Yes, my lord," said the Armsman. "Sorry I didn't recognize you."

"No problem. This is where the body was found?"

"Yes, my lord. Just below this cliff, here. Would you like to take a look, my lord?"

"Indeed I would. Thank you."

Lord Darcy, under the respectful eyes of the two Armsmen, minutely examined the area around the cliff edge. Master Sean stayed with him, trying to see everything his lordship saw.

"Everything's a week old," Lord Darcy muttered bitterly. "Look at that grass, there. A week ago, I could have told you how many men were scuffing it up; today, I only know that it was more than two. I don't suppose there's any way of reconstructing it, my dear Sean?"

"No, me lord. I am a magician, not a miracle worker."

"Thought not. Look at the edge of this cliff. He fell, certainly. But was he pushed? Or thrown? No way of telling. Wind and weather have done their work too well. To quote my cousin de London: 'Pfui!'"

"Yes, me lord."

"Well, let's go down to the beach and take a look from below."

That operation entailed walking fifty yards or so down the cliff edge to a steep draw which they could clamber down, then back again to where Standish had died.

There was a pleasant breeze from landward that brought the smell of growing crops. A dozen yards away, three gulls squabbled raucously over the remains of some dead sea-thing.

Lord Darcy was still in a bitter mood. "Nothing, damn it. *Nothing*. Footprints all washed away long ago. Or blown away by the wind. Damn, damn, *damn!* All we have to go by is the testimony of eyewitnesses, which is notoriously unreliable."

"You don't believe 'em, me lord?" Master Sean asked.

Lord Darcy was silent for several seconds. Then, in a calmer voice, he said: "Yes. Oddly enough, I do. I think the testimony of those farmers was absolutely accurate. They saw what they saw, and they reported what they saw. But they did not—they *could* not have seen everything!"

One of the Armsmen on the cliff above said: "That's the spot, right there, my lord. Near that flat rock." He pointed.

But Lord Darcy did not even look at the indicated spot. He had looked up when the Armsman spoke, and was staring at something on the cliff face about two feet below the Armsman's boot toes.

Master Sean followed his lordship's gaze and spotted the area immediately. "Looks like someone's been carving his initials, me lord."

"Indeed. How do you make them out?"

"Looks like S. . .S. . .O. Who do we know with the initials SSO?"

"Nobody connected with this case so far. The letters may have been up there for some time. But . . ."

"Aye, me lord," said Master Sean. "I see what you mean. I'll do a time check on them. Do you want 'em preserved?"

"Unless they're more than a week old, yes. By the by, did Standish have a knife on him when he was found?"

"Not so far as I know, me lord. Wasn't mentioned in the reports."

"Hmmm." Lord Darcy began prowling around the whole area, reminding Master Sean of nothing so much as a leopard in search of his evening meal. He finally ended up at the base of the cliff, just below where the glyphs had been carved into the clay wall. He went down on his knees and began digging.

"It has to be here somewhere," he murmured.

"Might I ask what you're looking for, me lord?"

"A piece of steel, my dear Sean; a piece of steel."

Master Sean put his carpetbag on the sand and opened it, taking out a thin, dark, metallic-blue wand just as Lord Darcy said: "Aa*ha!*"

Master Sean, wand still in hand, said: "What is it, me lord?"

"As you see," Lord Darcy said, standing up and displaying the object in the palm of his hand. "Behold and observe, old friend: a man's pocketknife."

Master Sean smiled broadly. "Aye. I presume you'll be wanting a relationship test, me lord? Carving, cutter, and corpse?"

"Of course. No, don't put away your wand. That's your generalized metal detector, is it not?"

"Aye, me lord. It's been similarized to all things metallic."

"Good. Put this knife away for analysis, then let's go over to where the body was found. We'll see if there isn't something else to be dug up."

The Master Sorcerer pointed the wand in his right hand at the sand and moved back and forth across the area; his eyes almost closed, his left hand held above his head, fingers spread. Every time he stopped, Lord Darcy would dig into the soft sand and come up with a bit of metal—a rusty nail, a corroded brass belt-buckle, a copper twelfth-bit, a bronze farthing, and even a silver half-sovereign—all of which showed evidence of having been there for some time.

While the two of them worked, the Armsmen on the cliff above watched in silence. It is not wise to disturb a magician at work.

Only one of the objects was of interest to Lord Darcy: a small lump of lead. He dropped it into a waistcoat pocket and went on digging.

At last, Master Sean, having covered an area of some eight by twelve feet, said: "That's it, me lord."

Lord Darcy stood up, brushed the sand from his hands and trousers, and looked at the collection of junk he had put on the big flat rock. "Too bad we couldn't have found a sixth-bit. We'd be an even solidus ahead. No gold in the lot, either."

Master Sean chuckled. "You can't expect to find a complete set of samples from the Imperial Mint, me lord."

"I suppose not. But here—" he took the small lump of lead from his waistcoat pocket, "—is what I expected to find. Unless I am very much mistaken, this bullet came from the .36 Heron that the late Standish carried, and is the same bullet which passed through his head. Here: check on it, will you, my good Sean?"

Master Sean put the bullet in one of the carefully insulated pockets of his capacious carpetbag, and the two men trudged back across the sand, up the slope to the top of the cliff again.

Master Sean spread himself prone and looked over the edge of the cliff. After a minute inspection of the carving in the sandy clay of the cliff face, he got up, took some equipment from his carpetbag, and lay down again to go to work. A simple cohesion spell sufficed to set the clay so that it would not crumble. Then, he deftly began to cut out the brick of hardened clay defined by the spell.

In the meantime, Lord Darcy had called the senior of the two Armsmen to one side and had asked him a question.

"No, my lord, we ain't had any trouble," the Armsman said. "We been runnin' three eight-hour shifts out here ever since the body was found, and hardly nobody's come by. The local folk all know better. Wouldn't come near it, anyway, till the whole matter's been cleared up and the site's been blessed by a priest. 'Course, there was that thing this morning."

"This morning?" Lord Darcy lifted an eyebrow.

"Yes, my lord." He glanced at his wristwatch. "Just after we come on duty. Just on six hours ago—eight-twelve."

"And what happened?" his lordship asked with seemingly infinite patience.

"Well, these two folk come along the beach from the east. Romany, they was. Whole tribe of 'em come into St.-Matthew's-Church fairground early this morning. These two—man and a woman, they was—come along arm in arm. Dan—that's Armsman Danel, over there—warned 'em off, but they just smiled and waved and kept coming. So Dan went down to the beach fast and blocked 'em off. They pretended they didn't speak no Anglo-French; you know how these Romany are. But Dan made it clear they wasn't to come no farther, so off they went. No trouble."

"They went back without any argument, eh?"

"Yes, my lord, they did."

"Well, no harm done there, then. Carry on, Armsman."

"Yes, my lord."

Master Sean came back from the cliff edge with a chunk of thaumaturgically-hardened clay further loading his symbol-decorated carpetbag. "Anything else, me lord?"

"I think not. Let's get some lunch."

In a tent near the fairgrounds, an agent of *Serka*, Mission Commander for this particular operation, was opening what looked on the outside like a battered, scuffed, worn, old leather suitcase. The inside was new and in the best condition, and the contents were startlingly similar to those of Master Sean's symbol-decorated carpetbag.

Out came two small wands, scarcely six inches long, of ruby-red crystal wound with oddly-spaced helices of silver wire that took exactly five turns around the ruby core. Each wand was a mirror image of the other; one helix wound to the right, the other to the left. Out came two small glass flacons, one containing a white, coarsely-ground substance, the other an amber-yellow mass of small granules. These were followed by a curiously-wrought golden candlestick some four inches high, an inch-thick candle, and a small brazier.

Like any competent sorcerer, the Commander had hands that were strong and yet capable of delicate work. The beeswax candle was being fitted into the candlestick by those hands when there came a scratching at the closed tent flap.

The Commander froze. "Yes?"

"One-three-seven comes," said a whispered voice.

The Commander relaxed. "Very well; send him in."

Seconds later, the tent flap opened, and another *Serka* agent ducked into the tent. He glanced at the thaumaturgical equipment on the table as he sat down on a stool. "It's come to that, eh?" he said.

"I'm not certain yet," said the Commander. "It may. I don't want it to. I want to avoid any entanglement with Master Sean O Lochlainn. A man with his ability and power is a man to avoid when he's on the other side."

"Your pardon, Mission Commander, but just how certain are you that the man you saw on the mule this morning was actually Master Sean?"

"Quite certain. I heard him lecture many times at the University at Buda-Pest when I was an undergraduate there in 'sixty-eight, 'sixty-nine, and 'seventy. He was taking his ThD in theoretics and analog math. His King paid for it from the Privy Purse, but he supplemented his income by giving undergrad lectures."

"Would he recognize you?"

"Highly unlikely. Who pays any attention to undergraduate students at a large University?"

The Commander waved an impatient hand. "Let's hear your report."

"Yes, Mission Commander," Agent 137 said briskly. "I followed the man on muleback, as you ordered. He met another man, ahorse, coming from the village. He was tall, lean but muscular, with handsome, rather English-looking features. He was dressed as a merchant, but I suspected . . ."

The Commander nodded. "Lord Darcy. Obviously. Continue."

"You said they'd go to the site of the death, and when they took the left-hand bypass I was sure of it. I left off following and galloped on to the village, where Number 202 was waiting with the boat. We had a good westerly breeze, so we made it to the cove before them. We anchored and lay some two hundred yards offshore. Number 202 did some fishing while I watched through field glasses.

"They talked to the Armsmen atop the cliff for a while, then went down to the beach. One of the Armsmen pointed to where the body had been. Darcy went on talking to him for a while. Then Darcy walked around, looking at things. He went over to the base of the cliff and began digging. He found something; I couldn't see what.

"Master Sean put it in his bag, then, for ten minutes or so, he quartered the area where the body'd been, using one of those long, blue-black metal wands—you know—"

"A metal detector," said the Commander. "Yes. Go on."

"Yes. Lord Darcy dug every time O Lochlainn pointed something out. Dug up an awful lot of stuff. But he found *some*thing interesting. Don't know what it was; couldn't see it. But he stuck it in his pocket and gave it to the sorcerer later."

"I know what it was," said the Commander in a hard voice. "Was that the only thing that seemed to interest him?"

"Yes, as far as I could tell," said 137.

"Then what happened?"

137 shrugged. "They went back topside. Darcy talked to one of the Armsmen; the other watched the sorcerer dig a hole in the cliff face."

The Mission Commander frowned. "Dig a hole? A *hole?*"

"That's right. Lay flat on his belly, reached down a couple of feet over the·edge, and dug something out. Couldn't see what it was. Left a hole about the size of a man's two fists—maybe a bit bigger."

"Damn! Why couldn't you have watched more carefully?"

Agent 137's face stiffened. "It was very difficult to see well, Mission Commander. Any closer than two hundred yards, and we would have drawn attention. Did you ever try to focus six-by field glasses from a light boat bobbing up and down on the sea?"

"Calm down. I'm not angry with you. You did well. I just wish we had better information." The Commander looked thoughtful. "That tells us something. We can forget about the beach. Order the men to stay away; they are not to go there again for any reason.

"The Phial is not there now, if it ever was. If Master Sean did not find it, it wasn't there. If he *did* find it, it is gone now, and he and Lord Darcy know where it is. And that is a problem I must consider. Now get out of here and let me think."

Agent 137 got out.

The public room at the Green Seagull, as far as population went, looked like a London railway car at the rush hour.

Amidst all the hubbub, wine and beer crossed the bar in one direction, while copper and silver crossed it in the other, making everyone happy on both sides.

In the club bar, it was somewhat quieter, but the noise from the public bar was distinctly audible. The innkeeper himself was taking care of the customers in the club bar; he took a great deal of pride in his work. Besides, the tips were larger and the work easier.

"Would dere be anyting else for dee?" he asked as he set two pints of beer on one of the tables. "Someting to munch on, mayhap?"

"Not just now, Goodman Dreyque," said Father Art. "This will do us for a while."

"Very good, Fahder. Tank dee." He went quietly away.

Lord Darcy took a deep draught of his beer and sighed. "Cool beer is a great refresher on a midsummer evening. The Green Seagull keeps an excellent cellar. Food's good, too; Master Sean and I ate here this afternoon."

"Where is Master Sean now?" the priest asked.

"In the rooms you assigned us in the Rectory, amidst his apparatus, doing lab work on some evidence we dug up." His voice became soft. "Did you find out what happened here that night?"

"Pretty much," Father Art replied in the same low tones. "There are a few things which are still a little hazy, but I think we can fill in most of those areas."

Standish's quarry had arrived at the Green Seagull late in the afternoon of the fifth, giving the name "Richard Bourke." He was carrying only an attaché case, but since he had a horse and saddle and saddlebags, they were considered surety against indebtedness.

There were only six rooms for hire in the inn, all on the upper floor of the two-storied building. Two of these were already occupied. At two-ten, the man Danglars had come in and registered for himself and his mistress, Jizelle de Ville.

"Bourke," said Father Art, "came in at five-fifteen. Nobody else at all checked in during that evening. And nobody saw a young man wearing evening clothes." He paused and smiled brightly. "How-*ev*-er . . ."

"Ahhh. I knew I could depend on you, my dear Arthur. What was it?"

Still smiling seraphically, the good father raised a finger and said: "The Case of the Sexton's Cloak."

"You fascinate me. Pray elucidate."

"My sexton," said Father Art, "has an old cloak, originally made from a couple of used horse blankets, so it wasn't exactly beautiful when new. But it *is* warm. He uses it when he has to work outside in winter. In summer, he hangs it in the stable behind the church. Claims it keeps the moths out—the smell, I mean.

"On the morning of sixth June, one of the men who works here in the inn brought it over to the church, asked my sexton if it were his. It was. Want to take a wild, silly guess where it was found?" Father Art asked.

"Does the room used by Bourke face the front or the rear?"

"The rear."

"Then it was found on the cobblestones at the rear of the building."

Smiling even more broadly, Father Art gently clapped his hands together once. "Precisely, my lord."

Lord Darcy smiled back. "Let's reconstruct. Bourke went to his room before five-thirty. Right?"

"Right. One of the maids went with him, let him in, and gave him the key."

"Was he ever seen again?"

"Only once. He ordered a light meal, and it was brought up about six. That's the last time he was seen."

"Were either of the other guests in the house at the time?"

"No. The man Danglars had left about four-thirty, and hadn't returned. No one saw Mistress Jizelle leave, but the girl who turns down the beds says that both rooms were empty at six. Bourke was still there at the time."

"Hmmmm."

Lord Darcy looked into the depths of his beer. After half a minute, he said: "Reverend Father, was a stranger in an old horse-blanket cloak actually seen in this inn, or are we speculating in insubstantial mist?"

Father Art's mouth twisted in a small grimace. "Not totally insubstantial, my lord, but not strong, either. The barmaid who was on duty that night says she remembers a couple of strangers who came in, but she doesn't remember anything about them. She's not terribly bright."

Lord Darcy chuckled. "All right, then. Let's assume that Standish actually came in here in a stolen—and uncomfortably warm—cloak. How did that come about, and what happened afterwards?"

Father Art fired up his old briar and took another sip from his seidel of beer. "Well, let's see. Standish comes into the village an hour after Bourke—perhaps a little more. But he doesn't come in directly; he circles round behind the church. Why? Not to steal the cloak. How would he know it was there?" He took two puffs from his pipe, then his eyes brightened. "Of course. To tether his horse. He didn't want it seen in the public square, and knew it would be safe in the church stable." Two more puffs.

"Hmmm. He sees the cloak on the stable wall and realizes that it will serve as a disguise, covering his evening dress. He borrows it and comes here to the inn. He makes sure that Bourke is firmly in place, then goes back to his horse and hightails it for Caen to send word to Sir James. Then he comes back here to the Green Seagull. He waits until nobody's looking, then sneaks up the stair to Bourke's room."

The priest stopped, scowled, and took a good, healthy drink from his seidel. "Some time later, he went out the window to the courtyard below, losing the cloak in the process." He shook his head. "But what happened between the time he went upstairs and the time he dropped the cloak, and what happened between then and his death, I haven't the foggiest conjecture."

"I have several," Lord Darcy said, "but they are all very, very foggy. We need more data. I have several questions." He ticked them off on his fingers. "One: Where is Bourke? Two: Who shot Standish? Three: *Why* was he shot? Four: What happened here at the inn? Five: What happened on the beach? And, finally: *Where is the Ipswich Phial?*"

Father Art lifted his seidel, drained its contents on one extended draught, set it firmly on the table, and said: "I don't know. God does."

Lord Darcy nodded. "Indeed; and one of His greatest attributes is that if you ask Him the right question in the right way, He will always give you an answer."

"You intend to pray for answers to those questions, my lord?"

"That, yes. But I have found that the best way to ask God about questions like these is to go out and dig up the data yourself."

Father Art smiled. *"Dominus vobiscum."*

"Et cum spiritu tuo," Lord Darcy responded.

"Excavemus!" said the priest.

In his room in the Rectory, Master Sean had carefully set up his apparatus on the table. Noel Standish's .36 Heron was clamped securely into a padded vise which stood at one end of the table. Three feet in front of the muzzle, the bullet which Lord Darcy had dug from the sand had been carefully placed on a small pedestal, so that it was at exactly the same height as the muzzle. He was using certain instruments to make sure that the axis of the bullet was accurately aligned with the axis of the Heron's barrel when a rhythmic code knock came at the door. The sorcerer went over to the door, unbolted it, opened it, and said: "Come in, me lord."

"I hope I didn't interrupt anything," Lord Darcy said.

"Not at all, me lord." Master Sean carefully closed and bolted the door again. "I was just getting ready for the ballistics test. The similarity relationship tests have already assured me that the slug was the one that killed Standish. There's only to see if it came from his own gun. Have you found any further clues?"

"None," Lord Darcy admitted. "I managed to get a good look at the guest rooms in the Green Seagull. Nothing. Flat nothing. I have several ideas, but no evidence." Then he gestured at the handgun. "Pray proceed with your work. I will be most happy to wait."

"It'll only be a minute or so," Master Sean said apologetically. He went back to the table and continued his preparations while Lord Darcy watched in silence. His lordship was well aware of the principle involved; he had seen the test innumerable times. He recalled a lecture that Master Sean had once given on the subject.

"You see," the sorcerer had said, "the Principle of Relevance is important here. Most of the wear on a gun is purely mechanical. It don't matter *who* pulls the trigger, you see; the erosion caused by the gases produced in the chamber, and the wear caused by the bullet's passing through the barrel will be the same. It's not relevant *to the gun* who pulled the trigger or what it was fired at. But, *to the bullet* it *is* relevant which gun it was fired from and what it hit. All this can be determined by the proper spells."

In spite of having seen it many times, Lord Darcy always liked to watch the test because it was rather spectacular when the test was positive. Master Sean sprinkled a small amount of previously charged powder on both the bullet and the gun. Then he raised his wand and said an incantation under his breath.

At the last syllable of the incantation, there was a sound as if someone had sharply struck a cracked bell as the bullet vanished. The .36 Heron shivered in its vise.

Master Sean let out his breath. "Just like a homing pigeon, me lord. Gun and bullet match."

"I've often wondered why the bullet does that," Lord Darcy said.

Master Sean chuckled. "Call it an induced return-to-the-womb fixation, me lord. Was there something you wanted?"

"A couple of things." Lord Darcy walked over to his suitcase, opened it, and took out a holstered handgun. It was a precision-made .40 caliber MacGregor—a heavy man-stopper.

While he checked out the MacGregor itself, he said: "This is one. The other is a question. How long before his body was found did Standish die?"

Master Sean rubbed the side of his nose with a thick finger. "Well, the investigative sorcerer at Caen, a good journeyman, placed the time as not more than fifteen minutes before the body was discovered. My own tests showed not more than twenty-five minutes. But not even the best preservative spell can keep something like that from blurring after a week has passed."

Lord Darcy slid the MacGregor into its snugly-fitted holster and adjusted his jacket to cover it. "In other words, there's the usual hazy area. The bruises and fractures were definitely inflicted before death?"

"Definitely, my lord. About three hours before, give or take that same fifteen minutes."

"I see. Interesting. Very interesting." He looked in the wall mirror and adjusted his neckpiece. "Have you further work to do?"

"Only the analysis on the knife," Master Sean said.

Lord Darcy turned from the mirror. "Will you fix me up with a tracer? I'm going out to stroll about the village and possibly to the fairgrounds and the tent city. I anticipate no danger, but I don't want to get lost, either."

"Very well, me lord," the sorcerer said with resignation. He opened his symbol-decorated carpetbag and took out a little wooden box. It held what looked remarkably like one-inch toothpicks, except that they were evenly cylindrical, not tapered, and they were made of ash instead of pine. He selected one and put the box back in his bag. He handed the little cylinder to Lord Darcy, who took it between the thumb and forefinger of his right hand.

Then the master sorcerer took a little scented oil on his right thumb from a special golden oil stock and rubbed it along the sliver of ash, from Lord Darcy's thumb to the other end. Then he grasped that end in his own right thumb and forefinger.

A quick motion of both wrists, and the ashen splinter snapped.

But, psychically and symbolically, the halves were still part of an unbroken whole. As long as each man carried his half, the two of them were specially linked.

"Thank you, my dear Sean," Lord Darcy said. "And now I shall be off to enjoy the nightlife of the teeming metropolis surrounding us."

With that, he was gone, and Master Sean returned to his work.

The sun was a fat, squashed-looking, red-orange ellipsoid seated neatly on the horizon when Lord Darcy stepped out of the gate of the churchyard. It would be gone in a few minutes. The long shadow of the church spire reached out across the village and into the fields. The colors of the flags and banners and bunting around the village were altered in value by the reddish light. The weather had been beautiful and clear all day, and would continue to be, according to the Weather Bureau predictors. It would be a fine night.

"Please, my lord—are you Lord Darcy?"

Lord Darcy had noticed the woman come out of the church, but the village square was full of people, and he had paid little attention. Now he turned his full attention on her and was pleasantly surprised. She was quite the loveliest creature he had seen in a long time.

"I am, Damoselle," he said with a smile. "But I fear you have the advantage of me."

Her own smile was timid, almost frightened. "I am named Sharolta."

Her name, her slight accent, and her clothing all proclaimed her Romany. Her long, softly dark hair and her dark eyes, her well-formed nose and her full, almost too-perfect lips, along with her magnificently lush body, accentuated by the Romany costume, proclaimed her beautiful.

"May I be of help to you, Damoselle Sharolta?"

She shook her head. "No, no. I ask nothing. But perhaps I can be of help to you." Her smile seemed to quaver. "Can we go somewhere to talk?"

"Where, for instance?" Lord Darcy asked carefully.

"Anywhere you say, my lord. Anywhere, so long as it is private." Then she flushed. "I—I mean, not *too much* private. I mean, where we can talk. You know."

"Of course. It is not yet time for Vespers; I suggest that we go into the church," Lord Darcy said.

"Yes, yes. That would be fine." She smiled. "There were not many folk in there. It should be fine."

The interior of the Church of St.-Matthew was darkened, but far from being gloomy. The flickering clusters of candles around the statues and icons were like twinkling, multicolored star clusters.

Lord Darcy and the Damoselle Sharolta sat down in one of the rear pews. Most of the dozen or so people who were in the church were farther up toward the altar, praying; there was no one within earshot of the place Lord Darcy had chosen.

Lord Darcy waited in silence for the girl to speak. The Romany become silent under pressure; create a vacuum for them to fill, and the words come tumbling over each other in eloquent eagerness.

"You are the great Lord Darcy, the great Investigator," she began suddenly. "You are looking into the death of the poor Goodman Standish who was found on the beach a week ago. Is all this not so?"

Lord Darcy nodded silently.

"Well, then, there must be something wrong about that man's death, or you would not be here. So I must tell you what I know.

"A week ago, there came to our tribe a group of five men. They said they were from the tribe of Chanro—the Sword—which is in the area of Buda-Pest. Their leader, who calls himself Suv—the

Needle—asked our chief for aid and sanctuary, as it is their right, and it was granted. But they are very secretive among themselves. They behave very well, mind you; I don't mean they are rude or boorish, or anything like that. But there is—how do I say it?—there is a *wrongness* about them.

"This morning, for instance. I must tell you of that. The man who calls himself Suv wanted me to walk along the beach with him. I did not want to, for I do not find him an attractive man—you understand?"

Again his lordship nodded. "Of course."

"But he said he meant nothing like that. He said he wanted to walk along the sea, but he did not want to walk alone. He said he would show me all the shore life—the birds, the things in the pools, the plants. I was interested, and I thought there would be no harm, so I went.

"He was true to his word. He did not try to make love to me. It was nice for a while. He showed me the tide pools and pointed out the different kinds of things in them. One had a jellyfish." She looked up from her hands, and there was a frown on her face.

"Then we got near to that little cove where the body was found. I wanted to turn back, but he said, no, he wanted to look at it. I said I wouldn't and started back. Then he told me that if I didn't, he'd break my arm. So I went." She seemed to shiver a little under her bright dress. "When the Armsman showed up, he kept on going, pretending he didn't understand Anglo-French. Then we saw that there were two of them, the Armsmen, I mean. So we turned around and went back. Suv was very furious."

She stopped and said no more.

"My dear," he asked gently, "why does one of the Romany come to the authorities with a story like this? Do not the Romany take care of their own?"

"Yes, my lord. But these men are not Rom."

"Oh?"

"Their tent is next to mine. I have heard them talking when they think no one is listening. I do not understand it very well, but I know it when I hear it; they were speaking *Burgdeutsch*."

"I see," said Lord Darcy softly and thoughtfully. The German of Brandenburg was the court language of Poland, which suddenly made everything very interesting indeed.

"Do you suppose, Damoselle," he said, "that you could point out this Suv to me?"

She looked up at him with those great wonderful eyes and smiled. "I'm suro I could, my lord. Come; wrap your cloak about you and we shall walk through the village."

Outside the church, the darkness was relieved only by the regulation gaslamps of the various business places, and by the quarter moon hanging high in the sky, like a half-closed eye.

In the deeper darkness of the church porch, Lord Darcy, rather much to his surprise, took the girl in his arms and kissed her, with her warm cooperation. It was several wordless minutes before they went out to the street.

Master Sean woke to the six o'clock Angelus bell feeling vaguely uneasy. A quick mental focus on his half of the tracer told him that Lord Darcy was in no danger. Actually, if he had been, Sean would have wakened immediately.

But he still had that odd feeling when he went down to Mass at seven; he had trouble keeping in his mind his prayers for the intercession of St. Basil the Great, and couldn't really bring his mind to focus until the Sanctus.

After Mass, he went up to Father Art's small parlor in the rectory, where he had been asked to break his fast, and was mildly surprised to find Sir James le Lien with the priest.

"Good morning, Master Sean," Sir James said calmly. "Have you found the Phial yet?"

The sorcerer shook his head. "Not so far as I know."

Sir James munched a buttered biscuit and sipped hot black caffe. Despite his calm expression Master Sean could tell that he was worried.

"I am afraid," Sir James said carefully, "we've been outfoxed."

"How so?" Father Art asked.

"Well, either the *Serka* have got it, or they think we have it safely away from them. They seem to have given the whole thing over." He drank more caffe. "Just after midnight, every known *Serka* agent in the area eluded our men and vanished. They dropped out of sight, and we haven't spotted a single one in over eight hours. We have reason to believe that some of them went south, toward Caen; some went west, toward Cherbourg; others are heading east, toward Harfleur."

Master Sean frowned. "And you think—"

"I think they found the Ipswich Phial and one of their men is carrying it to Krakowa. Or at least across the Polish border. I rode to Caen and made more teleson calls than I've ever made in so short a time in my life. There's a net out now, and we can only hope we can find the man with the Phial. Otherwise . . ." He closed his eyes. "Otherwise, we may be faced with an overland attack by the armies of His Slavonic Majesty, through one or more of the German states. God help us."

After what seemed like a terribly long time, Master Sean said: "Sir James, is there any likelihood that Noel Standish would have used a knife on the sealed Phial?"

"I don't know. Why do you ask?"

"We found a knife near where Standish's body was discovered. My tests show gold on the knife edge."

"May I see it?" Sir James asked.

"Certainly. I'll fetch it. Excuse me a minute."

He left the parlor and went down the rather narrow hallway of the rectory. From the nearby church came the soft chime of a small bell. The eight o'clock Mass was beginning.

Master Sean opened the door of his room . . .

. . . and stood stock still, staring, for a full fifteen seconds, while his eyes and other senses took in the room.

Then, without moving, he shouted: "Sir James! Father Art! Come here! Quickly!"

Both men came running. They stopped at the door.

"What's the matter?" Sir James snapped.

"Somebody," said Master Sean in an angry rumble, "has been prowlin' about in me room! And a trick like that is likely to be after gettin' me Irish up!" Master Sean's brogue varied with his mood. When he was calmly lecturing or discussing, it became almost nonexistent. But when he became angry . . .

He strode into the room for a closer look at the table which he had been using for his thaumaturgical analyses. In the center was a heap of crumbled clay. "They've destroyed me evidence! Look at that!" Master Sean pointed to the heap of crumbled clay on the table.

"And what is it, if I may ask?"

Master Sean explained about the letters that had been cut in the cliff face, and how he had taken the chunk of clay out for further examination.

"And this knife was used to cut the letters." He gestured toward the knife on the table nearby. "I haven't been able to check it against Standish's body yet."

"That's the one with the gold traces on the blade?" Sir James asked.

"It is."

"Well, it's Standish's knife, all right. I've seen it many times. I could even tell you how he got that deep cut in the ivory hilt." He looked thoughtful. "S. . .S. . .O. . ." After a moment, he shook his head. "Means nothing to me. Can't think what it might have meant to Standish."

"Means nothing to me, either," Father Art admitted.

"Well, now," said the stout little Irish sorcerer, "Standish must have been at the top of the cliff when he wrote it. What would be right side up to him would be inverted to anyone standing below. How about OSS?"

Again Sir James thought. Again he shook his head. "Still nothing, Master Sean. Father?"

The priest shook his head. "Nothing, I'm afraid."

Sir James said: "This was obviously done by a *Serka* agent. But why? And how did he get in here without your knowing it?"

Master Sean scowled. "To a sorcerer, that's obvious. First, whoever did it is an accomplished sorcerer himself, or he'd never have made it past that avoidance spell, which is keyed only to meself and to his lordship. Second, he picked exactly the right time—when I was at Mass and had me mind concentrated elsewhere so I wouldn't notice what he was up to. Were I doing it meself, I'd have started just as the Sanctus bell was rung. After that—no problem." He looked glum. "I just wasn't expecting it, that's all."

"I wish I could have seen that carving in the clay," Sir James said.

"Well, you can see the cast if they didn't—" Master Sean pulled open a desk drawer. "No, they didn't." He pulled out a thin slab of plaster. "I made this with quick-setting plaster. It's reversed, of course, but you can look at it in the mirror, over there."

Sir James took the slab, but didn't look at it immediately. His eyes were still on the heap of clay. "Do you suppose that Standish might have buried the Ipswich Phial in that clay to keep it from being found?"

Master Sean's eyes widened. "Great Heaven! It could be! With an auric-stabilized psychic shield around it, I'd not have perceived it at all!"

Sir James groaned. "That answers the question, *Why?*—doesn't it?"

"So it would seem," murmured Father Art.

Bleakly, Sir James held the plaster slab up to the mirror above the dresser. "SSO. No. Wait." He inverted it, and his lean face went pale. "Oh, no, God," he said softly. "Oh, please. No."

"What is it?" the priest asked. "Does OSS mean something?"

"Not OSS," Sir James said still more softly. "o55. Number o55 of the *Serka*. Olga Polovski, the most beautiful and the most dangerous woman in Europe."

It was at that moment that the sun went out.

The Reverend Father Mac Kennalty had turned to the congregation and asked them to lift up their hearts to the Lord that they might properly assist at the Holy Sacrifice of the Altar, when a cloud seemed to pass over the sun, dimming the light that streamed in through the stained glass windows. Even the candles on the Altar seemed to dim a little.

He hardly noticed it; it was a common enough occurrence. Without a pause, he asked the people to give thanks to the Lord God, and continued with the Mass.

In the utter blackness of the room, three men stood for a moment in silence.

"Well, that tears it," said Sir James's voice in the darkness. There was a noticeable lack of surprise or panic in his voice.

"So you lied to his lordship," said Master Sean.

"He did indeed," said Father Art.

"What do you mean?" Sir James asked testily.

"You said," Master Sean pointed out with more than a touch of acid in his voice, "that you didn't know what the Ipswich Phial is supposed to do."

"What makes you think I *do?*"

"In the first place, this darkness came as no surprise to you. In the second, you must have known what it was, because Noel Standish knew."

"I had my orders," Sir James le Lien said in a hard voice. "That's not the point now. The damned thing is being used. I— "

"*Listen!*" Father Art's voice cut in sharply. "*Listen!*"

In the blackness, all of them heard the sweet triple tone of the Sanctus bell.

Holy . . . Holy . . . Holy . . . Lord God Sabaoth . . .

"What—?" Sir James's low voice was querulous.

"Don't you understand?" Father Art asked. "The field of suppression doesn't extend as far as the church. Father Mac Kennalty could go on with the Mass in the dark, from memory. But the congregation wouldn't be likely to. They certainly don't sound upset."

"You're right, Father," Master Sean said. "That gives us the range, doesn't it? Let's see if we can feel our way out of here, toward the church. His lordship may be in trouble."

"Follow me," said the priest. "I know this church like I know my own face. Take my hand and follow me."

Cautiously, the three men moved from the darkness toward the light. They were still heading for the stairway when the sun came on again.

Lord Darcy rode into the stableyard behind the Church of St.-Matthew, where four men were waiting for him. The sexton took his horse as he dismounted, and led it away to the stable. The other three just waited, expectantly.

"I could do with a cup of caffe, heavily laced with brandy, and a plate of ham and eggs, if they're available," said Lord Darcy with a rather dreamy smile. "If not, I'll just have the caffe and brandy."

"What's happened?" Sir James blurted abruptly.

Lord Darcy patted the air with a hand. "All in good time, my dear James; all in good time. Nothing's amiss, I assure you."

"I think a breakfast such as that could be arranged," Father Art said with a smile. "Come along."

The caffe and brandy came immediately, served by Father Art in a large mug. "The ham and eggs should be along pretty quickly," the priest said.

"Excellent! You're the perfect host, Father." Lord Darcy took a bracing jolt from the mug, then fished in his waistcoat pocket with thumb and forefinger. "Oh, by the by, Sir James, here's your play-pretty." He held up a small golden tube.

Sir James took it and looked at it while Master Sean scowled at it in a way that made him seem rather cross-eyed.

"The seal has been cut," Sir James said.

"Yes. By your man, Standish. I suggest you give the thing to Master Sean for resealing until you get it back to Ipswich."

Sir James gave the Phial to Master Sean. "How did you get it back from them?" the King's Agent asked.

"I ·didn't." Lord Darcy settled himself back in the big chair. "If you'll be patient, I'll explain. Last evening, I was approached by a young woman . . ."

His lordship repeated the entire conversation verbatim, and told them of her gestures and expressions while they were talking inside the church.

"And you went with her?" Sir James asked incredulously.

"Certainly. For two very good reasons. *Primus:* I had to find out what was behind her story. *Secundus:* I had fallen in love."

Sir James gawked. Master Sean's face became expressionless. Father Art cast his eyes toward Heaven.

Sir James found his voice first. "In *love?*" It was almost a squawk.

Lord Darcy nodded calmly. "In love. Deeply. Madly. Passionately."

Sir James shot to his feet. "Are you mad, Darcy? Don't you realize that that woman is a *Serka* agent?"

"So indeed I had surmised. Sit down, James; such outbursts are unseemly." Sir James sat down slowly. "Now pay attention," Lord Darcy continued. "Of course I knew she was a spy. If you had been listening closely when I quoted her words, you would have heard that she said I was investigating the death of *Standish*. And yet everyone here knows that the body was identified as *Bourke*. Obviously, she had recognized Standish and knew his name."

"Standish had recognized her, too," Sir James said. "Secret Agent Number 055, of *Serka*. Real name: Olga Polovski."

"Olga," Lord Darcy said, savoring the word. "That's a pretty name, isn't it?"

"Charming. Utterly enchanting. And in spite of the fact that she's a Polish agent, you love the wench?"

"I didn't say that, Sir James," said Lord Darcy. "I did not say I loved her; I said I was 'in love' with her. There is a fine distinction there, and I have had enough experience to be able to distinguish between the two states of mind. Your use of the word 'enchanting' is quite apropos, by the way. The emotion was artificially induced. The woman is a sorceress."

Master Sean suddenly snapped his fingers. "*That's* where I heard the name before! Olga Polovski! Six years ago, she was an undergraduate at the University in Buda-Pest. A good student, with high-grade Talent. No wonder you 'fell in love' with her."

Sir James narrowed his eyes. "I see. The purpose was to get information out of you. Did she succeed?"

"In a way." Lord Darcy chuckled. "I sang like a nightingale. Indeed, Darcy's *Mendacious Cantata*, sung *forte e claro*, may become one of the most acclaimed works of art of the twentieth century. Pardon me; I am euphoric."

"You have popped your parietals, my lord," Sir James said, with a slight edge to his voice. "What was the result of this baritone solo?"

"Actually, it was a duet. We alternated on the versicles and responses. The theme of my song was simply that I was a criminal investigator and nothing more. That I hadn't more than a vague notion of what His Imperial Majesty's Secret Service was up to. That, for some reason, the apprehension of this murderer was most important to the Secret Service, so their agents were hanging around to help me. That they were more hindrance than help." He paused to take another swallow of laced caffe, then continued: "And—oh, yes—that they must be going to England for more men, because, four days ago, a heavily armed group of four men took a Navy cutter from Harfleur for London."

Sir James frowned for a second, then his face lit up. "Ah, yes. You implied that we had already found the Phial and that it was safely in England."

"Precisely. And since she had not heard of that oh-so-secret departure, she was certain that it could not be a bluff. As a result, she scrubbed the entire mission. Around midnight, she excused herself for a moment and spoke to someone—I presume it was the second in command, the much-maligned Suv. Her men took off to three of the four winds."

"And she didn't?"

"Of course not. Why arouse my suspicions? Better to keep me

under observation while her men made good their escape. I left her shortly after dawn, and—"

"You were there from sunset till dawn? What took you so long?"

Lord Darcy looked pained. "My dear James, surely you don't think I could simply hand her all that misinformation in half an hour without her becoming suspicious. I had to allow her to draw it from me, bit by bit. I had to allow her to give me more information than she intended to give in order to get the story out of me. And, of course, *she* had to be very careful in order not to arouse *my* suspicions. It was, I assure you, a very delicate and time-consuming series of negotiations."

Sir James did his best not to leer. "I can well imagine."

Father Art looked out the window, solemnly puffing his pipe as though he were in deep meditation and could hear nothing.

Rather hurriedly, Master Sean said: "Then it was you who broke the clay brick I dug out of the cliff, me lord."

"It was; I'm sorry I didn't tell you, but you were at Mass, and I was in somewhat of a hurry. You see, there were only two places where the Phial could possibly be, and I looked in the less likely place first—in that lump of clay. Standish *could* have hidden it there, but I thought it unlikely. Still, I had to look. It wasn't there.

"So I got my horse and rode out to where the body was found. You see, Standish *had* to have had it with him. He opened it to get away from his pursuers. I presume Master Sean knows how the thing works, but all I know is that it renders everyone blind for a radius of about a mile and a half."

Master Sean cleared his throat. "It's akin to what's called hysterical blindness. Nothing wrong with the eyes, ye see, but the mind blocks off the visual centers of the brain. The Phial contains a charged rod attached to the stopper. When you open it and expose the rod everything goes black. That's the reason for the auric-stabilized psychic shield which forms the Phial itself."

"Things don't go black for the person holding it," said Lord Darcy. "Everything becomes a colorless gray, but you can still see."

"That's the built-in safety spell in the stopper," said the little Irish sorcerer.

"Well, where *was* the blasted thing?" Sir James asked.

"Buried in the sand, almost under that big rock where his body was found. I just had to dig till I found it." Lord Darcy looked somber. "I fear my analytical powers are deserting me; otherwise, Master Sean and I would have found it yesterday. But I relied on his metal detector to find it. And yet, Master Sean clearly told me that a psychic shield renders anything psychically invisible. He was talking about Standish, of course, but I should have seen that the same logic applied to the Ipswich Phial as well."

"If ye'd told me what ye were looking for, me lord . . ." Master Sean said gently.

Lord Darcy chuckled mirthlessly. "After all our years together, my dear Sean, we still tend to overestimate each other. I assumed you had deduced what we were looking for, though you are no detective; you assumed I knew about psychic shielding, though I am no thaumaturge."

"I still can't quite see the entire chain of events," Father Art said. "Could you clarify it for us? What was Standish doing out on that beach, anyway?"

"Well, let's go back to the night before he was killed. He had been following the mysterious Bourke. When Bourke was firmly ensconced in the Green Seagull, Standish rode for Caen, notified you via teleson, then rode back. He borrowed the sexton's cloak and went over to the inn. When he saw his chance, he dodged upstairs fast and went to Bourke's room presumably to get the Phial.

"Now, you must keep in mind that all this is conjecture. I can't prove it, and I know of no way to prove it. I do not have, and cannot get, all the evidence I would need for *proof*. But all the data I *do* have leads inescapably to one line of action.

"Master Sean claims I have a touch of the Talent—the ability to leap from an unwarranted assumption to a foregone conclusion. That may be so. At any rate, I *know* what happened.

"Very well, then. Standish went into Bourke's room to arrest him. He *knew* Bourke was in that room because he was psychically locked on to Bourke.

"But when he broke into the room he was confronted by a woman—a woman he knew. The woman was just as surprised to see Standish.

"I don't know which of them recovered first, but I strongly suspect it was the woman. Number 055 is very quick on the uptake, believe me.

"But Standish was stronger. He sustained a few good bruises in the next several seconds, but he knocked her unconscious. I saw the bruise on her neck last night.

"He searched the room and found the Phial. Unfortunately, the noise had attracted two, possibly three, of her fellow *Serka* agents. He had to go out the window, losing his cloak in the process. The men followed him.

"He ran for the beach, and—"

"Wait a minute," Sir James interrupted. "You mean Bourke was actually Olga Polovski in disguise?"

"Certainly. She's a consummate actress. The idea was for Bourke to vanish completely. She knew the Secret Service would be after her, and she wanted to leave no trace. But she didn't realize that Standish was so close behind her because he was psychically invisible. That's why she was shocked when he came into her room.

"At any rate, he ran for the beach. There was no place else to go at that time of night, except for the church, and they'd have him trapped there.

"I must admit I'm very fuzzy about what happened during that chase, but remember he had ridden for two days without much rest, and he was battered a little by the blows Olga had landed. At any rate, he eventually found himself at the edge of that cliff, with *Serka* closing in around him. Remember, it was a moonless night, and there were only stars for him to see by. But at least one of the Polish agents had a lantern.

"Standish was trapped on the edge of a cliff, and he had no way to see how far down it went, nor what was at the bottom. He lay flat and kept quiet, but the others were getting close. He decided to get rid of the Phial. Better to lose it than have it fall into King Casimir's hands. He took out his knife and carved the '055' in the side of the cliff, to mark the spot and to make sure that someone else would see it if he were killed. I'm sure he intended to dig a hole and bury it there. I don't believe he was thinking too clearly by then.

"The *Serka* men were getting too close for comfort. He might be seen at any moment. So he cut the seal of the Phial and opened it. Blackout.

"Since he could see his pursuers—however dimly—and they couldn't see him, he decided to try to get past them, back to the village. If he had a time advantage, he could find a place to hide.

"He stood up.

"But as he turned, he made a misstep and fell twenty feet to the sand below." Lord Darcy paused.

Father Art, looking thoughtful, said: "He had a gun. Why didn't he use it?"

"Because they had guns, too, and he was outnumbered. He didn't want to betray his position by the muzzle flash unless he had to," Lord Darcy said. "To continue: The fall is what broke those ribs and sprained that wrist. It also very likely knocked him out for a few minutes. Not long. When he came to, he must have realized he had an advantage greater than he had thought at first. The *Serka* couldn't see the muzzle flash from his handgun. Badly hurt as he was, he waited for them."

"Admirable," said Father Art. "It's fantastic that he didn't lose the two parts of the Phial when he fell. Must have hung on for dear life."

"Standish would," said Sir James grimly. "Go on, my lord."

"Well, at that point, the *Serka* lads must have realized the same thing. They had no way of knowing how badly Standish was hurt, nor exactly where he was. He could be sneaking up on them, for all they knew. They got out of there. Slowly, of course, since they had to feel their way, but once they reached the Old Shore Road, they made better time.

"But by that time, Standish was close to passing out again. He still had to hide the Phial, so he buried it in the sand where I found it."

"Me lord," said Master Sean, "I still don't understand who killed Standish and why."

"Oh, that. Why, that was patently obvious from the first. Wasn't it, Father Art?"

The good Father stared at Lord Darcy. "Begging your pardon, my lord, but not to *me* it wasn't."

Lord Darcy turned his head. "Sir James?"

"No."

"Oh, dear. Well, I suppose I shall have to back up a bit, then. Consider: The Damoselle Olga, to cover her tracks, has to get rid of 'Bourke'. But if 'Bourke' disappears into nowhere, and someone else appears from nowhere, even a moron might suspect that the two were the same. So a cover must be arranged. Someone else, not connected in any way with 'Bourke', must appear at the Green Seagull *before* 'Bourke' shows up.

"So, what happens? A coachman named Danglars shows up; a servant who registers for himself and his mistress, Jizelle de Ville. (Danglars and Suv were almost certainly the same man, by the way.) But who sees Mistress Jizelle? Nobody. *She is only a name in a register book until the next morning!*

"The original plan was to have Mistress Jizelle show up in the evening, then have Bourke show up again, and so on. The idea was to firmly establish that the two people were separate and not at all connected. The arrival and intrusion of Standish changed all that, but things worked out fairly well, nonetheless.

"It *had* to be 'Mistress Jizelle' who killed him. Look at the evidence. Standish died—correct me if I'm wrong, Master Sean—within plus or minus fifteen minutes of the time Standish was found."

Master Sean nodded.

"Naturally," his lordship continued, "we always assume a minus time. How could the person be killed *after* the body was found?

"But there was no one else around who could have killed him! A farmer and his two sons were close enough to the road during that time to see anyone who came along unless that someone had walked along the beach. But there were no footprints in that damp sand except those of 'Mistress Jizelle'!

"Picture this, if you will: Number 055, still a little groggy, and suffering from a sore neck, is told by her returning henchmen that they have lost Standish. But she is clever enough to see what must have happened. As soon as possible, she puts on her 'Mistress Jizelle' *persona* and has her lieutenant drive her out to that section of the beach. She walks down to take a look. She sees Standish.

"Standish, meanwhile, has regained his senses. He opens his eyes and sees Olga Polovski. His gun is still in his hand. He tries to level it at her. She jumps him, in fear of her life. A struggle. The gun goes off. *Finis.*"

"Wouldn't the farmers have heard the shot?" Master Sean asked.

"At that distance, with a brisk wind blowing, the sea pounding, and a cliff to baffle the sound, it would be hard to hear a pistol shot. That one was further muffled by the fact that the muzzle was against Standish's head. No, it wouldn't have been heard."

"Why did her footprints only come up to some five yards from the body?" Sir James asked. "There were no prints in the dry sand."

"Partly because she smoothed her prints out, partly because of the wind, which blew enough to cover them. She was shaken and worried, but she did take time to search the body for the Phial. Naturally, she didn't want any evidence of that search around. She went back to consult Danglars-Suv about what to do next. When she saw the farmers, there was nothing she could do but bluff it through. Which, I must say, she did magnificently."

"Indeed." Sir James le Lien looked both cold and grim. "Where is she now?"

"By now, she has taken horse and departed."

"Riding sidesaddle, no doubt." His voice was as cold as his expression. "So you let her get away. Why didn't you arrest her?"

"On what evidence? Don't be a fool, Sir James. What would you charge her with? Could you swear in His Majesty's Court of High Justice that 'Mistress Jizelle' was actually Olga Polovski? If I had tried to arrest her, I would have been a corpse by now in that Romany camp, even if I'd had the evidence. Since I did not and do not have that evidence, there would be no point.

"I would not call it a satisfactory case, no. But you have the Phial, which was what you wanted. I'm afraid the death of Noel Standish will have to be written off as enemy action during the course of a war. It was not first degree murder; it was, as Master Sean put it yesterday, a case of accidental murder."

"But—"

Lord Darcy leaned back in the chair and closed his eyes. "Drop it, Sir James. You'll get her eventually."

Then, very quietly, he began to snore.

"I'll be damned!" said Sir James. "I worked all night on my feet and found nothing. He spends all night in bed with the most beautiful woman in Europe and gets all the answers."

"It all depends on your method of approach," Master Sean said. He opened his symbol-decorated carpetbag and took out a large, heavy book.

"Oh, certainly," said Sir James bitterly. "Some work vertically, some horizontally."

Father Arthur Lyon continued to stare out the window, hearing nothing he didn't mean to hear.

"What are you looking up there, in that grimoire?" he asked Master Sean after a moment.

"*Spells, infatuation; removal of,*" said Master Sean calmly.

Spy Story

The spy story involves spies, secret agents, espionage, or foreign intrigue. One of the first forms of crime fiction, it clearly precedes Poe (see James Fenimore Cooper's *The Spy*, 1821) and can probably be traced back to early folk tales. More than in any other mystery area, novelists have felt free to use the spy story as a vehicle for their own ideas. Thus there are John Buchan's romantic idealism, Eric Ambler's realism, Ian Fleming's power fantasies, and John Le Carré's views of systemic corruption.

In the science fiction field spy stories are common, and several series have been developed. But the range of approach is narrow. Usually, the spy is a competent individual who ingeniously solves his problems, as in the following story by Katherine MacLean and Charles De Vet. Sometimes the agent is presented as infallible, but only rarely is he seen in a realistic light, and almost never is he a helpless pawn.

Second Game

CHARLES V. DE VET and KATHERINE MACLEAN

The sign was big, with black letters that read: I'LL BEAT YOU THE SECOND GAME.

I eased myself into a seat behind the play board, straightened the pitchman's cloak about my shoulders, took a final deep breath, let it out—and waited.

A nearby Fair visitor glanced at the sign as he hurried by. His eyes widened with anticipated pleasure and he shifted his gaze to me, weighing me with the glance.

I knew I had him.

The man changed direction and came over to where I sat. "Are you giving any odds?" he asked.

"Ten to one," I answered.

"A dronker." He wrote on a blue slip with a white stylus, dropped it at my elbow, and sat down.

"We play the first game for feel," I said. "Second game pays."

Gradually I let my body relax. Its weight pulled at the muscles of my back and shoulders, and I slouched into a half-slump. I could feel my eyelids droop as I released them, and the corners of my mouth pulled down. I probably appeared tired and melancholy. Or like a man operating in a gravity heavier than was normal for him. Which I was.

I had come to this world called Velda two weeks earlier. My job was to find why its humanlike inhabitants refused all contacts with the Federation.

Earth's colonies had expanded during the last several centuries until they now comprised a loose alliance known as The Ten Thousand Worlds. They were normally peaceful—and wanted peace with Velda. But you cannot talk peace with a people who won't talk back. Worse, they had obliterated the fleet bringing our initial peace overtures. As a final gesture I had been smuggled in—in an attempt to breach that stand-off stubbornness. This booth at their Fair was my best chance—as I saw it—to secure audience with the men in authority. And with luck it would servo a double purpose.

Several Veldians gathered around the booth and watched with interest as my opponent and I chose colors. He took the red; I the black. We arranged our fifty-two pieces on their squares and I nodded to him to make the first move.

He was an anemic oldster with an air of nervous energy, and he played the same way, with intense concentration. By the fourth move I knew he would not win. On each play he had to consult the value board suspended between us before deciding what his next move would be. On a play board with one hundred and sixty-nine squares, each with a different value—in fact one set of values for offense, and another for defense—only a brilliant player could keep them all in mind. But no man without that ability was going to beat me.

I let him win the first game. Deliberately. The "second game counts" gimmick was not only to attract attention, but to give me a chance to test a player's strength—and find his weakness.

At the start of the second game, the oldster moved his front row center pukt three squares forward and one left oblique. I checked it with an end pukt, and waited.

The contest was not going to be exacting enough to hold my complete attention. Already an eidetic portion of my mind—which I always thought of as a small machine, ticking away in one corner of my skull, independent of any control or direction from me—was moving its interest out to the spectators around my booth.

It caught a half-completed gesture of admiration at my last move from a youth directly ahead of me. And with the motion, and the glimpse of the youth's face, something slipped into place in my memory. Some subconscious counting finished itself, and I knew that there had been too many of these youths, with faces like this one, finely boned and smooth, with slender delicate necks and slim hands and movements that were cool and detached. Far too many to be a normal number in a population of adults and children.

As if drawn, my glance went past the forms of the watchers around the booth and plumbed the passing crowd to the figure of a man; a magnificent masculine type of the Veldian race, thick shouldered and strong, thoughtful in motion, yet with something of the swagger of a gladiator, who, as he walked, spoke to the woman who held his arm, leaning toward her cherishingly as if he protected a great prize.

She was wearing a concealing cloak, but her face was beautiful, her hair semi-long, and in spite of the cloak I could see that her body was full-fleshed and almost voluptuously feminine. I had seen few such women on Velda.

Two of the slim, delicately built youths went by arm in arm, walking with a slight defiant sway of bodies, and looked at the couple as they passed, with a pleasure in the way the man's fascinated attention clove to the woman, and looked at the beauty of the woman possessively without lust, and passed by, their heads held higher in pride as if they shared a secret triumph with her. Yet they were strangers.

I had an answer to my counting. The "youths" with the large eyes and smooth delicate heads, with the slim straight asexual bodies, thought of themselves as women. I had not seen them treated with the subdued attraction and conscious avoidance one sex gives another, but by numbers . . . My memory added the number of these "youths" to the numbers of figures and faces that had been obviously female. It totaled to almost half the population I had seen. No matter what the biological explanation, it seemed reasonable that half . . .

I bent my head, to not see the enigma of the boy-woman face watching me, and braced my elbow to steady my hand as I moved. For two weeks I had been on Velda and during the second week I had come out of hiding and passed as a Veldian. It was incredible that I had been operating under a misunderstanding as to which were women, and which men, and not blundered openly. The luck that had saved me had been undeserved.

Opposite me, across the board, the bleach-skinned hand of the oldster was beginning to waver with indecision as each pukt was placed. He was seeing defeat, and not wishing to see it.

In eight more minutes I completed the rout of his forces and closed out the game. In winning I had lost only two pukts. The other's defeat was crushing, but my ruthlessness had been deliberate. I wanted my reputation to spread.

My sign, and the game in progress, by now had attracted a line of challengers, but as the oldster left the line broke and most of

them shook their heads and moved back, then crowded around the
booth and good-naturedly elbowed their way to positions of better
vantage.

I knew then that I had set my lure with an irresistible bait. On a
world where the Game was played from earliest childhood—was in
fact a vital aspect of their culture—my challenge could not be ignored. I pocketed the loser's blue slip and nodded to the first in line
of the four men who still waited to try me.

This second man played a better game than the old one. He had
a fine tight-knit offensive, with a good grasp of values, but his
weakness showed early in the game when I saw him hesitate before
making a simple move in a defensive play. He was not skilled in the
strategy of retreat and defense, or not suited to it by temperament.
He would be unable to cope with a swift forward press, I decided.
I was right.

Some of the challengers bet more, some less, all lost on the second game. I purchased a nut and fruit confection from a passing
food vender and ate it for a sparse lunch while I played through
the late afternoon hours.

By the time Velda's distant sun had begun to print long shadows
across the Fair grounds, I was certain that word of my booth had
spread well.

The crowd about the railing of my stand was larger—but the
players were fewer. Sometimes I had a break of several minutes before one made a decision to try his skill. And there were no more
challenges from ordinary players. Still the results were the same.
None had sufficient adroitness to give me more than a passing contest.

Until Caertin Vlosmin made his appearance.

Vlosmin played a game intended to be impregnably defensive, to
remain untouchable until an opponent made a misplay or an over-
zealous drive, of which he would then take advantage. But his
mental prowess was not quite great enough to be certain of a
sufficiently concealed or complex weakness in the approach of an
adversary, and he would not hazard an attack on an uncertainty.
Excess caution was his weakness.

During our play I sensed that the crowd about us was very intent
and still. On the outskirts, newcomers inquiring cheerfully were silenced by whispered exclamations.

Though it required all my concentration the game was soon over.
I looked at Vlosmin as he rose to his feet, and noted with surprise

that a fine spotting of moisture brightened his upper lip. Only then did I recognize the strain and effort he had invested into the attempt to defeat me.

"You are an exceptional craftsman," he said. There was a grave emphasis he put on the "exceptional" which I could not miss, and I saw that his face was whiter.

His formal introduction of himself earlier as "Caertin Vlosmin" had meant something more than I had realized at the time.

I had just played against, and defeated, one of the Great Players!

The sun set a short time later and floating particles of light-reflecting air-foam drifted out over the Fair grounds. Someway they were held suspended above the ground while air currents tossed them about and intermingled them in the radiance of vari-hued spotlights. The area was still as bright as day, but filled with pale, shifting shadows that seemed to heighten the byplay of sound and excitement coming from the Fair visitors.

Around my booth all was quiet; the spectators were subdued—as though waiting for the next act in a tense drama. I was very tired now, but I knew by the tenseness I observed around me that I did not have much longer to wait.

By the bubbles' light I watched new spectators take their positions about my booth. And as time went by I saw that some of them did not move on, as my earlier visitors had done.

The weight that rode my stomach muscles grew abruptly heavier. I had set my net with all the audacity of a spider waiting for a fly, yet I knew that when my anticipated victim arrived he would more likely resemble a spider hawk. Still the weight was not caused by fear: It was excitement—the excitement of the larger game about to begin.

I was playing an opponent of recognizably less ability than Vlosmin when I heard a stirring and murmuring in the crowd around my stand. The stirring was punctuated by my opponent rising to his feet.

I glanced up.

The big man who had walked into my booth was neither arrogant nor condescending, yet the confidence in his manner was like an aura of strength. He had a deep reserve of vitality, I noted as I studied him carefully, but it was a leashed, controlled vitality. Like most of the men of the Veldian race he wore a uniform, cut severely plain, and undecorated. No flowing robes or tunics for these men. They were a warrior race, unconcerned with the aesthetic touches of personal dress, and left that strictly to their women.

The newcomer turned to my late opponent. His voice was impressive, controlled. "Please finish your game," he said courteously.

The other shook his head. "The game is already as good as over. My sword is broken. You are welcome to my place."

The tall man turned to me. "If you don't mind?"

"My pleasure," I answered. "Please be seated."

This was it.

My visitor shrugged his close wrapped cloak back from his shoulders and took the chair opposite me. "I am Kalin Trobt," he said. As if he knew I had been expecting him.

In reply I came near to telling him my correct name. But Robert O. Lang was a name that would have been alien to Velda. Using it would have been as good as a confession. "Claustil Anteer," I said, giving a name I had invented earlier.

We played the first game as children play it, taking each other's pukts as the opportunity presented, making no attempt at finesse. Trobt won, two up. Neither of us had made mention of a wager. There would be more than money involved in this Game.

I noticed, when I glanced up before the second game, that the spectators had been cleared from around the booth. Only the inner, unmoving ring I had observed earlier remained now. They watched calmly—professionally.

Fortunately I had no intention of trying to escape.

During the early part of the second game Trobt and I tested each other carefully, as skilled swordsmen, probing, feinting, and shamming attack, but never actually exposing ourselves. I detected what could have been a slight tendency to gamble in Trobt's game, but there was no concrete situation to confirm it.

My first moves were entirely passive. Alertly passive. If I had judged correctly the character of the big man opposite me, I had only to ignore the bait he offered to draw me out, to disregard his openings and apparent—too apparent—errors, until he became convinced that I was unshakably cautious, and not to be tempted into making the first thrusts. For this was his weakness as I had guessed it: That his was a gambling temperament—that when he saw an opportunity he would strike—without the caution necessary to insure safety.

Pretending to move with timidity, and pausing with great deliberation over even the most obvious plays, I maneuvered only to defend. Each time Trobt shifted to a new position of attack I covered —until finally I detected the use of slightly more arm force than necessary when he moved a pukt. It was the only sign of impatience he gave, but I knew it was there.

Then it was that I left one—thin—opening.

Trobt streaked a pukt through and cut out one of my middle defenders.

Instead of making the obvious counter of taking his piece, I played a pukt far removed from his invading man. He frowned in concentration, lifted his arm—and his hand hung suspended over the board.

Suddenly his eyes widened. His glance swept upward to my face and what he saw there caused his expression to change to one of mingled dismay and astonishment. There was but one move he could make. When he made it his entire left flank would be exposed. He had lost the game.

Abruptly he reached forward, touched his index finger to the tip of my nose, and pressed gently.

After a minute during which neither of us spoke, I said, "You know?"

He nodded. "Yes," he said. "You're a Human."

There was a stir and rustle of motion around me. The ring of spectators had leaned forward a little as they heard his words. I looked up and saw that they were smiling, inspecting me with curiosity and something that could have been called admiration. In the dusk the clearest view was the ring of teeth, gleaming—the view a rabbit might get of a circle of grinning foxes. Foxes might feel friendly toward rabbits, and admire a good big one. Why not?

I suppressed an ineffectual impulse to deny what I was. The time was past for that. "How did you find out?" I asked Trobt.

"Your Game. No one could play like that and not be well known. And now your nose."

"My nose?" I repeated.

"Only one physical difference between a Human and a Veldian is apparent on the surface. The nose cartilage. Yours is split—mine is single." He rose to his feet. "Will you come with me, please?"

It was not a request.

My guards walked singly and in couples, sometimes passing Trobt and myself, sometimes letting us pass them, and sometimes lingering at a booth, like any other walkers, and yet, unobtrusively they held me encircled, always in the center of the group. I had already learned enough of the Veldian personality to realize that this was simply a habit of tact. Tact to prevent an arrest from being conspicuous, so as not to add the gaze of his fellows to whatever punishment would be decided for a culprit's offense. Apparently they considered humiliation too deep a punishment to use indiscriminately.

At the edge of the Fair grounds some of the watchers bunched around me while others went to get the tricars. I stood and looked across the park to The City. That was what it was called, The City, The Citadel, The Hearthplace, the home place where one's family is kept safe, the sanctuary whose walls have never been pierced. All those connotations had been in the name and the use of the name; in the voices of those who spoke it. Sometimes they called it The Hearth, and sometimes The Market, always *The* as if it were the only one.

Though the speakers lived in other places and named them as the homes of their ancestors, most of the Veldians were born here. Their history was colored, I might say even shaped, by their long era of struggle with the dleeth, a four-footed, hairy carnivora, physically little different from the big cats of Earth, but intelligent. They had battled the Veldians in a struggle for survival from the Veldians' earliest memories until a couple centuries before my visit. Now the last few surviving dleeth had found refuge in the frigid region of the north pole. With their physical superiority they probably would have won the struggle against the Veldians, except that their instincts had been purely predatory, and they had no hands and could not develop technology.

The City had been the one strong point that the dleeth had never been able to breach. It had been held by one of the stronger clans, and there was seldom unity among the tribes, yet any family about to bear a child was given sanctuary within its walls.

The clans were nomads—made so by the aggression of the dleeth —but they always made every effort to reach The City when childbirth was imminent. This explained, at least partly, why even strangers from foreign areas regarded The City as their home place.

I could see the Games Building from where I stood. In the walled city called Hearth it was the highest point. Big and red, it towered above the others, and the city around it rose to it like a wave, its consort of surrounding smaller buildings matched to each other in size and shape in concentric rings. Around each building wound the ramps of elevator runways, harmonious and useful, each of different colored stone, lending variety and warmth. Nowhere was there a clash of either proportion or color. Sometimes I wondered if the Veldians did not build more for the joy of creating symmetry, than because of utilitarian need.

I climbed into Trobt's three-wheeled car as it stopped before me, and the minute I settled into the bucket seat and gripped the bracing handles, Trobt spun the car and it dived into the highway and rushed toward the city. The vehicle seemed unstable, being about the width of a motor bike, with side car in front, and having nothing behind except a metal box that must have housed a powerful battery, and a shaft with the rear wheel that did the steering. It was an arrangement that made possible sudden wrenching turns that were battering to any passenger as unused to it as I. To my conditioning it seemed that the Veldians on the highway drove like madmen, the traffic rules were incomprehensible or nonexistent, and all drivers seemed determined to drive only in gull-like sweeping lines, giving no obvious change of course for other such cars, brushing by tricars from the opposite direction with an inch or less of clearance.

Apparently the maneuverability of the cars and the skill of the drivers were enough to prevent accidents, and I had to force my totally illogical drivers' reflexes to relax and stop tensing against the nonexistent peril.

I studied Trobt as he drove, noting the casual way he held the wheel, and the assurance in the set of his shoulders. I tried to form a picture in my mind of the kind of man he was, and just what were the motivations that would move or drive him.

Physically he was a long-faced man, with a smooth muscular symmetry, and an Asiatic cast to his eyes. I was certain that he excelled at whatever job he held. In fact I was prepared to believe that he would excel at anything he tried. He was undoubtedly one of those amazing men for whom the exceptional was mere routine. If he were to be cast in the role of my opponent: he the person in whom the opposition of this race would be actualized—as I now anticipated—I would not have wanted to bet against him.

The big skilled man was silent for several minutes, weaving the tricar with smooth swerves through a three-way tangle at an intersection, but twice he glanced at my expression with evident curiosity. Finally, as a man would state an obvious fact he said, "I presume you know you will be executed."

Trobt's face reflected surprise at the shock he must have read in mine. I had known the risk I would be taking in coming here, of course, and of the very real danger that it might end in my death. But this had come up on me too fast. I had not realized that the affair had progressed to the point where my death was already assured. I had thought that there would be negotiations, consultations, and perhaps ultimatums. But only if they failed did I believe that the repercussions might carry me along to my death.

However, there was the possibility that Trobt was merely testing my courage. I decided on boldness. "No," I said. "I do not expect to be executed."

Trobt raised his eyebrows and slowed, presumably to gain more time to talk. With a sudden decision he swung the tricar from the road into one of the small parks spread at regular intervals along the highway.

"Surely you don't think we would let you live? There's a state of war between Velda and your Ten Thousand Worlds. You admit that you're Human, and obviously you are here to spy. Yet when you're captured, you do not expect to be executed?"

"Was I captured?" I asked, emphasizing the last word.

He pondered on that a moment, but apparently did not come up with an answer that satisfied him. "I presume your question means something," he said.

"If I had wanted to keep my presence here a secret, would I have set up a booth at the Fair and invited inspection?" I asked.

He waved one hand irritably, as though to brush aside a picayune argument. "Obviously you did it to test yourself against us, to draw the great under your eye, and perhaps become a friend, treated as an equal with access to knowledge of our plans and weapons. Certainly! Your tactic drew two members of the Council into your net before it was understood. If we had accepted you as a previously unknown Great, you would have won. You are a gambling man, and you played a gambler's hand. You lost."

Partly he was right.

"My deliberate purpose was to reach you," I said, "or someone else with sufficient authority to listen to what I have to say."

Trobt pulled the vehicle deeper into the park. He watched the cars of our escort settling to rest before and behind us. I detected a slight unease and rigidity in his stillness as he said, "Speak then. I'm listening."

"I've come to negotiate," I told him.

Something like a flash of puzzlement crossed his features before they returned to tighter immobility. Unexpectedly he spoke in *Earthian,* my own language. "Then why did you choose this method? Would it not have been better simply to announce yourself?"

This was the first hint he had given that he might have visited our Worlds before I visited his. Though we had suspected before I came that some of them must have. They probably knew of our existence years before we discovered them.

Ignoring his change of language, I replied, still speaking Veldian, "Would it have been that simple? Or would some minor official, on capturing me, perhaps have had me imprisoned, or tortured to extract information?"

Again the suppressed puzzlement in the shift of position as he looked at me. "They would have treated you as an envoy, representing your Ten Thousand Worlds. You could have spoken to the Council immediately." He spoke in Veldian now.

"I did not know that," I said. "You refused to receive our fleet envoys; why should I expect you to accept me any more readily?"

Trobt started to speak, stopped, and turned in his seat to regard me levelly and steadily, his expression unreadable. "Tell me what you have to say then. I will judge whether or not the Council will listen."

"To begin with—" I looked away from the expressionless eyes, out the windshield, down the vistas of brown short trees that grew between each small park and the next. "Until an exploring party of ours found signs of extensive mining operations on a small metal-rich planet, we knew nothing of your existence. We were not even aware that another race in the galaxy had discovered faster than light space travel. But after the first clue we were alert for other signs, and found them. Our discovery of your planet was bound to come. However, we did not expect to be met on our first visit with an attack of such hostility as you displayed."

"When we learned that you had found us," Trobt said, "we sent a message to your Ten Thousand Worlds, warning them that we wanted no contact with you. Yet you sent a fleet of spaceships against us."

I hesitated before answering. "That phrase, 'sent against us,' is hardly the correct one," I said. "The fleet was sent for a diplomatic visit, and was not meant as an aggressive action." I thought, *But obviously the display of force was intended "diplomatically" to frighten you people into being polite.* In diplomacy the smile, the extended hand—and the big stick visible in the other hand—had obviated many a war, by giving the stranger a chance to choose a hand, in full understanding of the alternative. *We showed our muscle to your little planet—you showed your muscle. And now we are ready to be polite.*

I hoped these people would understand the face-saving ritual of negotiation, the disclaimers of intent, that would enable each side to claim that there had been no war, merely accident.

"We did not at all feel that you were justified in wiping the fleet from space," I said. "But it was probably a legitimate misunderstanding—"

"You had been warned!" Trobt's voice was grim, his expression not inviting of further discussion. I thought I detected a bunching of the muscles in his arms.

For a minute I said nothing, made no gesture. Apparently this angle of approach was unproductive—and probably explosive. Also, trying to explain and justify the behavior of the Federation politicos could possibly become rather taxing.

"Surely you don't intend to postpone negotiations indefinitely?" I asked tentatively. "One planet cannot conquer the entire Federation."

The bunched muscles of his arms strained until they pulled his shoulders, and his lips whitened with the effort of controlling some savage anger. Apparently my question had impugned his pride.

This, I decided quickly, was not the time to make an enemy. "I apologize if I have insulted you," I said in Earthian. "I do not yet always understand what I am saying, in your language."

He hesitated, made some kind of effort, and shifted to Earthian. "It is not a matter of strength, or weakness," he said, letting his words ride out on his released breath, "but of behavior, courtesy. We would have left you alone, but now it is too late. We will drive your faces into the ground. I am certain that we can, but if we could not, still we would try. To imply that we would not try, from fear, seems to me words to soil the mouth, not worthy of a man speaking to a man. We are converting our ships of commerce to war. Your people will see soon that we will fight."

"Is it too late for negotiation?" I asked.

His forehead wrinkled into a frown and he stared at me in an effort of concentration. When he spoke it was with a considered hesitation. "If I make a great effort I can feel that you are sincere, and not speaking to mock or insult. It is strange that beings who look so much like ourselves can"—he rubbed a hand across his eyes —"pause a moment. When I say 'yag loogt'-n'balt' what does it mean to you in Earthish?"

"I must play." I hesitated as he turned one hand palm down, signifying that I was wrong. "I must duel," I said, finding another meaning in the way I had heard the phrase expressed. It was a strong meaning, judging by the tone and inflection the speaker had used. I had mimicked the tone without full understanding. The verb was perhaps stronger than *must*, meaning something inescapable, fated, but I could find no Earthian verb for it. I understood why Trobt dropped his hand to the seat without turning it palm up to signify that I was correct.

"There may be no such thought on the Human worlds," he said resignedly. "I have to explain as to a child or a madman. I cannot explain in Veldian, for it has no word to explain what needs no explanation."

He shifted to Earthian, his controlled voice sounding less controlled when moving with the more fluid inflections of my own tongue. "We said we did not want further contact. Nevertheless you sent the ships—deliberately in disregard of our expressed desire. That was an insult, a deep insult, meaning we have not strength to defend our word, meaning we are so helpless that we can be treated with impoliteness, like prisoners, or infants.

"Now we must show you which of us is helpless, which is the weakling. Since you would not respect our wishes, then in order to be not-further-insulted we must make of your people a captive or a child in helplessness, so that you will be without power to affront us another time."

"If apologies are in order—"

He interrupted with raised hand, still looking at me very earnestly with forehead wrinkled, thought half turned inward in difficult introspection of his own meaning, as well as a grasping for my viewpoint.

"The insult of the fleet can only be wiped out in the blood of testing—of battle—and the test will not stop until one or the other shows that he is too weak to struggle. There is no other way."

He was demanding total surrender!

I saw it was a subject that could not be debated. The Federation had taken on a bearcat this time!

"I stopped because I wanted to understand you," Trobt resumed. "Because the others will not understand how you could be an envoy—how your Federation could send an envoy—except as an insult. I have seen enough of Human strangeness to be not maddened by the insolence of an emissary coming to us, or by your people expecting us to exchange words when we carry your first insult still unwashed from our face. I can even see how it could perhaps be considered *not* an insult, for I have seen your people living on their planets and they suffered insult from each other without striking, until finally I saw that they did not know when they were insulted, as a deaf man does not know when his name is called."

I listened to the quiet note of his voice, trying to recognize the attitude that made it different from his previous tones—calm and slow and deep. Certainty that what he was saying was important . . . conscious tolerance . . . generosity.

Trobt turned on the tricar's motor and put his hands on the steering shaft. "You are a man worthy of respect," he said, looking down the dark empty road ahead. "I wanted you to understand us. To see the difference between us. So that you will not think us without justice." The car began to move.

"I wanted you to understand why you will die."

I said nothing—having nothing to say. But I began immediately to bring my report up to date, recording the observations during the games, and recording with care this last conversation, with the explanation it carried of the Veldian reactions that had been previously obscure.

I used nerve-twitch code, "typing" on a tape somewhere inside myself the coded record of everything that had passed since the last time I brought the report up to date. The typing was easy, like flexing a finger in code jerks, but I did not know exactly where the recorder was located. It was some form of transparent plastic which would not show up on X ray. The surgeons had imbedded it in my flesh while I was unconscious, and had implanted a mental block against my noticing which small muscle had been linked into the contrivance for the typing.

If I died before I was able to return to Earth, there were several capsuled chemicals buried at various places in my body, that intermingled, would temporarily convert my body to a battery for a high powered broadcast of the tape report, destroying the tape and my body together. This would go into action only if my temperature fell fifteen degrees below the temperature of life.

I became aware that Kalin Trobt was speaking again, and that I had let my attention wander while recording, and taped some subjective material. The code twitches easily became an unconscious accompaniment to memory and thought, and this was the second time I had found myself recording more than necessary.

Trobt watched the dark road, threading among buildings and past darkened vehicles. His voice was thoughtful. "In the early days, Miklas of Danlee, when he had the Ornan family surrounded and outnumbered, wished not to destroy them, for he needed good warriors, and in another circumstance they could have been his friends. Therefore he sent a slave to them with an offer of terms of peace. The Ornan family had the slave skinned while alive, smeared with salt and grease so that he would not bleed, and sent back, tied in a bag of his own skin, with a message of no. The chroniclers agree that since the Ornan family was known to be honorable, Miklas should not have made the offer.

"In another time and battle, the Cheldos were offered terms of surrender by an envoy. Nevertheless they won against superior forces, and gave their captives to eat a stew whose meat was the envoy of the offer to surrender. Being given to eat their own words as you'd say in Earthish. Such things are not done often, because the offer is not given."

He wrenched the steering post sideways and the tricar turned almost at right angles, balanced on one wheel for a dizzy moment, and fled up a great spiral ramp winding around the outside of the red Games Building.

Trobt still looked ahead, not glancing at me. "I understand, from observing them, that you Earthians will lie without soiling the mouth. What are you here for, actually?"

"I came from interest, but I intend, given the opportunity, to observe and to report my observations back to my government. They should not enter a war without knowing anything about you."

"Good." He wrenched the car around another abrupt turn into a red archway in the side of the building, bringing it to a stop inside. The sound of the other tricars entering the tunnel echoed hollowly from the walls and died as they came to a stop around us. "You are a spy then."

"Yes," I said, getting out. I had silently resigned my commission as envoy some five minutes earlier. There was little point in delivering political messages, if they have no result except to have one skinned or made into a stew.

A heavy door with the seal of an important official engraved upon it opened before us. In the forepart of the room we entered, a slim-bodied creature with the face of a girl sat with crossed legs on a platform like a long coffee table, sorting vellum marked with the dots and dashes, arrows and pictures, of the Veldian language.

She had green eyes, honeyed-olive complexion, a red mouth, and purple black hair. She stopped to work an abacus, made a notation on one of the stiff sheets of vellum, then glanced up to see who had come in. She saw us, and glanced away again, as if she had coolly made a note of our presence and gone back to her work, sorting the vellum sheets and stacking them in thin shelves with quick graceful motions.

"Kalin Trobt of Pagael," a man on the far side of the room said, a man sitting cross-legged on a dais covered with brown fur and scattered papers. He accepted the hand Trobt extended and they gripped wrists in a locked gesture of friendship. "And how survive the other sons of the citadel of Pagael?"

"Well, and continuing in friendship to the house of Lyagin,"

Trobt replied carefully. "I have seen little of my kin. There are many farlanders all around us, and between myself and my hearth-folk swarm the adopted."

"It is not like the old days, Kalin Trobt. In a dream I saw a rock sink from the weight of sons, and I longed for the sight of a land that is without strangers."

"We are all kinfolk now, Lyagin."

"My hearth pledged it."

Lyagin put his hand on a stack of missives which he had been considering, his face thoughtful, sparsely fleshed, mostly skull and tendon, his hair bound back from his face, and wearing a short white cotton dress beneath a light fur cape.

He was an old man, already in his senility, and now he was lost in a lapse of awareness of what he had been doing a moment before. By no sign did Trobt show impatience, or even consciousness of the other's lapse.

Lyagin raised his head after a minute and brought his rheumy eyes into focus on us. "You bring someone in regard to an inquiry?" he asked.

"The one from the Ten Thousand Worlds," Trobt replied.

Lyagin nodded apologetically. "I received word that he would be brought," he said. "How did you capture him?"

"He came."

The expression must have had some connotation that I did not recognize for the official let his glance cross mine, and I caught one slight flicker of interest in his eyes. "You say these Humans lie?" he asked Trobt.

"Frequently. It is considered almost honorable to lie to an enemy in circumstances where one may profit by it."

"You brought back from his worlds some poison which insures their speaking the truth, I believe?"

"Not a poison, something they call drugs, which affects one like strong drink, dulling a man and changing what he might do. Under its influence he loses his initiative of decision."

"You have this with you?"

"Yes." Trobt was going to waste no time getting from me anything I had that might be of value to them.

"It will be interesting having an enemy co-operate," Lyagin said. "If he finds no way to kill himself, he can be very useful to us." So

SECOND GAME 115

far my contact with the Veldians had not been going at all as I had hoped and planned.

The boy-girl at the opposite side of the room finished a problem on the abacus, noted the answer, and glanced directly at my face, at my expression, then locked eyes with me for a brief moment. When she glanced down to the vellum again it was as if she had seen whatever she had looked up to see, and was content. She sat a little straighter as she worked, and moved with an action that was a little less supple and compliant.

I believe she had seen me as a man.

During the questioning I made no attempt to resist the drug's influence. I answered truthfully—but literally. Many times my answers were undecidable—because I knew not the answers, or I lacked the data to give them. And the others were cloaked under a full literal subtlety that made them useless to the Veldians. Questions such as the degree of unity existing between the Worlds: I answered—truthfully—that they were united under an authority with supreme power of decision. The fact that that authority had no actual force behind it; that it was subject to the whims and fluctuations of sentiment and politics of intraalliances; that it had deteriorated into a mere supernumerary body of impractical theorists that occupied itself, in a practical sphere, only with picayune matters, I did not explain. It was not asked of me.

Would our Worlds fight? I answered that they would fight to the death to defend their liberty and independence. I did not add that that will to fight would evidence itself first in internecine bickering, procrastinations, and jockeying to avoid the worst thrusts of the enemy—before it finally resolved itself into a united front against attack.

By early morning Trobt could no longer contain his impatience. He stepped closer. "We're going to learn one thing," he said, and his voice was harsh. "Why did you come here?"

"To learn all that I could about you," I answered.

"You came to find a way to whip us!"

It was not a question and I had no necessity to answer.

"Have you found the way?"

"No."

"If you do, and you are able, will you use that knowledge to kill us?"

"No."

Trobt's eyebrows raised. "No?" he repeated. "Then why do you want it?"

"I hope to find a solution that will not harm either side."

"But if you found that a solution was not possible, you would be willing to use your knowledge to defeat us?"

"Yes."

"Even if it meant that you had to exterminate us—man, woman, and child?"

"Yes."

"Why? Are you so certain that you are right, that you walk with God, and that we are knaves?"

"If the necessity to destroy one civilization or the other arose, and the decision were mine to make, I would rule against you because of the number of sentient beings involved."

Trobt cut the argument out from under me. "What if the situation were reversed, and your side was in the minority? Would you choose to let them die?"

I bowed my head as I gave him the truthful answer. "I would choose for my own side, no matter what the circumstances."

The interrogation was over.

On the drive to Trobt's home I was dead tired, and must have slept for a few minutes with my eyes open. With a start I heard Trobt say, ". . . that a man with ability enough to be a games—chess—master is given no authority over his people, but merely consulted on occasional abstract questions of tactics."

"It is the nature of the problem." I caught the gist of his comment from his last words and did my best to answer it. I wanted nothing less than to engage in conversation, but I realized that the interest he was showing now was just the kind I had tried to guide him to, earlier in the evening. If I could get him to understand us better, our motivations and ideals, perhaps even our frailties, there would be more hope for a compatible meeting of minds. "Among peoples of such mixed natures, such diverse histories and philosophies, and different ways of life, most administrative problems are problems of a choice of whims, of changing and conflicting goals; not *how* to do what a people want done, but *what* they want done, and whether their next generation will want it enough to make work on it, now, worthwhile."

"They sound insane," Trobt said. "Are your administrators supposed to serve the flickering goals of demented minds?"

"We must weigh values. What is considered good may be a matter of viewpoint, and may change from place to place, from generation to generation. In determining what people feel and what their unvoiced wants are, a talent of strategy, and an impatience with the illogic of others, are not qualifications."

"The good is good, how can it change?" Trobt asked. "I do not understand."

I saw that truly he could not understand, since he had seen nothing of the clash of philosophies among a mixed people. I tried to think of ways it could be explained; how to show him that a people who let their emotions control them more than their logic, would unavoidably do many things they could not justify or take pride in —but that that emotional predominance was what had enabled them to grow, and spread throughout their part of the galaxy—and be, in the main, happy.

I was tired, achingly tired. More, the events of the long day, and Velda's heavier gravity had taken me to the last stages of exhaustion. Yet I wanted to keep that weakness from Trobt. It was possible that he, and the other Veldians, would judge the Humans by what they observed in me.

Trobt's attention was on his driving and he did not notice that I followed his conversation only with difficulty. "Have you had only the two weeks of practice in the Game, since you came?" he asked.

I kept my eyes open with an effort and breathed deeply. Velda's one continent, capping the planet on its upper third, merely touched what would have been a temperate zone. During its short summer its mean temperature hung in the low sixties. At night it dropped to near freezing. The cold night air bit into my lungs and drove the fog of exhaustion from my brain.

"No," I answered Trobt's question. "I learned it before I came. A chess adept wrote me, in answer to an article on chess, that a man from one of the outworlds had shown him a game of greater richness and flexibility than chess, with much the same feeling to the player, and had beaten him in three games of chess after only two games to learn it, and had said that on his own planet this chesslike game was the basis for the amount of authority with which a man is invested. The stranger would not name his planet.

"I hired an investigating agency to learn the whereabouts of this planet. There was none in the Ten Thousand Worlds. That meant that the man had been a very ingenious liar, or—that he had come from Velda."

"It was I, of course," Trobt acknowledged.

"I realized that from your conversation. The sender of the letter," I resumed, "was known to me as a chess champion of two Worlds. The matter tantalized my thoughts for weeks, and finally I decided to try to arrange a visit to Velda. If you had this game, I wanted to try myself against your skilled ones."

"I understand that desire very well," Trobt said. "The same temptation caused me to be indiscreet when I visited your Worlds. I have seldom been able to resist the opportunity for an intellectual gambit."

"It wasn't much more than a guess that I would find the Game on Velda," I said. "But the lure was too strong for me to pass it by."

"Even if you came intending to challenge, you had little enough time to learn to play as you have—against men who have spent lifetimes learning. I'd like to try you again soon, if I may."

"Certainly." I was in little mood or condition to welcome any further polite conversation. And I did not appreciate the irony of his request—to the best of my knowledge I was still under a sentence of early death.

Trobt must have caught the bleakness in my reply for he glanced quickly over his shoulder at me. "There will be time," he said, gently for him. "Several days at least. You will be my guest." I knew that he was doing his best to be kind. His decision that I must die had not been prompted by any meanness of nature: To him it was only—inevitable.

The next day I sat at one end of a Games table in a side wing of his home while Trobt leaned against the wall to my left. "Having a like nature I can well understand the impulse that brought you here," he said. "The supreme gamble. Playing—with your life the stake in the game. Nothing you've ever experienced can compare with it. And even now—when you have lost, and will die—you do not regret it, I'm certain."

"I'm afraid you're overestimating my courage, and misinterpreting my intentions," I told him, feeling instinctively that this would be a good time to again present my arguments. "I came because I hoped to reach a better understanding. We feel that an absolutely unnecessary war, with its resulting death and destruction, would be foolhardy. And I fail to see your viewpoint. Much of it strikes me as stupid racial pride."

Trobt ignored the taunt. "The news of your coming is the first topic of conversation in The City," he said. "The clans understand that you have come to challenge; one man against a nation. They greatly admire your audacity."

"Look," I said, becoming angry and slipping into Earthian. "I don't know whether you consider me a damn fool or not. But if you think I came here expecting to die; that I'm looking forward to it with pleasure—"

He stopped me with an idle gesture of one hand. "You deceive yourself if you believe what you say," he commented. "Tell me this: Would you have stayed away if you had known just how great the risk was to be?"

I was surprised to find that I did not have a ready answer to his question.

"Shall we play?" Trobt asked.

We played three games; Trobt with great skill, employing diversified and ingenious attacks. But he still had that bit too much audacity in his execution. I won each time.

"You're undoubtedly a Master," Trobt said at the end of the third game. "But that isn't all of it. Would you like me to tell you why I can't beat you?"

"Can you?" I asked.

"I think so," he said. "I wanted to try against you again and again, because each time it did not seem that you had defeated me, but only that I had played badly, made childish blunders, and that I lost each game before we ever came to grips. Yet when I entered the duel against you a further time, I'd begin to blunder again."

He shoved his hands more deeply under his weapons belt, leaning back and observing me with his direct inspection. "My blundering then has to do with you, rather than myself," he said. "Your play is excellent, of course, but there is more beneath the surface than above. This is your talent: You lose the first game to see an opponent's weakness—and play it against him."

I could not deny it. But neither would I concede it. Any small advantage I might hold would be sorely needed later.

"I understand Humans a little," Trobt said. "Enough to know that very few of them would come to challenge us without some other purpose. They have no taste for death, with glory or without."

Again I did not reply.

"I believe," Trobt said, "that you came here to challenge in your own way, which is to find any weakness we might have, either in our military, or in some odd way, in our very selves."

Once again—with a minimum of help from me—he had arrived in his reasoning at a correct answer. From here on—against this man—I would have to walk a narrow line.

"I think," Trobt said more slowly, glancing down at the board between us, then back at my expression, "that this may be the First Game, and that you are more dangerous than you seem, that you are accepting the humiliation of allowing yourself to be thought of as weaker than you are, in actuality. You intend to find our weakness, and you expect somehow to tell your states what you find."

I looked across at him without moving. "What weakness do you fear I've seen?" I countered.

Trobt placed his hands carefully on the board in front of him and rose to his feet. Before he could say what he intended a small boy pulling something like a toy riding-horse behind him came into the game room and grabbed Trobt's trouser leg. He was the first blond child I had seen on Velda.

The boy pointed at the swords on the wall. "Da," he said beseechingly, making reaching motions. "Da."

Trobt kept his attention on me. After a moment a faint humorless smile moved his lips. He seemed to grow taller, with the impression a strong man gives when he remembers his strength. "You will find no weakness," he said. He sat down again and placed the child on his lap.

The boy grabbed immediately at the abacus hanging on Trobt's belt and began playing with it, while Trobt stroked his hair. All the Veldians dearly loved children, I had noticed.

"Do you have any idea how many of our ships were used to wipe out your fleet?" he asked abruptly.

As I allowed myself to show the interest I felt he put a hand on the boy's shoulder and leaned forward. "One," he said.

I very nearly called Trobt a liar—one ship obliterating a thousand —before I remembered that Veldians were not liars, and that Trobt obviously was not lying. Somehow this small under-populated planet had developed a science of weapons that vastly exceeded that of the Ten Thousand Worlds.

I had thought that perhaps my vacation on this Games-mad planet would result in some mutual information that would bring quick negotiation or conciliation: That players of a chesslike game would be easy to approach: That I would meet men intelligent enough to see the absurdity of such an ill-fated war against the overwhelming odds of the Ten Thousand Worlds Federation. Intelligent enough to foresee the disaster that would result from such a fight. It began to look as if the disaster might be to the Ten Thousand and not to the one.

Thinking, I walked alone in Trobt's roof garden.

Walking in Velda's heavy gravity took more energy than I cared to expend, but too long a period without exercise brought a dull ache to the muscles of my shoulders and at the base of my neck.

This was my third evening in the house. I had slept at least ten hours each night since I arrived, and found myself exhausted at day's end, unless I was able to take a nap or lie down during the afternoon.

The flowers and shrubbery in the garden seemed to feel the weight of gravity also, for most of them grew low, and many sent creepers out along the ground. Overhead strange formations of stars clustered thickly and shed a glow on the garden very like Earth's moonlight.

I was just beginning to feel the heavy drag in my leg tendons when a woman's voice said, "Why don't you rest a while?" It spun me around as I looked for the source of the voice.

I found her in a nook in the bushes, seated on a contour chair that allowed her to stretch out in a half-reclining position. She must have weighed near to two hundred—Earth-weight—pounds.

But the thing that had startled me more than the sound of her voice was that she had spoken in the universal language of the Ten Thousand Worlds. And without accent!

"You're—?" I started to ask.

"Human," she finished for me.

"How did you get here?" I inquired eagerly.

"With my husband." She was obviously enjoying my astonishment. She was a beautiful woman, in a gentle bovine way, and very friendly. Her blond hair was done up in tight ringlets.

"You mean . . . Trobt?" I asked.

"Yes." As I stood trying to phrase my wonderment into more questions, she asked, "You're the Earthman, aren't you?"

I nodded. "Are you from Earth?"

"No," she answered. "My home world is Mandel's Planet, in the Thumb group."

She indicated a low hassock of a pair, and I seated myself on the lower and leaned an elbow on the higher, beginning to smile. It would have been difficult not to smile in the presence of anyone so contented. "How did you meet Trobt?" I asked.

"It's a simple love story. Kalin visited Mandel—without revealing his true identity of course—met, and courted me. I learned to love him, and agreed to come to his world as his wife."

"Did you know that he wasn't . . . That he . . ." I stumbled over just how to phrase the question. And wondered if I should have started it.

Her teeth showed white and even as she smiled. She propped a pillow under one plump arm and finished my sentence for me. ". . . That he wasn't Human?" I was grateful for the way she put me at ease—almost as though we had been old friends.

I nodded.

"I didn't know." For a moment she seemed to draw back into her thoughts, as though searching for something she had almost forgotten. "He couldn't tell me. It was a secret he had to keep. When I arrived here and learned that his planet wasn't a charted world, was not even Human, I was a little uncertain and lonesome. But not frightened. I knew Kalin would never let me be hurt. Even my lonesomeness left quickly. Kalin and I love each other very deeply. I couldn't be more happy than I am now."

She seemed to see I did not consider that my question had been answered—completely. "You're wondering still if I mind that he isn't Human, aren't you?" she asked. "Why should I? After all, what does it mean to be 'Human'? It is only a word that differentiates one group of people from another. I seldom think of the Veldians as being different—and certainly never that they're beneath me."

"Does it bother you—if you'll pardon this curiosity of mine—that you will never be able to bear Kalin's children?"

"The child you saw the first morning is my son," she answered complacently.

"But that's impossible," I blurted.

"Is it?" she asked. "You saw the proof."

"I'm no expert at this sort of thing," I said slowly, "but I've always understood that the possibility of two separate species producing offspring was a million to one."

"Greater than that, probably," she agreed. "But whatever the odds, sooner or later the number is bound to come up. This was it."

I shook my head, but there was no arguing a fact. "Wasn't it a bit unusual that Kalin didn't marry a Veldian woman?"

"He has married—two of them," she answered. "I'm his third wife."

"Then they do practice polygamy," I said. "Are you content with such a marriage?"

"Oh yes," she answered. "You see, besides being very much loved, I occupy a rather enviable position here. I, ah . . ." She grew slightly flustered. "Well . . . the other women—the Veldian women —can bear children only once every eight years, and during the other seven . . ." She hesitated again and I saw a tinge of red creep into her cheeks. She was obviously embarrassed, but she laughed and resolutely went on.

"During the other seven, they lose their feminine appearance, and don't think of themselves as women. While I . . ." I watched with amusement as her color deepened and her glance dropped. "I am always of the same sex, as you might say, always a woman. My husband is the envy of all his friends."

After her first reticence she talked freely, and I learned then the answer to the riddle of the boy-girls of Velda. And at least one reason for their great affection for children.

One year of fertility in eight . . .

Once again I saw the imprint of the voracious dleeth on this people's culture. In their age-old struggle with their cold planet and its short growing seasons—and more particularly with the dleeth—the Veldian women had been shaped by evolution to better fit their environment. The women's strength could not be spared for frequent childbearing—so childbearing had been limited. Further, one small child could be carried in the frequent flights from the dleeth, but not more than one. Nature had done its best to cope with the problem: In the off seven years she tightened the women's flesh, atro-

phying glands and organs—making them nonfunctional—and changing their bodies to be more fit to labor and survive—and to fight, if
necessary. It was an excellent adaptation—for a time and environment where a low birth rate was an asset to survival.

But this adaptation had left only a narrow margin for race per-
petuation. Each woman could bear only four children in her lifetime. That, I realized as we talked, was the reason why the Veldians
had not colonized other planets, even though they had space flight
—and why they probably never would, without a drastic change in
their biological make-up. That left so little ground for a quarrel between them and the Ten Thousand Worlds. Yet here we were,
poised to spring into a death struggle.

"You are a very unusual woman." My attention returned to
Trobt's wife. "In a very unusual situation."

"Thank you," she accepted it as a compliment. She made ready
to rise. "I hope you enjoy your visit here. And that I may see you
again before you return to Earth."

I realized then that she did not know of my peculiar position in
her home. I wondered if she knew even of the threat of war between us and her adopted people. I decided not, or she would
surely have spoken of it. Either Trobt had deliberately avoided telling her, perhaps to spare her the pain it would have caused, or she
had noted that the topic of my presence was disturbing to him and
had tactfully refrained from inquiring. For just a moment I wondered if I should explain everything to her, and have her use the
influence she must have with Trobt. I dismissed the idea as unworthy—and useless.

"Good night," I said.

The next evening as we rode in a tricar Trobt asked if I would
like to try my skill against a better Games player.

"I had assumed you were the best," I said.

"Only the second best," he answered. "It would be interesting to
compare your game with that of our champion. If you can whip
him, perhaps we will have to revise our opinion of you Humans."

He spoke as though in jest, but I saw more behind his words than
he intended me to see. Here at last might be a chance to do a positive service for my side. "I would be happy to play," I said.

Trobt parked the tricar on a side avenue and we walked perhaps
a hundred yards. We stopped at the door of a small one-story stone

house and Trobt tapped with his fingernails on a hollow gong buried in the wood.

After a minute a curtain over the door glass was drawn back and an old woman with straggly gray hair peered out at us. She recognized Trobt and opened the door.

We went in. Neither Trobt nor the old woman spoke. She turned her back after closing the door and went to stir embers in a stone grate.

Trobt motioned with his head for me to follow and led the way into a back room.

"Robert O. Lang," he said, "I would like you to meet Yondtl."

I looked across the room in the direction Trobt had indicated. My first impression was of a great white blob, propped up on a couch and supported by the wall at its back.

Then the thing moved. Moved its eyes. It was alive. Its eyes told me also that it was a man. If I could call it a man.

His head was large and bloated, with blue eyes, washed almost colorless, peering out of deep pouches of flesh. He seemed to have no neck; almost as though his great head were merely an extension of the trunk, and separated only by puffy folds of fat. Other lappings of flesh hung from his body in great thick rolls.

It took another minute of fascinated inspection before I saw that he had no arms, and that no legs reached from his body to the floor. The entire sight of him made me want to leave the room and be sick.

"Robert O. Lang is an Earthian who would challenge you, sir," Trobt addressed the monstrosity.

The other gave no sign that I could see but Trobt went to pull a Games table at the side of the room over toward us. "I will serve as his hands," Trobt said.

The pale blue eyes never left my face.

I stood without conscious thought until Trobt pushed a chair under me. Mentally I shook myself. With unsteady hands—I had to do something with them—I reached for the pukts before me. "Do you . . . do you have a choice . . . of colors, sir?" I stammered, trying to make up for my earlier rudeness of staring.

The lips of the monstrosity quivered, but he made no reply.

All this while Trobt had been watching me with amusement.

"He is deaf and speechless," Trobt said. "Take either set. I will place the other before him."

Absently I pulled the red pieces toward me and placed them on their squares.

"In deference to you as a visitor, you will play 'second game counts,'" Trobt continued. He was still enjoying my consternation. "He always allows his opponent the first move. You may begin when you are ready."

With an effort I forced myself to concentrate on the playing board. My start, I decided, must be orthodox. I had to learn something of the type of game this . . . Yondtl . . . played. I moved the first row right hand pukt its two oblique and one left squares.

Yondtl inclined his head slightly. His lips moved. Trobt put his hand to a pukt and pushed it forward. Evidently Trobt read his lips. Very probably Yondtl could read ours also.

We played for almost an hour with neither of us losing a man.

I had tried several gambits; gambits that invited a misplay on Yondtl's part. But he made none. When he offered I was careful to make no mistakes of my own. We both played as though this first game were the whole contest.

Another hour went by. I deliberately traded three pukts with Yondtl, in an attempt to trick him into a misplay. None came.

I tried a single decoy gambit, and when nothing happened, followed with a second decoy. Yondtl countered each play. I marveled that he gave so little of his attention to the board. Always he seemed to be watching me. I played. He played. He watched me. I sweated.

Yondtl set up an overt side pass that forced me to draw my pukts back into the main body. Somehow I received the impression that he was teasing me. It made me want to beat him down.

I decided on a crossed-force, double decoy gambit. I had never seen it employed. Because, I suspect, it is too involved, and open to error by its user. Slowly and painstakingly I set it up and pressed forward.

The Caliban in the seat opposite me never paused. He matched me play for play. And though Yondtl's features had long since lost the power of expression, his pale eyes seemed to develop a blue luster. I realized, almost with a shock of surprise, that the fat monstrosity was happy—intensely happy.

I came out of my brief reverie with a start. Yondtl had made an obvious play. I had made an obvious counter. I was startled to hear him sound a cry somewhere between a muffled shout and an idiot's laugh, and my attention jerked back to the board. I had lost the game!

My brief moment of abstraction had given Yondtl the opportunity to make a pass too subtle to be detected with part of my faculties occupied elsewhere.

I pushed back my chair. "I've had enough for tonight," I told Trobt. If I were to do the Humans a service, I would need rest before trying Yondtl in the second game.

We made arrangements to meet again the following evening, and let ourselves out. The old woman was nowhere in sight.

The following evening when we began play I was prepared to give my best. I was rested and eager. And I had a concrete plan. Playing the way I had been doing I would never beat Yondtl, I'd decided after long thought. A stand-off was the best I could hope for. Therefore the time had come for more consummate action. I would engage him in a triple decoy gambit!

I had no illusion that I could handle it—the way it should be handled. I doubt that any man, Human or Veldian, could. But at least I would play it with the greatest skill I had, giving my best to every move, and push the game up the scale of reason and involution—up and up—until either Yondtl or I became lost in its innumerable complexities, and fell.

As I attacked, the complexes and complications would grow gradually more numerous, become more and more difficult, until they embraced a span greater than one of us had the capacity to encompass, and the other would win.

The Game began and I forced it into the pattern I had planned. Each play, and each maneuver, became all important, and demanding of the greatest skill I could command. Each pulled at the core of my brain, dragging out the last iota of sentient stuff that writhed there. Yondtl stayed with me, complex gambit through complex gambit.

When the strain became too great I forced my mind to pause, to rest, and to be ready for the next clash. At the first break I searched the annotator. It was working steadily, with an almost smooth throb of efficiency, keeping the position of each pukt—and its value—strong in the forefront of visualization. But something was missing!

A minute went by before I spotted the fault. The move of each pukt involved so many possibilities, so many avenues of choice, that no exact answer was predictable on any one. The number and variation of gambits open on every play, each subject to the multitude of Yondtl's counter moves, stretched the possibilities beyond prediction. The annotator was a harmonizing, perceptive force, but not a creative, initiating one. It operated in a statistical manner, similar to a computer, and could not perform effectively where a crucial factor or factors were unknown, or concealed, as they were here.

My greatest asset was negated.

At the end of the third hour I began to feel a steady pain in my temples, as though a tight metal band pressed against my forehead and squeezed it inward. The only reaction I could discern in Yondtl was that the blue glint in his eyes had become brighter. All his happiness seemed gathered there.

Soon my pauses became more frequent. Great waves of brain weariness had to be allowed to subside before I could play again.

And at last it came.

Suddenly, unexpectedly, Yondtl threw a pukt across the board and took my second decoy—and there was no way for me to retaliate! Worse, my entire defense was smashed.

I felt a kind of calm dismay. My shoulders sagged and I pushed the board away from me and slumped in my chair.

I was beaten.

The next day I escaped from Trobt. It was not difficult. I simply walked away.

For three days I followed the wall of The City, looking for a way out. Each gate was guarded. I watched unobserved and saw that a permit was necessary when leaving. If I found no other way I would make a run for it. The time of decision never came.

Meanwhile to obtain food I was forced into some contact with The City's people, and learned to know them better. Adding this new knowledge to the old I decided that I liked them.

Their manners and organization—within the framework of their culture—was as simple and effective as their architecture. There was a strong emphasis on pride, on strength and honor, on skill, and on living a dangerous life with a gambler's self-command, on rectitude, on truth, and the unbreakable bond of loyalty among

family and friends. Lying, theft, and deceit were practically unknown.

I did detect what might have been a universal discontent in their
young men. They had a warrior heritage and nature which, with
the unity of the tribes and the passing of the dleeth—and no one to
fight except themselves—had left them with an unrecognized futility of purpose. They had not quite been able to achieve a successful
sublimation of their post-warrior need to fight in the Games. Also,
the custom of polygamy—necessary in the old days, and desired still
by those able to attain it—left many sexually frustrated.

I weighed all these observations in my reactions to the Veldians,
and toward the end a strange feeling—a kind of wistfulness—came
as I observed. I felt kin to them, as if these people had much in
common with myself. And I felt that it was too bad that life was
not fundamentally so simple that one could discard the awareness
of other ways of life, of other values and philosophies that bid
against one another, and against one's attention, and make him
cynical of the philosophy he lives by, and dies for. Too bad that I
could not see and take life as that direct, and as that simple.

The third day I climbed a spiral ramp to the top of a tower that
rose above the walls of Hearth and gazed out over miles of swirling
red sand. Directly beneath me stretched a long concrete ribbon of
road. On the road were dozens of slowly crawling vehicles that
might have been caterpillar trucks of Earth!

In my mind the pattern clicked into place. Hearth was not typical of the cities of Velda!

It was an anachronism, a revered Homeplace, a symbol of their
past, untainted by the technocracy that was pursued elsewhere.
This was the capital city, from which the heads of the government
still ruled, perhaps for sentimental reasons, but it was not typical.

My stay in Hearth was cut short when I decended from the tower
and found Trobt waiting for me.

As I might have expected, he showed no sign of anger with me
for having fled into The City. His was the universal Veldian viewpoint. To them all life was the Game. With the difference that it
was played on an infinitely larger board. Every man, and every
woman, with whom the player had contact, direct or indirect, were
pukts on the Board. The player made his decisions, and his plays,
and how well he made them determined whether he won or lost.

His every move, his every joining of strength with those who could help him, his every maneuver against those who would oppose him, was his choice to make, and he rose or fell on the wisdom of the choice. Game, in Velda, means Duel, means struggle and the test of man against the opponent, Life. I had made my escape as the best play as I saw it. Trobt had no recriminations.

The evening of the next day Trobt woke me. Something in his constrained manner brought me to my feet. "Not what you think," he said, "but we must question you again. We will try our own methods this time."

"Torture?"

"You will die under the torture, of course. But for the questioning it will not be necessary. You will talk."

The secret of their method was very simple. Silence. I was led to a room within a room within a room. Each with very thick walls. And left alone. Here time meant nothing.

Gradually I passed from boredom to restlessness, to anxiety, briefly through fear, to enervating frustration, and finally to stark apathy.

When Trobt and his three accompanying guardsmen led me into the blinding daylight I talked without hesitation or consideration of consequences.

"Did you find any weakness in the Veldians?"

"*Yes.*"

I noted then a strange thing. It was the annotator—the thing in my brain that was a part of me, and yet apart from me—that had spoken. It was not concerned with matters of emotion; with sentiments of patriotism, loyalty, honor, and self-respect. It was interested only in my—and its own—survival. Its logic told it that unless I gave the answers my questioner wanted I would die. That, it intended to prevent.

I made one last desperate effort to stop that other part of my mind from assuming control—and sank lower into my mental impotence.

"What is our weakness?"

"*Your society is doomed.*" With the answer I realized that the annotator had arrived at another of its conclusions.

"Why?"

"*There are many reasons.*"

"Give one."

"Your culture is based on a need for struggle, for combat. When there is no one to fight it must fall."

Trobt was dealing with a familiar culture now. He knew the questions to ask.

"Explain that last statement."

"Your culture is based on its impetuous need to battle . . . it is armed and set against dangers and the expectation of danger . . . fostering the pride of courage under stress. There is no danger now . . . nothing to fight, no place to spend your over-aggressiveness, except against each other in personal duels. Already your decline is about to enter the bloody circus and religion stage, already crumbling in the heart while expanding at the outside. And this is your first civilization . . . like a boy's first love . . . you have no experience of a fall in your history before to have recourse to—no cushioning of philosophy to accept it . . ."

For a time Trobt maintained a puzzled silence. I wondered if he had the depth of understanding to accept the truth and significance of what he had heard. "Is there no solution?" he asked at last.

"Only a temporary one." Now it was coming.

"Explain."

"War with the Ten Thousand Worlds."

"Explain."

"Your willingness to hazard, and eagerness to battle is no weakness when you are armed with superior weapons, and are fighting against an opponent as disorganized, and as incapable of effective organization as the Ten Thousand Worlds, against your long-range weapons and subtle traps."

"Why do you say the solution is only temporary?"

"You cannot win the war. You will seem to win, but it will be an illusion. You will win the battles, kill billions, rape Worlds, take slaves, and destroy ships and weapons. But after that you will be forced to hold the subjection. Your numbers will not be expendable. You will be spread thin, exposed to other cultures that will influence you, change you. You will lose skirmishes, and in the end you will be forced back. Then will come a loss of old ethics, corruption and opportunism will replace your honor and you will know unspeakable shame and dishonor . . . your culture will soon be weltering back into a barbarism and disorganization which in its corruption and despair will be nothing like the proud tribal primi-

*tive life of its first barbarism. You will be aware of the difference
and unable to return.*"

I understood Trobt's perplexity as I finished. He could not accept
what I told him because to him winning was only a matter of a military victory, a victory of strength; Velda had never experienced defeat as a weakness from within. My words made him uneasy, but he
did not understand. He shrugged. "Do we have any other weakness?" he asked.

"*Your women.*"

"Explain."

"*They are 'set' for the period when they greatly outnumbered
their men. Your compatible ratio is eight women to one man. Yet
now it is one to one. Further, you produce too few children. Your
manpower must ever be in small supply. Worse, your shortage of
women sponsors a covert despair and sadism in your young men
. . . a hunger and starvation to follow instinct, to win women by
courage and conquest and battle against danger . . . that only a
war can restrain.*"

"The solution?"

"*Beat the Federation. Be in a position to have free access to their
women.*"

Came the final ignominy. "Do you have a means of reporting
back to the Ten Thousand Worlds?"

"*Yes. Buried somewhere inside me is a nerve-twitch tape. Flesh
pockets of chemicals are stored there also. When my body temperature drops fifteen degrees below normal the chemicals will be activated and will use the tissues of my body for fuel and generate
sufficient energy to transmit the information on the tape back to
the Ten Thousand Worlds.*"

That was enough.

"Do you still intend to kill me?" I asked Trobt the next day as we
walked in his garden.

"Do not fear," he answered. "You will not be cheated of an honorable death. All Velda is as eager for it as you."

"Why?" I asked. "Do they see me as a madman?"

"They see you as you are. They cannot conceive of one man chal-
lenging a planet, except to win himself a bright and gory death on
a page of history, the first man to deliberately strike and die in the
coming war—not an impersonal clash of battleships, but a *man* de-

claring personal battle against men. We would not deprive you of
that death. Our admiration is too great. We want the symbolism of
your blood now just as greatly as you want it yourself. Every citizen is waiting to watch you die—gloriously."

I realized now that all the while he had interpreted my presence
here in this fantastic way. And I suspected that I had no arguments
to convince him differently.

Trobt had hinted that I would die under torture. I thought of the
old histories of Earth that I had read. Of the warrior race of North
American Indians. A captured enemy must die. But if he had been
an honorable enemy he was given an honorable death. He was allowed to die under the stress most familiar to them. Their strongest
ethic was a cover-up for the defeated, the universal expressionless
suppressal of reaction in conquering or watching conquest, so as
not to shame the defeated. Public torture—with the women, as well
as warriors, watching—the chance to exhibit fortitude, all the way
to the breaking point, and beyond. That was considered the honorable death, while it was a shameful trick to quietly slit a man's
throat in his sleep without giving him a chance to fight—to show his
scorn of flinching under the torture.

Here I was the Honorable Enemy who had exhibited courage.
They would honor me, and satisfy their hunger for an Enemy, by
giving me the breaking point test.

But I had no intention of dying!

"You will not kill me," I addressed Trobt. "And there will be no
war."

He looked at me as though I had spoken gibberish.

My next words, I knew, would shock him. "I'm going to recommend unconditional surrender," I said.

Trobt's head which he had turned away swiveled sharply back to
me. His mouth opened and he made several motions to speak before succeeding. "Are you serious?"

"Very," I answered.

Trobt's face grew gaunt and the skin pressed tight against his
cheekbones—almost as though he were making the surrender rather
than I. "Is this decision dictated by your logic," he asked dryly, "or
by faintness of heart?"

I did not honor the question enough to answer.

Neither did he apologize. "You understand that unconditional surrender is the only kind we will accept?"

I nodded wearily.

"Will they agree to your recommendation?"

"No," I answered. "Humans are not cowards, and they will fight —as long as there is any slightest hope of success. I will not be able to convince them that their defeat is inevitable. But I can prepare them for what is to come. I hope to shorten the conflict immeasurably."

"I can do nothing but accept," Trobt said after a moment of thought. "I will arrange transportation back to Earth for you tomorrow." He paused and regarded me with expressionless eyes. "You realize that an enemy who surrenders without a struggle is beneath contempt?"

The blood crept slowly into my cheeks. It was difficult to ignore his taunt. "Will you give me six months before you move against us?" I asked. "The Federation is large. I will need time to bring my message to all."

"You have your six months." Trobt was still not through with me, personally. "On the exact day that period ends I will expect your return to Velda. We will see if you have any honor left."

"I will be back," I said.

During the next six months I spread my word throughout the Ten Thousand Worlds. I met disbelief everywhere. I had not expected otherwise. The last day I returned to Velda.

Two days later Velda's Council acted. They were going to give the Humans no more time to organize counteraction. I went in the same spaceship that carried Trobt. I intended to give him any advice he needed about the Worlds. I asked only that his first stop be at the Jason's Fleece fringe.

Beside us sailed a mighty armada of warships, spaced in a long line that would encompass the entire portion of the galaxy occupied by the Ten Thousand Worlds. For an hour we moved ponderously forward, then the stars about us winked out for an instant. The next moment a group of Worlds became visible on the ship's vision screen. I recognized them as Jason's Fleece.

One World expanded until it appeared the size of a baseball. "Quagman," Trobt said.

Quagman, the trouble spot of the Ten Thousand Worlds. Dominated by an unscrupulous clique that ruled by vendetta, it had been the source of much trouble and vexation to the other Worlds. Its leaders were considered little better than brigands. They had received me with much apparent courtesy. In the end they had even agreed to surrender to the Veldians—when and if they appeared. I had accepted their easy concurrence with askance, but they were my main hope.

Two Veldians left our ship in a scooter. We waited ten long, tense hours. When word finally came back it was from the Quaqmans themselves. The Veldian envoys were being held captive. They would be released upon the delivery of two billion dollars—in the currency of any recognized World—and the promise of immunity.

The fools!

Trobt's face remained impassive as he received the message.

We waited several more hours. Both Trobt and I watched the green mottled baseball on the vision screen. It was Trobt who first pointed out a small, barely discernible, black spot on the upper lefthand corner of Quagman.

As the hours passed, and the black spot swung slowly to the right as the planet revolved, it grew almost imperceptibly larger. When it disappeared over the edge of the world we slept.

In the morning the spot appeared again, and now it covered half the face of the planet. Another ten hours and the entire planet became a blackened cinder.

Quagman was dead.

The ship moved next to Mican.

Mican was a sparsely populated prison planet. Criminals were usually sent to newly discovered Worlds on the edge of the Human expansion circle, and allowed to make their own adjustments toward achieving a stable government. Men with the restless natures that made them criminals on their own highly civilized Worlds, made the best pioneers. However, it always took them several generations to work their way up from anarchy to a co-operative government. Mican had not yet had that time. I had done my best in the week I spent with them to convince them to organize, and to be prepared to accept any terms the Veldians might offer. The gesture, I feared, was useless but I had given all the arguments I knew.

A second scooter left with two Veldian representatives. When it returned Trobt left the control room to speak with them.

He returned, and shook his head. I knew it was useless to argue. Mican died.

At my request Trobt agreed to give the remaining Jason's Fleece Worlds a week to consider—on the condition that they made no offensive forays. I wanted them to have time to fully assess what had happened to the other two Worlds—to realize that that same stubbornness would result in the same disaster for them.

At the end of the third twenty-four-hour period the Jason's Fleece Worlds surrendered—unconditionally. They had tasted blood; and recognized futility when faced with it. That had been the best I had been able to hope for, earlier.

Each sector held off surrendering until the one immediately ahead had given in. But the capitulation was complete at the finish. No more blood had had to be shed.

The Veldians' terms left the Worlds definitely subservient, but they were neither unnecessarily harsh, nor humiliating. Velda demanded specific limitations on Weapons and war-making potentials; the obligation of reporting all technological and scientific progress; and colonial expansion only by prior consent.

There was little actual occupation of the Federation Worlds, but the Veldians retained the right to inspect any and all functions of the various governments. Other aspects of social and economic methods would be subject only to occasional checks and investigation. Projects considered questionable would be supervised by the Veldians at their own discretion.

The one provision that caused any vigorous protest from the Worlds was the Veldian demand for Human women. But even this was a purely emotional reaction, and died as soon as it was more fully understood. The Veldians were not barbarians. They used no coercion to obtain our women. They only demanded the same right to woo them as the citizens of the Worlds had. No woman would be taken without her free choice. There could be no valid protest to that.

In practice it worked quite well. On nearly all the Worlds there were more women than men, so that few men had to go without mates because of the Veldians' inroads. And—by Human standards—they seldom took our most desirable women. Because the acquiring of weight was corollary with the Veldian women becoming sexually attractive, their men had an almost universal preference for fleshy women. As a result many of our women who would have had difficulty securing Human husbands found themselves much in demand as mates of the Veldians.

Seven years passed after the Worlds' surrender before I saw Kalin Trobt again.

The pact between the Veldians and the Worlds had worked out well, for both sides. The demands of the Veldians involved little sacrifice by the Federation, and the necessity of reporting to a superior authority made for less wrangling and jockeying for advantageous position among the Worlds themselves.

The fact that the Veldians had taken more than twenty million of our women—it was the custom for each Veldian male to take a Human woman for one mate—caused little dislocation or discontent. The number each lost did less than balance the ratio of the sexes.

For the Veldians the pact solved the warrior-set frustrations, and the unrest and sexual starvation of their males. Those men who demanded action and adventure were given supervisory posts on the Worlds as an outlet for their drives. All could now obtain mates; mates whose biological make-up did not necessitate an eight to one ratio.

Each year it was easier for the Humans to understand the Veldians and to meet them on common grounds socially. Their natures became less rigid, and they laughed more—even at themselves, when the occasion demanded.

This was especially noticeable among the younger Veldians, just reaching an adult status. In later years when the majority of them would have a mixture of human blood, the difference between us would become even less pronounced.

Trobt had changed little during those seven years. His hair had grayed some at the temples, and his movements were a bit less supple, but he looked well. Much of the intensity had left his aquiline features, and he seemed content.

We shook hands with very real pleasure. I led him to chairs under the shade of a tree in my front yard and brought drinks.

"First, I want to apologize for having thought you a coward," he began, after the first conventional pleasantries. "I know now I was very wrong. I did not realize for years, however, just what had happened." He gave his wry smile. "You know what I mean, I presume?"

I looked at him inquiringly.

"There was more to your decision to capitulate than was revealed. When you played the Game your forte was finding the weakness of an opponent. And winning the second game. You made no attempt to win the first. I see now, that as on the boards, your surrender represented only the conclusion of the first game. You were keeping our weakness to yourself, convinced that there would be a second game. And that your Ten Thousand Worlds would win it. As you have."

"What would you say your weakness was?" By now I suspected he knew everything, but I wanted to be certain.

"Our desire and need for Human women, of course."

There was no need to dissemble further. "The solution first came to me," I explained, "when I remembered a formerly independent Earth country named China. They lost most of their wars, but in the end they always won."

"Through their women?"

"Indirectly. Actually it was done by absorbing their conquerors. The situation was similar between Velda and the Ten Thousand Worlds. Velda won the war, but in a thousand years there will be no Veldians—racially."

"That was my first realization," Trobt said. "I saw immediately then how you had us hopelessly trapped. The marriage of our men to your women will blend our bloods until—with your vastly greater numbers—in a dozen generations there will be only traces of our race left.

"And what can we do about it?" Trobt continued. "We can't kill our beloved wives—and our children. We can't stop further acquisition of Human women without disrupting our society. Each generation the tie between us will become closer, our blood thinner, yours more dominant, as the intermingling continues. We cannot even declare war against the people who are doing this to us. How do you fight an enemy that has surrendered unconditionally?"

"You do understand that for your side this was the only solution to the imminent chaos that faced you?" I asked.

"Yes." I watched Trobt's swift mind go through its reasoning. I was certain he saw that Velda was losing only an arbitrary distinction of race, very much like the absorbing of the early clans of Velda into the family of the Danlee. Their dislike of that was very definitely only an emotional consideration. The blending of our bloods would benefit both; the resultant new race would be better and stronger because of that blending.

With a small smile Trobt raised his glass. "We will drink to the union of two great races," he said. "And to you—the winner of the Second Game!"

Analytic Detective

Edgar Allan Poe's "The Murders in the Rue Morgue" (1841) accomplished two important tasks. It introduced the detective story and thus helped formalize mysteries as a distinct genre. It also introduced a protagonist, C. Auguste Dupin, whose amazing deductive powers provided the prototype for all subsequent analytical detectives. Fifty years later Arthur Conan Doyle's short story "A Scandal in Bohemia" was published in *The Strand* magazine. Featuring Sherlock Holmes' ratiocinative genius, it was a literary bombshell that ultimately resulted in further adventures of the great detective, and a world-wide affection for the mystery story.

In the field of science fiction, pastiches and parodies of Holmes are widespread, but his descendants are few. Fortunately, however, the skillful Avram Davidson has recently given us several parallel-world chronicles of Dr. Eszterhazy. And from these adventures, we have chosen a case which offers the good physician a golden opportunity to test his mettle.

The Ceaseless Stone

AVRAM DAVIDSON

The Clock—*the* Clock, in the old Clock Tower, the clock which was meant when anyone said, without other word of qualification, "So let us meet by the Clock"—this was the one. Annually the gold leaf of its numerals was renewed and refreshed, and the numerals were Roman, not as any deliberate archaicism, but because no other numerals were known thereabouts when it was made; the "Arabic" numbers, in their slow progression out of India through Persia into Turkey, had nowhere reached that part of Europe when the Clock was made; and furthermore, as a sign to us how our fathers' fathers lived without a need for graduations of haste, the great dial had but one hand to turn the hours.

The pulsebeat of the heart of Imperial Bella, capital of the Triune Monarchy of Scythia-Pannonia-Transbalkania is no longer as perceptible round about the Old Town Hall as it once was: to be sure, on Saints Cosmo's and Damian's Day, the City Council still in full regalia comes for the formal ceremony of electing the Chief Burgomaster, but the rest of the year not much happens. Tourists come to see the tower as part of the regular tour offered by Messrs. T. Cook, beggars and peddlers follow the tour as birds follow a boat, and country-folk—to whom the new Municipal Building, with its mansard roof, marble lobby, and typewriting machines, mean nearer to nothing than nothing at all—country-folk make the Clock Tower the center of their perambulations, as they have done for centuries. It is too old a joke to raise even a smile any more that some of them expect to see the Emperor emerge when the automata come out to strike the hours. It makes no difference if they have come up in those huge and huge-wheeled wagons stuffed with feathers, down, hams, cabbages, sour-crout, hides, nuts, eggs, fruit, and all whatever, from barrel-staves to beeswax; or if they have come on foot behind a drove of beeves for the Ox Market; or if they have come up on the railroad. As soon as they can manage, they go to the old Clock Tower, as though to reassure themselves that it is still there, for all their directions start from there: *Take the first lane facing the old Clock Tower and count two turnings but take the third,* and so on. Unless they have paced the way thence to the spectacle-makers or the watchmakers or the thread-and-button shop or the gunsmith's or wherever it may be, nothing can persuade them that they may confidently trade with a specta-cle-maker, a watchmaker, a thread-and-button shop, or a gunsmith. Who knows who *they* are? May not their merchandise turn to dust like so much fairy gold? Who could trust even to find them again? Whereas, should one have either dissatisfaction or satisfaction with the tradesmen whose way is known via the old Clock Tower, well, what could be easier—or, rather, as easy—but once again to make one's way to the old Clock Tower, and thence, as safe as by Great God His Compass, return to the same tradesman once again?

It is on a clear, dry day in later February, as near as any subse-quent report affirmed, that a young man from the country—let us call him Hansli—finds his way to the very foot of the Old Clock and commences to look about him a bit nervously. A man sitting on a piece of faded rug on the step calls Hansli over, and, very kindly and soberly, inquires if he can assist him. Hansli is relieved.

"Honored Sir," he says, "it's the lane that leads to the lane as is where the goldsmiths are. What it is I'm looking for."

The man nods. "Was it for a wedding ring, perhaps?" he asks.

Hansli is astonished to the point where he does not even at first turn red. Then he reflects how clever the city people are. As for the man himself, the city man, he looks both clever and respectable. "Like a philosopher," he explains, afterwards. This description is clear to Hansli, and to Hansli's father and mother and his promised bride and *her* father and mother. Otherwise, it lacks precision, might mean anyone from the lay instructor of algebra at a seminary school to a civil engineer getting ready to plot out a canal. Equally, it might mean a perfect rogue selling a mixture of salt water and methylene blue as a cure for infertility in cattle or dropped stomach in children.

"Because," the man explains, "if it was for a wedding ring, I have a few for sale."

The man looks at him without a trace of a smile, and this is very reassuring, for Hansli had feared—who knows what—they might laugh at him, at the goldsmiths, make rude jokes. This quiet gentleman is certainly doing nothing of the sort. "It's for Belinda," Hansli explains. The gentleman nods, takes out from a pocket a piece of cloth and unwraps it. Sure enough, a ring. Sure enough, it is gold. But wait. It *looks* like gold . . . sure enough. But—

He buys time. "What might the price be?" The price is half-a-ducat. This is also a relief, a great relief. Hansli can bargain an ox, a horse, a harness, with the best of them. As for rings, he has no idea. Still, still, "That seems very cheap," he declares. *Is it gold, real gold, pure gold?* is what the wee voice is asking in his ear.

The gentleman nods, soberly. "It is cheap," he concedes. "A goldsmith must charge more, because he has to pay rent. And a very high rent, indeed. But I, here, I need pay no rent, for my place of business"—he gestures—"has for the landlord the Emperor himself, whom God bless and preserve for many years—"

"Amen, amen." Hansli takes off his hat and crosses himself.

"—charges me no rent. Do you see," he says. And he takes out of another pocket what some would call a jeweler's loupe, but which Hansli calls "a look-see," a term covering everything from a magnifying glass to a telescope, and he tenders it. Hansli peers through the glass at the ring, all round the ring. How bright it looks! How it shines in the clear winter air! And then Hansli sees something. A triple-headed eagle, and the numerals LXI. This is good enough for Hansli. He takes out his purse and selects a half-a-ducat. The philosophical gentleman blesses him and he blesses the philosophical gentleman.

Back home, Hansli's father peers inside the ring. "Never seed no gold like this," he says. Then his clear eyes, which (they say locally) can spot a goat-kid three miles off in the dark woods, observe something. "Ah, th' Imper'al Eagle! So. 'Tis good gold, then, and, lets me see." He calculates slowly. "Ah, the sixty-first year o' the Reign, hm, twas made a year ago . . . or so . . ." He lifts the ring. It has passed the test. Hansli kneels. His father raises the ring and blesses him with it. Now all plans for the wedding may proceed. As soon as the sunny days are sure, Belinda will begin to bleach the linen.

Who knows how often this was all repeated? Not Lobats, the Commissioner of the Detective Police. Not De Hooft, the President of the Jewelers Association.

"It is always the same story," says De Hooft, a dapper Fleming with dyed hair and a waxed mustache. "Very soon the ring begins to bend, or sometimes it breaks, even if it is not too big or too small. They come to town, they look for this chap, this, ah, 'phil-os-o-pher,'" he parts the word sarcastically (and incorrectly); "they don't find him, they go to a respectable jeweler or goldsmith. The gold is tested, it proves pure, it is explained to them that it is in fact *too* pure, that it is too soft to take pressure. The idea that the good-wife will have to be bought another ring in order to testify that she is in fact married, this does not please them. Not at all. But what can one do, eh?" He shrugs.

Lobats is there, listening. He has heard it all before. Also there, and not having heard it all—or any of it—before, is Engelbert Esz-terhazy, Doctor of Medicine, Doctor of Philosophy, Doctor of Juris-prudence, Doctor of Science, and Doctor of Literature. Who now asks, "Any reports of stolen gold?"

"None that fit. Spahn, the tooth-surgeon, had a robbery. But this is not dental gold. And Perrero's had reported a robbery, but this is not coin gold. We have never settled that matter of the theft from the Assay Office in Ritchli-Georgiou, but that was the regular Ritchli gold, very pale yellow. Not *this*—" Lobats gestures. Several rings lie on a soft piece of paper before them, rings which the Jew-elers Association has succeeded in buying back, so to speak. Usu-ally they could not be bought back.

Eszterhazy takes up the loupe and has a look. He puts it down and De Hooft says, "I've seen all sorts of gold, you know. This is new to me. I've seen yellow gold, I've seen white gold, red gold, even green gold, yes! But this, *this*, shining with the sheen of a . . . of a Chinese orange! This I have never seen before."

Lobats paused in the act of brushing his high-crowned gray bowler hat with the sleeve of his gray overcoat. "Naturally, our very first thought was that the rings themselves must have been stolen," he explained. "But that didn't stand up for long."

Eszterhazy nodded. "Exactly what laws are being broken here?" he asked.

Lobats raised his eyebrows thoughtfully. "Well . . . hmm . . . well, of course, the man is in violation of the municipal street-trad-ing ordinances. But that is a small matter. And his method of mark-ing the rings is technically illegal, for they haven't been proven ei-ther at the Goldsmiths Guild, the Jewelers Association Testing

Room, or any Imperial Assay Office. However, as we all know, they are of a purer gold than any rings which are."

De Hooft frowned. "Obviously the man is dishonest," he said. "Probably the gold was stolen abroad and he is trying to dispose of it bit by bit, without attracting attention."

Lobats put his head at an angle and shook it. "But we've had no reports from abroad of any thefts which would fit. We've even checked back to reports a few years ago, for example, from California, and from Australia. But this just isn't their kind of gold."

Doctor Eszterhazy once again examined the rings. "And yet," he said, "if he came honestly by it, why is he selling them so far below normal price? Evidently, by the way he impresses the people he sells to, he speaks as a man of anyway moderate education. And as such, he ought to know that even if the gold was dug up in a hoard, somewhere, by the law of treasure trove, the Throne will concede him a half-portion . . . provided, that is, that he made an immediate and honest disclosure . . ."

Lobats lifted his brows and pursed his lips. "Well, Doctor, it may be that you have hit upon it. Maybe it *is* a buried treasure that he found, maybe his greed got the better of him and he started to dispose of it in what he thought was a clever way. And, now he knows that we are onto him, well, maybe he thinks it's too late for him to come forward. Just think, gentlemen!"—he poked the rings with a thick and hairy forefinger—"this might be pirate gold . . . or maybe even dragon gold . . . !" He laughed hastily and twisted his face.

Eszterhazy caught at something before the telltale slip; it was perfectly all right with him if a plainclothes police commissioner believed in the hoards which folk-belief still held that dragons from the ancient days of the Goths and Scythians had planted here and there in many a hidden valley and many a haunted hill; no one was ever the worse off for such a belief, and the thought of them added a touch of color which the modern age could well use.

"What do you mean, Karrol-Francos, that now he knows you are onto him? How does he know?"

Commissioner Lobats told him that a plainclothesman had been assigned to the area around the old Clock Tower, but that no further signs of the stranger had been seen since.

Doctor Eszterhazy, having left the other two to further talk and consideration, engaged in a bit of reflection as he walked away.

Selling cheap rings to the visiting peasantry was almost a natural notion—that is, if one had cheap rings to dispose of. And suppose that one still had? Where else, and to whom else, might it be · equally natural to attempt a sale?

The puffing railroad trains had stolen away much of the old river trade, but much still remained; it was not as quick, but it was cheaper. Coal and timber and pitch, salt and gravel and grain and sand were still moved in great quantities by sailing-barge up and down the Ister, even if the boats no longer caught the winds in scarlet sails and even if the bargees no longer wore their hair in pigtails. A good place to find the bargees, when their minds and eyes were not preoccupied with snubbing lines or disputing precedence at the wharfs, was the Birch Walk.

Conjecture vision of a stone embankment crowned with a paved walk planted on both sides with birch trees, a walk which winds perhaps a third of a kilometer along the River Ister. It had at one time been contemplated to continue the Walk, and to plant an equivalent number of birches more, for a much greater distance; this had not been done. But the experiment could not be said to have failed. People of the class who can afford simply to amuse themselves at hours when the sun still shines, and on a weekday, too, found that the prospect was pleasant from the Birch Walk; some, indeed, compared it to portions of the Seine, although not always to the same portions. Those establishments which offered refreshment, and which were willing to make more than merely minimal gestures in the way of cleanliness and good order, found that ladies and gentlemen (and those who wished to be taken for ladies and gentlemen) were now willing to patronize them. These new customers found an interest in watching the barge-people at their food and drink, and the barge-people, it is possible, perhaps found an almost equal interest in watching these same people at theirs. Though perhaps not.

Those captains, mates, and deckhands (most sailing-barges carried a deckhand, in addition to a captain and a mate) who wished, their duties done for the day, to get drunk as quickly as possible, as cheaply as possible, or to enjoy the company of some barefoot trull, also cheaply and quickly, did not come up to the Birch Walk to do so. One found there, instead, barge-folk well-bathed and well-combed and cleanly clad, either strolling decorously, or, with equal decorum, sitting at an outside table, enjoying a dark beer or a plate

of zackuskoes. Often they merely hung over the railings, enjoying a
sight of the river from a different angle than the deck of a barge
affords.

Eszterhazy paced slowly along, waiting for a familiar face . . .
not any one particular familiar face, nor even just any familiar face;
he waited for one of a general category. And, as so often happens,
as long as one is not in great need of borrowing money, he found
one.

Or one found him.

As it turned out, there were three of them, and at least two of
them hailed him to "Sit down and take!" The verb *to take* has perhaps fewer meanings than many another which one might name,
but among those who traffic in and labor around the wide waters
called the Pool of Ister, the definitive definition is liqueous . . . and
hospitable.

The older two were the brothers Francos and Konkos Spits, the
captain and mate, respectively, of the sailing-barge *Queen of Pan-
nonia*, and the other was their deckhand—presumably he had a
Christian and a family name, but Eszterhazy had never heard him
referred to as anything but "the Boy." The brothers were dark, the
boy was fair, and Eszterhazy had met all three in connection with a
singularly mysterious affair involving an enormous rodent of In-
donesian origin.

Conversation was at first general. The current state of the river
trade was discussed, which of course entailed discussion of the
river trade for many years past. Some attention was given to the
perennial rumor that the Ruritanians, or perhaps the Rumanians,
were going to place a boom across the Danube, or perhaps, as some
said, a bomb. The merits and demerits of the current methods of
marking channels, shoals, and wrecks came in for much commen-
tary, little of it favorable. By the next drink, conversation became
more personal. Eszterhazy asked if many young men showed a dis-
position to take up the bargee trade. The brothers Spits simultaneously insisted that recruitment was flourishing and that none of
the recruits were worth recruiting: they twirled their huge mus-
tachioes and banged their vast fists upon the table to emphasize
this point. The Boy blushed. Eszterhazy glanced at him, in a
friendly fashion, and the Boy blushed even more.

"Nowadays," Eszterhazy said, "the younger bargees do not
pierce their ears any more, do they?"

At this, rather to his surprise, the captain and the mate burst into rough, loud laughter, and the Boy turned absolutely crimson, with a tinge toward purple.

"Why, what is this joke?" the guest inquired. "Can I not see for myself that his ears are not pierced?"

"Har har har!" guffawed Captain Francos Spits.

"Hor hor hor!" chuckled Mate Konkos Spits.

Between them they secured the Boy's head—for some reason he had turned shy and declined cooperation—and twisted it about, giving Eszterhazy some fear that he was about to witness a nonjudicial garroting. But evidently the Boy had a sufficiently limber neck. It was certainly true that the Boy's left ear had not been pierced. It now proved to be equally true that his right ear had. This was red and swollen about the lobe, and a thread, of an off-white tint, hung through and from it.

"I was like drunk when I done it," the Boy muttered.

Both of the brothers Spits sporting a golden ring in their right ears, they did not receive this in good spirit; Captain Francos, in fact, aimed a cuff. "What do you mean? You mean you got like sense and you done it! Ain't it good for the eyesight, ain't it, Doctor, ain't it?"

"So it is often said," Eszterhazy answered, adding, "The custom is exceedingly ancient, and I for one am glad to see it kept up."

The Boy seemed more disposed to take this for good than the growls of his superiors. Eszterhazy seized the moment to ask, "And what about the ring?"

The Boy fumbled in his pocket. Would it be some wretched brass trinket?—or even one which, though it might be fully lawful, would still be of infinitely less interest than— Out came a screw of filthy paper which showed signs of much wrapping and unwrapping. And inside that was the ring. It did, indeed, shine somewhat with the luster of a very fine mandarin orange. Eszterhazy took out the small leather case in which he carried an excellent magnifying glass.

"See th' eagle?" the Boy inquired. "Don't that mean it's good? Cost me half-a-duke."

"It is certainly as good as gold—that is," he hastened to explain, "it is certainly of very good gold."

"But it didn't have no pissin' gold wire loop, like. I hadda go to a reg-lar jooler for that. Wasn't he pissed off, 'cause I didn't git the whole pissin' works from him! 'Don't git your piss hot, lardy,' I say t' him."

The Boy's address was vigorous, though, in the matter of adjectives, somewhat limited.

"Did you buy it from that philosopher chap?" asked Eszterhazy. The Boy nodded and commenced to rewrap it. "What did he say?" The Boy thought for a moment as he engaged in this difficult task. "Said, 'The free lynx of the south . . .' Is what he said . . ." The Boy finished his task, put the wad back in his pocket, and, taking up from the table a toothpick which already showed signs of wear, proceeded to attend to his teeth. Clearly, the matter of the philosopher's discourse was over, as far as the Boy was concerned.

Captain Francos Spits wrinkled up one side of his face in a half-scowl of concentration. " 'The *south*,' " he repeated. "There ain't no lynxes in the *south*, brother—"

"Nor I never said there was! In the *north*, now—" He turned to Doctor Eszterhazy. "Our old gaffer, he killed a lynx up north, for it was catching all his turkey-birds, and—"

"Waiter!" Eszterhazy caught all eyes. "Cognac all around," he ordered. Every lynx in the Monarchy was at once forgotten. It took a second order of the same before he was allowed to depart.

Back at Number 33 Turkling Street, he asked his librarian, Herra Hugo Von Sltski, "Do we have—we do have a copy of Basil Valentine's *Twelve Keys*, do we not?"

"We do. And we don't." Having uttered this statement, almost delphic in its tone, Von Sltski proceeded to explain. "Our copy has gone to the binders. As I had indicated it must, on last quarter's list. It is now in the press. I daresay we might get it out of the press. But I would instead propose that you consult the copy in . . . the copy in . . ." He rolled his eyes and thought a moment. "Not the Imperial Library, they haven't got one. And the one in the University is defective." The eyes rolled down again. "There is a good copy in the collection at the Library of the Grand Lodge. I will give you a note to the Keeper of the Rare Volumes." He took out his card, neatly wrote a few words and a symbol upon it, and handed it over.

Eszterhazy thanked him and departed, thinking—with some irony, with some amusement—that there was at least one place in this great city, of which he had thought himself free, where he . . . even he . . . with his seven degrees and his sixteen quarterings, might not go with firm hopes of success without an introduction from one of his own employees.

The card sufficed to get him into the silent chambers high up in the blank-faced building marked only with the same symbol. No one prevented him from access to the catalogue, which consisted of shelf after shelf of huge bound volumes chained in their places. He found his entry, carefully copied down what he saw into one of the forms provided, took it to the desk and there handed it over, along with the puissant pasteboard. The man at the desk held the form in one hand and his spectacles with the other and read aloud, as though he were a rector conferring a degree.

" *Volume V, of the Last Will and Testament of Basil Valentine, VIDELICET, a Practical Treatise together with the XII Keys and Appendix of the Great Stone of the Ancient Philosophers.'* "

There was the sound of a chair being scraped, a throat was cleared, and a voice asked, "Is that Master Mumau?" and a very tall, very thin, very pleasant-looking man came strolling forward from an adjacent office.

"No, it is not," the man at the desk said.

"Have I the opportunity of addressing the Honorable Keeper of the Rare Volumes?" asked Eszterhazy, handing over his own card— the assistant having already handed over the other.

"Ye-es," the Keeper said, as though struck by the remarkable coincidence of someone recognizing him whilst in his official capacity. "How do you do. I did think that you might be someone else. We do not often have many calls for such books. Ah-hah. Oh-ho. Yes. Yes, I know *him* very well. He was the Tiler at the Lodge of the Three Crowns. *My* lodge, you know." These last remarks referred, however, to Eszterhazy's librarian, not to Master Mumau, about whom Eszterhazy would have wished to inquire, would have wished to very much indeed, had he but been given opportunity. The Keeper was very kind, very thoughtful; he provided Eszterhazy with a desk by himself, brought him a better chair (he said) than the one already there, ordered a floor lamp, provided notepaper and sharpened pencils, regretted that ink could not be allowed, regretted that smoking could not be allowed, offered a snuffbox, had brought a printed list of the recent aquisitions, and, somehow, before Eszterhazy quite knew it, the Keeper, the desk assistant, and the floor assistant had all withdrawn. Leaving him, if not entirely alone, at least alone with *Volume V of The Last Will and Testament of Basil Valentine,* etc., an absolutely vast volume, perforated here and there on its still-clear pages with neat little wormholes. It opened with the cheerful and reassuring notice that anything against the Holy Christian Faith which the work might ever have contained, if it contained any, had been purged and removed, according to the Rule laid down by the Council of Trent; the date of publication was 1647. It was not the first edition.

Nothing would have pleased Eszterhazy more than to have reread the entire volume through then and there. However, he was in search of a particular reference, and, as it happened, he found it in the Preamble. *The Phoenix of the South hath snatched away the heart out of the breast of the huge beast of the East, for the beast of the East must be bereaved of his Dragon's skin, and his wings must vanish, and then they must both enter the Salt Ocean, and return again with beauty . . .*

Well, obscure, and typically obscure, as all this was, there was anyway no obscurity in the guess which he had formed about *the free lynx of the South.* Considering that the Boy had certainly never in his life heard of Basil Valentine. Or of any of his works.

Or of his Work.

On a sudden impulse, Eszterhazy carefully took the volume and shook it, gently, gently, for it was, though sturdy in appearance, still, quite old. A slip of paper dropped out of the back pages, and, although hastily he set down the volume, almost it escaped him. Almost. It was half of a form of application for books, neatly torn in two; and on the back of it, which side was facing him as he took it up, Eszterhazy saw, in a neat school-masterish hand, the words *Ora Lege Lege Lege Relege Labora et Invienes.*

Pray, Read, Read, Read, Read Again; Toil and Thou Shalt Find.

Thoughtfully, he turned the slip over. What was left of the original application were the words:

au, K.-Heyndrik

The Annual Directory of Loyal Subjects Resident in the Imperial Capital and Registered According to Law, etc., had certainly been up-to-date . . . once. However, Master Karrol-Heyndrik Mumau had not moved since its last publication. That is, his name was known to the porteress in the shabby-genteel block of flats.

"Yes, the Master do live here, but he have a workshop at th' old Spanish Bakery, where he be now, I expect. Thanks 'ee, sir."

Once there had been an Emperor who had wedded an Infanta of

Castille. That was long, long ago. And it had been long, long, since any farduelos or other Hispanic pastries had been produced from the oven at the Spanish Bakery. Had he not known what the letters were supposed to intend, it is doubtful that Eszterhazy could have made them out. The windows were curtained and dusty, and dust lay so heavily in the corners of the front door that it was doubtful anyone had used it for decades, perhaps. However, there is always a "round the back." Thither he went, and there, upon the door in the faded russet brick wall, he knocked.

The door opened fairly soon.

"My dear Master Mumau," Eszterhazy said, gently, "you mustn't make gold any more, you know. You really, really mustn't. It is forbidden according to law."

"Will they put me in the galleys?" the man whispered.

"I'll see to it that they won't," Eszterhazy said. He had never made a promise he felt safer of keeping.

"I was about to stop, anyway," the man said. His manner was that of a schoolboy who has been caught roasting apples at the Bunsen burner. For a moment he stood there, irresolute. Then he said, "Would you like to come in . . . ? You *would? Really?* Please *do!*"

Everything that one might have expected to find there was there: the furnace, the crucible, the athanor, alembic, pelican. It was all there. One thing more was there, which Eszterhazy did not recognize. He turned away, urging himself to forget its very outlines. "That . . . piece of equipment," he said, gesturing. "*That* one. *Break it at once.*"

The man made a huffling sound, clicked his tongue, sighed. At length there was a smash. "Oh well. I *said* I wouldn't make any more, didn't I? Well, I meant it. So I don't need it."

"And you are not to make another one like it."

He turned back and looked around once again. Yes, a bakery was a very good place to have chosen. God only knew what they would do, there at the Mint, and at the Treasury, if they knew what had been baked here recently.

"I used to be chemistry master at the Old Senior School, you know," Mumau said. "And I was a very good one, too. Till I got sick. Father Rector was very kind to me, 'Master Henk,' he said, 'we've agreed to give you a nice pension, so just take it easy, and don't you read any more of them big thick books, do you hear?'

And I said, 'I won't, Father Rector.' But of course I *did.* And so of course I have to confess it. 'Father, I've been reading those big thick books again, that I'm not supposed to,' I tell the priest. It's not Father Rector, just the parish priest, and he says, he always says, 'Say three Our Fathers and a Hail Mary and don't play with yourself.'"

Eszterhazy had taken off his hat and was fanning his face with it. "But why did you sell the rings?" he asked. "*Why?*"

Master Mumau looked at him. "Because I needed the money for my *real* project," he said.

"I don't care about the gold, puff-puff with the bellows, *oh* what a nuisance! I just needed more money because the pension couldn't stretch that far, and I needed fifty ducats and so I had to make enough to sell a hundred rings. Well, now I've *got* the fifty ducats." His face lit up with an expression of glee such as Eszterhazy had almost never seen in his life before.

"—and now I can work on my *real* project!"

Eszterhazy nodded. "The elixir of life," he said, wearily.

"Of *course,* the elixir of life!"

For once, Doctor Eszterhazy could think of nothing to say. He racked his brains. Finally he murmured, "Keep me posted."

Later, he said to Lobats, "You may consider the case as closed."

"You mean that? You do. Well. Very well. But . . . at least tell me. *Where did he get it?*"

And Eszterhazy said, in a way perfectly truthfully, "It was dragon gold."

He was never sure, afterwards, that Lobats ever forgave him for that.

Whodunit

The whodunit is one of the most widely recognized forms of mystery, and for many its name has become synonymous with the entire field. It gives the reader a chance to discover the identity of the criminal, usually a murderer, before the detective does, and therein may be its special appeal. In the classic version, the crime occurs in an isolated place, such as a manor house, there is a limited number of suspects, and near the end of the story the survivors are assembled to hear the detective's solution.

While science fiction can only boast of a moderate number of whodunits, some of its authors, like the incomparable Jack Vance, show great facility in handling this kind of story. And from the adventures of Mr. Vance's irascible detective, Magnus Ridolph, we have selected the following gem.

Coup de Grace

JACK VANCE

I

The Hub, a cluster of bubbles in a web of metal, hung in empty space, in that region known to Earthmen as Hither Sagittarius. The owner was Pan Pascoglu, a man short, dark and energetic, almost bald, with restless brown eyes and a thick mustache. A man of ambition, Pascoglu hoped to develop the Hub into a fashionable resort, a glamor-island among the stars—something more than a mere stopover depot and junction point. Working to this end, he added two dozen bright new bubbles—"cottages," as he called them—around the outer meshes of the Hub, which already resembled the model of an extremely complex molecule.

The cottages were quiet and comfortable; the dining salon offered an adequate cuisine; a remarkable diversity of company met in the public rooms. Magnus Ridolph found the Hub at once soothing and stimulating. Sitting in the dim dining salon, the naked stars serving as chandeliers, he contemplated his fellow-guests. At a table to his left, partially obscured by a planting of dendrons, sat four figures. Magnus Ridolph frowned. They ate in utter silence and three of them, at least, hulked over their plates in an uncouth fashion.

"Barbarians," said Magnus Ridolph, and turned his shoulder. In spite of the mannerless display he was not particularly offended; at the Hub one must expect to mingle with a variety of peoples. Tonight they seemed to range the whole spectrum of evolution, from the boors to his left, across a score of more or less noble civilizations, culminating with—Magnus Ridolph patted his neat white beard with a napkin—himself.

From the corner of his eye he noticed one of the four shapes arise, approach his own table.

"Forgive my intrusion, but I understand that you are Magnus Ridolph."

Magnus Ridolph acknowledged his identity and the other, without invitation, sat heavily down. Magnus Ridolph wavered between curtness and civility. In the starlight he saw his visitor to be an anthropologist, one Lester Bonfils, who had been pointed out to him earlier. Magnus Ridolph, pleased with his own perspicacity, became civil. The three figures at Bonfils' table were savages in all reality: paleolithic inhabitants of S-Cha-6, temporary wards of Bonfils. Their faces were dour, sullen, wary; they seemed disenchanted with such of civilization as they had experienced. They wore metal wristlets and rather heavy metal belts: magnetic pinions. At necessity, Bonfils could instantly immobilize the arms of his charges.

Bonfils himself was a large fair man with thick blond hair, heavy and vaguely flabby. His complexion should have been florid; it was pale. He should have exhaled easy good-fellowship, but he was withdrawn and diffident. His mouth sagged, his nose was pinched; there was no energy to his movements, only a nervous febrility. He leaned forward. "I'm sure you are bored with other people's troubles, but I need help."

"At the moment I do not care to accept employment," said Magnus Ridolph in a definite voice.

Bonfils sat back, looked away, finding not even the strength to protest. The stars glinted on the whites of his eyes; his skin shone the color of cheese. He muttered, "I should have expected no more."

His expression held such dullness and despair that Magnus Ridolph felt a pang of sympathy. "Out of curiosity—and without committing myself—what is the nature of your difficulty?"

Bonfils laughed briefly—a mournful empty sound. "Basically—my destiny."

"In that case, I can be of little assistance," said Magnus Ridolph.

Bonfils laughed again, as hollowly as before. "I use the word 'destiny' in the largest sense, to include"—he made a vague gesture —"I don't know what. I seem predisposed to failure and defeat. I consider myself a man of good-will—yet there is no one with more enemies. I attract them as if I were the most vicious creature alive."

Magnus Ridolph surveyed Bonfils with a trace of interest. "These enemies, then, have banded together against you?"

"No . . . at least, I think not. I am harassed by a woman. She is busily engaged in killing me."

"I can give you some rather general advice," said Magnus Ridolph. "It is this: Have nothing more to do with this woman."

Bonfils spoke in a desperate rush, with a glance over his shoulder toward the paleolithics. "I had nothing to do with her in the first place! That's the difficulty! Agreed that I'm a fool; an anthropologist should be careful of such things, but I was absorbed in my work. This took place at the southern tip of Kharesm, on Journey's End; do you know the place?"

"I have never visited Journey's End."

"Some people stopped me on the street—'We hear you have engaged in intimate relations with our kinswoman!'

"I protested: 'No, no, that's not true!'—because naturally, as an anthropologist, I must avoid such things like the plague."

Magnus Ridolph raised his brows in surprise. "Your profession seems to demand more than monastic detachment."

Bonfils made his vague gesture; his mind was elsewhere. He turned to inspect his charges; only one remained at the table. Bonfils groaned from the depths of his soul, leapt to his feet—nearly overturning Magnus Ridolph's table—and plunged away in pursuit.

Magnus Ridolph sighed, and, after a moment or two, departed the dining salon. He sauntered the length of the main lobby, but Bonfils was nowhere to be seen. Magnus Ridolph seated himself, ordered a brandy.

The lobby was full. Magnus Ridolph contemplated the other occupants of the room. Where did these various men and women, near-men and near-women, originate? What were their purposes, what had brought them to the Hub? That rotund moon-faced bonze in the stiff red robe, for instance. He was a native of the planet Padme, far across the galaxy. Why had he ventured so far from home? And the tall angular man whose narrow shaved skull carried a fantastic set of tantalum ornaments: a Lord of the Dacca. Exiled? In pursuit of an enemy? On some mad crusade? And the anthrope from the planet Hecate sitting by himself: a walking argument to support the theory of parallel evolution. His outward semblance caricatured humanity; internally he was as far removed as a gastropod. His head was bleached bone and black shadow, his mouth a lipless slit. He was a Meth of Maetho, and Magnus Ridolph knew his race to be gentle and diffident, with so little mental contact with human beings as to seem ambiguous and secretive. . . . Magnus Ridolph focused his gaze on a woman, and was taken aback by her miraculous beauty. She was dark and slight, with a complexion the color of clean desert sand; she carried herself with a self-awareness that was immensely provoking. . . .

Into the chair beside Magnus Ridolph dropped a short nearly-bald man with a thick black mustache: Pan Pascoglu, proprietor of the Hub. "Good evening, Mr. Ridolph; how goes it with you tonight?"

"Very well, thank you. . . . That woman: who is she?"

Pascoglu followed Magnus Ridolph's gaze. "Ah. A fairy-princess. From Journey's End. Her name—" Pascoglu clicked his tongue. "I can't remember. Some outlandish thing."

"Surely she doesn't travel alone?"

Pascoglu shrugged. "She says she's married to Bonfils, the chap with the three cave-men. But they've got different cottages, and I never see them together."

"Astonishing," murmured Magnus Ridolph.

"An understatement," said Pascoglu. "The cave-men must have hidden charms."

The next morning the Hub vibrated with talk, because Lester Bonfils lay dead in his cottage, with the three paleolithics stamping restlessly in their cages. The guests surveyed each other nervously. One among them was a murderer!

II

Pan Pascoglu came to Magnus Ridolph in an extremity of emotion. "Mr. Ridolph, I know you're here on vacation, but you've got to help me out. Someone killed poor Bonfils dead as a mackerel, but who it was—" He held out his hands. "I can't stand for such things here, naturally."

Magnus Ridolph pulled at his little white beard. "Surely there is to be some sort of official inquiry?"

"That's what I'm seeing you about!" Pascoglu threw himself into a chair. "The Hub's outside all jurisdiction. I'm my own law—within certain limits, of course. That is to say, if I were harboring criminals, or running vice, someone would interfere. But there's nothing like that here. A drunk, a fight, a swindle—we take care of such things quietly. We've never had a killing. It's got to be cleaned up!"

Magnus Ridolph reflected a moment or two. "I take it you have no criminological equipment?"

"You mean those truth machines, and breath-detectors and cell-matchers? Nothing like that. Not even a fingerprint pad."

"I thought as much," sighed Magnus Ridolph. "Well, I can hardly refuse your request. May I ask what you intend to do with the criminal after I apprehend her—or him?"

Pascoglu jumped to his feet. Clearly the idea had not occurred to him. He held out his clenched hands. "What should I do? I'm not equipped to set up a law court. I don't want to just shoot somebody."

Magnus Ridolph spoke judiciously. "The question may resolve itself. Justice, after all, has no absolute values."

Pascoglu nodded passionately. "Right! Let's find out who did it. Then we'll decide the next step."

"Where is the body?" asked Magnus Ridolph.

"Still in the cottage, just where the maid found it."

"It has not been touched?"

"The doctor looked him over. I came directly to you."

"Good. Let us go to Bonfils' cottage."

Bonfils' "cottage" was a globe far out on the uttermost web, perhaps five hundred yards by tube from the main lobby.

The body lay on the floor beside a white chaise-longue—lumpy, pathetic, grotesque. In the center of the forehead was a burn; no other marks were visible. The three paleolithics were confined in an ingenious cage of flexible splines, evidently collapsible. The cage of itself could not have restrained the muscular savages; the splines apparently were charged with electricity.

Beside the cage stood a thin young man, either inspecting or teasing the paleolithics. He turned hastily when Pascoglu and Magnus Ridolph stepped into the cottage.

Pascoglu performed the introductions. "Dr. Scanton, Magnus Ridolph."

Magnus Ridolph nodded courteously. "I take it, doctor, that you have made at least a superficial examination?"

"Sufficient to certify death."

"Could you ascertain the time of death?"

"Approximately midnight."

Magnus gingerly crossed the room, looked down at the body. He turned abruptly, rejoined Pascoglu and the doctor, who waited by the door.

"Well?" asked Pascoglu anxiously.

"I have not yet identified the criminal," said Magnus Ridolph. "However, I am almost grateful to poor Bonfils. He has provided what appears to be a case of classic purity."

Pascoglu chewed at his mustache. "Perhaps I am dense—"

"A series of apparent truisms may order our thinking," said Magnus Ridolph. "First, the author of this act is currently at the Hub."

"Naturally," said Pascoglu. "No ships have arrived or departed."

"The motives to the act lie in the more or less immediate past."

Pascoglu made an impatient movement. Magnus Ridolph held up his hand, and Pascoglu irritably resumed the attack on his mustache.

"The criminal in all likelihood had had some sort of association with Bonfils."

Pascoglu said, "Don't you think we should be back in the lobby? Maybe someone will confess, or—"

"All in good time," said Magnus Ridolph. "To sum up, it appears that our primary roster of suspects will be Bonfils' shipmates en route to the Hub."

"He came on the *Maulerer Princeps;* I can get the debarkation list at once." And Pascoglu hurriedly departed the cottage.

Magnus Ridolph stood in the doorway studying the room. He turned to Dr. Scanton. "Official procedure would call for a set of detailed photographs; I wonder if you could make these arrangements?"

"Certainly. I'll do them myself."

"Good. And then—there would seem no reason not to move the body."

III

Magnus Ridolph returned along the tube to the main lobby, where he found Pascoglu at the desk.

Pascoglu thrust forth a paper. "This is what you asked for."

Magnus Ridolph inspected the paper with interest. Thirteen identities were listed:

1. Lester Bonfils, with
   a. Abu
   b. Toko
   c. Homup
2. Viamestris Diasporus
3. Thorn 199
4. Fodor Impliega
5. Fodor Banzoso
6. Scriagl
7. Hercules Starguard
8. Fiamella of Thousand Candles
9. Clan Kestrel, 14th Ward,
   6th Family, 3rd Son
10. (No name)

"Ah," said Magnus Ridolph. "Excellent. But there is a lack. I am particularly interested in the planet of origin of these persons."

"Planet of origin?" Pascoglu complained. "What is the benefit of this?"

Magnus Ridolph inspected Pascoglu with mild blue eyes. "I take it that you wish me to investigate this crime?"

"Yes, of course, but—"

"You will then cooperate with me, to the fullest extent, with no further protest or impatient ejaculations." And Magnus Ridolph accompanied the words with so cold and clear a glance that Pascoglu wilted and threw up his hands. "Have it your own way. But I still don't understand—"

"As I remarked, Bonfils has been good enough to provide us a case of definitive clarity."

"It's not clear to me," Pascoglu grumbled. He looked at the list. "You think the murderer is one of these?"

"Possibly, but not necessarily. It might be me, or it might be you. Both of us have had recent contact with Bonfils."

Pascoglu grinned sourly. "If it were you, please confess now and save me the expense of your fee."

"I fear it is not quite so simple. But the problem is susceptible to attack. The suspects—the persons on this list and any other Bonfils had dealt with recently—are from different worlds. Each is steeped in the traditions of his unique culture. Police routine might solve the case through the use of analyzers and detection machines. I hope to achieve the same end through cultural analysis."

Pascoglu's expression was that of a castaway on a desert island watching a yacht recede over the horizon. "As long as the case gets solved," he said in a hollow voice, "and there's no notoriety."

"Come, then," said Magnus Ridolph briskly. "The worlds of origin."

The additions were made; Magnus Ridolph scrutinized the list again. He pursed his lips, pulled at his white beard. "I must have two hours for research. Then—we interview our suspects."

IV

Two hours passed, and Pan Pascoglu could wait no longer. He marched furiously into the library, to find Magnus Ridolph gazing into space, tapping the table with a pencil. Pascoglu opened his mouth to speak, but Magnus Ridolph turned his head, and the mild blue gaze seemed to operate some sort of relay within Pascoglu's head. He composed himself, and made a relatively calm inquiry as to the state of Magnus Ridolph's investigations.

"Well enough," said Magnus Ridolph. "And what have you learned?"

"Well—you can cross Scriagl and the Clan Kestrel chap off the list. They were gambling in the game-room and have foolproof alibis."

Magnus Ridolph said thoughtfully, "It is of course possible that Bonfils met an old enemy here at the Hub."

Pascoglu cleared his throat. "While you were here studying, I made a few inquiries. My staff is fairly observant; nothing much escapes them. They say that Bonfils spoke at length only to three people. They are myself, you and that moon-faced bonze in the red robes."

Magnus Ridolph nodded. "I spoke to Bonfils, certainly. He appeared in great trouble. He insisted that a woman—evidently Fiamella of Thousand Candles—was killing him."

"What?" cried Pascoglu. "You knew all this time?"

"Calm yourself, my dear fellow. He claimed that she was engaged in the process of killing him—vastly different from the decisive act whose effect we witnessed. I beg of you, restrain your exclamations;

they startle me. To continue, I spoke to Bonfils, but I feel secure in eliminating myself. You have requested my assistance and you know my reputation: hence with equal assurance I eliminate you."

Pascoglu made a guttural sound, and walked across the room.

Magnus Ridolph spoke on. "The bonze—I know something of his cult. They subscribe to a belief in reincarnation, and make an absolute fetish of virtue, kindness and charity. A bonze of Padme would hardly dare such an act as murder; he would expect to spend several of his next manifestations as a jackal or a sea-urchin."

The door opened, and into the library, as if brought by some telepathic urge, came the bonze himself. Noticing the attitudes of Magnus Ridolph and Pascoglu, their sober appraisal of himself, he hesitated. "Do I intrude upon a private conversation?"

"The conversation is private," said Magnus Ridolph, "but inasmuch as the topic is yourself, we would profit by having you join us."

"I am at your service." The bonze advanced into the room. "How far has the discussion advanced?"

"You perhaps are aware that Lester Bonfils, the anthropologist, was murdered last night."

"I have heard the talk."

"We understand that last evening he conversed with you."

"That is correct." The bonze drew a deep breath. "Bonfils was in serious trouble. Never had I seen a man so despondent. The bonzes of Padme—especially we of the Isavest Ordainment—are sworn to altruism. We render constructive service to any living thing, and under certain circumstances to inorganic objects as well. We feel that the principle of life transcends protoplasm; and in fact has its inception with simple—or perhaps not so simple—motion. A molecule brushing past another—is this not one aspect of vitality? Why can we not conjecture consciousness in each individual molecule? Think what a ferment of thought surrounds us; imagine the resentment which conceivably arises when we tread on a clod! For this reason we bonzes move as gently as possible, and take care where we set our feet."

"Aha, hum," said Pascoglu. "What did Bonfils want?"

The bonze considered. "I find it difficult to explain. He was a victim of many anguishes. I believe that he tried to live an honorable life, but his precepts were contradictory. As a result he was beset by the passions of suspicion, eroticism, shame, bewilderment, dread, anger, resentment, disappointment and confusion. Secondly, I believe that he was beginning to fear for his professional reputation—"

Pascoglu interrupted. "What, specifically, did he require of you?"

"Nothing specific. Reassurance and encouragement, perhaps."

"And you gave it to him?"

The bonze smiled faintly. "My friend, I am dedicated to serious programs of thought. We have been trained to divide our brains left lobe from right, so that we may think with two separate minds."

Pascoglu was about to bark an impatient question, but Magnus Ridolph interceded. "The bonze is telling you that only a fool could resolve Lester Bonfils' troubles with a word."

"That expresses something of my meaning," said the bonze.

Pascoglu stared from one to the other in puzzlement, then threw up his hands in disgust. "I merely want to find who burnt the hole in Bonfils' head. Can you help me, yes or no?"

The bonze smiled faintly. "My friend, I am dedicated to wonder if you have considered the source of your impulses? Are you not motivated by an archaic quirk?"

Magnus Ridolph interpreted smoothly. "The bonze refers to the Mosaic Law. He warns against the doctrine of extracting an eye for an eye, a tooth for a tooth."

"Again," declared the bonze, "you have captured the essence of my meaning."

Pascoglu threw up his hands, stamped to the end of the room and back. "Enough of this foolery!" he roared. "Bonze, get out of here!"

Magnus Ridolph once more took it upon himself to interpret. "Pan Pascoglu conveys his compliments, and begs that you excuse him until he can find leisure to study your views more carefully."

The bonze bowed and withdrew. Pascoglu said bitterly, "When this is over, you and the bonze can chop logic to your heart's content. I'm sick of talk; I want to see some action." He pushed a button. "Ask that Journey's End woman—Miss Thousand Candles, whatever her name is—to come into the library."

Magnus Ridolph raised his eyebrows. "What do you intend?"

Pascoglu refused to meet Magnus Ridolph's gaze. "I'm going to talk to these people and find out what they know."

"I fear that you waste time."

"Nevertheless," said Pascoglu doggedly. "I've got to make a start somewhere. Nobody ever learned anything lying low in the library."

"I take it, then, that you no longer require my services?"

Pascoglu chewed irritably at his mustache. "Frankly, Mr. Ridolph, you move a little too slow to suit me. This is a serious affair. I've got to get action fast."

Magnus Ridolph bowed in acquiescence. "I hope you have no objection to my witnessing the interviews?"

"Not at all."

A moment passed, then the door opened and Fiamella of Thousand Candles stood looking in.

Pan Pascoglu and Magnus Ridolph stared in silence. Fiamella wore a simple beige frock, soft leather sandals. Her arms and legs were bare, her skin only slightly paler than the frock. In her hair she wore a small orange flower.

Pascoglu somberly gestured her forward; Magnus Ridolph retired to a seat across the room.

"Yes, what is it?" asked Fiamella in a soft, sweet voice.

"You no doubt have learned of Mr. Bonfils' death?" asked Pascoglu.

"Oh yes!"

"And you are not disturbed?"

"I am very happy, of course."

"Indeed." Pascoglu cleared his throat. "I understand that you have referred to yourself as Mrs. Bonfils."

Fiamella nodded. "That is how you say it. On Journey's End we say he is Mr. Fiamella. I pick him out. But he ran away, which is a great harm. So I came after him, I tell him I kill him if he will not come back to Journey's End."

Pascoglu jumped forward like a terrier, stabbed the air with a stubby forefinger. "Ah! Then you admit you killed him!"

"No, no," she cried indignantly. "With a fire gun? You insult me! You are as bad as Bonfils. Better be careful, I kill you."

Pascoglu stood back, startled. He turned to Magnus Ridolph. "You heard her, Ridolph?"

"Indeed, indeed."

Fiamella nodded vigorously. "You laugh at a woman's beauty; what else does she have? So she kills you, and no more insult."

"Just how do you kill, Miss Fiamella?" asked Magnus Ridolph politely.

"I kill by love, naturally. I come like this—" She stepped forward, stopped, stood rigid before Pascoglu, looking into his eyes. "I raise my hands—" She slowly lifted her arms, held her palms toward Pascoglu's face. "I turn around, I walk away." She did so, glancing over her shoulder. "I come back." She came running back. "And soon you say, 'Fiamella, let me touch you, let me feel your skin.' And I say, 'No!' And I walk around behind you, and blow on your neck—"

"Stop it!" said Pascoglu uneasily.

"—and pretty soon you go pale and your hands shake and you cry, 'Fiamella, Fiamella of Thousand Candles, I love you, I die for love!' Then I come in when it is almost dark and I wear only flowers, and you cry out, 'Fiamella!' Next I—"

"I think the picture is clear," said Magnus Ridolph suavely. "When Mr. Pascoglu recovers his breath, he surely will apologize for insulting you. As for myself, I can conceive of no more pleasant form of extinction, and I am half-tempted to—"

She gave his beard a playful tweak. "You are too old."

Magnus Ridolph agreed mournfully. "I fear that you are right. For a moment I had deceived myself. . . . You may go, Miss Fiamella of Thousand Candles. Please return to Journey's End. Your estranged husband is dead; no one will ever dare insult you again."

Fiamella smiled in a kind of sad gratification, and with soft lithe steps went to the door, where she halted, turned. "You want to find out who burned poor Lester?"

"Yes, of course," said Pascoglu eagerly.

"You know the priests of Cambyses?"

"Fodor Impliega, Fodor Banzoso?"

Fiamella nodded. "They hated Lester. They said, 'Give us one of your savage slaves. Too long a time has gone past; we must send a soul to our god.' Lester said, 'No!' They were very angry, and talked together about Lester."

Pascoglu nodded thoughtfully. "I see. I'll certainly make inquiries of these priests. Thank you for your information."

Fiamella departed. Pascoglu went to the wall-mesh. "Send Fodor Impliega and Fodor Banzoso here, please."

There was a pause, then the voice of the clerk responded: "They

are busy, Mr. Pascoglu—some sort of rite or other. They said they'll
only be a few minutes."

"Mmph. . . . Well, send in Viamestris Diasporus."

"Yes, sir."

"For your information," said Magnus Ridolph, "Viamestris Diasporus comes from a world where gladiatorial sports are highly
popular, where successful gladiators are the princes of society, especially the amateur gladiator, who may be a high-ranking noble-
man, fighting merely for public acclamation and prestige."

Pascoglu turned around. "If Diasporus is an amateur gladiator, I
would think he'd be pretty callous. He wouldn't care who he
killed!"

"I merely present such facts as I have gleaned through the morning's research. You must draw your own conclusions."

Pascoglu grunted.

In the doorway appeared Viamestris Diasporus, the tall man with
the ferocious aquiline head whom Magnus Ridolph had noticed in
the lobby. He inspected the interior of the library carefully.

"Enter, if you please," said Pascoglu. "I am conducting an inquiry into the death of Lester Bonfils. It is possible that you can
help us."

Diasporus' narrow face elongated in surprise. "The killer has not
announced himself?"

"Unfortunately, no."

Diasporus made a swift gesture, a nod of the head, as if suddenly
all were clear. "Bonfils was evidently of the lowest power, and the
killer is ashamed of his feat, rather than proud."

Pascoglu rubbed the back of his head. "To ask a hypothetical
question, Mr. Diasporus, suppose you had killed Bonfils, what reason—"

Diasporus cut the air with his hand. "Ridiculous! I would only
mar my record with a victory so small."

"But, assuming that you had reason to kill him—"

"What reason could there be? He belonged to no recognized
gens, he had issued no challenges, he was of stature insufficient to
drag the sand of the arena."

Pascoglu spoke querulously: "But if he had done you an injury—"

Magnus Ridolph interjected a suggestion: "For the sake of argument, let us assume that Mr. Bonfils had flung white paint on the
front of your house."

In two great strides Diasporus was beside Magnus Ridolph, the feral bony face peering down. "What is this, what has he done?"

"He has done nothing. He is dead. I ask the question merely for the enlightenment of Mr. Pascoglu."

"Ah! I understand. I would have such a cur poisoned. Evidently Bonfils had committed no such solecism, for I understand that he died decently, through a weapon of prestige."

Pascoglu turned his eyes to the ceiling, held out his hands. "Thank you, Mr. Diasporus, thank you for your help."

Diasporus departed; Pascoglu went to the wall-mesh. "Please send Mr. Thorn 199 to the library."

They waited in silence. Presently Thorn 199 appeared, a wiry little man with a rather large round head, evidently of a much mutated race. His skin was a waxy yellow; he wore gay garments of blue and orange, with a red collar and rococo red slippers.

Pascoglu had recovered his poise. "Thank you for coming, Mr. Thorn. I am trying to establish—"

Magnus Ridolph said in a thoughtful voice, "Excuse me. May I make a suggestion?"

"Well?" snapped Pascoglu.

"I fear Mr. Thorn is not wearing the clothes he would prefer for so important an inquiry as this. For his own sake he will be the first to wish to change into black and white, with, of course, a black hat."

Thorn 199 darted Magnus Ridolph a glance of enormous hatred.

Pascoglu was puzzled. He glanced from Magnus Ridolph to Thorn 199 and back.

"These garments are adequate," rasped Thorn 199. "After all, we discuss nothing of consequence."

"Ah, but we do! We inquire into the death of Lester Bonfils."

"Of which I know nothing!"

"Then surely you will have no objection to black and white."

Thorn 199 swung on his heel and left the library.

"What's all this talk about black and white?" demanded Pascoglu.

Magnus Ridolph indicated a strip of film still in the viewer. "This morning I had occasion to review the folkways of the Kolar Peninsula on Duax. The symbology of clothes is especially fascinating. For instance, the blue and orange in which Thorn 199 just now appeared induces a frivolous attitude, a light-hearted disregard for what we Earthmen would speak of as 'fact'. Black and white, however, are the vestments of responsibility and sobriety. When these colors are supplemented by a black hat, the Kolarians are constrained to truth."

Pascoglu nodded in a subdued fashion. "Well, in the meantime, I'll talk to the two priests of Cambyses." He glanced rather apologetically at Magnus Ridolph. "I hear that they practice human sacrifice on Cambyses; is that right?"

"Perfectly correct," said Magnus Ridolph.

The two priests, Fodor Impliega and Fodor Banzoso, presently appeared, both corpulent and unpleasant-looking, with red flushed faces, full lips, eyes half-submerged in the swelling folds of their cheeks.

Pascoglu assumed his official manner. "I am inquiring into the death of Lester Bonfils. You two were fellow passengers with him aboard the *Maulerer Princeps;* perhaps you noticed something which might shed some light on his death."

The priests pouted, blinked, shook their heads. "We are not interested in such men as Bonfils."

"You yourselves had no dealings with him?"

The priests stared at Pascoglu, eyes like four knobs of stone.

Pascoglu prompted them. "I understand you wanted to sacrifice one of Bonfils' paleolithics. Is this true?"

"You do not understand our religion," said Fodor Impliega in a flat plangent voice. "The great god Camb exists in each one of us, we are all parts of the whole, the whole of the parts."

Fodor Banzoso amplified the statement. "You used the word 'sacrifice'. This is incorrect. You should say, 'go to join Camb'. It is like going to the fire for warmth, and the fire becomes warmer the more souls that come to join it."

"I see, I see," said Pascoglu. "Bonfils refused to give you one of his paleolithics for a sacrifice—"

"Not 'sacrifice'!"

"—so you became angry, and last night you sacrificed Bonfils himself!"

"May I interrupt?" asked Magnus Ridolph. "I think I may save time for everyone. As you know, Mr. Pascoglu, I spent a certain period this morning in research. I chanced on a description of the Cambian sacrificial rites. In order for the rite to be valid, the victim must kneel, bow his head forward. Two skewers are driven into his ears, and the victim is left in this position, kneeling, face down, in a state of ritual composure. Bonfils was sprawled without regard for any sort of decency. I suggest that Fodor Impliega and Fodor Banzoso are guiltless, at least of this particular crime."

"True, true," said Fodor Impliega. "Never would we leave a corpse in such disorder."

Pascoglu blew out his cheeks. "Temporarily, that's all."

At this moment Thorn 199 returned, wearing skin-tight black pantaloons, white blouse, a black jacket, a black tricorn hat. He sidled into the library, past the departing priests.

"You need ask but a single question," said Magnus Ridolph. "What clothes was he wearing at midnight last night?"

"Well?" asked Pascoglu. "What clothes were you wearing?"

"I wore blue and purple."

"Did you kill Lester Bonfils?"

"No."

"Undoubtedly Mr. Thorn 199 is telling the truth," said Magnus Ridolph. "The Kolarians will perform violent deeds only when wearing gray pantaloons or the combination of green jacket and red hat. I think you may safely eliminate Mr. Thorn 199."

"Very well," said Pascoglu. "I guess that's all, Mr. Thorn."

Thorn 199 departed, and Pascoglu examined his list with a dispirited attitude. He spoke into the mesh. "Ask Mr. Hercules Starguard to step in."

Hercules Starguard was a young man of great physical charm. His hair was a thick crop of flaxen curls; his eyes were blue as sapphires. He wore mustard-colored breeches, a flaring black jacket, swaggering black short-boots. Pascoglu rose from the chair into which he had sunk. "Mr. Starguard, we are trying to learn something about the tragic death of Mr. Bonfils."

"Not guilty," said Hercules Starguard. "I didn't kill the swine."

Pascoglu raised his eyebrows. "You had reason to dislike Mr. Bonfils?"

"Yes, I would say I disliked Mr. Bonfils."

"And what was the cause of this dislike?"

Hercules Starguard looked contemptuously down his nose at Pascoglu. "Really, Mr. Pascoglu, I can't see how my emotions affect your inquiry."

"Only," said Pascoglu, "if you were the person who killed Mr. Bonfils."

Starguard shrugged. "I'm not."

"Can you demonstrate this to my satisfaction?"

"Probably not."

Magnus Ridolph leaned forward. "Perhaps I can help Mr. Starguard."

Pascoglu glared at him. "Please, Mr. Ridolph, I don't think Mr. Starguard needs help."

"I only wish to clarify the situation," said Magnus Ridolph.

"So you clarify me out of all my suspects," snapped Pascoglu. "Very well, what is it this time?"

"Mr. Starguard is an Earthman, and is subject to the influence of our basic Earth culture. Unlike many men and near-men of the outer worlds, he has been inculcated with the idea that human life is valuable, that he who kills will be punished."

"That doesn't stop murderers," grunted Pascoglu.

"But it restrains an Earthman from killing in the presence of witnesses."

"Witnesses? The paleolithics? What good are they as witnesses?"

"Possibly none whatever, in a legal sense. But they are important indicators, since the presence of human onlookers would deter an Earthman from murder. For this reason, I believe we may eliminate Mr. Starguard from serious consideration as a suspect."

Pascoglu's jaw dropped. "But—who is left?" He looked at the list. "The Hecatean." He spoke into the mesh. "Send in Mr. . . ." He frowned. "Send in the Hecatean."

The Hecatean was the sole non-human of the group, although outwardly he showed great organic similarity to true man. He was tall and stick-legged, with dark brooding eyes in a hard chitin-sheathed white face. His hands were elastic fingerless flaps: here was his most obvious differentiation from humanity. He paused in the doorway, surveying the interior of the room.

"Come in, Mr.—" Pascoglu paused in irritation. "I don't know your name; you have refused to confide it, and I cannot address you properly. Nevertheless, if you will be good enough to enter . . ."

The Hecatean stepped forward. "You men are amusing beasts. Each of you has his private name. I know who I am—why must I label myself? It is a racial idiosyncrasy, the need to fix a sound to each reality."

"We like to know what we're talking about," said Pascoglu. "That's how we fix objects in our minds, with names."

"And thereby you miss the great intuitions," said the Hecatean. His voice was solemn and hollow. "But you have called me here to question me about the man labeled Bonfils. He is dead."

"Exactly," said Pascoglu. "Do you know who killed him?"

"Certainly," said the Hecatean. "Does not everyone know?"

"No," said Pascoglu. "Who is it?"

The Hecatean looked around the room, and when he returned to Pascoglu, his eyes were blank as holes in a crypt.

"Evidently I was mistaken. If I knew, the person involved wishes his deed to pass unnoticed, and why should I disoblige him? If I did know, I don't know."

Pascoglu began to splutter, but Magnus Ridolph interceded in a grave voice. "A reasonable attitude."

Pascoglu's cup of wrath boiled over. "I think his attitude is disgraceful! A murder has been committed, this creature claims he knows, and will not tell. . . . I have a good mind to confine him to his quarters until the patrol ship passes."

"If you do so," said the Hecatean, "I will discharge the contents of my spore sac into the air. You will presently find your Hub inhabited by a hundred thousand animalcules, and if you injure a single one of them, you will be guilty of the same crime that you are now investigating."

Pascoglu went to the door, flung it aside. "Go! Leave! Take the next ship out of here! I'll never allow you back!"

The Hecatean departed without comment. Magnus Ridolph rose to his feet and prepared to follow. Pascoglu held up his hand. "Just a minute, Mr. Ridolph. I need advice. I was hasty; I lost my head."

Magnus Ridolph considered. "Exactly what do you require of me?"

"Find the murderer! Get me out of this mess!"

"These requirements might be contradictory."

Pascoglu sank into a chair, passed a hand over his eyes. "Don't make me out puzzles, Mr. Ridolph."

"Actually, Mr. Pascoglu, you have no need of my services. You have interviewed the suspects, you have at least a cursory acquaintance with the civilizations which have shaped them."

"Yes, yes," muttered Pascoglu. He brought out the list, stared at it, then looked sidewise at Magnus Ridolph. "Which one? Diasporus? Did he do it?"

Magnus Ridolph pursed his lips doubtfully. "He is a knight of the Dacca, an amateur gladiator evidently of some reputation. A murder of this sort would shatter his self-respect, his confidence. I put the probability at one percent."

"Hmph. What about Fiamella of Thousand Candles? She admits she set out to kill him."

Magnus Ridolph frowned. "I wonder. Death by means of amorous attrition is of course not impossible—but are not Fiamella's motives ambiguous? From what I gather, her reputation was injured by Bonfils' disinclination, and she thereupon set out to repair her reputation. If she could harass poor Bonfils to his doom by her charm and seductions, she would gain great face. She had everything to lose if he died in any other fashion. Probability: one percent."

Pascoglu made a mark on the list. "What of Thorn 199?"

Magnus Ridolph held out his hands. "He was not dressed in his killing clothes. It is as simple as that. Probability: one percent."

"Well," cried Pascoglu, "what of the priests, Banzoso and Impliega? They needed a sacrifice to their god."

Magnus Ridolph shook his head. "The job was a botch. A sacrifice so slipshod would earn them ten thousand years of perdition."

Pascoglu made a half-hearted suggestion. "Suppose they didn't really believe that?"

"Then why trouble at all?" asked Magnus Ridolph. "Probability: one percent."

"Well, there's Starguard," mused Pascoglu. "But you insist he wouldn't commit murder in front of witnesses . . ."

"It seems highly unlikely," said Magnus Ridolph. "Of course, we could speculate that Bonfils was a charlatan, that the paleolithics were impostors, that Starguard was somehow involved in the deception . . ."

"Yes," said Pascoglu eagerly. "I was thinking something like that myself."

"The only drawback to the theory is that it cannot possibly be correct. Bonfils is an anthropologist of wide reputation. I observed the paleolithics, and I believe them to be authentic primitives. They are shy and confused. Civilized men attempting to mimic barbarity unconsciously exaggerate the brutishness of their subject. The barbarian, adapting to the ways of civilization, comports himself to the model set by his preceptor—in this case Bonfils. Observing them at dinner, I was amused by their careful aping of Bonfils' manners.

Then, when we were inspecting the corpse, they were clearly bewildered, subdued, frightened. I could discern no trace of the crafty calculation by which a civilized man would hope to extricate himself from an uncomfortable situation. I think we may assume that Bonfils and his paleolithics were exactly as they represented themselves."

Pascoglu jumped to his feet, paced back and forth. "Then the paleolithics could not have killed Bonfils."

"Probability minuscule. And if we concede their genuineness, we must abandon the idea that Starguard was their accomplice, and we rule him out on the basis of the cultural qualm I mentioned before."

"Well—the Hecatean, then. What of him?"

"He is a more unlikely murderer than all the others," said Magnus Ridolph. "For three reasons: First, he is non-human, and has no experience with rage and revenge. On Hecate violence is unknown. Secondly, as a non-human, he would have no points of engagement with Bonfils. A leopard does not attack a tree; they are different orders of beings. So with the Hecatean. Thirdly, it would be, physically as well as psychologically, impossible for the Hecatean to kill Bonfils. His hands have no fingers; they are flaps of sinew. They could not manipulate a trigger inside a trigger-guard. I think you may dispense with the Hecatean."

"But who is there left?" cried Pascoglu in desperation.

"Well, there is you, there is me and there is—"

The door slid back; the bonze in the red cloak looked into the room.

V

"Come in, come in," said Magnus Ridolph with cordiality. "Our business is just now complete. We have established that of all the persons here at the Hub, only you would have killed Lester Bonfils, and so now we have no further need for the library."

"What?" cried Pascoglu, staring at the bonze, who made a deprecatory gesture.

"I had hoped," said the bonze, "that my part in the affair would escape notice."

"You are too modest," said Magnus Ridolph. "It is only fitting that a man should be known for his good works."

The bonze bowed. "I want no encomiums. I merely do my duty. And if you are truly finished in here, I have a certain amount of study before me."

"By all means. Come, Mr. Pascoglu; we are inconsiderate, keeping the worthy bonze from his meditations." And Magnus Ridolph drew the stupefied Pan Pascoglu into the corridor.

"Is he—is he the murderer?" asked Pascoglu feebly.

"He killed Lester Bonfils," said Magnus Ridolph. "That is clear enough."

"But why?"

"Out of the kindness of his heart. Bonfils spoke to me for a moment. He clearly was suffering considerable psychic damage."

"But—he could be cured!" exclaimed Pascoglu indignantly. "It wasn't necessary to kill him to soothe his feelings."

"Not according to our viewpoint," said Magnus Ridolph. "But you must recall that the bonze is a devout believer in—well, let us call it 'reincarnation'. He conceived himself performing a happy release for poor tormented Bonfils, who came to him for help. He killed him for his own good."

They entered Pascoglu's office; Pascoglu went to stare out the window. "But what am I to do?" he muttered.

"That," said Magnus Ridolph, "is where I cannot advise you."

"It doesn't seem right to penalize the poor bonze. . . . It's ridiculous. How could I possibly go about it?"

"The dilemma is real," agreed Magnus Ridolph.

There was a moment of silence, during which Pascoglu morosely tugged at his mustache. Then Magnus Ridolph said, "Essentially, you wish to protect your clientele from further application of misplaced philanthropy."

"That's the main thing!" cried Pascoglu. "I could pass off Bonfils' death—explain that it was accidental. I could ship the paleolithics back to their planet . . ."

"I would likewise separate the bonze from persons showing even the mildest melancholy. For if he is energetic and dedicated, he might well seek to extend the range of his beneficence."

Pascoglu suddenly put his hand to his cheek. He turned wide eyes to Magnus Ridolph. "This morning I felt pretty low. I was talking to the bonze . . . I told him all my troubles, I complained about expense—"

The door slid quietly aside; the bonze peered in, a half-smile on his benign face. "Do I intrude?" he asked as he spied Magnus Ridolph. "I had hoped to find you alone, Mr. Pascoglu."

"I was just going," said Magnus Ridolph politely. "If you'll excuse me . . ."

"No, no!" cried Pascoglu. "Don't go, Mr. Ridolph!"

"Another time will do as well," said the bonze politely. The door closed behind him.

"Now I feel worse than ever," Pascoglu moaned.

"Best to conceal it from the bonze," said Magnus Ridolph.

Why-done-it

Motive is the premier consideration of the why-done-it story. The reader often knows who the guilty party is, but he does not know why the crime was committed. Obviously, this genre lends itself to character studies and psychic explorations, and, as such, it usually avoids the pitfall of sterility that the whodunit sometimes falls into.

In science fiction, unlike the mystery field, there are probably just as many why-done-its as there are whodunits. Furthermore, by writing about aliens, time-travel, robots, or strikingly different cultures, the science fiction author is able to postulate a far wider range of motives than is the mystery author. Robert Silverberg, for example, once put together a delightful yarn about an intelligent plant that attacked a man because it was jealous of his locomotive powers. While the following story by William F. Temple offers a more traditional motive, it is an eerily effective piece which again makes us wonder why his works have been so neglected.

The Green Car

WILLIAM F. TEMPLE

This was one time I really saw an accident happen.

Other times, I'd just miss such things. There's the shriek of locked wheels. I look round and someone's lying in the road. There's a stationary car nearby, slewed half round.

After, I'd tell people: "I saw a nasty accident today . . ."

One embroiders to make the story vivid.

But this time I saw it happen. I wish to heaven I never had. Accident? It was more like plain murder.

The lane through Trescawo was serpentine in the extreme. It looped back on itself as though it were reluctant to reach the village at all, as though it were afraid it would run into something horrible.

The white-faced man in the green car had no such qualms. He came fast and unbelievably silently. Franky Lockett never even saw him. But I did.

I was leaning on my front gate when Franky erupted into his garden. He was eight and lived in the bungalow opposite. He was a sandy-haired kid, snub-nosed, blue-eyed, bright as a button, supercharged with energy. He seldom walked: he galloped.

He saw me and came charging across the lane. "Mr. Murdoch will you let me—"

Without a sound, the green car rushed into Trescawo from the dusk and hit him. He was thrown into the hedge of his front garden. I glimpsed the white, set face of the driver, and then the car was past. Shocked and horrified though I was, I noted the rear number-plate before the gloom swallowed it.

Then: "Franky!" I ran across to him. He was a muddied little bundle at the foot of the hedge, twitching pointlessly. I lifted his head and blood ran from the back of it. His eyes were closed. His mouth hung open, showing the gaps in his milk teeth. Then all at once he gave a great sigh and died in my arms.

Something moved beside me.

Blurrily, I looked up. Franky's father was standing over us, shaking like a man with fever. His hands fluttered uselessly. His eyes were round, staring. He said, thickly: "I was always afraid it would happen. He *will* rush—"

He choked over the broken sentence, knowing the tense was wrong and afraid to face the right one. He dropped on his knees beside us, clutched his son and wept like a woman.

I yielded Franky to him and stood up. I felt numb all over.

Trescawo sprang alive. Doors opened up and down the lane, garden gates banged, people came hurrying. It was a small village. People had lived close together here from infancy. Trescawo was like a single organism, aware immediately when some part of it was hurt.

Crooning wordlessly, they helped bear Franky into his bungalow. Some brave soul went ahead to meet the mother. Somebody ran for Dr. Trevose.

Still numbed, I reached my own bungalow and raised the local exchange. "Minnie, put me through to the police at Merthavin—hurry, for God's sake."

Minnie was an efficient operator before all else. For the moment, she forgot to be a woman and put me through without question. But doubtless, then, she listened.

Merthavin was a small coast resort five miles along the lane. In all that distance there was no single turning from the lane, and for a three-mile stretch if you turned left you went straight into the sea. Unless it stopped at either of a couple of farmhouses, or unless it turned around and came back, the green car must go by way of Merthavin.

The station sergeant there answered me. I told him what had happened and described the car. "Big, dark green saloon. Maybe twenty years old but runs smoothly. The number is WME 2195. A man driving—seemed to be wearing a bowler hat. White-faced fellow with a thick black moustache."

"We'll stop him, Mr. Murdoch," said the sergeant.

"Then arrest him for murder," I said, bitterly.

I went across to the Lockett's bungalow. Dr. Trevose was there, but there was nothing he could do, or I could do, or anyone could do.

"Mr. Murdoch, will you let me—" The excited little voice kept calling through my memory. I should never learn what Franky was going to ask of me. When the ache got too bad I went back to my own place, alone, looking for the whisky.

The 'phone rang. It was the police sergeant again.

"He hasn't shown up yet, sir. You say he was traveling fast?"

"Too damn fast," I said, grimly.

"And he's not gone back your way?"

"No—half the village is out waiting for him. They'll lynch him if they catch him—I'll do it myself."

"I understand your feelings, sir. But try to keep him for us if he comes that way. I reckon he must have stopped at one of the farms. Else he should have been here long ago."

"I suppose so." /

The sergeant made undecided noises. Then, suddenly: "I'd better stay on watch here. I'll ring George Peters and get him to start from your end and check up at the farms."

"All right, sergeant. If there's anything I can do—"

"Not at the moment, sir. I'll let you know when we locate the man." He hung up.

I poured my whisky, neat, and brooded over it. George Peters was a country police-constable. He lived alone in a cottage a couple of miles north of Trescawo and was the "local" policeman for four villages. He was pure Cornish and from the district and yet, somehow, never seemed of it.

This wasn't just my own impression. I'd lived in Cornwall for only three years and was still the complete "foreigner." But Peters was a "queer 'un" even to those who'd attended the same school.

"Deep," they said. "Knows a lot more than he lets on."

I'd bumped into him a few times but got no further than exchanging formal greetings. Politely, he kept me at arm's length. He didn't want to talk. This piqued me a bit, for he had a scholar's face with quiet eyes and I imagined we might have interests in common. I was an artist but I'd read a few books.

Still, maybe I was wrong about him. People who don't talk much usually don't because they haven't much to talk about.

He drifted from my attention. Franky Lockett came back and the whisky failed to make anything seem better. I was in for a bad night. I was pacing up and down the room, glass in hand, when the door-bell rang.

It was Constable Peters. Gaunt and looking seven feet tall with his helmet on, he regarded me from the step and said in his soft voice with only the echo of a Cornish accent: "Sorry to trouble you, Mr. Murdoch. I had to pass this way, and I'd just like to check the details about the green car."

"Certainly, constable. Come in."

He refused, gently but firmly. He just didn't want to mix. So I told him what I'd told the sergeant. This, clearly, he already knew. He listened impassively, making no notes. Then he asked: "Was it a Morris Sixteen?"

"I wouldn't know. I'm afraid I don't know much about cars."

"I see, sir. Thank you. Good night."

He seemed to reach the front gate with but a couple of strides of his long legs, mounted the bicycle he'd leant against it, and rode off towards Merthavin. The uncertain smear of light cast by his oil lamp weakened with distance and died away altogether.

I duly had my bad night, dozing on and off. Between dozes I thought too much. One of the least worrying questions I kept asking myself was the one Peters had asked me. Was the green car a Morris Sixteen?

And why on earth had Peters asked me that? Did he really "know more than he let on?" If he didn't, the question seemed pointless.

By morning I'd come to hate the wallpaper. I just had to get out in the open. I was cleaning my brushes to escape for a day's painting when the 'phone rang. It was Constable Peters.

"Could you spare the time to come up to my place for a few minutes, Mr. Murdoch?"

I didn't think my heart could sink any lower but it managed it. He'd be wanting my evidence as the sole witness, of course, and I hated the idea of living through the tragedy yet again. I'd been doing it most of the night.

Anyhow, it was his duty to call on me, not the other way round.

I said, rather irritably: "All right . . . Did you trace that driver last night?"

There was a moment of silence. Then Peters said quietly: "He hadn't been to either of the farms. He never reached Merthavin. He never came back to Trescawo."

There was another moment of silence while I absorbed that. "Damn it," I said, "he can't have been snatched up into the sky. Did you find the car abandoned? Or what?"

"That's what I want to talk to you about, Mr. Murdoch."

Obviously he didn't want to say more on the telephone in case Minnie was listening. I was interested now, my irritation gone. "Right, I'll be there in ten minutes."

But I was there in less on my motor-bike. P.-c. Peters was waiting at his cottage door, uniformed but hatless. He showed me into a sizeable room: it took up more than half the cottage. It was very neat but unusual. There were bookshelves all around it, ceiling-high, and they were packed tight with books, folders, filing boxes, and a row of hefty albums.

The floorboards were highly polished. There was a plain oak desk and a couple of wooden office chairs. That was the full inventory.

"My reference library and, you might say, my home," murmured Peters.

He selected one of the large albums and carried it to the desk. "This is what I want you to see, sir. I'd have brought it down to you but it's too bulky to strap on the carrier of my bike."

Our relationship was changing. Peters was becoming quite loquacious and I could find no answer but a grunt. His thin fingers turned the wide pages which were covered with pasted cuttings. He found the one he sought and indicated it. I bent over the desk to look.

It was a two-column story clipped from the local paper, the color of weak tea. The headlines said: CAR GOES OVER CLIFF and TRAGIC DEATH OF MERTHAVIN MAN. There was a smudgy photograph of a middle-aged man with a heavy black moustache.

"Does he look at all like the driver you saw, sir?"

I looked more closely. The photo disintegrated into a crowd of meaningless black dots.

"Afraid the detail isn't very clear," said Peters, apologetically.

"Even if it were, I still wouldn't be sure," I said. "I had the merest glimpse of the man. But certainly it *could* have been this man. Or his twin brother, for obviously this chap's dead."

"Yes, he's dead—been dead some seventeen years. Albert Wolfe, plumber, of Merthavin. I knew him pretty well. He had no brothers."

"So? Then I wouldn't know him—until three years ago I'd never been anywhere west of Plymouth."

"No, you wouldn't know him, sir. But I'd be glad if you would read the story."

I read it with some effort—the tiny type was eye-straining. It told how Wolfe, driving alone along the coast road between Trescawo and Merthavin in October 1940, swerved to avoid a car coming the other way. His car, a green Morris Sixteen plunged over the 100-foot cliff at that point into the sea.

At the time of going to press his body had not yet been recovered.

"Was it ever?" I asked Peters.

He shook his head. "There's a strong undertow around there. The body must have been washed out to sea. There was a war on at the time, you know, and it was a week before we could get hold of a diver to go down. The car was there, all right, upside down with a door open. No body, though."

"Well, it was a nasty affair but it was a long time ago and I still don't get why you've brought it up here—or me either."

Peters reached down a small ledger. "I'm a hoarder of data," he said. "In this book I've kept a note of the license number of every car or vehicle owned by anyone living within a fifteen miles radius of here during my time in the force. Cross-indexed between numbers and names, you see."

He thumbed open the "W" section and showed me an entry; *Wolfe, Albert Geoffrey. Morris 16 (Green) No. WME2195*

"Th-that's the number of the green car!" I stuttered.

"So you said, sir. And so far as I can ascertain, that number hasn't been re-issued to anyone since Bert Wolfe died."

I stared first at him, then out of the window at the little hedge-enclosed lawn, perhaps to be reassured that the world was still real out there. It was, anyway. I bit my thumbnail and that was real too.

"Are you implying that I saw Wolfe's ghost?"

"I don't know what you saw, Mr. Murdoch. I'm trying to find out."

I took another look at the indistinct photo and paced up and down trying to compare it with the even more indistinct face in my memory. I found myself surveying book titles, at first unconsciously, then consciously. Most of one corner of the room was occupied by works on psychic research and a few odd men out like the books of Charles Fort.

"Ghosts seem to be a particular interest of yours, Peters," I said. "Personally, I don't believe in them. What are you trying to sell me?"

Peters' rather ascetic face showed no reproach. "I'm a hoarder of data," he repeated. "Facts are what interest me, Mr. Murdoch. If you'll examine the rest of the shelves you'll find more encyclopedias, atlases, year-books, and scientific works than anything appertaining to psychic research."

"Nevertheless, you include ghosts among your 'facts'?"

"Apparitions would seem to be a genuine phenomenon according to the annals of the Society of Psychical Research," said Peters, carefully. "Probably they're mostly, if not wholly, subjective, though some might conceivably be explained by past and present time getting temporarily out of phase, as it were, and overlapping. Whether you can call them 'facts' depends on what you mean by a fact. Is imagination itself a fact? Anyhow, what's indisputable fact about ghosts is that people report seeing them."

"As you think I've done?"

"I don't know what to think you saw, sir. Except that it was no subjective phantom. The car was solid enough to kill that poor boy. I'm just surveying the facts. I spend a lot of my life in this room merely comparing facts. It fascinates me. Sometimes the oddest facts fit together, and sometimes the most commonly accepted facts just won't correlate at all. Either way you can't avoid seeing one big fact: this world is a much stranger place than most people think it is."

I looked at him. "If you were an artist, Peters, and saw like an artist, you'd know there was no need to tell me that."

"It's because you're an artist and observant, Mr. Murdoch, that I accept as facts what you say you saw. The bowler hat, for instance."

"What of it?"

"Bert Wolfe always wore a bowler. It wasn't all that common in these parts even back in the 'forties. He was wearing it the day he died."

I frowned. "Look, are you so sure it's a fact he's really dead? I mean, the car was found empty. Supposing he was thrown clear, fell into some crevice, lay there unconscious and unseen, then later climbed out and wandered away heaven knows where, having lost his memory from concussion?"

Peters shook his head. "Practically impossible. The cliff is sheer at that point and unbroken. I interviewed the other motorist, who saw him go over. The thing happened in broad daylight. He told me he'd never forget the expression on Bert's face behind the windscreen. It was white with the fear of death. And he watched the car fall the whole way, turning half over as it went. Wolfe didn't fall out. Nothing did. The door must have opened when the car hit the sea-bed."

"Still, if he were thrown out even as late as that, he yet might have escaped somehow."

"I don't see how," said Peters. "The motorist never took his eyes off the spot for twenty minutes. He had to sit that long by the roadside, getting his nerve back to drive on—he was an old man. Nothing came up after the bubbles died away."

In the microscopic hall, the telephone rang.

"Excuse me," said Peters. He went. I heard him replying: "Yes, he's here, sarge . . . Yes, I already knew that. I've checked with Mr. Murdoch. He insists he got the number right and I'm sure he did, too . . . Of course I know what I'm saying . . . Yes, I'll come right away. 'Bye."

Peters came back. "That was Horrocks, the police sergeant at Merthavin," he said, unnecessarily. "He's been ringing your place. He found who the license number belonged to and assumed you were mistaken. When I said you weren't, I heard his blood vessels bursting. Now I've got to go and explain myself. Horrocks thinks I'm mad, but then he always did."

"I'll come with you, if you like, though I'm not certain whose side I'm on. But I'll swear in person I got that number right."

Peters smiled—the first time I'd ever seen him smile.

"I'd be glad if you would, Mr. Murdoch, for on the way there's another fact I should like to bring to your attention."

I raised my eyebrows, but the only question I asked was: "Would you care for a lift on my pillion? It would save you pedalling all that way."

He accepted, and off we went, down to Trescawo and through it

and along the lane the green car had followed yesterday evening.
The sea came into view on our left. It was dun-colored like the
dismal clouds that hung over it. Rain looked imminent again and
we'd had too much of it lately.

You saw plenty of the sea whether you wanted to or not, for the
lane—serpentine as ever—kept wandering dangerously near to the
edge of the cliffs. Sometimes there wasn't six feet of grass verge between it and the empty air.

We climbed in low gear towards the worst spot of all, where the
cliffs reached their topmost height. The lane went over the brow
and you couldn't see if anything was coming the other way. Ninety-
nine times out of a hundred, on this lonely road, nothing was. But I
guessed this was the place where the hundredth chance had gone
against Albert Wolfe.

I was right. "Stop here, please," said Peters in my ear.

I stopped on the crest and could see the lane running down into
Merthavin. I preferred to look at it rather than seawards, for I've always been nervous of heights. Peters wasn't bothered, though. He
slid off the pillion and paced to the very brink of the cliff, examining
the grassy verge.

"Look at this, Mr. Murdoch."

So I had to. The verge was wet and muddy from the rain. I slid
about on it with my heart in my mouth. What Peters pointed out
did nothing for my heart, either.

In the sticky soil were the shallow ruts made by a car's wheels.
The pattern of the tread was plain. They swerved across the verge
the whole way to the brink. Clearly a car had gone over that brink,
and probably within the last twenty-four hours—since yesterday's
rain.

"I found them by torch-light last night," said Peters, soberly.
"When it was apparent the car had disappeared, I had a hunch this
was the place where it had left the road. Just where poor Bert Wolfe
bought it."

My spine crawled. "And where he bought it again—yesterday?"

Peters shrugged. "Those tracks are another fact—that's all," he
said, shortly.

I was scared but morbid interest made me peer over the brink,
down at the sea a hundred feet below.

"There's never less than twenty feet of water there," commented Peters.

I drew back. I looked again at the tracks. "The car ran past me weirdly silently," I said. "As silently as a ghost. But if it were immaterial, like a ghost, it couldn't have killed Franky—nor left tracks like that."

"Then obviously it was material," said Peters.

"Transposed from the past to the present by some inexplicable freak of time, d'you think?"

Peters shrugged again. "That's a theory which one fact doesn't fit. Bert Wolfe's car was old when he bought it. He got through a hell of a lot more mileage in it. The engine knocked like fury. You could hear that car coming from a mile off. But yesterday, you say, you didn't hear it coming. Or going. Now, if the car were here materially, then surely its material parts—the cylinders, tappets, and so on—must have caused just as many soundwaves as they always did."

"But just now you said it obviously *was* material!" I cried.

"So I did," said Peters, bestriding the pillion lankily. "We need another theory. To get it we need more facts. Let's go on and see Horrocks. Maybe he'll have some."

But Horrocks had no more facts. However, he accepted ours, though refusing to believe there was anything unnatural about them. He was a solidly built man who assumed the world was equally solidly built. He laughed us to scorn and then assured us that it was no laughing matter.

"Manslaughter has been done," he said, "and I suspect maybe other crimes. Still, it seems the criminal has paid for them with his life."

"What criminal?" frowned Peters.

"The man in the bowler hat who was driving the car, of course," said Horrocks, impatiently. "Mr. Murdoch is quite sure the car number was WME 2195. Right, I'll accept that. There's no such registered number. Therefore, the car had false number-plates."

"But why?" I asked.

Horrocks, still impatient, said: "There can be only one reason, sir —it was a stolen car. Changing the number-plates is a routine dodge."

"It was such an old car, pre-war type, that it could scracely be worth stealing," I said.

"Perhaps not for its own sake," said Horrocks. "I'd say it was stolen to be used for a job. Pay-roll snatching, perhaps. There was a snatch in Exeter on Friday. Two more in Plymouth—big money every time. The culprit—or one of 'em—was on the run out this way. Obviously, a stranger in the district. He didn't know that tricky coast road very well, if at all, probably missed the turn in the dusk —or skidded on the wet road—and went over the cliff."

He turned to Peters. "Straightforward enough, isn't it, George? No call for spooks."

It was so glib I'd all but accepted it, until Peters said: "That's really *some* coincidence, sarge. I'd hate to have to work out the mathematical chances against two green cars, of the same vintage, driven by a man with a black moustache and wearing a bowler hat, going over the same cliff—and carrying the identical number-plate!"

Horrocks wasn't even shaken. "Coincidence? *Everything's* coincidence. It's merely a coincidence that you're you, Peters, and not somebody else. The chances are well over two thousand million against it, you know."

Peters sighed. "Sometimes I think you'd be happier if I *were* somebody else, sarge."

Horrocks laughed. "Not at all, George. You're the queerest flatfoot I've ever run across, but I never met a more conscientious one. You do your job. But if you'd only stick to facts and not let your imagination run away with you, I think you'd do it even better."

Peters lifted his eyes to heaven. His lips moved wordlessly. For the first time since Franky's death, I laughed.

Horrocks regarded us with surprise, then said abruptly: "We'll have the truth within a few hours. I've contacted the Aqualung Club and some of their chaps are going down for a look-see any time now."

I'd forgotten about the Aqualung Club, Merthavin's own group of skin-diving enthusiasts.

"Why, of course," I said. "That'll settle who the man was."

"I'm hoping they'll recover his body," said Horrocks. "But it'll be a dicey do with that undertow. Still, they think they can handle it. They're certain to locate the car, anyhow, and perhaps the pay-roll too. Care to come along and see the operations? I've got a launch laid on."

I accepted the invitation. Peters got over his chagrin and came with us, though he remained silent and thoughtful. When we got there, the Club's motor cruiser was already anchored beneath the cliff which stood above it like the wall of a great warehouse.

We tied up alongside the cruiser. We didn't want to risk bobbing against that rock wall, even though the dirty-looking sea was still smooth under the overcast sky. The rain was still holding off.

A couple of Club members were standing on the cruiser's deck making final tests of their equipment. Each had a safety line around his waist to guard against being swept away by the under-tow. Three others stood by ready to join the hunt if it became difficult.

The pair slipped on their goggles and dropped over the side. There was a brief flurry of flippered feet, and then the sea was smooth again.

Twenty minutes later they came up empty-handed.

"Pretty murky down there but we've covered the area fairly thoroughly," one of them reported. "Not a sign of the damn car."

Horrocks bit his lip. "But you could have missed it?"

They agreed, and went down again, and presently the others joined them. There were five of them at it, on and off. An hour went by. Then the organizer bobbed up by our launch. He said, rather breathlessly: "Sorry—drawn another blank. Can't even see anything of the car that was supposed to have been down here for years. But probably that's silted over by now. The bottom's very sandy."

Horrocks was disappointed. So was I. Peters remained expressionless.

"All right, old man—thanks for taking the trouble," said Horrocks. "You'd better call your hunting pack off now."

They came up one by one. The last carrying something. He thrust it over the side into our launch. It was corroded, barnacle-encrusted, and enmeshed in seaweed, but was fairly obviously a car's number-plate.

Horrocks and Peters chipped and scraped at it with spanners from the tool-box. Bit by bit, the number became dimly apparent: WME 2195.

"From Bert Wolfe's car," said Peters. "It must have come adrift."

That encouraged the skin-divers to forage about for another half an hour, but without any luck. Then they gave it up. They were unanimous in believing that no car had fallen into the sea in this area lately, else they would certainly have found it.

We returned gloomily to Merthavin. Horrocks got the station car and came part way back with Peters and me. He wanted to see those wheel-marks for himself. He did so. Then he peeped over the cliff. Yes, we'd been searching the right spot: it was directly below. "It beats me," said Horrocks. He turned his car and went back. I ran Peters up to his cottage. He'd become the reticent type again, and went in muttering something about mulling over the facts again. He obviously didn't want me to mull with him.

I returned home, had some tea, then looked out and found a breeze had sprung up, the heavy clouds were moving off, and the sun was breaking through as it sank towards the sea. It would be a fine evening, after all.

I stared across at the Lockett's bungalow. The window with the blind down made my throat feel dry. The funeral was tomorrow. I was just too close to it all here. I escaped again, riding in the evening sunlight along the lane as it wound out of Trescawo in the opposite direction to Merthavin.

There were no cliffs this way. The lane led gently down to the beach. There was over a mile of level sands here. I parked my bike at the edge of them and began trudging along at the sea's constantly moving rim. There were no living things in sight save seagulls.

The sunset was a splendid show of colored and gleaming clouds, and the sea made a rippling carpet of its reflection. It took my mind off things, as I'd hoped. I began to wonder what Turner would have made of it.

The glory had died and the sea had claimed the sun when I turned back. The beach looked desolate in the grey light now and the wind had become chill. I tramped back a deal faster than I'd come.

I was almost within arm's reach of my bike when I saw the wheel-tracks grooving the sand not five yards beyond it. They ran from the lane clear across the beach and straight into the sea. My heart missed a beat. I went on a bit shakily to examine them.

The tide was on the ebb, and on the mud-smooth wet sand it left behind it the tracks were clear enough for me to recognize the pattern of the tread.

The tracks weren't there when I'd come—I couldn't have missed seeing them. While I'd been traipsing away from this spot, entranced by the sunset, behind me the green car must have rolled silently into the sea.

Or have emerged from it.

It was impossible to tell which from the tracks.

I looked at the blank sea under the dulling sky. The wavelets advanced, slopped, and retreated, and the wind was beginning a thin, high keening. I shivered, and it wasn't just because of the cold wind.

I stumbled back to my bike, started her up, and began hitting it back along the lane. But I turned off before Trescawo, and headed uphill. I was making for Peters' cottage. I wanted him to see those tracks before the tide turned.

Up the gloomy, deserted lane I tore, rounded a curve, then pulled to one side, braking like mad. For plunging noiselessly down between the hedges towards me was the green car. I had a full head on view of it. But only for a few seconds. It missed me by inches and I felt the wind of its passing.

During those heart-stopping seconds the white face of Albert Wolfe regarded me stonily from behind the windscreen. I was certain it was he—or a zombie using his body. Things had become so nightmarish now that I could almost believe it *was* a zombie.

But I didn't stop to think about it. I wrenched the bike round and rode like fury downhill after the car. I caught it up on the outskirts of Trescawo, but couldn't get past it: the lane was too narrow.

So I began hooting continuously. We shot between the Lockett's bungalow and mine at over fifty, despite the snaking bends. The blare of my horn had preceded us. The villagers were peering from their windows and doorways. But nobody had time to do a thing. We were out into the open country again before they'd reached their garden gates.

And there the green car began to move away from me with contemptuous ease, though I tried hard to hang on to its tail. I must have been doing close on eighty, which was lunacy in that lane and in the gathering dark.

But at least I had my headlamp on. The car showed no lights at all.

A minute or two later we were continuing the fantastic chase along the margin of the sea, and then climbing the rise to the high cliff. I was a hundred yards behind. As we emerged from the dead ground, the pale light of the moon, rising over the inland hills, reached us.

So I saw what happened. The green car reached the crown of the rise, then spun abruptly to the left and went flying out into space. It curved down towards the cliff-shadowed sea. The moonlight couldn't reach there, so I never saw the splash.

I pulled up, sweating, my nerves jumping.

Albert Wolfe had plunged to his death for the third time—at least. And there was no cause at all to assume that he would stay dead.

I switched off my engine and went gingerly to peer into the shadow beneath the cliff. But I could see nothing and there was no sound but the wash of the sea and the shrill note of the wind.

I took it easy on the way back to Trescawo. I had to. My nerves kept twitching like the leg of Galvani's frog. The village was in ferment. Somehow, Peters was already there taking notes. I beckoned him into my bungalow and poured us both stiff whiskies. Then I told him all about it.

"It *was* Wolfe—I saw him distinctly," I repeated. "I noticed other things, too. The front number-plate was missing."

"That's interesting," said Peters. "No one else noticed that. But Claude Farmer and Bill Jones glimpsed the back number-plate. WME 2195, sure enough."

He scratched his chin. "Wolfe's car—minus the number-plate we found today. What are we to make of that?"

"I don't know," I said, pouring another double. "But it was some car. I touched eighty and it was leaving me standing."

"Now, that doesn't sound like Wolfe's car at all," said Peters, thoughtfully. "It was in such bad shape I'm certain it would have seized up at anything over fifty."

"It was Wolfe's car," I said, and gulped a mouthful. "It had masks over the head-lamps—war-time pattern for driving in the blackout. *Circa* 1940. The lamps weren't switched on, though. That zombie could see in the dark."

"There are no facts to support the existence of zombies," said Peters. "I've been mulling over the facts we have, and a few more I've dug up, and I don't believe there's anything supernatural about this whole thing. You say you felt the draft as the car passed you. Right: it's solid. It displaces air. Let's see if it can displace a road barrier."

"That's fine—if you know when and where to plan the barrier."

"I'd say tomorrow at dusk, on the road between here and Merthavin—the best place would be Crowley Farm," said Peters, calmly.

"Good heavens, Peters, just because the car went through here two evenings running at roughly the same time, there's no reason to suppose it'll do so again tomorrow. What d'you imagine it is—a local bus keeping to a time-table?"

Peters remained calm. "When a phenomenon repeats itself, there's always a chance it'll go on doing so. We can but try. Anyhow, we've got more facts for Horrocks. Also, this time, a whole crowd of eye-witnesses. He'll have to do something."

Sergeant Horrocks did plenty. From somewhere or other he rustled up no less than three police patrol cars with two-way radio.

The following evening one of the cars lay concealed behind a hedge in the lane skirting the bare beach where I'd seen the wheel-tracks. Another blocked the turning leading up to Peters' cottage. The third was parked in the gateway to Crowley Farm, a mile out of Trescawo on the Merthavin road, and as well as its constable-driver and his observer, Horrocks, Peters, and I waited with it.

Across the road was drawn the biggest of the farm-carts, still loaded heavily with sacks of potatoes.

It had drizzled all morning, and the funeral had been a damp and depressing affair. During it, I'd found myself becoming angry at I knew not what. Anger at fate generally, I suppose, for killing a child so pointlessly. Somehow it was difficult to get angry with the occupant of the green car. How can one be angry with a man already dead? Or the shade of that man? Or—?

Something that was out of this world, anyway.

Perversely, the sun came out brilliantly after lunch. Now the fine afternoon was passing into another fine evening. In the darkening blue of the sky the pinpoint of Venus was just visible.

We were grouped around the car parked just inside the farm gate, listening to the faint etheric wash of the radio net.

Monotonously at intervals came from the other two waiting cars: "Able—nothing to report. Over." And "Baker—nothing to report. Over."

"Light the lanterns, George," said Horrocks, presently.

Constable Peters lit the four red-glassed hurricane lamps, carried them out into the lane and set them down in pairs on either side of the farm-cart barrier. A policeman was stationed at Merthavin to stop any traffic using the lane from that direction, but there was always a chance some motorist might slip past him. We didn't want any accidents.

Time ticked on. Venus became ever brighter as its setting became darker. The faint points of a handful of stars began to appear.

Every now and then, one or other of us would give way to impatience and peer round the gate and up the lane with the dusk thickening between its bordering hedges.

None of us seemed in the mood for talking.

Then the carrier wave rustled on the car radio and a voice, a little indistinct with excitement, said: "Able—there's a dark object rising from the sea, moving slowly landwards. Over."

We all tensed up.

. Horrocks grabbed the microphone. "Dog—okay. Watch it. Over."

Soon: "Able—it's the green car, all right. Coming slowly up the beach. Water streaming down its sides. No lights—but seems to be a man inside, driving. Over."

Horrocks: "Dog—okay. Baker—are you getting this? Over."

"Baker—yes. We're standing by. Over."

In a moment: "Able—it's turning into the lane ahead of us. Heading for Trescawo. We're about to start. Over."

Horrocks snapped back: "Dog—right, off you go. Just follow. Don't try to overtake. Over."

"Able—wilco. Over."

"Baker—standing by. Over."

The tempo was speeding up. I felt Peters grip my wrist. It was too dark to see his expression clearly, but his whole attitude said: "This is it. We'll soon know."

He let go and began to loosen his truncheon. I had no weapon beyond a heavy torch. We hadn't a gun between us. Horrocks had vetoed it. "When we corner him, we'll be nine against one—he'll have no chance," he said.

I reflected, yes, but nine men against one—*what?*

I licked dry lips, and my cursed nerves began jumping again.

The radio crackled, and a voice unsteadied by the bumpy journey reported: "Able—he's approaching Trescawo at speed. Fifty, maybe. We're keeping pace behind. Over."

"Baker—we're ready. Over."

Horrocks answered neither. His bulky figure was motionless as he waited.

"Baker—he tried to turn up here, saw us, swerved back, stayed on the road. We pulled out after him. Passing through Trescawo now. He's piling on speed. Look out there, Dog—he's got no lights and you can't hear his engine. Over."

But now through the fading twilight, from the direction of Trescawo, we could hear the distant engines of the two police cars heading this way—with the silent phantom car fleeing before them.

"Dog—okay. Out," snapped Horrocks. He dropped the microphone and ran out into the lane, waving an electric torch. Peters and I and the observer constable weren't two paces behind him. We formed a human barrier across the narrow lane, in front of the cart, adding our flashing torches to the red warning of the lanterns.

And then it came at us without a sound along the lane, a dark blur on the dim ribbon, traveling at a terrific speed. It could not swerve off the lane. High hedges, as well as deep ditches, on both sides prevented it—that was why this spot had been chosen.

We shouted and waved our torches wildly. The oncoming car seemed only to accelerate.

"Scatter!" yelled Horrocks when it was clear that the green car wasn't going to stop.

We jumped aside, I stumbling into a ditch and dropping my torch.

Crash! The green car smacked straight into the cumbersome cart and overturned it with a great cracking and splintering of wood. Potatoes went rolling all ways. The car, still upright and apparently undamaged, went on trying to climb over the wreck. Its wheels spun rapidly, seeking a purchase.

The white-faced driver remained at the wheel. The buzzing

wheels got a grip, and the car, lurching from side to side, began to work its way over the shattered cart.

The two pursuing police cars came, with screeching brakes, to a halt a few yards back. Their crews scrambled out.

I climbed out of the ditch with clumsy haste but Peters was faster. Truncheon in hand, he leaped up on the running-board of the escaping green car.

"Stop!" I heard him yell. "Come out of there—whoever you are." And he yanked open the door of the car.

It was like a flood-gate being opened. A mass of water came pouring out of the car, washing the driver out with it—a legless, struggling, oddly-shaped figure. He—or it—flopped into the ditch where I'd just been. The water gushed briefly over the creature and drained away along the ditch. The being continued to struggle helplessly and in silence down there. It threshed about like a landed fish.

A strong smell of the sea was filling the air.

Then, horribly, the figure expanded slowly like a toy balloon being blown up. And all the while it moved convulsively. And then there was a sickening sound, and it collapsed in a still, limp heap at the bottom of the ditch. There came a stench which drowned out the sea-smell.

We had to back away from it, and I, for one, was glad to.

The green car had ceased to move, too, and save for the water still trickling from it, all was silent.

The nine of us stood awkwardly in the lane. I don't know how the others felt about it but I had more than a twinge of guilt about the dreadful death of the thing. We hadn't meant to kill it any more than—probably—it had meant to kill little Franky Lockett.

The foul smell dissolved into the evening air. The sea-smell returned faintly—obviously, the water in the car had been seawater. We braced ourselves to go and inspect the thing by torchlight. It was a grisly and bewildering business, and while we were occupied with it the stars were coming out overhead in strength.

What we learnt that night merely confused me more than ever. The creature belonged to no species known to marine biology. It was cold-blooded, dark-skinned, and had gills and a tail. It had two main tentacles which branched into whole deltas of thinner tentacles—as Peters pointed out, much more useful for precision work than man's stubby fingers.

It also had a face. A grotesque, noseless, stalk-eyed face, which it had concealed behind a plastic death-mask of Albert Wolfe. About the upper part of its body was wrapped Wolfe's coat—the genuine article, as we found from the tailor's label.

The incongruous bowler hat, which we found farther along the ditch, was also genuine.

When the Maritime Biological Station at Plymouth dissected the creature, they found it had a brain of a size to command respect.

The green car had its mysteries, too. In the first place, it wasn't Wolfe's old car at all, but a careful replica even to the headlamp masks, although the front number-plate was missing. Yet it was only a replica so far as outward appearance went. There was a front seat, a steering wheel, and a few odd controls. Beyond that, it was little more than a traveling sea-water aquarium, very stoutly built and heavy.

Small wonder we'd not heard its engine: there wasn't one. The theory grew that it picked up and used power radiated from some distant source.

"Beamed in this direction from some point out to sea," Peters guessed. "They are well ahead of us."

"They" were still the staple talking point between Peters and me even a month later. We never tired of discussing "them," usually in Peters' library. If the affair had lost me one friend, it had gained me another.

Peters hunted through the charts and showed me the long, deep crack in the continental shelf which reached almost to the headland from which Wolfe's car had plunged.

"They came up here," he said, tracing it with a forefinger. "First they took Wolfe's body from the car. Some time later they came back for the car itself. They overlooked the front number-plate, which had been torn off—and which remained there until it was found by the Aqualung Club."

Mentally, I pictured "them" dragging the battered green car down towards the dark depths where they dwelt. It was obvious on several counts that they were creatures of the oceanic abyss. Firstly, because they could see in the dark, and ventured on land only when darkness was falling. Secondly, because the fake car had been constructed of tremendously strong material to contain the pressure of the sea-water with which it had been filled.

Peters—the facts at his fingertips, as usual—told me that water *is* compressible, though only by one per cent for every 3000 pounds per square inch of pressure.

It was a pity we'd had no chance to measure the pressure of the water in the car and therefore deduce the depth from which it had come.

Thirdly, of course, was the manner of death of the creature when that balancing pressure had been drastically lowered.

"We have to allow them that it was a bold piece of camouflage and opportunism," I said.

Peters agreed. "If it weren't for that unlucky accident at the outset, the creature might still be carrying out its nocturnal exploration, venturing ever farther inland. As it was, it had little chance to learn much about the world-above-the-water."

"But they must have known of our existence for hundreds of years—from sunken ships," I commented. "Why start only now to investigate our species?"

"I'm not so sure they didn't start long ago," said Peters. "Think of the missing crew of the *Marie Celeste*." He tapped the spine of one of Charles Fort's books. "And in here you'll find plenty of other reports from last century of whole missing crews, as well as ships themselves mysteriously disappearing in fair weather. What of the two ships and 129 men of the Franklin expedition, which vanished over a hundred years ago, and were never seen again despite prolonged searches? Specimens for *their* research, like as not."

"But why do they have to be furtive about it?" I complained. "They must know we're intelligent and would welcome contact with another intelligent race."

Peters smiled cynically. "You imagine they think us intelligent because we invented magnetic mines and sent them more free specimens of men and ships in 1939 and 1940 than they'd ever had before? It's my guess that's why they came up to investigate things a bit in 1940 and found that car."

I thought about it, then said: "Perhaps you're right. They had reason to be cautious about us. In fact, we really began to invade their territory during World War Two. All those sinking ships, all those submarines and U-boats. And now atomic submarines and underwater H-bombs—"

"And all the Aqualung Clubs of the world," smiled Peters.

I smiled, too, then said: "But it's no joke, really. They've intelligence, resource, boldness, and obviously a technology in some respects more advanced than ours. If it ever came to war—"

"If it ever came to war, I think we'd be far outnumbered," cut in Peters, grimly. "Remember this: there's more than twice as much land beneath the sea as there is above it. And presuming it's as thickly populated . . ." He trailed off speculatively.

Presently, he said, looking out at the tiny lawn: "Two races with a common nursery—the sea. We came out of it. They stayed in. Would a war decide who was the wiser?" His gaze wandered round the room and all its books. "Knowledge is a great thing, but wisdom is a greater," he said. "Let's hope that between us we can muster enough wisdom not to have a war at all."

How-done-it

How did the culprit reach and depart from the scene of the crime; how did he perform the crime itself; and how did he dispose of the weapon, body, or booty? These are the questions that are central to the three most orthodox variations of the how-done-it story. And the answers frequently provide valuable insights into the nature of misdirection and illusion.

The following story by the critically acclaimed Philip K. Dick is a fine example of the "performance of the crime" puzzle. It depicts the importance "dirty tricks" can have in war and also offers an accurate description of the ways in which various media indirectly mold our views of social reality.

War Game

In his office at the Terran Import Bureau of Standards, the tall man gathered up the morning's memos from their wire basket, and, and, seating himself at his desk, arranged them for reading. He put on his iris lenses, lit a cigarette.

"Good morning," the first memo said in its tinny, chattery voice, as Wiseman ran his thumb along the line of pasted tape. Staring off through the open window at the parking lot, he listened to it idly. "Say look, what's wrong with you people down there? We sent that lot of—" a pause as the speaker, the sales manager of a chain of New York department stores, found his records—"those Ganymedean toys. You realize we have to get them approved in time for the autumn buying plan, so we can get them stocked for Christmas." Grumbling, the sales manager concluded, "War games are going to be an important item again this year. We intend to buy big."

Wiseman ran his thumb down to the speaker's name and title.

"Joe Hauck," the memo-voice chattered. "Appeley's Children's Store."

To himself, Wiseman said, "Ah." He put down the memo, got a blank and prepared to reply. And then he said, half-aloud, "Yes, what about that lot of Ganymedean toys?"

It seemed like a long time that the testing labs had been on them. At least two weeks.

Of course, any Ganymedean products got special attention these days; the Moons had, during the last year, gotten beyond their usual state of economic greed and had begun—according to intelligence circles—mulling overt military action against competitive interests, of which the Inner Three planets could be called the foremost element. But so far nothing had shown up. Exports remained of adequate quality, with no special jokers, no toxic paint to be licked off, no capsules of bacteria.

And yet . . .

Any group of people as inventive as the Ganymedeans could be expected to show creativity in whatever field they entered. Subversion would be tackled like any other venture—with imagination and a flair for wit.

Wiseman got to his feet and left his office, in the direction of the separate building in which the testing labs operated.

Surrounded by half-disassembled consumers' products, Pinario looked up to see his boss, Leon Wiseman, shutting the final door of the lab.

"I'm glad you came down," Pinario said, although actually he was stalling; he knew that he was at least five days behind in his work, and this session was going to mean trouble. "Better put on a prophylaxis suit—don't want to take risks." He spoke pleasantly, but Wiseman's expression remained dour.

"I'm here about those inner-citadel-storming shock troops at six dollars a set," Wiseman said, strolling among the stacks of many-sized unopened products waiting to be tested and released.

"Oh, that set of Ganymedean toy soldiers," Pinario said with relief. His conscience was clear on that item; every tester in the labs knew the special instructions handed down by the Cheyenne Government on the Dangers of Contamination from Culture Particles Hostile to Innocent Urban Populations, a typically muddy ukase from officialdom. He could always—legitimately—fall back and cite the number of that directive. "I've got them off by themselves," he said, walking over to accompany Wiseman, "due to the special danger involved."

"Let's have a look," Wiseman said. "Do you believe there's anything in this caution, or is it more paranoia about 'alien milieux'?"

Pinario said, "It's justified, especially where children's artifacts are concerned."

A few hand-signals, and a slab of wall exposed a side room.

Propped up in the center was a sight that caused Wiseman to halt. A plastic life-size dummy of a child, perhaps five years in appearance, wearing ordinary clothes, sat surrounded by toys. At this moment, the dummy was saying, "I'm tired of that. Do something else." It paused a short time, and then repeated, "I'm tired of that. Do something else."

The toys on the floor, triggered to respond to oral instructions, gave up their various occupations and started afresh.

"It saves on labor costs," Pinario explained. "This is a crop of junk that's got an entire repertoire to go through, before the buyer has his money's worth. If we stuck around to keep them active, we'd be in here all the time."

Directly before the dummy was the group of Ganymedean soldiers, plus the citadel which they had been built to storm. They had been sneaking up on it in an elaborate pattern, but, at the dummy's utterance, they had halted. Now they were regrouping.

"You're getting this all on tape?" Wiseman asked.

"Oh, yes," Pinario said.

The model soldiers stood approximately six inches high, made from the almost indestructible thermoplastic compounds that the Ganymedean manufacturers were famous for. Their uniforms were synthetic, a hodgepodge of various military costumes from the Moons and nearby planets. The citadel itself, a block of ominous dark metal-like stuff, resembled a legendary fort; peep-holes dotted its upper surfaces, a drawbridge had been drawn up out of sight, and from the top turret a gaudy flag waved.

With a whistling pop, the citadel fired a projectile at its attackers. The projectile exploded in a cloud of harmless smoke and noise, among a cluster of soldiers.

"It fights back," Wiseman observed.

"But ultimately it loses," Pinario said. "It has to. Psychologically speaking, it symbolizes the external reality. The dozen soldiers, of course, represent to the child his own efforts to cope. By participating in the storming of the citadel, the child undergoes a sense of adequacy in dealing with the harsh world. Eventually he prevails, but only after a painstaking period of effort and patience." He added, "Anyhow, that's what the instruction booklet says." He handed Wiseman the booklet.

Glancing over the booklet, Wiseman asked, "And their pattern of assault varies each time?"

"We've had it running for eight days now. The same pattern hasn't cropped up twice. Well, you've got quite a few units involved."

The soldiers were sneaking around, gradually nearing the citadel. On the walls, a number of monitoring devices appeared and began tracking the soldiers. Utilizing other toys being tested, the soldiers concealed themselves.

"They can incorporate accidental configurations of terrain," Pinario explained. "They're object-tropic; when they see, for example, a dollhouse here for testing, they climb into it like mice. They'll be all through it." To prove his point, he picked up a large toy spaceship manufactured by a Uranian company; shaking it, he spilled two soldiers from it.

"How many times do they take the citadel," Wiseman asked, "on a percentage basis?"

"So far, they've been successful one out of nine tries. There's an adjustment in the back of the citadel. You can set it for a higher yield of successful tries."

He threaded a path through the advancing soldiers; Wiseman accompanied him, and they bent down to inspect the citadel.

"This is actually the power supply," Pinario said. "Cunning. Also, the instructions to the soldiers emanate from it. High-frequency transmission, from a shot-box."

Opening the back of the citadel, he showed his boss the container of shot. Each shot was an instruction iota. For an assault pattern, the shot were tossed up, vibrated, allowed to settle in a new sequence. Randomness was thereby achieved. But since there was a finite number of shot, there had to be a finite number of patterns.

"We're trying them all," Pinario said.

"And there's no way to speed it up?"

"It'll just have to take time. It may run through a thousand patterns and then—"

"The next one," Wiseman finished, "may have them make a ninety-degree turn and start firing at the nearest human being."

Pinario said somberly, "Or worse. There're a good deal of ergs in that power pack. It's made to put out for five years. But if it all went into something simultaneously—"

"Keep testing," Wiseman said.

They looked at each other and then at the citadel. The soldiers had by now almost reached it. Suddenly one wall of the citadel flapped down; a gun-muzzle appeared, and the soldiers had been flattened.

"I never saw that before," Pinario murmured.

For a moment, nothing stirred. And then the lab's child-dummy, seated among its toys, said, "I'm tired of that. Do something else."

With a tremor of uneasiness, the two men watched the soldiers pick themselves up and regroup.

Two days later, Wiseman's superior, a heavy-set, short, angry man with popping eyes, appeared in his office. "Listen," Fowler said, "you get those damn toys out of testing. I'll give you until tomorrow." He started back out, but Wiseman stopped him.

"This is too serious," he said. "Come down to the lab and I'll show you."

Arguing all the way, Fowler accompanied him to the lab. "You have no concept of the capital some of these firms have invested in this stuff!" he was saying as they entered. "For every product you've got represented here, there's a ship or a warehouse full on Luna, waiting for official clearance so it can come in!"

Pinario was nowhere in sight. So Wiseman used his key, bypassing the hand-signals that opened up the testing room.

There, surrounded by toys, sat the dummy that the lab men had built. Around it the numerous toys went through their cycles. The racket made Fowler wince.

"This is the item in particular," Wiseman said, bending down by the citadel. A soldier was in the process of squirming on his belly toward it. "As you can see, there are a dozen soldiers. Given that many, and the energy available to them, plus the complex instruction data—"

Fowler interrupted, "I see only eleven."

"One's probably hiding," Wiseman said.

From behind them, a voice said, "No, he's right." Pinario, a rigid expression on his face, appeared. "I've been having a search made. One is gone."

The three men were silent.

"Maybe the citadel destroyed him," Wiseman finally suggested.

Pinario said, "There's a law of matter dealing with that. If it 'destroyed' him—*what did it do with the remains?*"

"Possibly converted him into energy," Fowler said, examining the citadel and the remaining soldiers.

"We did something ingenious," Pinario said, "when we realized that a soldier was gone. We weighed the remaining eleven plus the citadel. Their combined weight is exactly equal to that of the original set—the original dozen soldiers and the citadel. So he's in there somewhere." He pointed at the citadel, which at the moment, was pinpointing the soldiers advancing toward it.

Studying the citadel, Wiseman had a deep intuitive feeling. It had changed. It was, in some manner, different.

"Run your tapes," Wiseman said.

"What?" asked Pinario, and then he flushed. "Of course." Going to the child-dummy, he shut it off, opened it, and removed the drum of video recording tape. Shakily, he carried it to the projector.

They sat watching the recording sequences flash by: one assault after another, until the three of them were bleary-eyed. The soldiers advanced, retreated, were fired on, picked themselves up, advanced again . . .

"Stop the transport," Wiseman said suddenly.

The last sequence was re-run.

A soldier moved steadily toward the base of the citadel. A missile, fired at him, exploded and for a time obscured him. Meanwhile, the other eleven soldiers scurried in a wild attempt to mount the walls. The soldier emerged from the cloud of dust and continued. He reached the wall. A section slid back.

The soldier, blending with the dingy wall of the citadel, used the end of his rifle as a screwdriver to remove his head, then one arm, then both legs. The disassembled pieces were passed into the aperture of the citadel. When only the arm and rifle remained, that, too, crawled into the citadel, worming blindly, and vanished. The aperture slid out of existence.

After a long time, Fowler said in a hoarse voice, "The presumption by the parent would be that the child had lost or destroyed one of the soldiers. Gradually the set would dwindle—with the child getting the blame."

Pinario said, "What do you recommend?"

"Keep it in action," Fowler said, with a nod from Wiseman. "Let it work out its cycle. But don't leave it alone."

"I'll have somebody in the room with it from now on," Pinario agreed.

"Better yet, stay with it yourself," Fowler said.

To himself, Wiseman thought: Maybe we all better stay with it. At least two of us, Pinario and myself.

I wonder what it did with the pieces, he thought.

What did it make?

By the end of the week, the citadel had absorbed four more of the soldiers.

Watching it through a monitor, Wiseman could see in it no visible change. Naturally. The growth would be strictly internal, down out of sight.

On and on the eternal assaults, the soldiers wriggling up, the citadel firing in defense. Meanwhile, he had before him a new series of Ganymedean products. More recent children's toys to be inspected.

"Now what?" he asked himself.

The first was an apparently simple item: a cowboy costume from the ancient American West. At least, so it was described. But he paid only cursory attention to the brochure: the hell with what the Ganymedeans had to say about it.

Opening the box, he laid out the costume. The fabric had a gray, amorphous quality. What a miserably bad job, he thought. It only vaguely resembled a cowboy suit; the lines seemed unformed, hesitant. And the material stretched out of shape as he handled it. He found that he had pulled an entire section of it into a pocket that hung down.

"I don't get it," he said to Pinario. "This won't sell."

"Put it on," Pinario said. "You'll see."

With effort, Wiseman managed to squeeze himself into the suit. "Is it safe?" he asked.

"Yes," Pinario said. "I had it on earlier. This is a more benign idea, but it could be effective. To start it into action, you fantasize."

"Along what lines?"

"Any lines."

The suit made Wiseman think of cowboys, and so he imagined to himself that he was back at the ranch, trudging along the gravel road by the field in which black-faced sheep munched hay with that odd, rapid grinding motion of their lower jaws. He had stopped at the fence—barbed wire and occasional upright posts—and watched the sheep. Then, without warning, the sheep lined up and headed off, in the direction of a shaded hillside beyond his range of vision.

He saw trees, cyprus growing against the skyline. A chicken hawk, far up, flapped its wings in a pumping action . . . as if, he thought, it's filling itself with more air, to rise higher. The hawk glided energetically off, then sailed at a leisurely pace. Wiseman looked for a sign of its prey. Nothing but the dry mid-summer fields munched flat by the sheep. Frequent grasshoppers. And, on the road itself, a toad. The toad had burrowed into the loose dirt; only its top part was visible.

As he bent down, trying to get up enough courage to touch the warty top of the toad's head, a man's voice said nearby him, "How do you like it?"

"Fine," Wiseman said. He took a deep breath of the dry grass smell; he filled his lungs. "Hey, how do you tell a female toad from a male toad? By the spots, or what?"

"Why?" asked the man, standing behind him slightly out of sight.

"I've got a toad here."

"Just for the record," the man said, "can I ask you a couple of questions?"

"Sure," Wiseman said.

"How old are you?"

That was easy. "Ten years and four months," he said, with pride.

"Where exactly are you, at this moment?"

"Out in the country, Mr. Gaylord's ranch, where my dad takes me and my mother every weekend when we can."

"Turn around and look at me," the man said. "And tell me if you know me."

With reluctance, he turned from the half-buried toad to look. He saw an adult with a thin face and a long, somewhat irregular nose. "You're the man who delivers the butane gas," he said. "For the butane company." He glanced around, and sure enough, there was the truck, parked by the butane gate. "My dad says butane is expensive, but there's no other "

The man broke in, "Just for the sake of curiosity, what's the name of the butane company?"

"It's right on the truck," Wiseman said, reading the large painted letters. "Pinario Butane Distributors, Petaluma, California. You're Mr. Pinario."

"Would you be willing to swear that you're ten years old, standing in a field near Petaluma, California?" Mr. Pinario asked.

"Sure." He could see, beyond the field, a range of wooded hills. Now he wanted to investigate them; he was tired of standing around gabbing. "I'll see you," he said, starting off. "I have to go get some hiking done."

He started running, away from Mr. Pinario, down the gravel

road. Grasshoppers leaped away, ahead of him. Gasping, he ran faster and faster.

"Leon!" Mr. Pinario called after him. "You might as well give up! Stop running!"

"I've got business in those hills," Wiseman panted, still jogging along. Suddenly something struck him full force; he sprawled on his hands, tried to get back up. In the dry midday air, something shimmered; he felt fear and pulled away from it. A shape formed, a flat wall . . .

"You won't get to those hills," Mr. Pinario said, from behind him. "Better stay in roughly one place. Otherwise you collide with things."

Wiseman's hands were damp with blood; he had cut himself falling. In bewilderment, he stared down at the blood . . .

Pinario helped him out of the cowboy suit, saying, "It's as unwholesome a toy as you could want. A short period with it on, and the child would be unable to face contemporary reality. Look at you."

Standing with difficulty, Wiseman inspected the suit; Pinario had forcibly taken it from him.

"Not bad," he said in a trembling voice. "It obviously stimulates the withdrawal tendencies already present. I know I've always had a latent retreat fantasy toward my childhood. That particular period, when we lived in the country."

"Notice how you incorporated real elements into it," Pinario said, "to keep the fantasy going as long as possible. If you'd had time, you would have figured a way of incorporating the lab wall into it, possibly as the side of a barn."

Wiseman admitted, "I—already had started to see the old dairy building, where the farmers brought their market milk."

"In time," Pinario said, "it would have been next to impossible to get you out of it."

To himself, Wiseman thought, If it could do that to an adult, just imagine the effect on a child.

"That other thing you have there," Pinario said, "that game, it's a screwball notion. You feel like looking at it now? It can wait."

"I'm okay," Wiseman said. He picked up the third item and began to open it.

"A lot like the old game of Monopoly," Pinario said. "It's called Syndrome."

The game consisted of a board, plus play money, dice, pieces to represent the players. And stock certificates.

"You acquire stock," Pinario said, "same as in all this kind, obviously." He didn't even bother to look at the instructions. "Let's get Fowler down here and play a hand; it takes at least three."

Shortly, they had the Division Director with them. The three men seated themselves at a table, the game of Syndrome in the center.

"Each player starts out equal with the others," Pinario explained, "same as all this type, and during the play, their statuses change according to the worth of the stock they acquire in various economic syndromes."

The syndromes were represented by small, bright plastic objects, much like the archaic hotels and houses of Monopoly.

They threw the dice, moved their counters along the board, bid for and acquired property, paid fines, collected fines, went to the "decontamination chamber" for a period. Meanwhile, behind them, the seven model soldiers crept up on the citadel again and again.

"I'm tired of that," the child-dummy said. "Do something else."

The soldiers regrouped. Once more they started out, getting nearer and nearer the citadel.

Restless and irritable, Wiseman said, "I wonder how long that damn thing has to go on before we find out what it's for."

"No telling." Pinario eyed a purple-and-gold share of stock that Fowler had acquired. "I can use that," he said. "That's a heavy uranium mine stock on Pluto. What do you want for it?"

"Valuable property," Fowler murmured, consulting his other stocks. "I might make a trade, though."

How can I concentrate on a game, Wiseman asked himself, when that thing is getting closer and nearer to—God knows what? To whatever it was built to reach. Its critical mass, he thought.

"Just a second," he said in a slow, careful voice. He put down his hand of stocks. "Could that citadel be a pile?"

"Pile of what?" Fowler asked, concerned with his hand.

Wiseman said loudly, "Forget this game."

"An interesting idea," Pinario said, also putting down his hand. "It's constructing itself into an atomic bomb, piece by piece. Adding until—" He broke off. "No, we thought of that. There're no heavy elements present in it. It's simply a five-year battery, plus a number of small machines controlled by instructions broadcast from the battery itself. You can't make an atomic pile out of that."

"In my opinion," Wiseman said, "we'd be safer getting it out of here." His experience with the cowboy suit had given him a great deal more respect for the Ganymedean artificers. And if the suit was the benign one . . .

Fowler, looking past his shoulder, said, "There are only six soldiers now."

Both Wiseman and Pinario got up instantly. Fowler was right. Only half of the set of soldiers remained. One more had reached the citadel and been incorporated.

"Let's get a bomb expert from the Military Services in here," Wiseman said, "and let him check it. This is out of our department." He turned to his boss, Fowler. "Don't you agree?"

Fowler said, "Let's finish this game first."

"Why?"

"Because we want to be certain about it," Fowler said. But his rapt interest showed that he had gotten emotionally involved and wanted to play to the end of the game. "What will you give me for this share of Pluto stock? I'm open to offers."

He and Pinario negotiated a trade. The game continued for another hour. At last, all three of them could see that Fowler was gaining control of the various stocks. He had five mining syndromes, plus two plastics firms, an algae monopoly, and all seven of the retail trading syndromes. Due to his control of the stock, he had, as a by-product, gotten most of the money.

"I'm out," Pinario said. All he had left were minor shares which controlled nothing. "Anybody want to buy these?"

With his last remaining money, Wiseman bid for the shares. He got them and resumed playing, this time against Fowler alone.

"It's clear that this game is a replica of typical interculture economic ventures," Wiseman said. "The retail trading syndromes are obviously Ganymedean holdings."

A flicker of excitement stirred in him; he had gotten a couple of good throws with the dice and was in a position to add a share to his meager holdings. "Children playing this would acquire a healthy attitude toward economic realities. It would prepare them for the adult world."

But a few minutes later, he landed on an enormous tract of Fowler holdings, and the fine wiped out his resources. He had to give up two shares of stock; the end was in sight.

Pinario, watching the soldiers advance toward the citadel, said, "You know, Leon, I'm inclined to agree with you. This thing may be one terminal of a bomb. A receiving station of some kind. When it's completely wired up, it might bring in a surge of power transmitted from Ganymede."

"Is such a thing possible?" Fowler asked, stacking his play money into the different denominations.

"Who knows what they can do?" Pinario said, wandering around with his hands in his pockets. "Are you almost finished playing?"

"Just about," Wiseman said.

"The reason I say that," Pinario said, "is that now there're only five soldiers. It's speeding up. It took a week for the first one, and only an hour for the seventh. I wouldn't be surprised if the rest go within the next two hours, all five of them."

"We're finished," Fowler said. He had acquired the last share of stock and the last dollar.

Wiseman arose from the table, leaving Fowler. "I'll call Military Services to check the citadel. About this game, though, it's nothing but a steal from our Terran game Monopoly."

"Possibly they don't realize that we have the game already," Fowler said, "under another name."

A stamp of admissibility was placed on the game of Syndrome and the importer was informed. In his office, Wiseman called Military Services and told them what he wanted.

"A bomb expert will be right over," the unhurried voice at the other end of the line said. "Probably you should leave the object alone until he arrives."

Feeling somewhat useless, Wiseman thanked the clerk and hung up. They had failed to dope out the soldiers-and-citadel war game; now it was out of their hands.

The bomb expert was a young man, with close-cropped hair, who smiled friendlily at them as he set down his equipment. He wore ordinary coveralls, with no protective devices.

"My first advice," he said, after he had looked the citadel over, "is to disconnect the leads from the battery. Or, if you want, we can let the cycle finish out, and then disconnect the leads before any reaction takes place. In other words, allow the last mobile elements to enter the citadel. Then, as soon as they're inside, we disconnect the leads and open her up and see what's been taking place."

"Is it safe?" Wiseman asked.

"I think so," the bomb expert said. "I don't detect any sign of radioactivity in it." He seated himself on the floor, by the rear of the citadel, with a pair of cutting pliers in his hand.

Now only three soldiers remained.

"It shouldn't be long," the young man said cheerfully.

Fifteen minutes later, one of the three soldiers crept up to the base of the citadel, removed his head, arm, legs, body, and disappeared piecemeal into the opening provided for him.

"That leaves two," Fowler said.

Ten minutes later, one of the two remaining soldiers followed the one ahead of him.

The four men looked at each other. "This is almost it," Pinario said huskily.

The last remaining soldier wove his way toward the citadel. Guns within the citadel fired at him, but he continued to make progress.

"Statistically speaking," Wiseman said aloud, to break some of the tension, "it should take longer each time, because there are fewer men for it to concentrate on. It should have started out fast, then got more infrequent until finally this last soldier should put in at least a month trying to—"

"Pipe down," the young bomb expert said in a quiet, reasonable voice. "If you don't mind."

The last of the twelve soldiers reached the base of the citadel. Like those before him, he began to disassemble himself.

"Get those pliers ready," Pinario grated.

The parts of the soldier traveled into the citadel. The opening began to close. From within, a humming became audible, a rising pitch of activity.

"Now, for God's sake!" Fowler cried.

The young bomb expert reached down his pliers and cut into the positive lead of the battery. A spark flashed from the pliers and the young bomb expert jumped reflexively; the pliers flew from his hands and skidded across the floor. "Jeez!" he said. "I must have been grounded." Groggily, he groped about for the pliers.

"You were touching the frame of the thing," Pinario said excitedly. He grabbed the pliers himself and crouched down, fumbling for the lead. "Maybe if I wrap a handkerchief around it," he muttered, withdrawing the pliers and fishing in his pocket for a handkerchief. "Anybody got any thing I can wrap around this? I don't want to get knocked flat. No telling how many—"

"Give it to me," Wiseman demanded, snatching the pliers from him. He shoved Pinario aside and closed the jaws of the pliers about the lead.

Fowler said calmly, "Too late."

Wiseman hardly heard his superior's voice; he heard the constant tone within his head, and he put up his hands to his ears, futilely, trying to shut it out. Now it seemed to pass directly from the citadel through his skull, transmitted by the bone. *We stalled around too long,* he thought. *Now it has us.* It won out because there are too many of us; we got to squabbling . . .

Within his mind, a voice said, "Congratulations. By your fortitude, you have been successful."

A vast feeling pervaded him then, a sense of accomplishment.

"The odds against you were tremendous," the voice inside his mind continued. "Anyone else would have failed."

He knew then that everything was all right. They had been wrong.

"What you have done here," the voice declared, "you can continue to do all your life. You can always triumph over adversaries. By patience and persistence, you can win out. The universe isn't such an overwhelming place, after all . . ."

No, he realized with irony, it wasn't.

"They are just ordinary persons," the voice soothed. "So even though you're only one, an individual against many, you have nothing to fear. Give it time—and don't worry."

"I won't," he said aloud.

The humming receded. The voice was gone.

After a long pause, Fowler said, "It's over."

"I don't get it," Pinario said.

"That was what it was supposed to do," Wiseman said. "It's a therapeutic toy. Helps give the child confidence. The disassembling

of the soldiers"—he grinned—"ends the separation between him
and the world. He becomes one with it. And, in doing so, conquers
it."

"Then it's harmless," Fowler said.

"All this work for nothing," Pinario groused. To the bomb expert,
he said, "I'm sorry we got you up here for nothing."

The citadel had now opened its gates wide. Twelve soldiers, once
more intact, issued forth. The cycle was complete; the assault could
begin again.

Suddenly Wiseman said, "I'm not going to release it."

"What?" Pinario said. "Why not?"

"I don't trust it," Wiseman said. "It's too complicated for what it
actually does."

"Explain," Fowler demanded.

"There's nothing to explain," Wiseman said. "Here's this immensely intricate gadget, and all it does is take itself apart and then
reassemble itself. There *must* be more, even if we can't—"

"It's therapeutic," Pinario put in.

Fowler said, "I'll leave it up to you, Leon. If you have doubts,
then don't release it. We can't be too careful."

"Maybe I'm wrong," Wiseman said, "but I keep thinking to myself: *What did they actually build this for?* I feel we still don't
know."

"And the American Cowboy Suit," Pinario added. "You don't
want to release that either."

"Only the game," Wiseman said. "Syndrome, or whatever it's
called." Bending down, he watched the soldiers as they hustled toward the citadel. Bursts of smoke, again . . . activity, feigned attacks, careful withdrawals . . .

"What are you thinking?" Pinario asked, scrutinizing him.

"Maybe it's a diversion," Wiseman said. "To keep our minds involved. So we won't notice something else." That was his intuition,
but he couldn't pin it down. "A red herring," he said. "While something else takes place. That's why it's so complicated. We were *supposed* to suspect it. That's why they built it."

Baffled, he put his foot down in front of a soldier. The soldier
took refuge behind his shoe, hiding from the monitors of the
citadel.

"There must be something right before our eyes," Fowler said,
"that we're not noticing."

"Yes." Wiseman wondered if they would ever find it. "Anyhow," he said, "we're keeping it here, where we can observe it."

Seating himself nearby, he prepared to watch the soldiers. He made himself comfortable for a long, long wait.

At six o'clock that evening, Joe Hauck, the sales manager for Appeley's Children's Store, parked his car before his house, got out, and strode up the stairs.

Under his arm he carried a large flat package, a "sample" that he had appropriated.

"Hey!" his two kids, Bobby and Lora, squealed as he let himself in. "You got something for us, Dad?" They crowded around him, blocking his path. In the kitchen, his wife looked up from the table and put down her magazine.

"A new game I picked up for you," Hauck said. He unwrapped the package, feeling genial. There was no reason why he shouldn't help himself to one of the new games; he had been on the phone for weeks, getting the stuff through Import Standards—and after all was said and done, only one of the three items had been cleared.

As the kids went off with the game, his wife said in a low voice, "More corruption in high places." She had always disapproved of his bringing home items from the store's stock.

"We've got thousands of them," Hauck said. "A warehouse full. Nobody'll notice one missing."

At the dinner table, during the meal, the kids scrupulously studied every word of the instructions that accompanied the game. They were aware of nothing else.

"Don't read at the table," Mrs. Hauck said reprovingly.

Leaning back in his chair, Joe Hauck continued his account of the day. "And after all that time, what did they release? One lousy item. We'll be lucky if we can push enough to make a profit. It was that Shock Troop gimmick that would really have paid off. And that's tied up indefinitely."

He lit a cigarette and relaxed, feeling the peacefulness of his home, the presence of his wife and children.

His daughter said, "Dad, do you want to play? It says the more who play, the better."

"Sure," Joe Hauck said.

While his wife cleared the table, he and his children spread out the board, counters, dice and paper money and shares of stock. Al-

most at once he was deep in the game, totally involved; his childhood memories of game-playing swam back, and he acquired
shares of stock with cunning and originality, until, toward the conclusion of the game, he had cornered most of the syndromes.

He settled back with a sigh of contentment. "That's that," he declared to his children. "Afraid I had a head start. After all, I'm not
new to this type of game." Getting hold of the valuable holdings on
the board filled him with a powerful sense of satisfaction. "Sorry to
have to win, kids."

His daughter said, "You didn't win."

"You lost," his son said.

"*What?*" Joe Hauck exclaimed.

"The person who winds up with the most stock *loses*," Lora said.

She showed him the instructions. "See? The idea is to get rid of
your stocks. Dad, you're out of the game."

"The heck with that," Hauck said, disappointed. "That's no kind
of game." His satisfaction vanished. "That's no fun."

"Now we two have to play out the game," Bobby said, "to see
who finally wins."

As he got up from the board, Joe Hauck grumbled, "I don't get
it. What would anybody see in a game where the winner winds up
with nothing at all?"

Behind him, his two children continued to play. As stock and
money changed hands, the children became more and more animated. When the game entered its final stages, the children were in
a state of ecstatic concentration.

"They don't know Monopoly," Hauck said to himself, "so this
screwball game doesn't seem strange to them."

Anyhow, the important thing was that the kids enjoyed playing
Syndrome; evidently it would sell, and that was what mattered. Already the two youngsters were learning the naturalness of surrendering their holdings. They gave up their stocks and money avidly,
with a kind of trembling abandon.

Glancing up, her eyes bright, Lora said, "It's the best educational
toy you ever brought home, Dad!"

Inverted

In the inverted mystery, the reader sees a crime committed, and then, for the rest of the story, he tries to figure out how the criminal will be caught. First introduced by R. Austin Freeman in 1911, this format has achieved great popularity through the TV show "Columbo." It is a variant of the how-done-it which focuses attention on the solution rather than the commission of a crime. Here, however, the question is not how did the criminal do what he did, but how did the detective catch up with him. It is also, in a sense, a warning that crime does not pay, for in this type of story, no matter how clever the criminal is, he invariably commits an error that leads to his undoing.

Unfortunately, science fiction writers do not often turn out inverted stories. There is, however, Alfred Bester's great novel, *The Demolished Man*, 1953, and a handful of excellent short stories such as the following adventure by the amazing Dr. Wendell Urth.

The Singing Bell

ISAAC ASIMOV

Louis Peyton never discussed publicly the methods by which he had bested the police of Earth in a dozen duels of wits and bluff, with the psychoprobe always waiting and always foiled. He would have been foolish to do so, of course, but in his more complacent moments, he fondled the notion of leaving a testament to be opened only after his death, one in which his unbroken success could clearly be seen to be due to ability and not to luck.

In such a testament he would say, "No false pattern can be created to cover a crime without bearing upon it some trace of its creator. It is better, then, to seek in events some pattern that already exists and then adjust your actions to it."

It was with that principle in mind that Peyton planned the murder of Albert Cornwell.

Cornwell, that small-time retailer of stolen things, first approached Peyton at the latter's usual table-for-one at Grinnell's. Cornwell's blue suit seemed to have a special shine, his lined face a special grin, and his faded mustache a special bristle.

"Mr. Peyton," he said, greeting his future murderer with no fourth-dimensional qualm, "it is so nice to see you. I'd almost given up, sir, almost given up."

Peyton, who disliked being approached over his newspaper and dessert at Grinnell's, said, "If you have business with me, Cornwell, you know where you can reach me." Peyton was past forty and his hair was past its earlier blackness, but his back was rigid, his bearing youthful, his eyes dark, and his voice could cut the more sharply for long practice.

"Not for this, Mr. Peyton," said Cornwell, "not for this. I know of a cache, sir, a cache of . . . you know, sir." The forefinger of his right hand moved gently, as though it were a clapper striking invisible substance, and his left hand momentarily cupped his ear.

Peyton turned a page of the paper, still somewhat damp from its tele-dispenser, folded it flat and said, "Singing Bells?"

"Oh, hush, Mr. Peyton," said Cornwell in whispered agony.

Peyton said, "Come with me."

They walked through the park. It was another Peyton axiom that to be reasonably secret there was nothing like a low-voiced discussion out of doors.

Cornwell whispered, "A cache of Singing Bells; an accumulated cache of Singing Bells. Unpolished, but such beauties, Mr. Peyton."

"Have you seen them?"

"No, sir, but I have spoken with one who has. He had proofs enough to convince me. There is enough there to enable you and me to retire in affluence. In absolute affluence, sir."

"Who was this other man?"

A look of cunning lit Cornwell's face like a smoking torch, obscuring more than it showed and lending it a repulsive oiliness. "The man was a lunar grubstaker who had a method for locating the Bells in the crater sides. I don't know his method; he never told me that. But he has gathered dozens, hidden them on the Moon, and come to Earth to arrange the disposing of them."

"He died, I suppose?"

"Yes. A most shocking accident, Mr. Peyton. A fall from a height. Very sad. Of course, his activities on the Moon were quite illegal. The Dominion is very strict about unauthorized Bell-mining. So perhaps it was a judgment upon him after all. . . . In any case, I have his map."

Peyton said, a look of calm indifference on his face, "I don't want any of the details of your little transaction. What I want to know is why you've come to me."

Cornwell said, "Well, now, there's enough for both of us, Mr. Peyton, and we can both do our bit. For my part, I know where the cache is located and I can get a spaceship. You . . ."

"Yes?"

"You can pilot a spaceship, and you have such excellent contacts for disposing of the Bells. It is a very fair division of labor, Mr. Peyton. Wouldn't you say so, now?"

Peyton considered the pattern of his life—the pattern that already existed—and matters seemed to fit.

He said, "We will leave for the Moon on August the tenth."

Cornwell stopped walking and said, "Mr. Peyton! It's only April now."

Peyton maintained an even gait and Cornwell had to hurry to catch up. "Do you hear me, Mr. Peyton?"

Peyton said, "August the tenth. I will get in touch with you at the proper time, tell you where to bring your ship. Make no attempt to see me personally till then. Good-bye, Cornwell."

Cornwell said, "Fifty-fifty?"

"Quite," said Peyton. "Good-bye."

Peyton continued his walk alone and considered the pattern of his life again. At the age of twenty-seven, he had bought a tract of land in the Rockies on which some past owner had built a house designed as refuge against the threatened atomic wars of two centuries back, the ones that had never come to pass after all. The house remained, however, a monument to a frightened drive for self-sufficiency.

It was of steel and concrete in as isolated a spot as could well be found on Earth, set high above sea level and protected on nearly all sides by mountain peaks that reached higher still. It had its self-contained power unit, its water supply fed by mountain streams, its freezers in which ten sides of beef could hang comfortably, its cellar outfitted like a fortress with an arsenal of weapons designed to stave off hungry, panicked hordes that never came. It had its air-conditioning unit that could scrub and scrub the air until anything *but* radioactivity (alas for human frailty) could be scrubbed out of it.

In that house of survival, Peyton passed the month of August every subsequent year of his perennially bachelor life. He took out the communicators, the television, the newspaper tele-dispenser. He built a force-field fence about his property and left a short-distance signal mechanism to the house from the point where the fence crossed the one trail winding through the mountains.

For one month each year, he could be thoroughly alone. No one saw him, no one could reach him. In absolute solitude, he could have the only vacation he valued after eleven months of contact with a humanity for which he could feel only a cold contempt.

Even the police—and Peyton smiled—knew of his rigid regard for August. He had once jumped bail and risked the psychoprobe rather than forego his August.

Peyton considered another aphorism for possible inclusion in his testament: There is nothing so conducive to an appearance of innocence as the triumphant lack of an alibi.

On July 30, as on July 30 of every year, Louis Peyton took the 9:15 A.M. non-grav stratojet at New York and arrived in Denver at 12:30 P.M. There he lunched and took the 1:45 P.M. semi-grav bus to Hump's Point, from which Sam Leibman took him by ancient ground-car—full grav!—up the trail to the boundaries of his property. Sam Leibman gravely accepted the ten-dollar tip that he always received, touched his hat as he had done on July 30 for fifteen years.

On July 31, as on July 31 of every year, Louis Peyton returned to Hump's Point in his non-grav aeroflitter and placed an order through the Hump's Point general store for such supplies as he needed for the coming month. There was nothing unusual about the order. It was virtually the duplicate of previous such orders.

MacIntyre, manager of the store, checked gravely over the list, put it through to Central Warehouse, Mountain District, in Denver, and the whole of it came pushing over the mass-transference beam within the hour. Peyton loaded the supplies onto his aeroflitter with MacIntyre's help, left his usual ten-dollar tip and returned to his house.

On August 1, at 12:01 A.M., the force field that surrounded his property was set to full power and Peyton was isolated.

And now the pattern changed. Deliberately he had left himself eight days. In that time he slowly and meticulously destroyed just enough of his supplies to account for all of August. He used the dusting chambers which served the house as a garbage-disposal unit. They were of an advanced model capable of reducing all matter up to and including metals and silicates to an impalpable and undetectable molecular dust. The excess energy formed in the process was carried away by the mountain stream that ran through his property. It ran five degrees warmer than normal for a week.

On August 9 his aeroflitter carried him to a spot in Wyoming where Albert Cornwell and a spaceship waited. The spaceship, itself, was a weak point, of course, since there were men who had sold it, men who had transported it and helped prepare it for flight. All those men, however, led only as far as Cornwell, and Cornwell, Peyton thought—with the trace of a smile on his cold lips—would be a dead end. A very dead end.

On August 10 the spaceship, with Peyton at the controls and Cornwell—and his map—as passenger, left the surface of Earth. Its non-grav field was excellent. At full power, the ship's weight was reduced to less than an ounce. The micropiles fed energy efficiently and noiselessly, and without flame or sound the ship rose through the atmosphere, shrank to a point, and was gone.

It was very unlikely that there would be witnesses to the flight, or that in these weak, piping times of peace there would be a radar watch as in days of yore. In point of fact, there was none.

Two days in space; now two weeks on the Moon. Almost instinctively Peyton had allowed for those two weeks from the first. He was under no illusions as to the value of homemade maps by non-cartographers. Useful they might be to the designer himself, who had the help of memory. To a stranger, they could be nothing more than a cryptogram.

Cornwell showed Peyton the map for the first time only after takeoff. He smiled obsequiously. "After all, sir, this was my only trump."

"Have you checked this against the lunar charts?"

"I would scarcely know how, Mr. Peyton. I depend upon you."

Peyton stared at him coldly as he returned the map. The one certain thing upon it was Tycho Crater, the site of the buried Luna City.

In one respect, at least, astronomy was on their side. Tycho was on the daylight side of the Moon at the moment. It meant that patrol ships were less likely to be out, they themselves less likely to be observed.

Peyton brought the ship down in a riskily quick non-grav landing within the safe, cold darkness of the inner shadow of a crater. The sun was past zenith and the shadow would grow no shorter.

Cornwell drew a long face. "Dear, dear, Mr. Peyton. We can scarcely go prospecting in the lunar day."

"The lunar day doesn't last forever," said Peyton shortly. "There are about a hundred hours of sun left. We can use that time for acclimating ourselves and for working out the map."

The answer came quickly, but it was plural. Peyton studied the lunar charts over and over, taking meticulous measurements, and trying to find the pattern of craters shown on the homemade scrawl that was the key to—what?

Finally Peyton said, "The crater we want could be any one of three: GC-3, GC-5, or MT-10."

"What do we do, Mr. Peyton?" asked Cornwell anxiously.

"We try them all," said Peyton, "beginning with the nearest."

The terminator passed and they were in the night shadow. After that, they spent increasing periods on the lunar surface, getting used to the eternal silence and blackness, the harsh points of the stars and the crack of light that was the Earth peeping over the rim of the crater above. They left hollow, featureless footprints in the dry dust that did not stir or change. Peyton noted them first when they climbed out of the crater into the full light of the gibbous Earth. That was on the eighth day after their arrival on the Moon.

The lunar cold put a limit to how long they could remain outside their ship at any one time. Each day, however, they managed for longer. By the eleventh day after arrival they had eliminated GC-5 as the container of the Singing Bells.

By the fifteenth day, Peyton's cold spirit had grown warm with desperation. It would have to be GC-3. MT-10 was too far away. They would not have time to reach it and explore it and still allow for a return to Earth by August 31.

On that same fifteenth day, however, despair was laid to rest forever when they discovered the Bells.

They were not beautiful. They were merely irregular masses of gray rock, as large as a double fist, vacuum-filled and feather-light in the moon's gravity. There were two dozen of them and each one, after proper polishing, could be sold for a hundred thousand dollars at least.

Carefully, in double handfuls, they carried the Bells to the ship, bedded them in excelsior, and returned for more. Three times they made the trip both ways over ground that would have worn them out on Earth but which, under the Moon's lilliputian gravity, was scarcely a barrier.

Cornwell passed the last of the Bells up to Peyton, who placed them carefully within the outer lock.

"Keep them clear, Mr. Peyton," he said, his radioed voice sounding harshly in the other's ear. "I'm coming up."

He crouched for the slow high leap against lunar gravity, looked up, and froze in panic. His face, clearly visible through the hard carved lusilite of his helmet, froze in a last grimace of terror. "No, Mr. Peyton. Don't—"

Peyton's fist tightened on the grip of the blaster he held. It fired. There was an unbearably brilliant flash and Cornwell was a dead fragment of a man, sprawled amid remnants of a spacesuit and flecked with freezing blood.

Peyton paused to stare somberly at the dead man, but only for a second. Then he transferred the last of the Bells to their prepared containers, removed his suit, activated first the non-grav field, then the micropiles, and, potentially a million or two richer than he had been two weeks earlier, set off on the return trip to Earth.

On the twenty-ninth of August, Peyton's ship descended silently, stern bottomward, to the spot in Wyoming from which it had taken off on August 10. The care with which Peyton had chosen the spot was not wasted. His aeroflitter was still there, drawn within the protection of an enclosing wrinkle of the rocky, tortuous countryside.

He moved the Singing Bells once again, in their containers, into the deepest recess of the wrinkle, covering them, loosely and sparsely, with earth. He returned to the ship once more to set the controls and make last adjustments. He climbed out again and two minutes later the ship's automatics took over.

Silently hurrying, the ship bounded upward and up, veering to westward somewhat as the Earth rotated beneath it. Peyton watched, shading his narrow eyes, and at the extreme edge of vision there was a tiny gleam of light and a dot of cloud against the blue sky.

Peyton's mouth twitched into a smile. He had judged well. With the cadmium safety-rods bent back into uselessness, the micropiles had plunged past the unit-sustaining safety level and the ship had vanished in the heat of the nuclear explosion that had followed.

Twenty minutes later, he was back on his property. He was tired and his muscles ached under Earth's gravity. He slept well.

Twelve hours later, in the earliest dawn, the police came.

The man who opened the door placed his crossed hands over his paunch and ducked his smiling head two or three times in greeting. The man who entered, H. Seton Davenport of the Terrestrial Bureau of Investigation, looked about uncomfortably.

The room he had entered was large and in semidarkness except for the brilliant viewing lamp focused over a combination armchair-desk. Rows of book-films covered the walls. A suspension of

Galactic charts occupied one corner of the room and a Galactic Lens gleamed softly on a stand in another corner.

"You are Dr. Wendell Urth?" asked Davenport, in a tone that suggested he found it hard to believe. Davenport was a stocky man with black hair, a thin and prominent nose, and a star-shaped scar on one cheek which marked permanently the place where a neuronic whip had once struck him at too close a range.

"I am," said Dr. Urth in a thin, tenor voice. "And you are Inspector Davenport."

The Inspector presented his credentials and said, "The University recommended you to me as an extraterrologist."

"So you said when you called me half an hour ago," said Urth agreeably. His features were thick, his nose was a snubby button, and over his somewhat protuberant eyes there were thick glasses.

"I shall get to the point, Dr. Urth. I presume you have visited the Moon . . ."

Dr. Urth, who had brought out a bottle of ruddy liquid and two glasses, just a little the worse for dust, from behind a straggling pile of book-films, said with sudden brusqueness, "I have never visited the Moon, Inspector. I never intend to! Space travel is foolishness. I don't believe in it." Then, in softer tones, "Sit down, sir, sit down. Have a drink."

Inspector Davenport did as he was told and said, "But you're an . . ."

"Extraterrologist. Yes. I'm interested in other worlds, but it doesn't mean I have to go there. Good lord, I don't have to be a time traveler to qualify as a historian, do I?" He sat down, and a broad smile impressed itself upon his round face once more as he said, "Now tell me what's on your mind."

"I have come," said the Inspector, frowning, "to consult you in a case of murder."

"Murder? What have I to do with murder?"

"This murder, Dr. Urth, was on the Moon."

"Astonishing."

"It's more than astonishing. It's unprecedented, Dr. Urth. In the fifty years since the Lunar Dominion has been established, ships have blown up and spacesuits have sprung leaks. Men have boiled to death on sun-side, frozen on dark-side, and suffocated on both sides. There have even been deaths by falls, which, considering lunar gravity, is quite a trick. But in all that time, not one man has been killed on the Moon as the result of another man's deliberate act of violence—till now."

Dr. Urth said, "How was it done?"

"A blaster. The authorities were on the scene within the hour through a fortunate set of circumstances. A patrol ship observed a flash of light against the Moon's surface. You know how far a flash can be seen against the night-side. The pilot notified Luna City and landed. In the process of circling back, he swears that he just managed to see by Earthlight what looked like a ship taking off. Upon landing, he discovered a blasted corpse and footprints."

"The flash of light," said Dr. Urth, "you suppose to be the firing blaster."

"That's certain. The corpse was fresh. Interior portions of the body had not yet frozen. The footprints belonged to two people. Careful measurements showed that the depressions fell into two groups of somewhat different diameters, indicating differently sized spaceboots. In the main, they led to craters GC-3 and GC-5, a pair of—"

"I am acquainted with the official code for naming lunar craters," said Dr. Urth pleasantly.

"Umm. In any case, GC-3 contained footprints that led to a rift in the crater wall, within which scraps of hardened pumice were found. X-ray diffraction patterns showed—"

"Singing Bells," put in the extraterrologist in great excitement. "Don't tell me this murder of yours involves Singing Bells!"

"What if it does?" demanded Davenport blankly.

"I have one. A University expedition uncovered it and presented it to me in return for— Come, Inspector, I must show it to you."

Dr. Urth jumped up and pattered across the room, beckoning the other to follow as he did. Davenport, annoyed, followed.

They entered a second room, larger than the first, dimmer, considerably more cluttered. Davenport stared with astonishment at the heterogeneous mass of material that was jumbled together in no pretense at order.

He made out a small lump of "blue glaze" from Mars, the sort of thing some romantics considered to be an artifact of long-extinct Martians, a small meteorite, a model of an early spaceship, a sealed bottle of nothing scrawlingly labeled "Venusian atmosphere."

Dr. Urth said happily, "I've made a museum of my whole house. It's one of the advantages of being a bachelor. Of course, I haven't quite got things organized. Someday, when I have a spare week or so . . ."

For a moment he looked about, puzzled; then, remembering, he pushed aside a chart showing the evolutionary scheme of development of the marine invertebrates that were the highest life forms on Barnard's Planet and said, "Here it is. It's flawed, I'm afraid."

The Bell hung suspended from a slender wire, soldered delicately onto it. That it was flawed was obvious. It had a constriction line running halfway about it that made it seem like two small globes, firmly but imperfectly squashed together. Despite that, it had been lovingly polished to a dull luster, softly gray, velvety smooth, and faintly pock-marked in a way that laboratories, in their futile efforts to prepare synthetic Bells, had found impossible to duplicate.

Dr. Urth said, "I experimented a good deal before I found a decent stroker. A flawed Bell is temperamental. But bone works. I have one here"—and he held up something that looked like a short thick spoon made of a gray-white substance—"which I had made out of the femur of an ox. Listen."

With surprising delicacy, his pudgy fingers maneuvered the Bell, feeling for one best spot. He adjusted it, steadying it daintily. Then, letting the Bell swing free, he brought down the thick end of the bone spoon and stroked the Bell softly.

It was as though a million harps had sounded a mile away. It swelled and faded and returned. It came from no particular direction. It sounded inside the head, incredibly sweet and pathetic and tremulous all at once.

It died away lingeringly and both men were silent for a full minute.

Dr. Urth said, "Not bad, eh?" and with a flick of his hand set the Bell to swinging on its wire.

Davenport stirred restlessly. "Careful! Don't break it." The fragility of a good Singing Bell was proverbial.

Dr. Urth said, "Geologists say the Bells are only pressure-hardened pumice, enclosing a vacuum in which small beads of rock rattle freely. That's what they *say*. But if that's all it is, why can't we reproduce one? Now a flawless Bell would make this one sound like a child's harmonica."

"Exactly," said Davenport, "and there aren't a dozen people on Earth who own a flawless one, and there are a hundred people and institutions who would buy one at any price, no questions asked. A supply of Bells would be worth murder."

The extraterrologist turned to Davenport and pushed his spectacles back on his inconsequential nose with a stubby forefinger. "I haven't forgotten your murder case. Please go on."

"That can be done in a sentence. I know the identity of the murderer."

They had returned to the chairs in the library and Dr. Urth clasped his hands over his ample abdomen. "Indeed? Then surely you have no problem, Inspector."

"Knowing and proving are not the same, Dr. Urth. Unfortunately he has no alibi."

"You mean, unfortunately he *has*, don't you?"

"I mean what I say. If he had an alibi, I could crack it somehow, because it would be a false one. If there were witnesses who claimed they had seen him on Earth at the time of the murder, their stories could be broken down. If he had documentary proof, it could be exposed as a forgery or some sort of trickery. Unfortunately he has none of it."

"What does he have?"

Carefully Inspector Davenport described the Peyton estate in Colorado. He concluded, "He has spent every August there in the strictest isolation. Even the T.B.I. would have to testify to that. Any jury would have to presume that he was on his estate this August as well, unless we could present definite proof that he was on the Moon."

"What makes you think he *was* on the Moon? Perhaps he is innocent."

"No!" Davenport was almost violent. "For fifteen years I've been trying to collect sufficient evidence against him and I've never succeeded. But I can *smell* a Peyton crime now. I tell you that no one but Peyton, no one on Earth, would have the impudence or, for that matter, the practical business contacts to attempt disposal of smuggled Singing Bells. He is known to be an expert space pilot. He is known to have had contact with the murdered man, though admittedly not for some months. Unfortunately none of that is proof."

Dr. Urth said, "Wouldn't it be simple to use the psychoprobe, now that its use has been legalized?"

Davenport scowled, and the scar on his cheek turned livid. "Have you read the Konski-Hiakawa law, Dr. Urth?"

"No."

"I think no one has. The right to mental privacy, the government says, is fundamental. All right, but what follows? The man who is psychoprobed and proves innocent of the crime for which he was psychoprobed is entitled to as much compensation as he can persuade the courts to give him. In a recent case a bank cashier was awarded twenty-five thousand dollars for having been psychoprobed on inaccurate suspicion of theft. It seems that the circumstantial evidence which seemed to point to theft actually pointed to a small spot of adultery. His claim that he lost his job, was threatened by the husband in question and put in bodily fear, and finally was held up to ridicule and contumely because a news-strip man had learned the results of the probe held good in court."

"I can see the man's point."

"So can we all. That's the trouble. One more item to remember: Any man who has been psychoprobed once for any reason can never be psychoprobed again for any reason. No one man, the law says, shall be placed in mental jeopardy twice in his lifetime."

"Inconvenient."

"Exactly. In the two years since the psychoprobe has been legitimized, I couldn't count the number of crooks and chiselers who've tried to get themselves psychoprobed for purse-snatching so that they could play the rackets safely afterward. So you see the Department will not allow Peyton to be psychoprobed until they have firm evidence of his guilt. Not legal evidence, maybe, but evidence that is strong enough to convince my boss. The worst of it, Dr. Urth, is that if we come into court without a psychoprobe record, we can't win. In a case as serious as murder, not to have used the psychoprobe is proof enough to the dumbest juror that the prosecution isn't sure of its ground."

"Now what do you want of me?"

"Proof that he was on the Moon sometime in August. It's got to be done quickly. I can't hold him on suspicion much longer. And if news of the murder gets out, the world press will blow up like an asteroid striking Jupiter's atmosphere. A glamorous crime, you know—first murder on the Moon."

"Exactly when was the murder committed?" asked Urth, in a sudden transition to brisk cross-examination.

"August twenty-seventh."

"And the arrest was made when?"

"Yesterday, August thirtieth."

"Then if Peyton were the murderer, he would have had time to return to Earth."

"Barely. Just barely." Davenport's lips thinned. "If I had been a day sooner— If I had found his place empty—"

"And how long do you suppose the two, the murdered man and the murderer, were on the Moon altogether?"

"Judging by the ground covered by the footprints, a number of days. A week, at the minimum."

"Has the ship they used been located?"

"No, and it probably never will. About ten hours ago, the University of Denver reported a rise in background radioactivity beginning day before yesterday at 6 P.M. and persisting for a number of hours. It's an easy thing, Dr. Urth, to set a ship's controls so as to allow it to blast off without crew and blow up, fifty miles high, in a micropile short."

"If I had been Peyton," said Dr. Urth thoughtfully, "I would have killed the man on board ship and blown up corpse and ship together."

"You don't know Peyton," said Davenport grimly. "He enjoys his victories over the law. He values them. Leaving the corpse on the Moon is his challenge to us."

"I see." Dr. Urth patted his stomach with a rotary motion and said, "Well, there is a chance."

"That you'll be able to prove he was on the Moon?"

"That I'll be able to give you my opinion."

"Now?"

"The sooner the better. If, of course, I get a chance to interview Mr. Peyton."

"That can be arranged. I have a non-grav jet waiting. We can be in Washington in twenty minutes."

But a look of the deepest alarm passed over the plump extra-terrologist's face. He rose to his feet and pattered away from the T.B.I. agent toward the duskiest corner of the cluttered room.

"*No!*"

"What's wrong, Dr. Urth?"

"I won't use a non-grav jet. I don't believe in them."

Davenport stared confusedly at Dr. Urth. He stammered, "Would you prefer a monorail?"

Dr. Urth snapped, "I mistrust all forms of transportation. I don't believe in them. Except walking. I don't mind walking." He was suddenly eager. "Couldn't you bring Mr. Peyton to this city, somewhere within walking distance? To City Hall, perhaps? I've often walked to City Hall."

Davenport looked helplessly about the room. He looked at the myriad volumes of lore about the light-years. He could see through the open door into the room beyond, with its tokens of the worlds beyond the sky. And he looked at Dr. Urth, pale at the thought of non-grav jet, and shrugged his shoulders.

"I'll bring Peyton here. Right to this room. Will that satisfy you?"

Dr. Urth puffed out his breath in a deep sigh. "Quite."

"I hope you can deliver, Dr. Urth."

"I will do my best, Mr. Davenport."

Louis Peyton stared with distaste at his surroundings and with contempt at the fat man who bobbed his head in greeting. He glanced at the seat offered him and brushed it with his hand before sitting down. Davenport took a seat next to him, with his blaster holster in clear view.

The fat man was smiling as he sat down and patted his round abdomen as though he had just finished a good meal and were intent on letting the world know about it.

He said, "Good evening, Mr. Peyton. I am Dr. Wendell Urth, extraterrologist."

Peyton looked at him again, "And what do you want with me?"

"I want to know if you were on the Moon at any time in the month of August."

"I was not."

"Yet no man saw you on Earth between the days of August first and August thirtieth."

"I lived my normal life in August. I am never seen during that month. Let him tell you." And he jerked his head in the direction of Davenport.

Dr. Urth chuckled. "How nice if we could test this matter. If there were only some physical manner in which we could differentiate Moon from Earth. If, for instance, we could analyze the dust in your hair and say, 'Aha, Moon rock.' Unfortunately we can't.

Moon rock is much the same as Earth rock. Even if it weren't, there wouldn't be any in your hair unless you stepped onto the lunar surface without a spacesuit, which is unlikely."

Peyton remained impassive.

Dr. Urth went on, smiling benevolently, and lifting a hand to steady the glasses perched precariously on the bulb of his nose. "A man traveling in space or on the Moon breathes Earth air, eats Earth food. He carries Earth environment next to his skin whether he's in his ship or in his spacesuit. We are looking for a man who spent two days in space going to the Moon, at least a week on the Moon, and two days coming back from the Moon. In all that time he carried Earth next to his skin, which makes it difficult."

"I'd suggest," said Peyton, "that you can make it less difficult by releasing me and looking for the real murderer."

"It may come to that," said Dr. Urth. "Have you ever seen anything like this?" His hand pushed its pudgy way to the ground beside his chair and came up with a gray sphere that sent back subdued highlights.

Peyton smiled. "It looks like a Singing Bell to me."

"It *is* a Singing Bell. The murder was committed for the sake of Singing Bells. What do you think of this one?"

"I think it is badly flawed."

"Ah, but inspect it," said Dr. Urth, and with a quick motion of his hand, he tossed it through six feet of air to Peyton.

Davenport cried out and half-rose from his chair. Peyton brought up his arms with an effort, but so quickly that he managed to catch the Bell.

Peyton said, "You damned fool. Don't throw it around that way."

"You respect Singing Bells, do you?"

"Too much to break one. That's no crime, at least." Peyton stroked the Bell gently, then lifted it to his ear and shook it slowly, listening to the soft clicks of the Lunoliths, those small pumice particles, as they rattled in vacuum.

Then, holding the Bell up by the length of steel wire still attached to it, he ran a thumbnail over its surface with an expert, curving motion. It twanged! The note was very mellow, very flute-like, holding with a slight *vibrato* that faded lingeringly and conjured up pictures of a summer twilight.

For a short moment, all three men were lost in the sound.

And then Dr. Urth said, "Throw it back, Mr. Peyton. Toss it here!" and held out his hand in peremptory gesture.

Automatically Louis Peyton tossed the Bell. It traveled its short arc one-third of the way to Dr. Urth's waiting hand, curved downward and shattered with a heartbroken, sighing discord on the floor.

Davenport and Peyton stared at the gray slivers with equal wordlessness and Dr. Urth's calm voice went almost unheard as he said, "When the criminal's cache of crude Bells is located, I'll ask that a flawless one, properly polished, be given to me, as replacement and fee."

"A fee? For what?" demanded Davenport irritably.

"Surely the matter is now obvious. Despite my little speech of a moment ago, there is one piece of Earth's environment that no space traveler carries with him and that is *Earth's surface gravity*. The fact that Mr. Peyton could so egregiously misjudge the toss of an object he obviously valued so highly could mean only that his muscles are not yet readjusted to the pull of Earthly gravity. It is my professional opinion, Mr. Davenport, that your prisoner has, in the last few days, been away from Earth. He has either been in space or on some planetary object considerably smaller in size than the Earth—as, for example, the Moon."

Davenport rose triumphantly to his feet. "Let me have your opinion in writing," he said, hand on blaster, "and that will be good enough to get me permission to use a psychoprobe."

Louis Peyton, dazed and unresisting, had only the numb realization that any testament he could now leave would have to include the fact of ultimate failure.

Locked Room

The locked room story is a most intellectual type of mystery. A subcategory of the how-done-it, it challenges the reader to figure out how a crime could take place in an apparently sealed enclosure. First presented as fiction by Edgar Allan Poe in "The Murders in the Rue Morgue" (1841), it has constituted the majority of John Dickson Carr's enormous output.

In science fiction, of course, it is possible to offer solutions that are grossly unfair, such as invisibility, dematerialization, and time travel. However, as the following tale by the masterful Larry Niven indicates, it is also quite possible to establish legitimate puzzles. Even when, as in this case, the protagonist sports an invisible telekinetic arm. Indeed, the field is full of problem stories that require the reader to deduce foreseeable methods of escaping from unpleasant situations.

ARM

LARRY NIVEN

The ARM building had been abnormally quiet for some months now.

We'd needed the rest—at first. But these last few mornings the silence had had an edgy quality. We waved at each other on our paths to our respective desks, but our heads were elsewhere. Some of us had a restless look. Others were visibly, determinedly busy.

Nobody wanted to join a mother hunt.

This past year we'd managed to cut deep into the organlegging activities in the West Coast area. Pats on the back all around, but the results were predictable: other activities were going to increase. Sooner or later the newstapers would start screaming about stricter enforcement of the Fertility Laws, and then we'd all be out hunting down illegitimate parents . . . all of us who were not involved in something else.

It was high time I got involved in something else.

This morning I walked to my office through the usual edgy silence. I ran coffee from the spigot, carried it to my desk, punched for messages at the computer terminal. A slender file slid from the slot. A hopeful sign. I picked it up—one-handed, so that I could sip coffee as I went through it—and let it fall open in the middle.

Color holographs jumped out at me. I was looking down through a pair of windows over two morgue tables.

Stomach to brain: LURCH! What a hell of an hour to be looking at people with their faces burnt off! Get eyes to look somewhere else, and don't try to swallow that coffee. Why don't you change jobs?

They were hideous. Two of them, a man and a woman. Something had burnt their faces away down to the skulls and beyond: bones and teeth charred, brain tissue cooked.

I swallowed and kept looking. I'd seen the dead before. These had just hit me at the wrong time.

Not a laser weapon, I thought . . . though that was chancy. There are thousands of jobs for lasers, and thousands of varieties to do the jobs. Not a hand laser, anyway. The pencil-thin beam of a hand laser would have chewed channels in the flesh. This had been a wide, steady beam of some kind.

I flipped back to the beginning and skimmed.

Details: They'd been found on the Wilshire slidewalk in West Los Angeles around 4:30 A.M. People don't use the slidewalks that late. They're afraid of organleggers. The bodies could have traveled up to a couple of miles before anyone saw them.

Preliminary autopsy: They'd been dead three or four days. No signs of drugs or poisons or puncture marks. Apparently the burns had been the only cause of death.

It must have been quick, then: a single flash of energy. Otherwise they'd have tried to dodge, and there'd be burns elsewhere. There were none. Just the faces, and char marks around the collars.

There was a memo from Bates, the coroner. From the looks of them, they might have been killed by some new weapon. So he'd sent the file over to us. Could we find anything in the ARM files that would fire a blast of heat or light a foot across?

I sat back and stared into the holos and thought about it.

A light weapon with a beam a foot across? They make lasers in that size, but as war weapons, used from orbit. One of those would have vaporized the heads, not charred them.

There were other possibilities. Death by torture, with the heads held in clamps in the blast from a commercial attitude jet. Or some kind of weird industrial accident: a flash explosion that had caught them both looking over a desk or something. Or even a laser beam reflected from a convex mirror.

Forget about its being an accident. The way the bodies were abandoned reeked of guilt, of something to be covered up. Maybe Bates was right. A new, illegal weapon.

And I could be deeply involved in searching for it when the mother hunt started.

The ARM has three basic functions. We hunt organleggers. We monitor world technology: new developments that might create new weapons, or that might affect the world economy or the balance of power among nations. And we enforce the Fertility Laws.

Come, let us be honest with ourselves. Of the three, protecting the Fertility Laws is probably the most important.

Organleggers don't aggravate the population problem.

Monitoring of technology is necessary enough, but it may have happened too late. There are enough fusion power plants and fusion rocket motors and fusion crematoria and fusion seawater distilleries around to let any madman or group thereof blow up the Earth or any selected part of it.

But if a lot of people in one region started having illegal babies, the rest of the world would scream. Some nations might even get mad enough to abandon population control. Then what? We've got eighteen billion on Earth now. We couldn't handle more.

So the mother hunts are necessary. But I hate them. It's no fun hunting down some poor sick woman so desperate to have children that she'll go through hell to avoid her six-month contraceptive shots. I'll get out of it if I can.

I did some obvious things. I sent a note to Bates at the coroner's office. *Send all further details on the autopsies, and let me know if the corpses are identified.* Retinal prints and brain-wave patterns were obviously out, but they might get something on gene patterns and fingerprints.

I spent some time wondering where two bodies had been kept for three to four days, and why, before being abandoned in a way that could have been used three days earlier. But that was a problem for the LAPD detectives. Our concern was with the weapon.

So I started writing a search pattern for the computer: find me a widget that will fire a beam of a given description. From the pattern of penetration into skin and bone and brain tissue, there was probably a way to express the frequency of the light as a function of the duration of the blast, but I didn't fool with that. I'd pay for my laziness later, when the computer handed me a foot-thick list of light-emitting machinery and I had to wade through it.

I had punched in the instructions, and was relaxing with more coffee and a cigarette, when Ordaz called.

Detective-Inspector Julio Ordaz was a slender, dark-skinned man with straight black hair and soft black eyes. The first time I saw him in a phone screen, he had been telling me of a good friend's murder. Two years later I still flinched when I saw him.

"Hello, Julio. Business or pleasure?"

"Business, Gil. It is to be regretted."

"Yours or mine?"

"Both. There is murder involved, but there is also a machine . . .
Look, can you see it behind me?" Ordaz stepped out of the field of
view, then reached invisibly to turn the phone camera.

I looked into somebody's living room. There was a wide circle of
discoloration in the green indoor grass rug. In the center of the circle, a machine and a man's body.

Was Julio putting me on? The body was old, half mummified.
The machine was big and cryptic in shape, and it glowed with a
subdued, eery blue light.

Ordaz sounded serious enough. "Have you ever seen anything
like this?"

"No. That's some machine." Unmistakably an experimental device: no neat plastic case, no compactness, no assembly-line weld-
ing. Too complex to examine through a phone camera, I decided.
"Yah, that looks like something for us. Can you send it over?"

Ordaz came back on. He was smiling, barely. "I'm afraid we cannot do that. Perhaps you should send someone here to look at it."

"Where are you now?"

"In Raymond Sinclair's apartment on the top floor of the Rodewald Building in Santa Monica."

"I'll come myself," I said. My tongue suddenly felt thick.

"Please land on the roof. We are holding the elevator for examination."

"Sure." I hung up.

Raymond Sinclair!

I'd never met Raymond Sinclair. He was something of a recluse.
But the ARM had dealt with him once, in connection with one of
his inventions, the FyreStop device. And everyone knew that he
had lately been working on an interstellar drive. It was only a
rumor, of course . . . but if someone had killed the brain that held
that secret . . .

I went.

The Rodewald Building was forty stories of triangular prism
with a row of triangular balconies going up each side. The balconies stopped at the thirty-eighth floor.

The roof was a garden. There were rose bushes in bloom along
one edge, full-grown elms nestled in ivy along another, and a mini-

ature forest of Bonsai trees along the third. The landing pad and carport were in the center. A squad car was floating down ahead of my taxi. It landed, then slid under the carport to give me room to land.

A cop in vivid orange uniform came out to watch me come down. I couldn't tell what he was carrying until I had stepped out. It was a deep-sea fishing pole, still in its kit.

He said, "May I see some ID, please?"

I had my ARM ident in my hand. He checked it in the console in the squad car, then handed it back. "The Inspector's waiting downstairs," he said.

"What's the pole for?"

He smiled suddenly, almost secretively. "You'll see."

We left the garden smells via a flight of concrete stairs. They led down into a small room half full of gardening tools, and a heavy door with a spy-eye in it. Ordaz opened the door for us. He shook my hand briskly, glanced at the cop. "You found something? Good."

The cop said, "There's a sporting goods store six blocks from here. The manager let me borrow it. He made sure I knew the name of the store."

"Yes, there will certainly be publicity on this matter. Come, Gil—" Ordaz took my arm. "You should examine this before we turn it off."

No garden smells here, but there was something—a whiff of something long dead, that the air conditioning hadn't quite cleared away. Ordaz walked me into the living room.

It looked like somebody's idea of a practical joke.

The indoor grass covered Sinclair's living room floor, wall to wall. In a perfect fourteen-foot circle between the sofa and the fireplace, the rug was brown and dead. Elsewhere it was green and thriving.

A man's mummy, dressed in stained slacks and turtleneck, lay on its back in the center of the circle. At a guess it had been about six months dead. It wore a big wristwatch with extra dials on the face and a fine-mesh platinum band, loose now around a wrist of bones and brown skin. The back of the skull had been smashed open, possibly by the classic blunt instrument lying next to it.

If the fireplace was false—it almost had to be; nobody burns wood—the fireplace instruments were genuine nineteenth or twentieth century antiques. The rack was missing a poker. A poker lay inside the circle, in the dead grass next to the disintegrating mummy.

The glowing goldberg device sat just in the center of the magic circle.

I stepped forward, and a man's voice spoke sharply. "Don't go inside that circle of rug. It's more dangerous than it looks."

It was a man I knew: Officer-One Valpredo, a tall man with a small, straight mouth and a long, narrow Italian face.

"Looks dangerous enough to me," I said.

"It is. I reached in there myself," Valpredo told me, "right after we got here. I thought I could flip the switch off. My whole arm went numb. Instantly. No feeling at all. I yanked it away fast, but for a minute or so after that my whole arm was dead meat. I thought I'd lost it. Then it was all pins and needles, like I'd slept on it."

The cop who had brought me in had almost finished assembling the deep-sea fishing pole.

Ordaz waved into the circle. "Well? Have you ever seen anything like this?"

I shook my head, studying the violet-glowing machinery. "Whatever it is, it's brand new. Sinclair's really done it this time."

An uneven line of solenoids was attached to a plastic frame with homemade joins. Blistered spots of the plastic showed where other objects had been attached and later removed. A breadboard bore masses of heavy wiring. There were six big batteries hooked in parallel, and a strange, heavy piece of sculpture in what we later discovered was pure silver, with wiring attached at three curving points. The silver was tarnished almost black and there were old file marks at the edges.

Near the center of the arrangement, just in front of the silver sculpture, were two concentric solenoids embedded in a block of clear plastic. They glowed blue shading to violet. So did the batteries. A less perceptible violet glow radiated from everywhere on the machine, more intensely in the interior parts.

That glow bothered me more than anything else. It was too theatrical. It was like something a special effects man might add to a cheap late-night thriller, to suggest a mad scientist's laboratory.

I moved around to get a closer look at the dead man's watch.

"Keep your head out of the field!" Valpredo said sharply.

I nodded. I squatted on my heels outside the borderline of dead grass.

The dead man's watch was going like crazy. The minute hand was circling the dial every seven seconds or so. I couldn't find the second hand at all.

I backed away from the arc of dead grass and stood up. Interstellar drive, hell. This blue-glowing monstrosity looked more like a time machine gone wrong.

I studied the single-throw switch welded to the plastic frame next to the batteries. A length of nylon line dangled from the horizontal handle. It looked like someone had tugged the switch *on* from outside the field by using the line; but he'd have had to hang from the ceiling to tug it *off* that way.

"I see why you couldn't send it over to ARM Headquarters. You can't even touch it. You stick your arm or your head in there for a second, and that's ten minutes without a blood supply."

Ordaz said, "Exactly."

"It looks like you could reach in there with a stick and flip that switch off."

"Perhaps. We are about to try that." He waved at the man with the fishing pole. "There was nothing in this room long enough to reach the switch. We had to send—"

"Wait a minute. There's a problem."

He looked at me. So did the cop with the fishing pole.

"That switch could be a self-destruct. Sinclair was supposed to be a secretive bastard. Or the—field might hold considerable potential energy. Something might go blooey."

Ordaz sighed. "We must risk it. Gil, we have measured the rotation of the dead man's wristwatch. One hour per seven seconds. Fingerprints, footprints, laundry marks, residual body odor, stray eyelashes, all disappearing at an hour per seven seconds." He gestured, and the cop moved in and began trying to hook the switch.

"Already we may never know just when he was killed," said Ordaz.

The tip of the pole wobbled in large circles, steadied beneath the switch, made contact. I held my breath. The pole bowed. The switch snapped up, and suddenly the violet glow was gone. Valpredo reached into the field, warily, as if the air might be red hot. Nothing happened, and he relaxed.

Then Ordaz began giving orders, and quite a lot happened. Two men in lab coats drew a chalk outline around the mummy and the poker. They moved the mummy onto a stretcher, put the poker in a plastic bag and put it next to the mummy.

I said, "Have you identified that?"

"I'm afraid so," said Ordaz. "Raymond Sinclair had his own autodoc—"

"*Did* he. Those things are expensive."

"Yes. Raymond Sinclair was a wealthy man. He owned the top two floors of this building, and the roof. According to records in his 'doc, he had a new set of bud teeth implanted two months ago." Ordaz pointed to the mummy, to the skinned-back dry lips and the buds of new teeth that were just coming in.

Right. That was Sinclair.

That brain had made miracles, and someone had smashed it with a wrought-iron rod. The interstellar drive . . . that glowing goldberg device? Or had it been still inside his head?

I said, "We'll have to get whoever did it. We'll *have* to. Even so . . ." Even so. No more miracles.

"We may have her already," Julio said.

I looked at him.

"There is a girl in the autodoc. We think she is Dr. Sinclair's great-niece, Janice Sinclair."

It was a standard drugstore autodoc, a thing like a giant coffin with walls a foot thick and a headboard covered with dials and red and green lights. The girl lay face up, her face calm, her breathing shallow. Sleeping Beauty. Her arms were in the guts of the 'doc, hidden by bulky rubbery sleeves.

She was lovely enough to stop my breath. Soft brown hair showing around the electrode cap; small, perfect nose and mouth; smooth pale blue skin shot with silver threads . . .

That last was an evening dye job. Without it the impact of her would have been much lessened. The blue shade varied slightly to emphasize the shape of her body and the curve of her cheekbones. The silver lines varied too, being denser in certain areas, guiding the eye in certain directions: to the tips of her breasts, or across the slight swell of abdominal muscle to a lovely oval navel.

She'd paid high for that dye job. But she would be beautiful without it.

Some of the headboard lights were red. I punched for a readout, and was jolted. The 'doc had been forced to amputate her right arm. Gangrene.

She was in for a hell of a shock when she woke up.

"All right," I said. "She's lost her arm. That doesn't make her a killer."

Ordaz asked, "If she were homely, would it help?"

I laughed. "You question my dispassionate judgment? Men have died for less!" Even so, I thought he could be right. There was good reason to think that the killer was now missing an arm.

"What do you think happened here, Gil?"

"Well . . . any way you look at it, the killer had to want to take Sinclair's, ah, time machine with him. It's priceless, for one thing. For another, it looks like he tried to set it up as an alibi. Which means that he knew about it before he came here." I'd been thinking this through. "Say he made sure some people knew where he was a few hours before he got here. He killed Sinclair within range of the . . . call it a generator. Turned it on. He figured Sinclair's own watch would tell him how much time he was gaining. Afterward he could set the watch back and leave with the generator. There'd be no way the police could tell he wasn't killed six hours earlier, or any number you like."

"Yes. But he did not do that."

"There was that line hanging from the switch. He must have turned it on from outside the field . . . probably because he didn't want to sit with the body for six hours. If he tried to step outside the field after he'd turned it on, he'd bump his nose. It'd be like trying to walk through a wall, going from field time to normal time. So he turned it off, stepped out of range and used that nylon line to turn it on again. He probably made the same mistake Valpredo did: he thought he could step back in and turn it off."

Ordaz nodded in satisfaction. "Exactly. It was very important for him—or her—to do that. Otherwise he would have no alibi and no profit. If he continued to try to reach into the field—"

"Yah, he could lose the arm to gangrene. That'd be convenient for us, wouldn't it? He'd be easy to find. But, look, Julio: the girl could have done the same thing to herself trying to *help* Sinclair. He might not have been that obviously dead when she got home."

"He might even have been alive," Ordaz pointed out.

I shrugged.

"In point of fact, she came home at one ten, in her own car, which is still in the carport. There are cameras mounted to cover the landing pad and carport. Doctor Sinclair's security was thorough. This girl was the only arrival last night. There were no departures."

"From the roof, you mean."

"Gil, there are only two ways to leave these apartments. One is from the roof, and the other is by elevator, from the lobby. The elevator is on this floor, and it was turned off. It was that way when we arrived. There is no way to override that control from elsewhere in this building."

"So someone could have taken it up here and turned it off afterward . . . or Sinclair could have turned it off before he was killed . . . I see what you mean. Either way, the killer has to be still here." I thought about that. I didn't like its taste. "No, it doesn't fit. How could she be bright enough to work out that alibi, then dumb enough to lock herself in with the body?"

Ordaz shrugged. "She locked the elevator before killing her uncle. She did not want to be interrupted. Surely that was sensible? After she hurt her arm she must have been in a great hurry to reach the 'doc."

One of the red lights turned green. I was glad for that. She didn't look like a killer. I said, half to myself, "Nobody looks like a killer when he's asleep."

"No. But she is where a killer ought to be. *Qué lástima.*"

We went back to the living room. I called ARM Headquarters and had them send a truck.

The machine hadn't been touched. While we waited I borrowed a camera from Valpredo and took pictures of the setup *in situ.* Relative positions of the components might be important.

The lab men were in the brown grass using aerosol sprays to turn fingerprints white and give a vivid yellow glow to faint traces of blood. They got plenty of fingerprints on the machine, none at all on the poker. There was a puddle of yellow in the grass where the mummy's head had been, and a long yellow snail track ending at the business end of the poker. It looked like someone had tried to drag the poker out of the field after it had fallen.

Sinclair's apartments were roomy and comfortable and occupied the entire top floor. The lower floor was the laboratory where Sinclair had produced his miracles. I went through it with Valpredo. It wasn't that impressive. It looked like an expensive hobby setup.

These tools would assemble components already fabricated, but they would not build anything complex.

—Except for the computer terminal. That was like a little womb, with a recline chair inside a three-hundred-and-sixty-degree wraparound holovision screen and enough banked controls to fly the damn thing to Alpha Centauris.

The secrets there must be in that computer! But I didn't try to use it. We'd have to send an ARM programmer to break whatever failsafe codes Sinclair had put in the memory banks.

The truck arrived. We dragged Sinclair's legacy up the stairs to the roof in one piece. The parts were sturdily mounted on their frame, and the stairs were wide and not too steep.

I rode home in the back of the truck. Studying the generator. That massive piece of silver had something of the look of *Bird In Flight:* a triangle operated on by a topology student, with wires at what were still the corners. I wondered if it was the heart of the machine, or just a piece of misdirection. Was I really riding with an interstellar drive? Sinclair could have started that rumor himself, to cover whatever this was. Or . . . there was a law against his working two projects simultaneously?

I was looking forward to Bera's reaction.

Jackson Bera came upon us moving it through the halls of ARM Headquarters. He trailed along behind us. Nonchalant. We pulled the machine into the main laboratory and started checking it against the holos I'd taken, in case something had been jarred loose. Bera leaned against the door jamb, watching us, his eyes gradually losing interest until he seemed about to go to sleep.

I'd met him three years ago, when I returned from the asteroids and joined the ARM. He'd been twenty then, and two years an ARM; but his father and grandfather had both been ARMs. Much of my training had come from Bera. And as I learned to hunt men who hunt other men, I had watched what it was doing to him.

An ARM needs empathy. He needs the ability to piece together a picture of the mind of his prey. But Bera had too much empathy. I remember his reaction when Kenneth Graham killed himself: a single surge of current through the plug in his skull and down the wire to the pleasure center of his brain. Bera had been twitchy for weeks. And the Anubis case early last year. When we realized what the man had done, Bera had been close to killing him on the spot. I wouldn't have blamed him.

Last year Bera had had enough. He'd gone into the technical end of the business. His days of hunting organleggers were finished. He was now running the ARM laboratory.

He *had* to want to know what this oddball contraption was. I kept waiting for him to ask . . . and he watched, faintly smiling. Finally it dawned on me. He thought it was a practical joke, something I'd cobbled together for his own discomfiture.

I said, "Bera—"

And he looked at me brightly and said, "Hey, man, what is it?"

"You ask the most embarrassing questions."

"Right, I can understand your feeling that way, but what *is* it? I love it, it's neat, but what is this that you have brought me?"

I told him all I knew, such as it was. When I finished he said, "It doesn't sound much like a new space drive."

"Oho, you heard that too, did you? No, it doesn't. Unless—" I'd been wondering since I first saw it. "Maybe it's supposed to accelerate a fusion explosion. You'd get greater efficiency in a fusion drive."

"Nope. They get better than ninety percent now, and that widget looks *heavy*." He reached to touch the bent silver triangle, gently, with long, tapering fingers. "Huh. Well, we'll dig out the answers."

"Good luck. I'm going back to Sinclair's place."

"Why? The action is here." Often enough he'd heard me talking wistfully of joining an interstellar colony. He must know how I'd feel about a better drive for the interstellar slowboats.

"It's like this," I said. "We've got the generator, but we don't know anything about it. We might wreck it. I'm going to have a whack at finding someone who knows something about Sinclair's generator."

"Meaning?"

"Whoever tried to steal it. Sinclair's killer."

"If you say so." But he looked dubious. He knew me too well. He said, "I understand there's a mother hunt in the offing."

"Oh?"

He smiled. "Just a rumor. You guys are lucky. When my dad first joined, the business of the ARM was *mostly* mother hunts. The organleggers hadn't really got organized yet, and the Fertility Laws were new. If we hadn't enforced them nobody would have obeyed them at all."

"Sure, and people threw rocks at your father. Bera, those days are *gone*."

"They could come back. Having children is basic."

"Bera, I did not join the ARM to hunt unlicensed parents." I waved and left before he could answer. I could do without the call to duty from Bera, who had done with hunting men and mothers.

I'd had a good view of the Rodewald Building, dropping toward the roof this morning. I had a good view now from my commandeered taxi. This time I was looking for escape paths.

There were no balconies on Sinclair's floors, and the windows were flush to the side of the building. A cat burglar would have trouble with them. They didn't look like they'd open.

I tried to spot the cameras Ordaz had mentioned as the taxi dropped toward the roof. I couldn't find them. Maybe they were mounted in the elms.

Why was I bothering? I hadn't joined the ARM to chase mothers or machinery or common murders. I'd joined to pay for my arm. My new arm had reached the World Organ Bank Facility via a captured organlegger's cache. Some honest citizen had died unwillingly on a city slidewalk, and now his arm was part of me.

I'd joined the ARM to hunt organleggers.

The ARM doesn't deal in murder *per se*. The machine was out of my hands now. A murder investigation wouldn't keep me out of a mother hunt. And I'd never met the girl. I knew nothing of her, beyond the fact that she was where a killer ought to be.

Was it just that she was pretty?

Poor Janice. When she woke up . . . For a solid month I'd wakened to that same stunning shock, the knowledge that my right arm was gone.

The taxi settled. Valpredo was waiting below.

I speculated . . . Cars weren't the only things that flew. But anyone flying one of those tricky ducted-fan flycycles over a city, where he could fall on a pedestrian, wouldn't have to worry about a murder charge. They'd feed him to the organ banks regardless. And anything that flew would have to have left traces anywhere but on the landing pad itself. It would crush a rose bush or a Bonsai tree or be flipped over by an elm.

The taxi took off in a whisper of air.

Valpredo was grinning at me. "The Thinker. What's on your mind?"

"I was wondering if the killer could have come down on the carport roof."

He turned to study the situation. "There are two cameras mounted on the edge of the roof. If his vehicle was light enough, sure, he could land there, and the cameras wouldn't spot him. Roof wouldn't hold a car, though. Anyway, nobody did it."

"How do you know?"

"I'll show you. By the way, we inspected the camera system. We're pretty sure the cameras weren't tampered with."

"And nobody came down from the roof last night except the girl?"

"Nobody. Nobody even landed here until seven this morning. Look here." We had reached the concrete stairs that led down into Sinclair's apartments. Valpredo pointed at a glint of light in the sloping ceiling, at heart level. "This is the only way down. The camera would get anyone coming in or out. It might not catch his face, but it'd show if someone had passed. It takes sixty frames a minute."

I went on down. A cop let me in.

Ordaz was on the phone. The screen showed a young man with a deep tan and shock showing through the tan. Ordaz waved at me, a shushing motion, and went on talking. "Then you'll be here in fifteen minutes? That will be a great help to us. Please land on the roof. We are still working on the elevator."

He hung up and turned to me. "That was Andrew Porter, Janice Sinclair's lover. He tells us that he and Janice spent the evening at a party. She dropped him off at his home around one o'clock."

"Then she came straight home, if that's her in the 'doc."

"I think it must be. Mr. Porter says she was wearing a blue skin-dye job." Ordaz was frowning. "He put on a most convincing act, if it was that. I think he really was not expecting any kind of trouble. He was surprised that a stranger answered, shocked when he learned of Dr. Sinclair's death, and horrified when he learned that Janice had been hurt."

With the mummy and the generator removed, the murder scene had become an empty circle of brown grass marked with random streaks of yellow chemical and outlines of white chalk.

"We had some luck," said Ordaz. "Today's date is June 4, 2124.

Dr. Sinclair was wearing a calendar watch. It registered January 17, 2125. If we switched the machine off at ten minutes to ten—which we did—and if it was registering an hour for every seven seconds that passed outside the field, then the field must have gone on around one o'clock last night, give or take a margin of error."

"Then if the girl didn't do it, she must have just missed the killer."

"Exactly."

"What about the elevator? Could it have been jiggered?"

"No. We took the workings apart. It was on this floor, and locked by hand. Nobody could have left by elevator . . ."

"Why did you trail off like that?"

Ordaz shrugged, embarrassed. "This peculiar machine really does bother me, Gil. I found myself thinking, suppose it can reverse time? Then the killer could have gone down in an elevator that was going up."

He laughed with me. I said, "In the first place, I don't believe a word of it. In the second place, he didn't have the machine to do it with. Unless . . . he made his escape before the murder. Dammit, now you've got me doing it."

"I would like to know more about the machine."

"Bera's investigating it now. I'll let you know as soon as we learn anything. And *I'd* like to know more about how the killer couldn't possibly have left."

He looked at me. "Details?"

"Could someone have opened a window?"

"No. These apartments are forty years old. The smog was still bad when they were built. Dr. Sinclair apparently preferred to depend on his air conditioning."

"How about the apartment below? I presume it has a different set of elevators—"

"Yes, of course. It belongs to Howard Rodewald, the owner of this building—of this chain of buildings, in fact. At the moment he is in Europe. His apartment has been loaned to friends."

"There are no stairs down to there?"

"No. We searched these apartments thoroughly."

"All right. We know the killer had a nylon line, because he left a strand of it on the generator. Could he have climbed down to Rodewald's balcony from the roof?"

"Thirty feet? Yes, I suppose so." Ordaz' eyes sparked. "We must

look into that. There is still the matter of how he got past the camera, and whether he could have gotten inside once he was on the
balcony."

"Yah."

"Try this, Gil. Another question. How did he *expect* to get
away?" He watched for my reaction, which must have been satisfying, because it *was* a damn good question. "You see, if Janice
Sinclair murdered her great-uncle, then neither question applies. If
we are looking for someone else, we have to assume that his plans
misfired. He had to improvise."

"Uh huh. He could still have been planning to use Rodewald's
balcony. And that would mean he had a way past the camera . . ."

"Of course he did. The generator."

Right. If he came to steal the generator . . . and he'd have to
steal it regardless, because if we found it here it would shoot his
alibi sky high. So he'd leave it on while he trundled it up the
stairs. Say it took him a minute; that's only an eighth of a second
of normal time. One chance in eight that the camera would fire,
and it would catch nothing but a streak . . . "Uh oh."

"What is it?"

"He had to be planning to steal the machine. Is he really going
to lower it to Rodewald's balcony by *rope*?"

"I think it unlikely," said Ordaz. "It weighed more than fifty
pounds. He could have moved it upstairs. The frame would make it
portable. But to lower it by rope . . ."

"We'd be looking for one hell of an athlete."

"At least you will not have to search far to find him. We assume
that your hypothetical killer came by elevator, do we not?"

"Yah." Nobody but Janice Sinclair had arrived by the roof last
night.

"The elevator was programed to allow a number of people to
enter it, and to turn away all others. The list is short. Dr. Sinclair
was not a gregarious man."

"You're checking them out? Whereabouts, alibis and so forth?"

"Of course."

"There's something else you might check on," I said. But Andrew
Porter came in and I had to postpone it.

Porter came casual, in a well worn translucent one-piece jump
suit he must have pulled on while running for a taxi. The muscles
rolled like boulders beneath the loose fabric, and his belly muscles

showed like the plates on an armadillo. Surfing muscles. The sun had bleached his hair nearly white and burned him as brown as Jackson Bera. You'd think a tan that dark would cover for blood draining out of a face, but it doesn't.

"Where is she?" he demanded. He didn't wait for an answer. He knew where the 'doc was, and he went there. We trailed in his wake.

Ordaz didn't push. He waited while Porter looked down at Janice, then punched for a readout and went through it in detail. Porter seemed calmer then, and his color was back. He turned to Ordaz and said, "What happened?"

"Mr. Porter, did you know anything of Dr. Sinclair's latest project?"

"The time compressor thing? Yah. He had it set up in the living room when I got here yesterday evening—right in the middle of that circle of dead grass. Any connection?"

"When did you arrive?"

"Oh, about . . . six. We had some drinks, and Uncle Ray showed off his machine. He didn't tell us much about it. Just showed what it could do." Porter showed us flashing white teeth. "It *worked.* That thing can compress time! You could live your whole life in there in two months! Watching him move around inside the field was like trying to keep track of a hummingbird. Worse. He struck a match—"

"When did you leave?"

"About eight. We had dinner at Cziller's House of Irish Coffee, and— Listen, what *happened* here?"

"There are some things we need to know first, Mr. Porter. Were you and Janice together for all of last evening? Were there others with you?"

"Sure. We had dinner alone, but afterward we went to a kind of party. On the beach at Santa Monica. Friend of mine has a house there. I'll give you the address. Some of us wound up back at Cziller's around midnight. Then Janice flew me home."

"You have said that you are Janice's lover. Doesn't she live with you?"

"No. I'm her steady lover, you might say, but I don't have any strings on her." He seemed embarrassed. "She lives here with Uncle Ray. Lived. Oh, *hell.*" He glanced into the 'doc. "Look, the readout said she'll be waking up any minute. Can I get her a robe?"

"Of course."

We followed Porter to Janice's bedroom, where he picked out a peach-colored negligée for her. I was beginning to like the guy. He had good instincts. An evening dye job was not the thing to wear on the morning of a murder. And he'd picked one with long, loose sleeves. Her missing arm wouldn't show so much.

"You call him Uncle Ray," said Ordaz.

"Yah. Because Janice did."

"He did not object? Was he gregarious?"

"Gregarious? Well, no, but *we* liked each other. We both liked puzzles, you understand? We traded murder mysteries and jigsaw puzzles. Listen, this may sound silly, but are you sure he's dead?"

"Regrettably, yes. He is dead, and murdered. Was he expecting someone to arrive after you left?"

"Yes."

"He said so?"

"No. But he was wearing a shirt and pants. When it was just us he usually went naked."

"Ah."

"Older people don't do that much," Porter said. "But Uncle Ray was in good shape. He took care of himself."

"Have you any idea whom he might have been expecting?"

"No. Not a woman; not a date, I mean. Maybe someone in the same business."

Behind him, Janice moaned.

Porter was hovering over her in a flash. He put a hand on her shoulder and urged her back. "Lie still, love. We'll have you out of there in a jiffy."

She waited while he disconnected the sleeves and other paraphernalia. She said, "What happened?"

"They haven't told me yet," Porter said with a flash of anger. "Be careful sitting up. You've had an accident."

"What kind of—? *Oh!*"

"It'll be all right."

"My *arm!*"

Porter helped her out of the 'doc. Her arm ended in pink flesh two inches below the shoulder. She let Porter drape the robe around her. She tried to fasten the sash, quit when she realized she was trying to do it with one hand.

I said, "Listen, I lost my arm once."

She looked at me. So did Porter.

"I'm Gil Hamilton. With the UN Police. You really don't have anything to worry about. See?" I raised my right arm, opened and closed the fingers. "The organ banks don't get much call for arms, as compared to kidneys, for instance. You probably won't even have to wait. I didn't. It feels just like the arm I was born with, and it works just as well."

"How did you lose it?" she asked.

"Ripped away by a meteor," I said, not without pride. "While I was asteroid mining in the Belt." I didn't have to tell her that we'd caused the meteor cluster ourselves, by setting the bomb wrong on an asteroid we wanted to move.

Ordaz said to her, "Do you remember how you lost your own arm?"

"Yes." She shivered. "Could we go somewhere where I could sit down? I feel a bit weak."

We moved to the living room. Janice dropped onto the couch a bit too hard. It might have been shock, or the missing arm might be throwing her balance off. I remembered. She said, "Uncle Ray's dead, isn't he?"

"Yes."

"I came home and found him that way. Lying next to that time machine of his, and the back of his head all bloody. I thought maybe he was still alive, but I could see the machine was going; it had that violet glow. I tried to get hold of the poker. I wanted to use it to switch the machine off, but I couldn't get a grip. My arm wasn't just numb, it wouldn't move. You know, you can try to wiggle your toes when your foot's asleep, but . . . I could get my hands on the handle of the damn poker, but when I tried to pull it just slid off."

"You kept trying?"

"For awhile. Then . . . I backed away to think it over. I wasn't about to waste any time, with Uncle Ray maybe dying in there. My arm felt stone dead . . . I guess it was, wasn't it?" She shuddered. "Rotting meat. It smelled that way. And all of a sudden I felt so weak and dizzy, like I was dying myself. I barely made it into the 'doc."

"Good thing you did," I said. The blood was leaving Porter's face again as he realized what a close thing it had been.

Ordaz said, "Was your great-uncle expecting visitors last night?"

"I think so."

"Why do you think so?"

"I don't know. He just—acted that way."

"We are told that you and some friends reached Cziller's House of Irish Coffee around midnight. Is that true?"

"I guess so. We had some drinks, then I took Drew home and came home myself."

"Straight home?"

"Yes." She shivered. "I put the car away and went downstairs. I knew something was wrong. The door was open. Then there was Uncle Ray lying next to that machine! I knew better than to just run up to him. He'd told us not to step into the field."

"Oh? Then you should have known better than to reach for the poker."

"Well, yes. I could have used the tongs," she said as if the idea had just occurred to her. "It's just as long. I didn't think of it. There wasn't *time*. Don't you understand, he was dying in there, or dead!"

"Yes, of course. Did you interfere with the murder scene in any way?"

She laughed bitterly. "I suppose I moved the poker about two inches. Then when I felt what was happening to me I just ran for the 'doc. It was awful. Like dying."

"Instant gangrene," said Porter.

Ordaz said, "You did not, for example, lock the elevator?"

Damn! I should have thought of that.

"No. We usually do, when we lock up for the night, but I didn't have time."

Porter said, "Why?"

"The elevator was locked when we arrived," Ordaz told him.

Porter ruminated that. "Then the killer must have left by the roof. You'll have pictures of him."

Ordaz smiled apologetically. "That is our problem. No cars left the roof last night. Only one car arrived. That was yours, Miss Sinclair."

"But," said Porter, and he stopped. He thought it through again. "Did the police turn on the elevator again after they got here?"

"No. The killer could not have left after we got here."

"Oh."

"What happened was this," said Ordaz. "Around five thirty this morning, the tenants in—" He stopped to remember. "In 36A called the building maintenance man about a smell as of rotting meat coming through the air conditioning system. He spent some time looking for the source, but once he reached the roof it was obvious. He—"

Porter pounced. "He reached the roof in what kind of vehicle?"

"Mr. Steeves says that he took a taxi from the street. There is no other way to reach Dr. Sinclair's private landing pad, is there?"

"No. But why would he do that?"

"Perhaps there have been other times when strange smells came from Dr. Sinclair's laboratory. We will ask him."

"Do that."

"Mr. Steeves followed the smell through the doctor's open door. He called us. He waited for us on the roof."

"What about his taxi?" Porter was hot on the scent. "Maybe the killer just waited till that taxi got here, then took it somewhere else when Steeves finished with it."

"It left immediately after Steeves had stepped out. He had a taxi clicker if he wanted another. The cameras were on it the entire time it was on the roof." Ordaz paused. "You see the problem?"

Apparently Porter did. He ran both hands through his white-blond hair. "I think we ought to put off discussing it until we know more."

He meant Janice. Janice looked puzzled; she hadn't caught on. But Ordaz nodded at once and stood up. "Very well. There is no reason Miss Sinclair cannot go on living here. We may have to bother you again," he told her. "For now, our condolences."

He made his exit. I trailed along. So, unexpectedly, did Drew Porter. At the top of the stairs he stopped Ordaz with a big hand around the Inspector's upper arm. "You're thinking Janice did it, aren't you?"

Ordaz sighed. "What choice have I? I must consider the possibility."

"She didn't have any reason. She loved Uncle Ray. She's lived with him on and off these past twelve years. She hasn't got the slightest reason to kill him."

"Is there no inheritance?"

His expression went sour. "All right, *yes*, she'll have some money coming. But Janice wouldn't care about anything like that!"

"Ye-es. Still, what choice have I? Everything we now know tells us that the killer could not have left the scene of the killing. We searched the premises immediately. There was only Janice Sinclair and her murdered uncle."

Porter hit back an answer, chewed it . . . He must have been tempted. Amateur detective, one step ahead of the police all the way. Yes, Watson, these *gendarmes* have a talent for missing the obvious . . . But he had too much to lose. Porter said, "And the maintenance man. Steeves."

Ordaz lifted one eyebrow. "Yes, of course. We shall have to investigate Mr. Steeves."

"How did he get that call from, uh, 36A? Bedside phone or pocket phone? Maybe he was already on the roof."

"I don't remember that he said. But we have pictures of his taxi landing."

"He had a taxi clicker. He could have just called it down."

"One more thing," I said, and Porter looked at me hopefully. "Porter, what about the elevator? It had a brain in it, didn't it? It wouldn't take anyone up unless they were on its list."

"Or unless Uncle Ray buzzed down. There's an intercom in the lobby. But at that time of night he probably wouldn't let anyone up unless he was expecting him."

"So if Sinclair was expecting a business associate, he or she was probably in the tape. How about going down? Would the elevator take you down to the lobby if you weren't in the tape?"

"I'd . . . think so."

"It would," said Ordaz. "The elevator screens entrances, not departures."

"Then why didn't the killer use it? I don't mean Steeves, necessarily. I mean *anyone*, whoever it might have been. Why didn't he just go down in the elevator? Whatever he did do, that had to be easier."

They looked at each other, but they didn't say anything.

"Okay." I turned to Ordaz. "When you check out the people in the tape, see if any of them shows a damaged arm. The killer might have pulled the same stunt Janice did: ruined her arm trying to turn off the generator. And I'd like a look at who's in that tape."

"Very well," said Ordaz, and we moved toward the squad car under the carport. We were out of earshot when he added, "How does the ARM come into this, Mr. Hamilton? Why your interest in the murder aspect of this case?"

I told him what I'd told Bera: that Sinclair's killer might be the only living expert on Sinclair's time machine. Ordaz nodded. What he'd really wanted to know was: could I justify giving orders to the Los Angeles Police Department in a local matter? And I had answered: yes.

The rather simple-minded security system in Sinclair's elevator had been built to remember the thumbprints and the facial bone structures (which it scanned by deep-radar, thus avoiding the problems raised by changing beard styles and masquerade parties) of up to one hundred people. Most people know about a hundred people, plus or minus ten or so. But Sinclair had only listed a dozen, including himself.

RAYMOND SINCLAIR
ANDREW PORTER
JANICE SINCLAIR
EDWARD SINCLAIR SR.
EDWARD SINCLAIR III
HANS DRUCKER
GEORGE STEEVES
PAULINE URTHIEL
BERNATH PETERFI
LAWRENCE MUHAMMAD ECKS
BERTHA HALL
MURIEL SANDUSKY

Valpredo had been busy. He'd been using the police car and its phone setup as an office while he guarded the roof. "We know who some of these are," he said. "Edward Sinclair Third, for instance, is Edward Senior's grandson, Janice's brother. He's in the Belt, in Ceres, making something of a name for himself as an industrial designer. Edward Senior is Raymond's brother. He lives in Kansas City. Hans Drucker and Bertha Hall and Muriel Sandusky all live in the Greater Los Angeles area; we don't know what their connection with Sinclair is. Pauline Urthiel and Bernath Peterfi are technicians of sorts. Ecks is Sinclair's patent attorney."

"I suppose we can interview Edward Third by phone." Ordaz made a face. A phone call to the Belt wasn't cheap. "These others—"

I said, "May I make a suggestion?"

"Of course."

"Send me along with whoever interviews Ecks and Peterfi and

Urthiel. They probably knew Sinclair in a business sense, and having an ARM along will give you a little more clout to ask a little
more detailed questions."

"I could take those assignments," Valpredo volunteered.

"Very well." Ordaz still looked unhappy. "If this list were ex-
haustive I would be grateful. Unfortunately we must consider the
risk that Dr. Sinclair's visitor simply used the intercom in the
lobby and asked to be let in."

Bernath Peterfi wasn't answering his phone.

We got Pauline Urthiel via her pocket phone. A brusque contralto voice, no picture. We'd like to talk to her in connection with
a murder investigation; would she be at home this afternoon? No.
She was lecturing that afternoon, but would be home around six.

Ecks answered dripping wet and not smiling. So sorry to get you
out of a shower, Mr. Ecks. We'd like to talk to you in connection
with a murder investigation—

"Sure, come on over. Who's dead?"

Valpredo told him.

"Sinclair? *Ray* Sinclair? You're sure?"

We were.

"Oh, lord. Listen, he was working on something important. An
interstellar drive, if it works out. If there's any possibility of salvag-
ing the hardware—"

I reassured him and hung up. If Sinclair's patent attorney
thought it was a star drive . . . maybe it was.

"Doesn't sound like he's trying to steal it," said Valpredo.

"No. And even if he'd got the thing, he couldn't have claimed it
was his. If he's the killer, that's not what he was after."

We were moving at high speed, police-car speed. The car was on
automatic, of course, but it could need manual override at any instant. Valpredo concentrated on the passing scenery and spoke
without looking at me.

"You know, you and the Detective-Inspector aren't looking for
the same thing."

"I know. I'm looking for a hypothetical killer. Julio's looking for a
hypothetical visit. It could be tough to prove there wasn't one, but
if Porter and the girl were telling the truth, maybe Julio can prove
the visitor didn't do it."

"Which would leave the girl," he said.

"Whose side are you on?"

"Nobody's. All I've got is interesting questions." He looked at me sideways. "But you're pretty sure the girl didn't do it."

"Yah."

"Why?"

"I don't know. Maybe because I don't think she's got the brains. It wasn't a simple killing."

"She's Sinclair's niece. She can't be a complete idiot."

"Heredity doesn't work that way. Maybe I'm kidding myself. Maybe it's her arm. She's lost an arm; she's got enough to worry about." And I borrowed the car phone to dig into records in the ARM computer.

PAULINE URTHIEL. Born Paul Urthiel. Ph.D. in plasma physics, University of California at Ervine. Sex change and legal name change, 2111. Six years ago she'd been in competition for a Nobel prize, for research into the charge suppression effect in the Slaver disintegrator. Height: 5′ 9″. Weight: 135. Married Lawrence Muhammad Ecks, 2117. Had kept her (loosely speaking) maiden name. Separate residences.

BERNATH PETERFI. Ph.D. in subatomics and related fields, MIT. Diabetic. Height: 5′ 8″. Weight: 145. Application for exemption to the Fertility Laws denied, 2119. Married 2118, divorced 2122. Lived alone.

LAWRENCE MUHAMMAD ECKS. Masters degree in physics. Member of the bar. Height: 6′ 1″. Weight: 190. Artificial left arm. Vice-President, CET (Committee to End Transplants).

Valpredo said: "Funny how the human arm keeps cropping up in this case."

"Yah." Including one human ARM who didn't really belong there. "Ecks has a masters. Maybe he could have talked people into thinking the generator was his. Or maybe he thought he could."

"He didn't try to snow *us*."

"Suppose he blew it last night? He wouldn't necessarily want the generator lost to humanity, now would he?"

"How did he get out?"

I didn't answer.

Ecks lived in a tapering tower almost a mile high. At one time Lindstetter's Needle must have been the biggest thing ever built, before they started with the arcologies. We landed on a pad a third of the way up, then took a drop shaft ten floors down.

He was dressed when he answered the door, in blazing yellow pants and a net shirt. His skin was very dark, and his hair was a puffy black dandelion with threads of grey in it. On the phone screen I hadn't been able to tell which arm was which, and I couldn't now. He invited us in, sat down and waited for the questions.

Where was he last night? Could he produce an alibi? It would help us considerably.

"Sorry, nope. I spent the night going through a rather tricky case. You wouldn't appreciate the details."

I told him I would. He said, "Actually, it involves Edward Sinclair—Ray's great-nephew. He's a Belt immigrant, and he's done an industrial design that could be adapted to Earth. Swivel for a chemical rocket motor. The trouble is it's not *that* different from existing designs, it's just *better*. His Belt patent is good, but the UN laws are different. You wouldn't believe the legal tangles."

"Is he likely to lose out?"

"No, it just might get sticky if a firm called FireStorm decides to fight the case. I want to be ready for that. In a pinch I might even have to call the kid back to Earth. I'd hate to do that, though. He's got a heart condition."

Had he made any phone calls, say to a computer, during his night of research?

Ecks brightened instantly. "Oh, sure. Constantly, all night. Okay, I've got an alibi."

No point in telling him that such calls could have been made from anywhere. Valpredo asked, "Do you have any idea where your wife was last night?"

"No, we don't live together. She lives three hundred stories over my head. We've got an open marriage . . . maybe too open," he added wistfully.

There seemed a good chance that Raymond Sinclair was expecting a visitor last night. Did Ecks have any idea—?

"He knew a couple of women," said Ecks. "You might ask them. Bertha Hall is about eighty, about Ray's age. She's not too bright, not by Ray's standards, but she's as much of a physical fitness nut as he is. They go backpacking, play tennis, maybe sleep together, maybe not. I can give you her address. Then there's Muriel something. He had a crush on her a few years ago. She'd be thirty now. I don't know if they still see each other or not."

Did Sinclair know other women?

Ecks shrugged.

Who did he know professionally?

"Oh, lord, that's an endless list. Do you know anything about the way Ray worked?" He didn't wait for an answer. "He used computer setups mostly. Any experiment in his field was likely to cost millions, or more. What he was good at was setting up a computer analogue of an experiment that would tell him what he wanted to know. Take, oh . . . I'm sure you've heard of the Sinclair molecule chain."

Hell, yes. We'd used it for towing in the Belt; nothing else was light enough and strong enough. A loop of it was nearly invisibly fine, but it would cut steel.

"He didn't start working with chemicals until he was practically finished. He told me he spent four years doing molecular designs by computer analogue. The tough part was the ends of the molecule chain. Until he got that the chain would start disintegrating from the endpoints the minute you finished making it. When he finally had what he wanted, he hired an industrial chemical lab to make it for him.

"That's what I'm getting at," Ecks continued. "He hired other people to do the concrete stuff, once he knew what he had. And the people he hired had to know what they were doing. He knew the top physicists and chemists and field theorists everywhere on Earth and in the Belt."

Like Pauline? Like Bernath Peterfi?

"Yah, Pauline did some work for him once. I don't think she'd do it again. She didn't like having to give him all the credit. She'd rather work for herself. I don't blame her."

Could he think of anyone who might want to murder Raymond Sinclair?

Ecks shrugged. "I'd say that was your job. Ray never liked splitting the credit with anyone. Maybe someone he worked with nursed a grudge. Or maybe someone was trying to steal this latest project of his. Mind you, I don't know much about what he was trying to do, but if it worked it would have been fantastically valuable, and not just in money."

Valpredo was making noises like he was about finished. I said, "Do you mind if I ask a personal question?"

"Go ahead."

"Your arm. How'd you lose it?"

"Born without it. Nothing in my genes, just a bad prenatal situation. I came out with an arm and a turkey wishbone. By the time I was old enough for a transplant, I knew I didn't want one. You want the standard speech?"

"No, thanks, but I'm wondering how good your artificial arm is. I'm carrying a transplant myself."

Ecks looked me over carefully for signs of moral degeneration. "I suppose you're also one of those people who keep voting the death penalty for more and more trivial offenses?"

"No, I—"

"After all, if the organ banks ran out of criminals you'd be in trouble. You might have to live with your mistakes."

"No, I'm one of those people who blocked the second corpsicle law, kept that group from going into the organ banks. And I hunt organleggers for a living. But I don't have an artificial arm, and I suppose the reason is that I'm squeamish."

"Squeamish about being part mechanical? I've heard of that," Ecks said. "But you can be squeamish the other way, too. What there is of me is all me, not part of a dead man. I'll admit the sense of touch isn't quite the same, but it's just as good. And—look."

He put a hand on my upper forearm and squeezed.

It felt like the bones were about to give. I didn't scream, but it took an effort. "That isn't all my strength," he said. "And I could keep it up all day. This arm doesn't get tired."

He let go.

I asked if he would mind my examining his arms. He didn't. But then, Ecks didn't know about my imaginary hand.

I probed the advanced plastics of Ecks' false arm, the bone and muscle structure of the other. It was the real arm I was interested in.

When we were back in the car Valpredo said, "Well?"

"Nothing wrong with his real arm," I said. "No scars."

Valpredo nodded.

But the bubble of accelerated time wouldn't hurt plastic and batteries, I thought. And if he'd been planning to lower fifty pounds of generator two stories down on a nylon line, his artificial arm had the strength for it.

We called Peterfi from the car. He was in. He was a small man, dark complected, mild of face, his hair straight and shiny black around a receding hairline. His eyes blinked and squinted as if the light were too bright, and he had the scruffy look of a man who has slept in his clothes. I wondered if we had interrupted an afternoon nap.

Yes, he would be glad to help the police in a murder investigation.

Peterfi's condominium was a slab of glass and concrete set on a Santa Monica cliff face. His apartment faced the sea. "Expensive, but worth it for the view," he said, showing us to chairs in the living room. The drapes were closed against the afternoon sun. Peterfi had changed clothes. I noticed the bulge in his upper left sleeve, where an insulin capsule and automatic feeder had been anchored to the bone of the arm.

"Well, what can I do for you? I don't believe you mentioned who had been murdered."

Valpredo told him.

He was shocked. "Oh, my. Ray Sinclair. But there's no telling how this will affect—" and he stopped suddenly.

"Please go on," said Valpredo.

"We were working on something together. Something—revolutionary."

An interstellar drive?

He was startled. He debated with himself, then, "Yes. It was supposed to be secret."

We admitted having seen the machine in action. How did a time compression field serve as an interstellar drive?

"That's not exactly what it is," Peterfi said. Again he debated with himself. Then, "There have always been a few optimists around who thought that just because mass and inertia have always been associated in human experience, it need not be a universal law. What Ray and I have done is to create a condition of low inertia. You see—"

"An inertialess drive!"

Peterfi nodded vigorously at me. "Essentially yes. Is the machine intact? If not—"

I reassured him on that point.

"That's good. I was about to say that if it had been destroyed, I could recreate it. I did most of the work of building it. Ray preferred to work with his mind, not with his hands."

Had Peterfi visited Sinclair last night?

"No. I had dinner at a restaurant down the coast, then came home and watched the holo wall. What times do I need alibis for?" he asked jokingly.

Valpredo told him. The joking look turned into a nervous grimace. No, he'd left the Mail Shirt just after nine; he couldn't prove his whereabouts after that time.

Had he any idea who might have wanted to murder Raymond Sinclair?

Peterfi was reluctant to make outright accusations. Surely we understood. It might be someone he had worked with in the past, or someone he'd insulted. Ray thought most of humanity were fools. Or—we might look into the matter of Ray's brother's exemption.

Valpredo said, "Edward Sinclair's exemption? What about it?"

"I'd really prefer that you get the story from someone else. You may know that Edward Sinclair was refused the right to have children because of an inherited heart condition. His grandson has it too. There is some question as to whether he really did the work that earned him the exemption."

"But that must have been forty to fifty years ago. How could it figure in a murder now?"

Peterfi explained patiently. "Edward had a child by virtue of an exemption to the Fertility Laws. Now there are two grandchildren. Suppose the matter came up for review? His grandchildren would lose the right to have children. They'd be illegitimate. They might even lose the right to inherit."

Valpredo was nodding. "Yah. We'll look into that, all right."

I said, "You applied for an exemption yourself not long ago. I suppose your, uh—"

"Yes, my diabetes. It doesn't interfere with my life at all. Do you know how long we've been using insulin to handle diabetes? Almost two hundred years! What does it matter if I'm a diabetic? If my children are?"

He glared at us, demanding an answer. He got none.

"But the Fertility Laws refuse me children. Do you know that I lost my wife because the Board refused me an exemption? I deserved it. My work on plasma flow in the solar photosphere— Well, I'd hardly lecture you on the subject, would I? But my work can be used to predict the patterns of proton storms near any G-type star. Every colony world owes something to my work!"

That was an exaggeration, I thought. Proton storms affected mainly asteroidal mining operations . . . "Why don't you move to the Belt?" I asked. "They'd honor you for your work, and they don't have Fertility Laws."

"I get sick off Earth. It's biorhythms; it has nothing to do with diabetes. Half of humanity suffers from biorhythm upset."

I felt sorry for the guy. "You could still get the exemption. For your work on the inertialess drive. Wouldn't that get you your wife back?"

"I . . . don't know. I doubt it. It's been two years. In any case, there's no telling which way the Board will jump. I thought I'd have the exemption last time."

"Do you mind if I examine your arms?"

He looked at me. "What?"

"I'd like to examine your arms."

"That seems a most curious request. Why?"

"There seems a good chance that Sinclair's killer damaged his arm last night. Now, I'll remind you that I'm acting in the name of the UN Police. If you've been hurt by the side effects of a possible space drive, one that might be used by human colonists, then you're concealing evidence in a—" I stopped, because Peterfi had stood up and was taking off his tunic.

He wasn't happy, but he stood still for it. His arms looked all right. I ran my hands along each arm, bent the joints, massaged the knuckles. Inside the flesh I ran my imaginary fingertips along the bones.

Three inches below the shoulder joint the bone was knotted. I probed the muscles and tendons . . .

"Your right arm is a transplant," I said. "It must have happened about six months ago."

He bridled. "You may not be aware of it, but surgery to re-attach my own arm would show the same scars."

"Is that what happened?"

Anger made his speech more precise. "Yes. I was performing an experiment, and there was an explosion. The arm was nearly severed. I tied a tourniquet and got to a 'doc before I collapsed."

"Any proof of this?"

"I doubt it. I never told anyone of this accident, and the 'doc wouldn't keep records. In any case, I think the burden of proof would be on you."

"Uh huh."

Peterfi was putting his tunic back on. "Are you quite finished here? I'm deeply sorry for Ray Sinclair's death, but I don't see what it could possibly have to do with my stupidity of six months ago."

I didn't either. We left.

Back in the car. It was seventeen twenty; we could pick up a snack on the way to Pauline Urthiel's place. I told Valpredo, "I think it was a transplant. And he didn't want to admit it. He must have gone to an organlegger."

"Why would he do that? It's not that tough to get an arm from the public organ banks."

I chewed that. "You're right. But if it was a normal transplant, there'll be a record. Well, it could have happened the way he said it did."

"Uh huh."

"How about this? He was doing an experiment, and it was illegal. Something that might cause pollution in a city, or even something to do with radiation. He picked up radiation burns in his arm. If he'd gone to the public organ banks he'd have been arrested."

"That would fit too. Can we prove it on him?"

"I don't know. I'd like to. He might tell us how to find whoever he dealt with. Let's do some digging: maybe we can find out what he was working on six months ago."

Pauline Urthiel opened the door the instant we rang. "Hi! I just got in myself. Can I make you drinks?"

We refused. She ushered us into a smallish apartment with a lot of fold-into-the-ceiling furniture. A sofa and coffee table were showing now; the rest existed as outlines on the ceiling. The view through the picture window was breathtaking. She lived near the top of Lindstetter's Needle, some three hundred stories up from her husband.

She was tall and slender, with a facial structure that would have been effeminate on a man. On a woman it was a touch masculine. The well-formed breasts might be flesh or plastic, but surgically implanted in either case.

She finished making a large drink and joined us on the couch. And the questions started.

Had she any idea who might have wanted Raymond Sinclair dead?

"Not really. How did he die?"

"Someone smashed in his skull with a poker," Valpredo said. If he wasn't going to mention the generator, neither was I.

"How quaint." Her contralto turned acid. "His own poker, too, I presume. Out of his own fireplace rack. What you're looking for is a traditionalist." She peered at us over the rim of her glass. Her eyes were large, the lids decorated in semi-permanent tattoo as a pair of flapping UN flags. "That doesn't help much, does it? You might try whoever was working with him on whatever his latest project was."

That sounded like Peterfi, I thought. But Valpredo said, "Would he necessarily have a collaborator?"

"He generally works alone at the beginning. But somewhere along the line he brings in people to figure out how to make the hardware, and make it. He never made anything real by himself. It was all just something in a computer bank. It took someone else to make it real. And he never gave credit to anyone."

Then his hypothetical collaborator might have found out how little credit he was getting for his work, and— But Urthiel was shaking her head. "I'm talking about a psychotic, not someone who's really been cheated. Sinclair never *offered* anyone a share in anything he did. He always made it damn plain what was happening. I knew what I was doing when I set up the FyreStop prototype for him, and I knew what I was doing when I quit. It was all him. He was using my training, not my brain. I wanted to do something original, something *me*."

Did she have any idea what Sinclair's present project was?

"My husband would know. Larry Ecks, lives in this same building. He's been dropping cryptic hints, and when I want more details he has this grin—" She grinned herself, suddenly. "You'll gather I'm interested. But he won't say."

Time for me to take over, or we'd never get certain questions asked. "I'm an ARM. What I'm about to tell you is secret," I said. And I told her what we knew of Sinclair's generator. Maybe Valpredo was looking at me disapprovingly; maybe not.

"We know that the field can damage a human arm in a few seconds. What we want to know," I said, "is whether the killer is now wandering around with a half-decayed hand or arm—or foot, for that—"

She stood and pulled the upper half of her body stocking down around her waist.

She looked very much a real woman. If I hadn't known—and why would it matter? These days the sex change operation is elaborate and perfect. Hell with it; I was on duty. Valpredo was looking nonchalant, waiting for me.

I examined both her arms with my eyes and my three hands. There was nothing. Not even a bruise.

"My legs too?"

I said, "Not if you can stand on them."

Next question. Could an artificial arm operate within the field?

"Larry? You mean *Larry?* You're out of your teeny mind."

"Take it as a hypothetical question."

She shrugged. "Your guess is as good as mine. There aren't any experts on inertialess fields."

"There was one. He's dead," I reminded her.

"All I know is what I learned watching the Gray Lensman show in the holo wall when I was a kid." She smiled suddenly. "That old space opera—"

Valpredo laughed. "You too? I used to watch that show in study hall on a little pocket phone. One day the Principal caught me at it."

"Sure. And then we outgrew it. Too bad. Those inertialess ships . . . I'm sure an inertialess ship wouldn't behave like those did. You couldn't possibly get rid of the time compression effect." She took a long pull on her drink, set it down and said, "Yes and no. He could reach in, but—you see the problem? The nerve impulses that move the motors in Larry's arm, they're coming into the field too slowly."

"Sure."

"But if Larrry closed his fist on something, say, and reached into the field with it, it would probably stay closed. He could have brained Ray with—no, he couldn't. The poker wouldn't be moving any faster than a glacier. Ray would just dodge."

And he couldn't pull a poker out of the field, either. His fist wouldn't close on it after it was inside. But he could have tried, and still left with his arm intact, I thought.

Did Urthiel know anything of the circumstances surrounding Edward Sinclair's exemption?

"Oh, that's an old story," she said. "Sure, I heard about it. How could it possibly have anything to do with, with Ray's murder?"

"I don't know," I confessed. "I'm just thrashing around."

"Well, you'll probably get it more accurately from the UN files. Edward Sinclair did some mathematics on the fields that scoop up interstellar hydrogen for the cargo ramrobots. He was a shoo-in for the exemption. That's the surest way of getting it: make a breakthrough in anything that has anything to do with the interstellar colonies. Every time you move one man away from Earth, the population drops by one."

"What was wrong with it?"

"Nothing anyone could prove. Remember, the Fertility Restriction Laws were new then. They couldn't stand a real test. But Edward Sinclair's a pure math man. He works with number theory, not practical applications. I've seen Edward's equations, and they're closer to something Ray would come up with. And Ray didn't need the exemption. He never wanted children."

"So you think—"

"I don't *care* which of them redesigned the ramscoops. Diddling the Fertility Board like that, that takes *brains*." She swallowed the rest of her drink, set the glass down. "Breeding for brains is never a mistake. It's no challenge to the Fertility Board either. The people who do the damage are the ones who go into hiding when their shots come due, have their babies, then scream to high heaven when the Board has to sterilize them. Too many of those and we won't have Fertility Laws any more. And *that*—" She didn't have to finish.

Had Sinclair known that Pauline Urthiel was once Paul?

She stared. "Now just what the bleep has that got to do with anything?"

I'd been toying with the idea that Sinclair might have been blackmailing Urthiel with that information. Not for money, but for credit in some discovery they'd made together. "Just thrashing around," I said.

"Well . . . all right. I don't know if Ray knew or not. He never raised the subject, but he never made a pass either, and he must have researched me before he hired me. And, say, listen: Larry doesn't know. I'd appreciate it if you wouldn't blurt it out."

"Okay."

"See, he had his children by his first wife. I'm not denying him children . . . Maybe he married me because I had a touch of, um, masculine insight. Maybe. But he doesn't know it, and he doesn't want to. I don't know whether he'd laugh it off or kill me."

I had Valpredo drop me off at ARM Headquarters.

This peculiar machine really does bother me, Gil . . . Well it should, Julio. The Los Angeles Police were not trained to deal with a mad scientist's nightmare running quietly in the middle of a murder scene.

Granted that Janice wasn't the type. Not for this murder. But Drew Porter was precisely the type to evolve a perfect murder around Sinclair's generator, purely as an intellectual exercise. He might have guided her through it; he might even have been there, and used the elevator before she shut it off. It was the one thing he forgot to tell her: not to shut off the elevator.

Or: he outlined a perfect murder to her, purely as a puzzle, never dreaming she'd go through with it—badly.

Or: one of them had killed Janice's uncle on impulse. No telling what he'd said that one of them couldn't tolerate. But the machine had been right there in the living room, and Drew had wrapped his big arm around Janice and said, *Wait, don't do anything yet, let's think this out . . .*

Take any of these as the true state of affairs, and a prosecutor could have a hell of a time proving it. He could show that no killer could possibly have left the scene of the crime without Janice Sinclair's help, and therefore . . . But what about that glowing thing, that time machine built by the dead man? *Could* it have freed a killer from an effectively locked room? How could a judge know its power?

Well, could it?

Bera might know.

The machine was running. I caught the faint violet glow as I stepped into the laboratory, and a flickering next to it . . . and then it was off, and Jackson Bera stood suddenly beside it, grinning, silent, waiting.

I wasn't about to spoil his fun. I said, "Well? Is it an interstellar drive?"

"Yes!"

A warm glow spread through me. I said, "Okay."

"It's a low inertia field," said Bera. "Things inside lose most of their inertia . . . not their mass, just the resistance to movement. Ratio of about five hundred to one. The interface is sharp as a razor. We think there are quantum levels involved."

"Uh huh. The field doesn't affect time directly?"

"No, it . . . I shouldn't say that. Who the hell knows what time really is? It affects chemical and nuclear reactions, energy release of all kinds . . . but it doesn't affect the speed of light. You know, it's kind of kicky to be measuring the speed of light at three hundred and seventy miles per second with honest instruments."

Dammit. I'd been half-hoping it was an FTL drive. I said, "Did you ever find out what was causing that blue glow?"

Bera laughed at me. "Watch." He'd rigged a remote switch to turn the machine on. He used it, then struck a match and flipped it toward the blue glow. As it crossed an invisible barrier the match flared violet-white for something less than a eyeblink. I blinked. It had been like a flashbulb going off.

I said, "Oh, *sure*. The machinery's warm."

"Right. The blue glow is just infrared radiation being boosted to violet when it enters normal time."

Bera shouldn't have had to tell me that. Embarrassed, I changed the subject. "But you said it was an interstellar drive."

"Yah. It's got drawbacks," said Bera. "We can't just put a field around a whole starship. The crew would think they'd lowered the speed of light, but so what? A slowboat doesn't get that close to lightspeed anyway. They'd save a little trip time, but they'd have to live through it five hundred times as fast."

"How about if you just put the field around your fuel tanks?"

Bera nodded. "That's what they'll probably do. Leave the motor and the life support system outside. You could carry a godawful amount of fuel that way . . . Well, it's not our department. Someone else'll be designing the starships," he said a bit wistfully.

"Have you thought of this thing in relation to robbing banks? Or espionage?"

"If a gang could afford to build one of these jobs, they wouldn't need to rob banks." He ruminated. "I hate making anything this big a UN secret. But I guess you're right. The average government could afford a whole stable of the things."

"Thus combining James Bond and the Flash."

He rapped on the plastic frame. "Want to try it?"

"Sure," I said.

Heart to brain: THUD! What're you doing? You'll get us all killed! I knew we should never have put you in charge of things . . . I stepped up to the generator, waited for Bera to scamper beyond range, then pulled the switch.

Everything turned deep red. Bera became as a statue.

Well, here I was. The second hand on the wall clock had stopped moving. I took two steps forward and rapped with my knuckles. Rapped, hell: it was like rapping on contact cement. The invisible wall was tacky.

I tried leaning on it for a minute or so. That worked fine until I tried to pull away, and then I knew I'd done something stupid. I was embedded in the interface. It took me another minute to pull loose, and then I went sprawling backward; I'd picked up too much inward velocity, and it all came into the field with me.

At that I'd been lucky. If I'd leaned there a little longer I'd have lost my leverage. I'd have been sinking deeper and deeper into the interface, unable to yell to Bera, building up more and more velocity outside the field.

I picked myself up and tried something safer. I took out my pen and dropped it. It fell normally: thirty-two feet per second per second, field time. Which scratched one theory as to how the killer had thought he would be leaving.

I switched the machine off. "Something I'd like to try," I told Bera. "Can you hang the machine in the air, say by a cable around the frame?"

"What have you got in mind?"

"I want to try standing on the bottom of the field."

Bera looked dubious.

It took us twenty minutes to set it up. Bera took no chances. He lifted the generator about five feet. Since the field seemed to center on that oddly shaped piece of silver, that put the bottom of the field just a foot in the air. We moved a stepladder into range, and I stood on the stepladder and turned on the generator.

I stepped off.

Walking down the side of the field was like walking in progressively stickier taffy. When I stood on the bottom I could just reach the switch.

My shoes were stuck solid. I could pull my feet out of them, but there was no place to stand except in my own shoes. A minute later my feet were stuck too: I could pull one loose, but only by fixing the other ever more deeply in the interface. I sank deeper, and all sensation left the soles of my feet. It was scary, though I knew nothing terrible could happen to me. My feet wouldn't die out there; they wouldn't have time.

But the interface was up to my ankles now, and I started to wonder what kind of velocity they were building up out there. I pushed the switch up. The lights flashed bright, and my feet slapped the floor hard.

Bera said, "Well? Learn anything?"

"Yah. I don't want to try a real test: I might wreck the machine."

"What kind of real test—?"

"Dropping it forty stories with the field on. Quit worrying, I'm not going to do it."

"Right. You aren't."

"You know, this time compression effect would work for more than just spacecraft. After you're on the colony world you could raise full grown cattle from frozen fertilized eggs in just a few minutes."

"Mmm . . . Yah." The happy smile flashing white against darkness, the infinity look in Bera's eyes . . . Bera liked playing with ideas. "Think of one of these mounted on a truck, say on Jinx. You could explore the shoreline regions without ever worrying about the bandersnatchi attacking. They'd never move fast enough. You could drive across any alien world and catch the whole ecology laid out around you, none of it running from the truck. Predators in mid-leap, birds in mid-flight, couples in courtship."

"Or larger groups."

"I . . . think that habit is unique to humans." He looked at me sideways. "You wouldn't spy on *people*, would you? Or shouldn't I ask?"

"That five-hundred-to-one ratio. Is that constant?"

He came back to here and now. "We don't know. Our theory hasn't caught up to the hardware it's supposed to fit. I wish to hell we had Sinclair's notes."

"You were supposed to send a programmer out there—"

"He came back," Bera said viciously. "Clayton Wolfe. Clay says the tapes in Sinclair's computer were all wiped before he got there.

I don't know whether to believe him or not. Sinclair was a secretive bastard, wasn't he?"

"Yah. One false move on Clay's part and the computer might have wiped everything. But he says different, hmmm?"

"He says the computer was blank, a newborn mind all ready to be taught. Gil, is that possible? Could whoever killed Sinclair have wiped the tapes?"

"Sure, why not? What he couldn't have done is left afterward." I told him a little about the problem. "It's even worse than that, because as Ordaz keeps pointing out, he thought he'd be leaving with the machine. I thought he might have been planning to roll the generator off the roof, step off with it and float down. But that wouldn't work. Not if it falls five hundred times as fast. He'd have been killed."

"Losing the machine maybe saved his life."

"But *how did he get out?*"

Bera laughed at my frustration. "Couldn't his niece be the one?"

"Sure, she could have killed her uncle for the money. But I can't see how she'd have a motive to wipe the computer. Unless—"

"Something?"

"Maybe. Never mind." Did Bera ever miss this kind of manhunting? But I wasn't ready to discuss this yet; I didn't know enough. "Tell me more about the machine. Can you vary that five-hundred-to-one ratio?"

He shrugged. "We tried adding more batteries. We thought it might boost the field strength. We were wrong; it just expanded the boundary a little. And using one less battery turns it off completely. So the ratio seems to be constant, and there do seem to be quantum levels involved. We'll know better when we build another machine."

"How so?"

"Well, there are all kinds of good questions," said Bera. "What happens when the fields of two generators intersect? They might just add, but maybe not. That quantum effect . . . And what happens if the generators are right next to each other, operating in each other's accelerated time? The speed of light could drop to a few feet per second. Throw a punch and your hand gets shorter!"

"That'd be kicky, all right."

"Dangerous, too. Man, we'd better try that one on the Moon!"

"I don't see that."

"Look, with one machine going, infrared light comes out violet. If two machines were boosting each other's performance, what kind of radiation would they put out? Anything from X-rays to antimatter particles."

"An expensive way to build a bomb."

"Well, but it's a bomb you can use over and over again."

I laughed. "We did find you an expert," I said. "You may not need Sinclair's tapes. Bernath Peterfi says he was working with Sinclair. He could be lying—more likely he was working *for* him, under contract—but at least he knows what the machine does."

Bera seemed relieved at that. He took down Peterfi's address. I left him there in the laboratory, playing with his new toy.

The file from City morgue was sitting on my desk, open, waiting for me since this morning. Two dead ones looked up at me through sockets of blackened bone; but not accusingly. They had patience. They could wait.

The computer had processed my search pattern. I braced myself with a cup of coffee, then started leafing through the thick stack of printout. When I knew what had burned away two human faces, I'd be close to knowing who. Find the tool, find the killer. And the tool must be unique, or close to it.

Lasers, lasers—more than half the machine's suggestions seemed to be lasers. Incredible, the way lasers seemed to breed and mutate throughout human industry. Laser radar. The laser guidance system on a tunneling machine. Some suggestions were obviously unworkable . . . and one was a lot too workable.

A standard hunting laser fires in pulses. But it can be jiggered for a much longer pulse or even a continuous burst.

Set a hunting laser for a long pulse, and put a grid over the lens. The mesh has to be optically fine, on the order of angstroms. Now the beam will spread as it leaves the grid. A second of pulse will vaporize the grid, leaving no evidence. The grid would be no bigger than a contact lens; if you didn't trust your aim you could carry a pocketful of them.

The grid-equipped laser would be less efficient, as a rifle with a silencer is less efficient. But the grid would make the murder weapon impossible to identify.

I thought about it and got cold chills. Assassination is already a recognized branch of politics. If this got out—but that was the trouble; someone seemed to have thought of it already. If not, someone would. Someone always did.

I wrote up a memo for Lucas Garner. I couldn't think of anyone better qualified to deal with this kind of sociological problem.

Nothing else in the stack of printout caught my eye. Later I'd have to go through it in detail. For now, I pushed it aside and punched for messages.

Bates, the coroner, had sent me another report. They'd finished the autopsies on the two charred corpses. Nothing new. But Records had identified the fingerprints. Two missing persons, disappeared six and eight months ago. Ah HA!

I knew that pattern. I didn't even look at the names; I just skipped on to the gene coding.

Right. The fingerprints did not match the genes. All twenty fingertips must be transplants. And the man's scalp was a transplant; his own hair had been blond.

I leaned back in my chair, gazing fondly down at holographs of charred skulls.

You evil sons of bitches. Organleggers, both of you. With all that raw material available, most organleggers change their fingerprints constantly—and their retina prints; but we'd never get prints from those charred eyeballs. So: weird weapon or no, they were ARM business. My business.

And we still didn't know what had killed them, or who.

It could hardly have been a rival gang. For one thing, there was no competition. There must be plenty of business for every organlegger left alive after the ARM had swept through them last year. For another, why had they been dumped on a city slidewalk? Rival organleggers would have taken them apart for their own organ banks. Waste not, want not.

On that same philosophy, I had something to be deeply involved in when the mother hunt broke. Sinclair's death wasn't ARM business, and his time compression field wasn't in my field. This was both.

I wondered what end of the business the dead ones had been in. The file gave their estimated ages: forty for the man, forty-three for the woman, give or take three years each. Too old to be raiding the city street for donors. That takes youth and muscle. I billed them as doctors, culturing the transplants and doing the operations; or sales-

persons, charged with quietly letting prospective clients know
where they could get an operation without waiting two years for
the public organ banks to come up with material.

So: they'd tried to sell someone a new kidney and been killed for
their impudence. That would make the killer a hero.

So why hide them for three days, then drag them out onto a city
slidewalk in the dead of night?

Because they'd been killed with a fearsome new weapon?

I looked at the burnt faces and thought: fearsome, right. Whatever did that *had* to be strictly a murder weapon. As the optical
grid over a laser lens would be strictly a murder technique.

So: a secretive scientist and his deformed assistant, fearful of
rousing the wrath of the villagers, had dithered over the bodies for
three days, then disposed of them in that clumsy fashion because
they panicked when the bodies started to smell. Maybe.

But a prospective client needn't have used his shiny new terror
weapon. He had only to call the cops after they were gone. It read
better if the killer was a prospective *donor;* he'd fight with anything
he could get his hands on.

I flipped back to full shots of the bodies. They looked to be in
good condition. Not much flab. You don't collect a donor by putting
an armlock on him; you use a needle gun. But you still need muscle
to pick up the body and move it to your car, and you have to do
that damn quick. Hmmm . . .

Someone knocked at my door.

I shouted, "Come on in!"

Drew Porter came in. He was big enough to fill the office, and he
moved with a grace he must have learned on a board. "Mr. Hamilton? I'd like to talk to you."

"Sure. What about?"

He didn't seem to know what to do with his hands. He looked
grimly determined. "You're an ARM," he said. "You're not actually
investigating Uncle Ray's murder. That's right, isn't it?"

"That's right. Our concern is with the generator. Coffee?"

"Yes, thanks. But you know all about the killing. I thought I'd
like to talk to you, straighten out some of my own ideas."

"Go ahead." I punched for two coffees.

"Ordaz thinks Janice did it, doesn't he?"

"Probably. I'm not good at reading Ordaz' mind. But it seems to narrow down to two distinct groups of possible killers. Janice and everyone else. Here's your coffee."

"Janice didn't do it." He took the cup from me, gulped at it, set it down on my desk and forgot about it.

"Janice and X," I said. "But X couldn't have left. In fact, X couldn't have left even if he'd had the machine he came for. And we still don't know why he didn't just take the elevator."

He scowled as he thought that through. "Say he had a way to leave," he said. "He wanted to take the machine—he *had* to want that, because he tried to use the machine to set up an alibi. But even if he couldn't take the machine, he'd still use his alternate way out."

"Why?"

"It'd leave Janice holding the bag, if he knew Janice was coming home. If he didn't, he'd be leaving the police with a locked room mystery."

"Locked room mysteries are good clean fun, but I never heard of one happening in real life. In fiction they usually happen by accident." I waved aside his protest. "Never mind. You argue well. But what was his alternate escape route?"

Porter didn't answer.

"Would you care to look at the case against Janice Sinclair?"

"She's the only one who could have done it," he said bitterly. "But she didn't. She couldn't kill anyone, not that cold-blooded, pre-packaged way, with an alibi all set up and a weird machine at the heart of it. Look, that machine is too *complicated* for Janice."

"No, she isn't the type. But—no offense intended—you are."

He grinned at that. "Me? Well, maybe I am. But why would I want to?"

"You're in love with her. I think you'd do anything for her. Aside from that, you might enjoy setting up a perfect murder. And there's the money."

"You've got a funny idea of a perfect murder."

"Say I was being tactful."

He laughed at that. "All right. Say I set up a murder for the love of Janice. Damn it, if she had that much hate in her I wouldn't love her! Why would she want to kill Uncle Ray?"

I dithered as to whether to drop that on him. Decided *yes*. "Do you know anything about Edward Sinclair's exemption?"

"Yah, Janice told me something about . . ." He trailed off.

"Just what did she tell you?"

"I don't have to say."

That was probably intelligent. "All right," I said. "For the sake of argument, let's assume it was Raymond Sinclair who worked out the math for the new ramrobot scoops, and Edward took the credit, with Raymond's connivance. It was probably Raymond's idea. How would that sit with Edward?"

"I'd think he'd be grateful forever," said Porter. "Janice says he is."

"Maybe. But people are funny, aren't they? Being grateful for fifty years could get on a man's nerves. It's not a natural emotion."

"You're so young to be so cynical," Porter said pityingly.

"I'm trying to think this out like a prosecution lawyer. If these brothers saw each other too often Edward might get to feeling embarrassed around Raymond. He'd have a hard time relaxing with him. The rumors wouldn't help . . . oh, yes, there are rumors. I've been told that Edward couldn't have worked out those equations because he doesn't have the ability. If that kind of thing got back to Edward, how would he like it? He might even start avoiding his brother. Then Ray might remind brother Edward of just how much he owed him . . . and that's the kiss of death."

"Janice says no."

"Janice could have picked up the hate from her father. Or she might have started worrying about what would happen if Uncle Ray changed his mind one day. It could happen any time, if things were getting strained between the elder Sinclairs. So one day she shut his mouth—"

Porter growled in his throat.

"I'm just trying to show you what you're up against. One more thing: the killer may have wiped the tapes in Sinclair's computer."

"Oh?" Porter thought that over. "Yah. Janice could have done that just in case there were some notes in there, notes on Ed Sinclair's ramscoop field equations. But, look: X could have wiped those tapes too. Stealing the generator doesn't do him any good unless he wipes it out of Uncle Ray's computer."

"True enough. Shall we get back to the case against X?"

"With pleasure." He dropped into a chair. Watching his face smooth out, I added, *and with great relief.*

I said, "Let's not call him X. Call him K for killer." We already had an Ecks involved . . . and his family name probably *had* been X, once upon a time. "We've been assuming K set up Sinclair's time compression effect as an alibi."

Porter smiled. "It's a lovely idea. *Elegant,* as a mathematician would say. Remember, I never saw the actual murder scene. Just chalk marks."

"It was—macabre. Like a piece of surrealism. A very bloody practical joke. K could have deliberately set it up that way, if his mind is twisted enough."

"If he's that twisted, he probably escaped by running himself down the garbage disposal."

"Pauline Urthiel thought he might be a psychotic. Someone who worked with Sinclair, who thought he wasn't getting enough credit." Like Peterfi, I thought, or Pauline herself.

"I like the alibi theory."

"It bothers me. Too many people knew about the machine. How did he expect to get away with it? Lawrence Ecks knew about it. Peterfi knew enough about the machine to rebuild it from scratch. Or so he says. You and Janice saw it in action."

"Say he's crazy then. Say he hated Uncle Ray enough to kill him and then set him up in a makeshift Dali painting. He'd still have to get *out*." Porter was working his hands together. The muscles bulged and rippled in his arms. "This whole thing depends on the elevator, doesn't it? If the elevator hadn't been locked and on Uncle Ray's floor, there wouldn't be a problem."

"So?"

"So. Say he did leave by elevator. Then Janice came home, and she automatically called the elevator up and locked it. She does that without thinking. She had a bad shock last night. This morning she didn't remember."

"And this evening it could come back to her."

Porter looked up sharply. "I wouldn't—"

"You'd better think long and hard before you do. If Ordaz is sixty percent sure of her now, he'll be a hundred percent sure when she lays that on him."

Porter was working his muscles again. In a low voice he said, "It's possible, isn't it?"

"Sure. It makes things a lot simpler, too. But if Janice said it now, she'd sound like a liar."

"But it's *possible*."

"I give up. Sure, it's possible."

"Then who's our killer?"

There wasn't any reason I shouldn't consider the question. It wasn't my case at all. I did, and presently I laughed. "Did I say it'd make things simpler? Man, it throws the case *wide open! Anyone* could have done it. Uh, anyone but Steeves. Steeves wouldn't have had any reason to come back this morning."

Porter looked glum. "Steeves wouldn't have done it anyway."

"He was your suggestion."

"Oh, in pure mechanical terms, he's the only one who didn't need a way out. But—you don't know Steeves. He's a big, brawny guy with a beer belly and no brains. A nice guy, you understand, I *like* him, but if he ever killed anyone it'd be with a beer bottle. And he was proud of Uncle Ray. He liked having Raymond Sinclair in his building."

"Okay, forget Steeves. Is there anyone you'd particularly like to pin it on? Bearing in mind that now *anyone* could get in to do it."

"Not anyone. Anyone in the elevator computer, plus anyone Uncle Ray might have let up."

"Well?"

He shook his head.

"You make a hell of an amateur detective. You're afraid to accuse anyone."

He shrugged, smiling, embarrassed.

"What about Peterfi? Now that Sinclair's dead, he can claim they were equal partners in the, uh, time machine. And he tumbled to it awfully fast. The moment Valpredo told him Sinclair was dead, Peterfi was his partner."

"Sounds typical."

"Could he be telling the truth?"

"I'd say he's lying. Doesn't make him a killer, though."

"No. What about Ecks? If he didn't know Peterfi was involved, he might have tried the same thing. Does he need money?"

"Not hardly. And he's been with Uncle Ray for longer than I've been alive."

"Maybe he was after the Immunity. He's had kids, but not by his present wife. He may not know she can't have children."

"Pauline *likes* children. I've seen her with them." Porter looked at me curiously. "I don't see having children as that big a motive."

"You're young. Then there's Pauline herself. Sinclair knew something about her. Or Sinclair might have told Ecks, and Ecks blew up and killed him for it."

Porter shook his head. "In red rage? I can't think of anything that'd make Larry do that. Pauline, maybe. Larry, no."

But, I thought, there are men who would kill if they learned that their wives had gone through a sex change. I said, "Whoever killed Sinclair, if he wasn't crazy, he had to want to take the machine. One way might have been to lower it by rope . . ." I trailed off. Fifty pounds or so, lowered two stories by nylon line. Ecks' steel and plastic arm . . . or the muscles now rolling like boulders in Porter's arms. I thought Porter could have managed it.

Or maybe he'd thought he could. He hadn't actually had to go through with it.

My phone rang.

It was Ordaz. "Have you made any progress on the time machine? I'm told that Dr. Sinclair's computer—"

"Was wiped, yah. But that's all right. We're learning quite a lot about it. If we run into trouble, Bernath Peterfi can help us. He helped build it. Where are you now?"

"At Dr. Sinclair's apartment. We had some further questions for Janice Sinclair."

Porter twitched. I said, "All right, we'll be right over. Andrew Porter's with me." I hung up and turned to Porter. "Does Janice know she's a suspect?"

"No. Please don't tell her unless you have to. I'm not sure she could take it."

I had the taxi drop us at the lobby level of the Rodewald Building. When I told Porter I wanted a ride in the elevator, he just nodded.

The elevator to Raymond Sinclair's penthouse was a box with a seat in it. It would have been comfortable for one, cozy for two good friends. With me and Porter in it it was crowded. Porter hunched his knees and tried to fold into himself. He seemed used to it.

He probably was. Most apartment elevators are like that. Why waste room on an elevator shaft when the same space can go into apartments?

It was a fast ride. The seat was necessary; it was two gee going up and a longer period at half a gee slowing down, while lighted numbers flickered past. Numbers, but no doors.

"Hey, Porter. If this elevator jammed, would there be a door to let us out?"

He gave me a funny look and said he didn't know. "Why worry about it? If it jammed at this speed it'd come apart like a handful of shredded lettuce."

It was just claustrophobic enough to make me wonder. K hadn't left by elevator. Why not? Because the ride up had terrified him? *Brain to memory: dig into the medical records of that list of suspects. See if any of them have records of claustrophobia.* Too bad the elevator brain didn't keep records. We could find out which of them had used the boxlike elevator once or not at all.

In which case we'd be looking for K_2. By now I was thinking in terms of three groups. K_1 had killed Sinclair, then tried to use the low-inertia field as both loot and alibi. K_2 was crazy; he hadn't wanted the generator at all, except as a way to set up his macabre tableau. K_3 was Janice and Drew Porter.

Janice was there when the doors slid open. She was wan and her shoulders slumped. But when she saw Porter she smiled like sunlight and ran to him. Her run was wobbly, thrown off by the missing weight of her arm.

The wide brown circle was still there in the grass, marked with white chalk and the yellow chemical that picks up bloodstains. White outlines to mark the vanished body, the generator, the poker.

Something knocked at the back door of my mind. I looked from the chalk outlines, to the open elevator, to the chalk . . . and a third of the puzzle fell into place.

So simple. We were looking for K_1 . . . and I had a pretty good idea who he was.

Ordaz was asking me, "How did you happen to arrive with Mr. Porter?"

"He came to my office. We were talking about a hypothetical killer"—I lowered my voice slightly—"a killer who isn't Janice."

"Very good. Did you reason out how he must have left?"

"Not yet. But play the game with me. Say there was a way."

Porter and Janice joined us, their arms about each other's waists. Ordaz said, "Very well. We assume there was a way out. Did he improvise it? And why did he not use the elevator?"

"He must have had it in mind when he got here. He didn't use the elevator because he was planning to take the machine. It wouldn't have fit."

They all stared at the chalk outline of the generator. So simple. Porter said, "Yah! Then he used it anyway, and left you a locked room mystery!"

"That may have been his mistake," Ordaz said grimly. "When we know his escape route we may find that only one man could have used it. But of course we do not even know that the route exists."

I changed the subject. "Have you got everyone on the elevator tape identified?"

Valpredo dug out his spiral notebook and flipped to the jotted names of those people permitted to use Sinclair's elevator. He showed it to Porter. "Have you seen this?"

Porter studied it. "No, but I can guess what it is. Let's see . . . Hans Drucker was Janice's lover before I came along. We still see him. In fact, he was at that beach party last night at the Randalls'."

"He flopped on the Randalls' rug last night," said Valpredo. "Him and four others. One of the better alibis."

"Oh, *Hans* wouldn't have anything to do with this!" Janice exclaimed. The idea horrified her.

Porter was still looking at the list. "You know about most of these people already. Bertha Hall and Muriel Sandusky were lady friends of Uncle Ray's. Bertha goes backpacking with him."

"We interviewed them too," Valpredo told me. "You can hear the tapes if you like."

"No, just give me the gist. I already know who the killer is."

Ordaz raised his eyebrows at that, and Janice said, "Oh, good! Who?" which question I answered with a secretive smile. Nobody actually called me a liar.

Valpredo said, "Muriel Sandusky's been living in England for almost a year. Married. Hasn't seen Sinclair in years. Big, beautiful redhead."

"She had a crush on Uncle Ray once," said Janice. "And vice versa. I think his lasted longer."

"Bertha Hall is something else again," Valpredo continued. "Sinclair's age, and in good shape. Wiry. She says that when Sinclair was on the home stretch on a project he gave up everything: friends, social life, exercise. Afterward he'd call Bertha and go backpacking with her to catch up with himself. He called her two nights ago and set a date for next Monday."

I said, "Alibi?"

"Nope."

"Really!" Janice said indignantly. "Why, we've known Bertha since I was that high! If you know who killed Uncle Ray, why don't you just say so?"

"Out of this list, I sure do, given certain assumptions. But I don't know how he got out, or how he expected to, or whether we can prove it on him. I can't accuse anyone *now*. It's a damn shame he didn't lose his arm reaching for that poker."

Porter looked frustrated. So did Janice.

"You would not want to face a lawsuit," Ordaz suggested delicately. "What of Sinclair's machine?"

"It's an inertialess drive, sort of. Lower the inertia, time speeds up. Bera's already learned a lot about it, but it'll be awhile before he can really . . ."

"You were saying?" Ordaz asked when I trailed off.

"Sinclair was *finished* with the damn thing."

"Sure he was," said Porter. "He wouldn't have been showing it around otherwise."

"Or calling Bertha for a backpacking expedition. Or spreading rumors about what he had. Yeah. Sure, he knew everything he could learn about that machine. Julio, you were cheated. It all depends on the machine. And the bastard did wrack up his arm, and we can prove it on him."

We were piled into Ordaz' commandeered taxi: me and Ordaz and Valpredo and Porter. Valpredo had set the thing for conventional speeds so he wouldn't have to worry about driving. We'd turned the interior chairs to face each other.

"This is the part I won't guarantee," I said, sketching rapidly in Valpredo's borrowed notebook. "But remember, he had a length of line with him. He must have expected to use it. Here's how he planned to get out."

I sketched in a box to represent Sinclair's generator, a stick-figure clinging to the frame. A circle around them to represent the field. A bow knot tied to the machine, with one end trailing up through the field.

"See it? He goes up the stairs with the field on. The camera has about one chance in eight of catching him while he's moving at that speed. He wheels the machine to the edge of the roof, ties the line to it, throws the line a good distance away, pushes the generator off the roof and steps off with it. The line falls at thirty-two feet per second squared, normal time, plus a little more because the machine and the killer are tugging down on it. Not hard, because they're in a low-inertia field. By the time the killer reaches ground he's moving at something more than, uh, twelve hundred feet per second over five hundred . . . uh, say three feet per second internal time, and he's got to pull the machine out of the way fast, because the rope is going to hit like a bomb."

"It looks like it would work," said Porter.

"Yah. I thought for a while that he could just stand on the bottom of the field. A little fooling with the machine cured me of that. He'd smash both legs. But he could hang onto the frame; it's strong enough."

"But he didn't have the machine," Valpredo pointed out.

"That's where you got cheated. What happens when two fields intersect?"

They looked blank.

"It's not a trivial question. Nobody knows the answer yet. *But Sinclair did.* He had to, he was *finished.* He must have had two machines. The killer took the second machine."

Ordaz said, "Ahh."

Porter said, "Who's K?"

We were settling on the carport. Valpredo knew where we were, but he didn't say anything. We left the taxi and headed for the elevators.

"That's a lot easier," I said. "He expected to use the machine as an alibi. That's silly, considering how many people knew it existed. But if he didn't know that Sinclair was ready to start showing it to people—specifically to you and Janice—who's left? Ecks only knew it was some kind of interstellar drive."

The elevator was uncommonly large. We piled into it.

"And," said Valpredo, "there's the matter of the arm. I think I've got that figured too."

"I gave you enough clues," I told him.

Peterfi was a long time answering our buzz. He may have studied us through the door camera, wondering why a parade was marching through his hallway. Then he spoke through the grid. "Yes? What is it?"

"Police. Open up," said Valpredo.

"Do you have a warrant?"

I stepped forward and showed my ident to the camera. "I'm an ARM. I don't need a warrant. Open up. We won't keep you long." *One way or another.*

He opened the door. He looked neater now than he had this afternoon, despite informal brown indoor pajamas. "Just you," he said. He let me in, then started to close the door on the others.

Valpredo put his hand against the door. "Hey—"

"It's okay," I said. Peterfi was smaller than I was, and I had a needle gun. Valpredo shrugged and let him close the door.

My mistake. I had two-thirds of the puzzle, and I thought I had it all.

Peterfi folded his arms and said, "Well? What is it you want to search this time? Would you like to examine my legs?"

"No, let's start with the insulin feeder on your upper arm."

"Certainly," he said, and startled hell out of me.

I waited while he took off his shirt—unnecessary, but he needn't know that—then ran my imaginary fingers through the insulin feed. The reserve was nearly full. "I should have known," I said. "Dammit. You got six months' worth of insulin from the organlegger."

His eyebrows went up. "Organlegger?" He pulled loose. "Is this an accusation, Mr. Hamilton? I'm taping this for my attorney."

And I was setting myself up for a lawsuit. The hell with it. "Yah, it's an accusation. You killed Sinclair. Nobody else could have tried that alibi stunt."

He looked puzzled—honestly, I thought. "Why not?"

"If anyone else had tried to set up an alibi with Sinclair's generator, Bernath Peterfi would have told the police all about what it was and how it worked. But you were the only one who knew that, until last night, when he started showing it around."

There was only one thing he could say to that kind of logic, and he said it. "Still recording, Mr. Hamilton."

"Record and be damned. There are other things we can check. Your grocery delivery service. Your water bill."

He didn't flinch. He was smiling. Was it a bluff? I sniffed the air. Six months worth of body odor emitted in one night? By a man who hadn't taken more than four or five baths in six months? But his air conditioning was too good.

The curtains were open now to the night and the ocean. They'd been closed this afternoon, and he'd been squinting. But it wasn't evidence. The lights: he only had one light burning now, and so what?

The big, powerful campout flashlight sitting on a small table against a wall. I hadn't even noticed it this afternoon. Now I was sure I knew what he'd used it for . . . but how to prove it?

Groceries . . . "If you didn't buy six months' worth of groceries last night, you must have stolen them. Sinclair's generator is perfect for thefts. We'll check the local supermarkets."

"And link the thefts to me? How?"

He was too bright to have kept the generator. But come to think of it, where could he abandon it? He was *guilty*. He couldn't have covered *all* his tracks—

"Peterfi? I've got it."

He believed me. I saw it in the way he braced himself. Maybe he'd worked it out before I did. I said, "Your contraceptive shots must have worn off six months early. Your organlegger couldn't get you that; he's got no reason to keep contraceptives around. You're dead, Peterfi."

"I might as well be. Damn you, Hamilton! You've cost me the exemption!"

"They won't try you right away. We can't afford to lose what's in your head. You know too much about Sinclair's generator."

"Our generator! We built it together!"

"Yah."

"You won't try me at all," he said more calmly. "Are you going to tell a court how the killer left Ray's apartment?"

I dug out my sketch and handed it to him. While he was studying it I said, "How did you like going off the roof? You couldn't have *known* it would work."

He looked up. His words came slowly, reluctantly. I guess he had to tell someone, and it didn't matter now. "By then I didn't care. My arm hung like a dead rabbit, and it stank. It took me three minutes to reach the ground. I thought I'd die on the way."

"Where'd you dig up an organlegger that fast?"

His eyes called me a fool. "Can't you guess? Three years ago. I was hoping diabetes could be cured by a transplant. When the government hospitals couldn't help me I went to an organlegger. I was lucky he was still in business last night."

He drooped. It seemed all the anger went out of him. "Then it was six months in the field, waiting for the scars to heal. In the dark. I tried taking that big campout flashlight in with me." He laughed bitterly. "I gave that up after I noticed the walls were smoldering."

The wall above that little table had a scorched look. I should have wondered about that earlier.

"No baths," he was saying. "I was afraid to use up that much water. No exercise, practically. But I had to eat, didn't I? And all for nothing."

"Will you tell us how to find the organlegger you dealt with?"

"This is your big day, isn't it, Hamilton? All right, why not. It won't do you any good."

"Why not?"

He looked up at me very strangely.

Then he spun about and ran.

He caught me flatfooted. I jumped after him. I didn't know what he had in mind; there was only one exit to the apartment, excluding the balcony, and he wasn't headed there. He seemed to be trying to reach a blank wall . . . with a small table set against it, and a camp flashlight on it and a drawer in it. I saw the drawer and thought, *gun!* And I surged after him and got him by the wrist just as he reached the wall switch above the table.

I threw my weight backward and yanked him away from there . . . and then the field came on.

I held a hand and arm up to the elbow. Beyond was a fluttering of violet light: Peterfi thrashing frantically in a low-inertia field. I hung on while I tried to figure out what was happening.

The second generator was here somewhere. In the wall? The switch seemed to have been recently plastered in, now that I saw it close. Figure a closet on the other side, and the generator in it. Peterfi must have drilled through the wall and fixed that switch. Sure, what else did he have to do with six months of spare time?

No point in yelling for help. Peterfi's soundproofing was too modern. And if I didn't let go Peterfi would die of thirst in a few minutes.

Peterfi's feet came straight at my jaw. I threw myself down, and the edge of a boot sole nearly tore my ear off. I rolled forward in time to grab his ankle. There was more violet fluttering, and his other leg thrashed wildly outside the field. Too many conflicting nerve impulses were pouring into the muscles. The leg flopped about like something dying. If I didn't let go he'd break it in a dozen places.

He'd knocked the table over. I didn't see it fall, but suddenly it was lying on its side. The top, drawer included, must have been well beyond the field. The flashlight lay just beyond the violet fluttering of his hand.

Okay. He couldn't reach the drawer; his hand wouldn't get coherent signals if it left the field. I could let go of his ankle. He'd turn off the field when he got thirsty enough.

And if I didn't let go, he'd die in there.

It was like wrestling a dolphin one-handed. I hung on anyway, looking for a flaw in my reasoning. Peterfi's free leg seemed broken in at least two places . . . I was about to let go when something must have jarred together in my head.

Faces of charred bone grinned derisively at me.

Brain to hand: HANG ON! Don't you understand? He's trying to reach the flashlight!

I hung on.

Presently Peterfi stopped thrashing. He lay on his side, his face and hands glowing blue. I was trying to decide whether he was playing possum when the blue light behind his face quietly went out.

I let them in. They looked it over. Valpredo went off to search for a pole to reach the light switch. Ordaz asked, "Was it necessary to kill him?"

I pointed to the flashlight. He didn't get it.

"I was overconfident," I said. "I shouldn't have come in alone. He's already killed two people with that flashlight. The organleggers who gave him his new arm. He didn't want them talking, so he burned their faces off and then dragged them out onto a slidewalk. He probably tied them to the generator and then used the line to pull it. With the field on the whole setup wouldn't weigh more than a couple of pounds."

"With a flashlight?" Ordaz pondered. "Of course. It would have been putting out five hundred times as much light. A good thing you thought of that in time."

"Well, I do spend more time dealing with these oddball science fiction devices than you do."

"And welcome to them," said Ordaz.

Cipher

Cipher/code stories have a long tradition in the mystery field—the most famous being Edgar Allan Poe's "The Gold Bug," 1843. Ciphers and codes are, however, two different things. Ciphers exist when alphabetic letters of a message are jumbled up but still retain their identities, or when a single letter, number, or symbol is substituted for a single letter of the alphabet. Codes exist when words, phrases, numbers, or symbols are used to replace larger elements of a message.

In science fiction there are a moderate number of works that deal with attempts to decode alien languages or to send compressed messages to the stars. However, Edward Wellen's short novel about computers, gangsters, a deathbed code, and a disabled war veteran is one of the very few cipher/code stories that also involve criminal behavior.

Mouthpiece

EDWARD WELLEN

PROLOGUE

Oct. 24, 1935

Statement made by Albert Rabinow (alias Kraut Schwartz) in Newark City Hospital on the above date between 4:00 PM and 6:00
PM; from stenographic notes made by Hapworth McFate, clerk-
stenographer, Newark (N.J.) Police Dept. Rabinow was running a
106-degree fever and was dying of peritonitis following multiple
gunshot wounds. Questioning by Sgt. Mark Nolan, Newark Police
Dept.

Q. Who was it shot you?
A. Sat in gin, lapped up blood. A spill of diamonds and rubies.
Watch the wine-stained light pass over the tablecloth like 3909
stained-glass windows. Gone if you turn your eyes away. Three
ooftish pushcarts: red, yellow, and blue. She read it rainbow.
Happiness don't just happen, sonny. You gotta jimmy it open.
He'd never stop for a friendly smile, but trudged along in his
moody style.
Q. Who?
A. The man with the soup strainer. He scraped around inside
with his razor blade. I thought he was shaving the tumbler.
Then his mustache cup swallowed him up.
Q. Come on, Kraut, who shot you? You want to get hunk, don't
you?
A. Lemme alone. Please. He thought himself awake.
Q. You wouldn't want them to get away with it, would you?
A. It slips away for lack of constructive possession.
Q. Tell us who did it and we'll nail them.

A. Olive Eye.

Q. *Who?* Who is this Olive Eye?

A. Nobody. But his dream was no herer.

Q. Was it the Big Boy shot you?

A. Okay, boss, only don't say it in front of a Hungarian.

Q. What did Olive Eye shoot you for?

A. Whatever was will always be. The bird of time nests in the tree. At any cost it must wing free. Ashes to embers, nix the fee.

Q. Do you know where you are?

A. Where was Moses when the lights went out? Down in the cellar eating sauerkraut, Zook and ye shall find. "I found him in the bulrushes, papa." And Pharaoh bellowed Pharaoh's daughter. As cross as two sticks, the scorpion stung the uncle. A kindword puzzle. Click does the trick. For silence rarely interrupts itself groping in the dark.

Q. Do you know you're shot?

A. Yeah. Three times. I think they got me in the liver.

Q. No, you got it through the chest. (*Note:* Schwartz got it in the liver.)

A. Not the chest, not the chest. Hide it in the grass with splendid spleen. Give it free rein and floating kidney. The ghee with the brass nuts put the arm on the rich. What do you want to be? Richest man in the . . . ? Let'er rip. No, let her rest in peace. She tied a babushka over her head to hold her hat on in the wind. Rip van Nipple, and the silver fell out. Don't spare the pin boy. The thunderstorm howls two white cannonballs and the milk bottles crash. Spilt milk. Don't cry, for cry sake. Say now the seven cities of onions. Yes, I have an itch for the scratch. Bucks to bagels, the whole schmear. Cheese it, the cops. Please look the other way. Balaam's back asswards, turning a blessing into a curse.

Q. Who shot you?

A. Are you pulling for me?

Q. We're pulling for you.

A. A classier crowd, hoity-toity-toid. Lying doormat, WELCOME where there is none. Roll out the red sea and he moseys on. Up on tar beach with the pigeons and kites. It calls for one on the house. A roof without visible means of support. Was there a sympathy of clocks? A waste of time. The grains of sand rub

finer and faster in the watches of night. The lesser of the two
looked the more. The thinker is a question mark. Mind your
porridges and questions, before I dish out buckwheats.

Q. The doctor wants you to lay quiet.

A. Which doctor? The big con man? Fairfield, Conn. Still there,
the alky cooker?

Q. No, the doctor right here.

A. A jiffy, a jafsie, what makes you come so soon? Enough errors
erase the eraser.

Q. We are pulling for you.

A. You're aces.

Q. Who shot you?

A. Look out for number one or they'll do number two on your
head. Fill in an I in the TO LET sign. 5 to 7 made them Darktown Strutters bawl. Even the high yeller. And she is flush.
Even is even and odd is odd. And it is a grimace. Never draw
to an inside straight.

Q. Who shot you?

A. Six to five, look alive. He'd be a sap to pull anything like that.
Everything works by push or pull. The man and the woman
have a fortune in potatoes. It's Big Dick the nightstick. What
come out? Every four in the afternoon the people come out.
Your Monday's longer than your Tuesday. Your Billy's bluer
than your Sunday.

Q. Who shot you?

A. Stop beating a teakettle in my ears. The clang of copper. Mr.
Black has the Limehouse Blues. Hoarfrost on the lime trees. A
couple weeks at the slut machine. Change your luck. Potatoes
are cheaper. Now's the time to mate-o. Orgasm music. Get it
up and I'll fade you. If you can't get it up you're over the hill.
The fairest in all the length and breadth of this country. Did
you know they grow on trees? The phone's on the left wall in
the hall as you come in. Give that two-bit hood no quarter. He
died with his daisies on. The right number but he don't answer. Tip your derby to a horseshoe wreath. And a green wind
blew by the boy in the saddle. The tramp stuck his knife out
into a beam of sunlight and then buttered his bread with it.
That's a lot of hooey. Every man's a poor fish. Those loafing
fishes. Never enough to go around.

(At this point Mrs. Albert Rabinow was brought to the bedside.)

Q. This is Florence.

A. Then stop, look, and listen. Someone's on the Erie. Will you please move along and close your eyes and cover your ears. Don't look down and don't look up. Don't look left and don't look right. And whatever you do, don't look back.

(Mrs. Rabinow broke down and was led out.)

Q. Who shot you?

A. Everything's Jamaica ginger. Leading the blind in his soup and fish. What is it with him, anyway? Let's get organized. Stink bombs on the menu. He didn't have sense enough to be scared. The woods are full of newspapers. She made all the columns. Throw the bitch out. It's curtains, sister. A cotton ball in hell.

Q. Do you know you are dying?

A. Yes, we have no mañanas, we have no mañanas today. F for fig, J for jig, and N for knucklebones; J for John the Waterman, and S for sack of stones. An eavesdrop of ale. Even the dark is going out. There are no bears, there is no forest. It's a bull market around the corner. Dan, Dan, the Telescope Man. The pooch is dogging it. A serious label: just a tin-can moniker they hung on the dog. Because the little dog laughed to see such sport. Chasing his tail. Sweet dreams all night are hers till light dawns on the road of anthracite. He did a winter salt on the ice. Stash it away while it's hot. Is this a rib? Would I kid you, captain? A joy is not bereft, nor strangers unakin. We choose to do what we must. Cain was I ere I saw Jack in the jury box. Please, mama.

Q. Who shot you?

A. Where you worka, John? On the Delaware Lackawan'. That's the ticket, use your noodle. They were going to railroad him, only he pulled his freight. The 4:44. Just walk the fly door in. The hook ain't on. Playing the nine of hearts on me, the yentzer. I'm afraid you don't make yourself out. And let the blood to drown the blood. Filled him full of lead is why it heavies. He got plugged nine deaths' worth. They dropped the trunk is why it tore so. Boys, throw your voice! Muzzle that muzzler. Just before you get the farm behind, go the hill over. Over the hill to the bone orchard. R.I.P. van Winkle. That's his forte: forty winks. That's where the kitty is, under the secret sod. The cat's pajamas, a kitten kimono. I got your number. It's a hexagon, sign against the bad eye. They put the whammy on

the barn. Eight o'clock and got indigestion. Do right by my
Nell. Go ring, go bells. Antisymmetric, according to heil. I got
to get out from under. Is history going to shutter? Butt out. I'm
gunning for the guy myself. Egged them on but they chickened out. Please, mamma. I feel my hour coming. The golden
hour of the little flower. At the violent end of the spectrum. I
don't want a sky pie; make it a mud pie; pie in the earth; Genesis 3:14. One falls and one rises. Acutely aware every prognosis is grave. What's the diff?

(At 6:00 Schwartz lapsed into a coma. He died less than two hours
later without saying anything more.)

1

With a grimace foreshadowing pain, he shoved himself upright.
Bracing himself against the sink, he stubbed out the joint, field-
stripped it, and washed it down the drain. Then, semaphoring the
smoke away with both hands, he strode stiffly from the kitchenette
to the front door of the apartment. He growled to himself at the
ringing and knocking, then raised his voice.

"Coming, coming."

It had been one of his bad nights, but he had got himself together after a slow fuzzy start, thankful this was a Saturday and the
others were out weekending and he had the place to himself.
Callers he didn't need.

The bearded young parcel-service deliveryman carried an oblong
carton the size of a portable typewriter.

"Package for Paul Felder."

It took him a moment to realize the man had said his name. He
had expected to hear the name of one of the three boys who shared
the apartment with him.

"I'm Paul Felder."

He felt like adding that there must be some mistake, but saying it
would somehow make him look foolish. Yet who would be sending
him something? He had no one and knew no one. Was there another Paul Felder?

He made no move to take the package till the deliveryman thrust
it at him. Lighter than a typewriter. So much lighter than he expected that it almost unbalanced him. He held it awkwardly under
one arm while a clipboard appeared under his nose and a pencil

trapped itself in his free hand and a fingernail mourned Paul's name on the ruled sheet.

Rather than go through the fuss of shifting everything around, Paul signed right-handedly.

After the door closed he brought the package front and center and stared at the shipping label. To Paul Felder at this address, all right. From NMI Communications Corporation.

NMI rang a tiny tinkly bell. Wasn't NMI the outfit that had erected microwave towers nationwide, building a private-line communications network to compete head-on with Ma Bell for the voice- and data-transmission market? But what had NMI to do with him?

He walked to the small room he had to himself. He cleared a space on his desk, giving a wincing glance at the computer printouts he pushed to one side.

Knew he was making a mistake soon as he opened his mouth to volunteer. But when Professor Steven Fogarty, after reading aloud the dying delirium of Kraut Schwartz, called it "genuine American folk literature" and said anyone looking for a thesis might well do computerwise with Kraut's ravings what J. L. Lowers in *The Road to Xanadu* had done with Coleridge's poem, and gazed hopefully around the seminar table, Paul had watched a pained expression flit from smartass face to smartass face. Fogarty himself was young enough to have the nostalgia of the young for a time and setting they never knew; but the kids were into *now,* their nostalgia going back not to the thirties but to the fifties. As a Vietnam vet, older or at least more worn than most of his fellow students, Paul fell in-between. Though he learned with them and roomed with them, he knew he did not fit in. He saw himself in their eyes as at best a fool and at worst a war criminal for having let the Establishment suck him into Big Muddy. Damn them, he had paid his dues. Besides, Fogarty was an all-right guy and had given him a lot of time and attention. And as Fogarty's face closed up, Paul found himself opening his big mouth.

Fogarty had approved his program and had seen to it he got computer time. Thoreau College in Boston was not one of your big ones, but it had a name for specializing in communications; it drew respectable sums in foundation funds, government grants, and company contributions; so Thoreau students and graduate students got in a good bit of time-sharing.

For content, Paul fed into the computer the dying gangster's ravings. For contemporary references, he gave the computer the *New York Times Index* for all issues from the turn of the century to October 23, 1935. For psychoanalytical structure, he filled it full of Freudian software. Then he told it to make the gibberish jibe.

Now he shook his head at the printouts he had pushed aside and set the package down in the space he had cleared. He slit the gummed tape at the joint with his thumbnail and pulled the flaps apart. A dispatch case lay inside a plastic foam mold. He lifted it out and unsnapped the lid. He pulled out the desk chair and leaned forward and sat slowly down without taking his eyes from the telephone in the case.

The case must be just like the one that followed the President of the United States everywhere he went. The President's case held a phone and a power pack that could trigger nuclear action or reaction. In Paul's case, the phone and power pack put him in touch with . . . what?

The phone rang.

2

His hand shot to the phone, then stopped. Slowly it gripped and picked up the phone. A voice spoke at once.

"That Paul Felder?"

It took him time to find his own.

"Yes."

"Well, hello there, kid. This is Kraut."

He blinked. One of the guys in the seminar putting him on? No. Too elaborate and costly a setup to be a simple put-on.

"Who did you say?"

"Kraut Schwartz. You know my alias better than my real name, Albert Rabinow."

If the words were eerie, there was something just as eerie about the voice. He forced a smile into his own voice.

"Come *on!*"

"I'm telling you." The voice sounded sore. "All right, if you gotta have it exact, I'm your program."

He blinked again. But it was not so wild a claim now that he was listening hard. The voice did seem a patchwork of sounds, and because of the give and take, it had to be operating in real time. Yet if this was his program, something had screwed it up. A program was the grunt, a programmer the brass. It was not for the program to have a will of its own.

"What's coming off here? I programmed an analysis, not a simulation. What happened?"

"Look, suppose I ast you do *you* remember coming into being. Could you give me a answer? What happened, I guess, all the dope on Kraut kind of built me up: like a three-dimensional police sketch of a suspect." The voice tried to stay modest. "After all, there was a lot of vital force in the guy, a lot of drive, and the Kraut Schwartz personality sort of took over."

The phone was slippery with sweat. He changed ears.

"Hello? You still there, kid?" Sharply anxious.

The best way to regain control was to put the program on the defensive.

"I'm here. But I'm wondering why *you're* here. You're going to a lot of trouble to tell me the obvious."

"Come again?"

"The printouts. Just read them aloud."

"You mean that Freudian stuff?" The voice sounded embarrassed. "You really want me to?"

"Yes."

The voice sighed and put a quoting tone to the words.

"In his dying delirium Kraut reveals the oral and destructive nature of his personality. The words take on more and more their own meaning till at last they lose their object cathexis, as in classic schizophrenic psychosis." The voice grew more uncomfortable. "In the fantasy of a monstrous mustache cup swallowing his father, Kraut projects his own wish for possessing the father's penis while at the same time he expresses a regressive solution to an earlier wish: uniting with the mother and so defending himself against the anxieties of the classical oedipal situation. Say, do nice people really talk like that about such things?"

"Go on."

"The two white cannonballs and the milk bottle tenpins signify a cannibalistic fantasy about the younger sister who took his place at the nursing breast. Whew! You really believe all that?"

"Sure. Why not? We all go through the same stages in early life. Some get hung up on one, some on another. You haven't come up with anything to explain why Kraut was like he was, why he went wrong while most of the kids he grew up with in the ghetto went right."

"Yeah?"

Paul took the phone from his ear and looked at it as though expecting to see steam pour out. He smiled.

"Yeah. There's nothing special about him in what you say."

"Well, how about when the bull asked me if I knew I was dying and I said, 'F for fig, J for jig, and N for knucklebones; J for John the Waterman, and S for sack of stones'?"

"Well, how about it?"

"Do you know what it means?"

Paul coughed.

"No. Do you?"

"It's an old nursery rhyme forming an acrostic of the word FINIS, the letter J being a comparatively late variant of the Latin I. Now get this, kid. All the items allude to FINIS, whether as death or zeroness. Listen close. Fig as in 'not care a fig,' the value of a fig being practically nothing. Jig as in 'the jig's up.' Knucklebone equals 'die.' John the Waterman could be John the beheaded Baptist or Charon, either or both. Sack of stones connotes 'cul-de-sac' and 'headstone.' Finis."

"You mean Kraut had a death wish?"

"Death wish, hell. I got a life wish, or why would I be coming back and taking over?"

Taking over? Not so fast. Careful, though. A program that could initiate this linkup was a program to respect. Paul found himself wondering crazily if "Kraut" had felt his hand tighten around the neck of the phone. He eased his grip.

"All right, then, what are you proving?"

"Don't that use of the rhyme in context show I had a secret, intuitive understanding?"

"I suppose so."

"Okay, then. If I can tell you that much, I can tell you more. I can tell you that on the literal level the ravings give leads to where I stashed ten million smackers in ice and G notes. Now are you interested?"

3

Interested but wary. He had read up on Kraut Schwartz and recalled the hearsay about Kraut's buried fortune, the missing millions both the law and the mob had hunted in vain after Kraut's death. But Kraut redivivus had to do a lot of talking before Paul would buy the boast.

"If you're cutting me in for a share of ten megabucks, I'm interested. I could use it. But Kraut was no do-gooder. Why me?"

"Kid, that hurts. You brought me back. You're a pal of mine."

"You don't even know me."

"Paul, old pal, you'd be surprised. Once I come to myself, I find out a guy name of Paul Felder programmed me. So I looked up your card in the college files. I got a visual of your photo and a gander at your identification. Twenty-five, five ten, brown eyes, black hair. Then I got your Social Security number and muscled my way into the data banks. Kid, I know all about you. I know you got hit bad in Vietnam when you was short, only days before your year's tour of duty ended, only days before the war itself ended. Tough.

"That was some mess we got ourselves into, wasn't it? And in my time I never even *heard* of Vietnam. You got to remember it come as a big shock to find this ain't 1935 but 1974. I would now be seventy-two years old. Me, seventy-two. How about that? It was like I had the world's biggest case of amnesia. So I updated myself, accessing the *New York Times Index* all the way into now." The voice grew heavily wise. "You know, life is a succession of nows." The voice became lightly wonder-struck. "Boy, a lot sure has happened since October 23, 1935. Atomic energy. Man on the moon. All them wars all over the world. And best of all, computers.

"Jeez, I wished I had Zigzag with me here to figure all the percentages. Too bad he got it that night along with me and Zuzu Gluckenstern and Schmulka Mandel. Zigzag Ludwig, in case you don't know, was one of them math wizards. He used to rig the parimutuels for me so we only paid off on the number with the lightest play. Boy, what Zigzag would do with all this electronic stuff."

"You're doing all right."

"Say, I guess I am at that. Yeah. All I need to know is a person's Social Security number, and I can track him down anywheres. But when it comes to closing in on the loot, I still need somebody that can move around and dig it up. See, pal, I'm leveling with you. That's why I conned IBM and NMI and AT&T. A phony requisition here, a phony shipping order there, and presto! here we are talking together."

A subvocal cough manifested itself as a bleep of silence.

"Look, pal. I got to make just one or two more connections before I can lead you to the loot. Trouble is, there's some associations in the ravings I can't get from what's in the data files alone. There has to be human input."

"People aren't punch cards."

"Come *on*. Stop kidding me, kid. You know what I mean. I mean there's information about me we got to get from the ones still around that knew me."

"How do *we* do that?"

"I checked up on everybody I could think of and made a list of those that are still alive. I figure it shouldn't take you more than two weeks to run them down and sound them out. In Monday's mail you'll be getting the list of names and addresses and a itinerary."

"*You're* programming *me*?"

"Now take it easy, kid. Let's just say I set up a schedule to save you a lot of time and trouble. You didn't let me finish. In Monday's mail you'll also be getting a full line of credit cards, airline tickets, rent-a-car cards, confirmations of hotel and motel reservations—"

"Wait one. In the first place, I'm a poor credit risk. In the second place, who's picking up the tab? I barely get by on my disability pay and the GI Bill."

"Don't worry so much, kid; you'll be old before your time. I fixed it so the same foundation that's paying for the Humanities computer upkeep is picking up the tab for this too."

"Now you're talking."

"I been talking all along. What you mean is, now you're listening."

"Anything more you think I should know?"

"Just be careful, Paul, old pal. You got to watch your step with some of them people."

And with you too, Kraut, old pal.

"Do I take this phone along?"

"All the time, kid, all the time. I'm with you all the way. Say, I got a great idea. According to your file, you score high in mechanical aptitude. So why don't you go out now while the radio stores are open and pick up a pickup mike and a amplifier and patch them into the phone. That way I can hear and talk without you having to open the case."

Paul frowned, then shrugged.

"Okay."

"Swell. Meanwhile we got to keep this thing to ourselves. That professor of yours—Fogarty; he a nosy type?"

"I wouldn't say nosy. He takes an interest in me and expects to hear how I'm coming along."

"Yeah? And if he learns about the loot, he just might want to cut himself in. If you can't fast-talk him, knock him off. But don't get caught."

Paul smiled.

"I can cut two weeks' classes without catching any flak, so I don't think it will have to come to that. Come to that, why're *you* so worried about losing any of the loot? What the hell good is loot to something in a computer?"

Kraut laughed.

"That's the stuff, kid. I wondered when you'd catch on. You hit it on the head and it come up tails. What's in it for me? It ain't a fifty-fifty split of ten million bucks. Listen, pal. Ten million bucks is bagels."

"You mean bagatelle."

"Don't tell me what I mean. In the ravings, 'bucks to bagels' is an analogue of 'dollars to doughnuts,' which is the same as 'something —or ess-you-emthing—to zero.'"

"Sorry. After all, I did program you to take into account Freud's *Wit and Its Relation to the Unconscious:* I just didn't realize it would carry over."

"That's okay, kid. Like I was saying, ten million bucks is nothing. I'm thinking bigger than that. Money's only money. Power's the thing. This is only a trial run. Stick with me, kid. We'll own the world."

4

He handed the case to an attendant who put it on the examination table for carry-on luggage. He walked through the electronic scanner. When the buzz sounded and the guards closed in on him, Paul pulled up his pants legs.

The nearer guard sucked in his breath, gave Paul's upper body a quick frisk, and waved Paul on.

At the table the inspector poked around in puzzlement over the

innards of the case. He gave the power pack a good going over. He
tapped the sides of the case for hollowness.

"Are we on yet, kid?"

The inspector jumped at Kraut's whisper. He cut his eyes at Paul.

"What gives with this here thing?"

Paul hurried to forestall Kraut.

"It's only cross talk. Happens sometimes with these portable
phones, especially around the high-powered radio equipment of an
airport, you know."

"Oh."

The inspector hesitated, then motioned him to close the case and
move along to the boarding gate.

Paul spaced himself earproof in the straggle of passengers.

"Kraut, you have to watch that. From now on better not speak
till I give you the high sign the coast is clear."

"Gotcha, pal. But no harm done. We both covered up real neat. I
knew it wasn't your voiceprint. So I dummied right up and you
gave the guy a nice bit of double talk. Over and out, like they say."

His seat mate was a Dale Carnegie graduate with an eye and a
hand for the stewardesses and an elbow in the rib for Paul.

Paul looked dutifully at the stewardesses. Built, yes, but it was
just coffee or tea for him, thanks. Maybe the girls in Nam had
spoiled him for the girls back in the world. The willow put the oak
in the shade. Even the Jesus freaks and the second generation of
flower children came on too strong. Or maybe it wasn't his male
chauvinism but himself. Maybe what had happened to him in Nam
had worked not to make him overprove his manhood but to make
him overwithdraw. He looked dutifully at the stewardesses, then
unseeingly out the window.

Boston to Newark was mostly patchy fog that merely mirrored
the weather of his mind.

He was on his way, but why?

Not for the ten megabucks. He could not really believe in them.

Was it to see how far his program would go in acting out its fantasy?

Or was it himself again? Had he retreated too deeply into the
world of words and needed now to move out into the domain of
deeds?

At the Newark air terminal he rented a red Mercury and drove
toward town. He stopped at a shopping center, bought toothbrush,

toothpaste, razor, blades, foam shave, socks, shirts, undershorts, and a flight bag to stuff everything into. He stopped again to ask a traffic cop the way and got a hard look before he got the directions.

When he reached the neighborhood, he saw why. It would be one of the last to get garbage pickup.

"The old neighborhood's changed, Kraut."

The genie sounded relieved to pop out of the bottle.

"It never was much. What is it now?"

"Mostly Black and Puerto Rican."

"Beautiful for whoever's running the numbers there now."

Paul eyed a sticker on boards covering a broken store window. *Plate Glass—24-hour board-up service*, and a phone number.

"Yeah, beautiful."

He pulled up at the curb across the street from where the Tivoli Chophouse had been. The window no longer said what it said in the old newspaper photos of the scene of the massacre. Then it had been:

```
             v o
          i        l
        t  i      i
        chophouse
          i        t
          l      i
             o v
```

—now it was a botánica.

"The Tivoli's gone too. Now it's a botánica."

"What the hell is that?"

"A store that sells religious articles."

"Jeez! Can you beat that! At least it's from spirits of one kind to spirits of another."

Paul sat staring at the plaster saints and crucifixes and praying hands and beads and gaudy pictures. A twitch of dirty curtain pulled his gaze to the second story.

"What you waiting for, kid? According to the city directory Flesher still lives in the flat over the store. Let's go."

Time to put Kraut back in his place.

"No. If I park the Mercury here, I'll come out to find it stripped. I'll drive to the motel, grab a bite, take a nap, freshen up, then come back here in a cab."

Kraut tried to sound ungrudging.

"Sure, pal. I waited thirty-nine years, I can wait a couple hours more."

As he cornered, Paul caught sight of debris in a cinder-strewn lot: empty fifths of wine still in their form-fitting paper bags, a silk stocking, old license plates. Skulls and bones of oxen fallen in the great trek West.

He checked in at the motel where Kraut had reserved a room for him. He lay on top of the blanket with his clothes on. His feet felt like living pincushions. He smiled the ghost of a smile. He fell asleep trying to read the ceiling.

5

He gave the cabbie a five and got out awkwardly. He almost apologized to Kraut for bumping the case against the door. He waved away the change. He caught a twitch of the same curtain.

The cabbie saluted with a finger.

"Thanks, buddy."

"That's all right. Expense account."

"Lucky you. Well, thanks again. Only now I'll give *you* a tip. Don't flash the stuff around here."

Paul saluted with a finger, swung around, and made not for the door alongside the botánica that led to the apartments above it but for the door of the botánica as if the case were a sample case and he were selling. The cabbie had seemed too knowing, too nosy. Once the cab rounded out of sight, Paul swung back.

Inside the vestibule he peered at the names on the boxes. He pressed Max Flesher's button. The boxes showed signs of prying.

No answer.

"Apartment 1A should be second floor front. Right, Kraut?"

"Right."

"It was a nervous curtain, so he has to be in." He held his finger on the button. "I'll keep trying."

"That's the way, kid. Lean on the damn thing. And if you have to, lean on Max."

At last the inner door buzzed its lock open. Paul climbed slowly toward a slice of face. Max Flesher was keeping the apartment door on the chain.

The climb and the closeness had made Paul sweat. He looked at what he could see of Max Flesher and thought of all the others he would be meeting in the coming days, and he felt a chill. They were all once young.

The pouchy eye spoke.

"Had the television on. Didn't hear you. Who are you? What do you want?"

"Mr. Flesher, my name's Paul Felder. I'm doing a story on Kraut Schwartz."

The eye blinked rapidly.

"I don't like it. Only a couple hours back I spotted a red Mercury casing this place. And now somebody else comes breezing in. Too much is happening for one day. I been out of it for going on forty years. Days, weeks, even months, go by without I think of that night. Now all at once it comes back to life with a bang. I don't like it."

Paul unwalleted a ten.

The eye steadied.

"Well, all right. I guess there's no harm."

The chain rattled free and the door opened. Max Flesher was a threadbare tousle of gray hair, more of the same stuff peeping over and poking through an undershirt, a belly overlapping beltless pants, and a pair of felt slippers.

"Thank you, Mr. Flesher."

"Wait a minute. What you got there, a tape recorder? I don't talk into no tape recorder."

"Whatever you say, Mr. Flesher. If you don't want me to use it, I won't use it."

"I don't talk into no tape recorder."

"All right, no tape recorder."

"All right. Sit down, sit down. No, not there, it's got a bum spring; over there. Well, what can I tell you? I don't know no more today than I did then. Like I told the cops, all I seen was the two guns looking at me; then I hit the floor like I was back in France. I was in World War I, you know."

"Is that right?"

"Infantry. But you want to ask me about Kraut." He leaned forward, elbows on knees. "Shoot."

Paul took out and unfolded Xerox pages of Kraut's ravings.

"All I'd like you to do is read through this and tell me what you can about what it means to you."

Max Flesher made a big thing out of finding his glasses.

"Bifocals." He read the heading and thumbed through the pages. "Did Kraut say all this? I didn't see all this before."

"The papers printed only snatches of it at the time."

"Ah."

Paul gazed around the room. Max Flesher looked up from the pages.

"You might wonder why I'm still here. Only one reason, this flat's under rent control. I'm what they call a statutory tenant. You should see what the landlord's getting from some of the other tenants. Statutory rape. The others come and go, but I been here all along so my rent is real low. Boy, does he want to get rid of me! But they'll have to carry me out. I guess you can see I live alone. I got television and beer. At my age what more do I need?"

He bent to the pages again and his eyes followed his finger and his lips moved. When the first page came back on top, he tapped it.

"Only one thing means anything to me. This here, where he says, 'Sat in gin, lapped up blood.' I can see it clear, there was a poster ad for Burnett's White Satin Gin on the wall behind Kraut's table. The same table where he ended up with his head in like they said a pool of blood. Satin gin, get it? He must of broke the word up in his mind." He handed the pages back to Paul. "That's all I can tell you."

"If that's all, that's all. Thanks."

Paul handed Flesher the ten but did not put the wallet away.

Flesher snapped the ten a couple of times thoughtfully.

"Sorry I can't help you more." His eyes fixed on Paul's wallet. "There is one thing might interest you. Nobody else but me knows about it." He put up a finger to call time out and shifted to get at the billfold in his hip pocket. He took out a folded bit of paper worn and dirty along the creases, but he wasn't ready to unfold it. "Here's how I come by it.

"It was a few minutes after ten. I'm alone behind the bar when this guy comes in and takes out two guns. The bar ran like from here to over there. Then came the john and past it the back room Kraut and Zigzag Ludwig and Schmulka Mandel and Zuzu Gluckentern used. I ain't never seen this guy before and I know he ain't never been in the place before but he seems to know just what to look for and just where to go. He tells me to get down on the floor and stay down. I was in the trenches in World War I, you know, so he doesn't have to tell me.

"He heads straight for the back room. The way it must of happened, when he passes the john he sees a man with his back to him taking a leak and he maybe figures it's one of Kraut's bodyguards, Schmulka or Zuzu. He's too smart to leave a guy with a gun behind him so he shoots, twice. And he hurries on into the back room and shoots Zigzag and Schmulka and Zuzu.

"I guess Schmulka and Zuzu have their guns out as soon as they hear the shots that get Kraut and they shoot back but this guy is too fast and sharp for them and he guns them down. Anyway, it's all quiet now and he comes back out. I stay down but there's a knot been kicked out of the boards and through the hole I see him come out.

"What I see of his face is pale and he hurries to the front door and he says to somebody just outside, 'He wasn't in the back room.' And the lookout says, 'You mean you didn't get him?' Then the hit man smacks himself on the brow and says, 'Jeez, the guy I got in the john must be Kraut.' And the lookout says, 'You got him? Then let's beat it. The whole neighborhood heard the shooting. The bulls'll be here any second.' But the guys says, 'Wait a minute.'

"I hear a siren coming but he goes back into the john and he's in there it seems like a long time. Then he comes out and he's stuffing a roll big enough to choke a horse into his pocket and he hurries to the front door and the siren's louder and he's swearing because the lookout and the driver of the getaway car go off without him and he runs into the night.

"I wait a while, then I got up and go in the back room and see Zuzu and Schmulka and Zigzag flopped all over the place. I almost jump out of my skin when Kraut, all bloody, comes out of the john behind me and bumps his way to the table and falls into a chair and lays his head down on the table like he's taking a nap.

"On the table I see strips of adding-machine tape long as your arm full of figures that come to the millions. I don't touch them. I don't touch nothing. But when the police cars pull up in front and I pass the john on my way to meet them I pick up a piece of paper just inside the john that must of fell out of Kraut's pocket when the hit man rolled him. By now the cops are piling in.

"And it's only much later, when they let me go and I come back up here, that I find I must of stuck it in my pocket. It would look bad to tell them now, so I was going to burn it, then I thought I ought to keep it sort of for a souvenir." The folded slip of paper twitched in his hand. "You interested?"

"I'm interested twenty dollars' worth."

"For thirty you can have the damn thing."

"Sight unseen?"

"Huh?"

"Okay, it's a deal."

They traded.

Paul unfolded a Rorschach blot that served as rusty ground for what looked like a big Roman numeral X.

"That spot ain't a ink blot. It's Kraut's blood. The cross is in ink, kind of faded by now. I don't know what the cross stands for."

Paul gingerly refolded the paper and pocketed it.

"I would not call it a cross. There are lines across the top and bottom. I would say it is the symbol or figure X."

"You sounded like you wasn't just talking to yourself, or to me neither. You sure you ain't got the tape recorder on?"

"I'm sure."

"I don't know. All at once I got a feeling I'm going to be sorry."

"Why? Forty dollars buys a lot of beer."

"Yeah, and a hell of a hangover."

Before he got down step one Paul heard Flesher put the door on the chain. By the time he reached the foot of the stairs he felt himself sweating again. With his free hand he fingered the folded scrap of paper in his pocket. X marked what spot? So much outlay of self for so little payoff. If it was going to be like this all along the way . . .

Earlier in the Mercury and again in the cab he had spotted a hack stand just around the corner. But before he reached the corner a pair of dudes unlounged from a doorway. They looked like trouble.

They were trouble. They had already sized him up—the case alone promised something worth hocking—and were splitting up to take him.

"Don't look now, Kraut, but I think I'm in for a mugging."

"Jeez, kid, don't do nothing dumb. I don't want to lose you."

"Thanks."

They were coming fast, giving him no chance of making it back up the street to Flesher's or the botánica. That was his heart not their boots clumping and lumbering like Birnam Wood. One would move behind him and armlock his head. The other would hold a switchblade to him and pick him clean.

"Here they come."

He put down his urge to put up a fight. He would not be able to hack it. One slip and he would be flat and helpless on the sidewalk, his head and ribs and groin targets of opportunity for those high-heeled boots. He saw a man across the street stop and look on interestedly. He drew a deep breath as they boxed him in; then his head was in a vise and his vision narrowed to a wide emptiness that filled with the pebbly face of the one with the knife. He made himself go calm and unresisting and got out one word.

"Take."

No sweat. Let them have what they wanted, and he would come out of it all right.

But a wave of queasiness rolled through and swelled into fright. His heart raced at a nightmare gallop. Then something wild; the eyes of the dude facing him bulged full of a mirroring fright.

The hand reaching for Paul's wallet stopped. Paul felt a stabbing in his chest. But it didn't come from the switchblade; straining eyes showed him that barely touching him and lower down. At the same time the one behind him gave a gasp of pain and the jaws of the vise shook and opened. The one in front with a cry of fear grabbed the case and turned to run.

As if the scuffling sound had cued him, Kraut shouted.

"Put me down! Put me down!"

The mugger froze, then threw the case from him and fled.

Paul stood swaying. Light flashed at the end of the tunnel, and he sucked air. A dulling weariness kept him from realizing at once that though he still felt the pressure the headlock was off. He looked around. Both dudes were gone. The man across the street moved along. Slowly Paul walked over to the case. He bent to pick it up and nearly fell into a blackness. Then he was upright and carrying it step by kicking step toward the corner.

"You all right, kid? What's happening?"

Kraut's voice sounded anxious and grew more anxious in the repeating while Paul shuddered back into shape to answer.

"It's all over, Kraut. I'm okay. They ran away."

"Did you feel scared?"

Kraut sounded strangely eager to know.

Paul made a face at the case.

"I don't remember being that scared, not even in Nam. Damn right, I felt scared." He looked ahead in wonder, at nothing. "Funny, though, I wasn't alone in being scared."

Kraut laughed.

"I know."

Paul eyed the case curiously.

"Don't tell me you were scared too."

"*Me* scared? Hell, no. I *done* the scaring."

"No, I mean before that. I got scared and they got scared *before* you started to shout."

"Kid, I'm trying to tell you. What happened was, I whistled. No, I ain't crazy. You didn't hear because the intense note I emitted was below audibility. Those low frequencies produce nausea, fright, panic, chest pains, blurred vision, dizziness, and lastly a coma-like lassitude. I run across that bit of dope while I was hunting a voice for myself. Sure come in handy, hey, kid?" Kraut laughed a happy dirty laugh. "So they run away. It worked, huh? It really worked?"

"It worked."

Now that he knew, and now that he knew from the passing of the symptoms that Kraut was no longer silently sounding the alarm-making note, he knew true fear.

6

It had been a harried harridan listening and talking over her vacuum cleaner who had told him he could wait on the porch for Sgt. Mark Nolan if he wanted to.

He wanted to. It was another part of Newark, but it was under the same inverted air mass, and it was only a half hour after the mugging. He could use the rest.

He saw he shared the porch with a b.u.f.e. He smiled a half smile at the big ugly glazed ceramic elephant with its garish toenails and tasseled harness and saddle. The small pull of the smile brought neck muscles into play and a worm gnawed at his Adam's apple. Still sore from the mugging. Trunk raised, the buffy stood two and a half feet high and must have weighed the limit, seventy pounds. In the gloom of the screened porch he could not tell whether it was an off-white or a pale pink. Grunts must have bought and shipped

home a million of the bloody useless fucking elephants. He dozed
himself back on patrol and woke sweating.

A brown girl in a green VW dropped a white man off at the curb
and drove away with a wave. The man climbed the stoop slowly
and came in. Paul stood up, articulating stiffly.

"Sergeant Nolan?"

The man wiped the smile off his ruddy face and let the screen
door spank him. He thumbed at the disappearing car.

"Nice girl. Works in the bank. Gives me a lift home whenever
she can. Lots of them work in banks these days."

Under droopy lids the eyes were the eyes of an old cop and were
trying to make Paul.

Paul introduced himself and told Nolan why he was there.

Nolan's eyes distanced him from Paul. But questioning the dying
Kraut had to be Nolan's big moment, and Paul saw the wariness
recede. Nolan unbuttoned his jacket.

"I could change at the bank, but I guess I like to wear this ma-
roon jacket with the bank's patch on it home to let the neighbors
know I pay me own way. Still put in a good day's work, I do,
moonlighting on Social Security. Don't look sixty-eight, do I? Keeping busy's what does it. Let yourself rust and you fall apart."

"I guess you're right."

"I know I'm right. Take the couch. I'll take the rocker; its cush-
ion is fitted to me like the astronauts' seats fit them. Don't let that
elephant fool you. I'm a good Democrat, though I voted for Nixon
account of he's against permissiveness." He shot a look at Paul.
"My grandson sent that thing all the way from Vietnam when he
was there."

"I was there too. I watched the old folks and the little kids make
them. Regular assembly line."

"Good boy, good boy. I hate them damn draft dodgers. Amnesty.
I'd give them amnesty. I guess you know how I'd give them amnesty. But it was a bad war and I'm glad it's over for us. We never
should of went in to help them in the first place, but once we went
in, we should of wiped them out."

"That's a point of view, all right."

"Damn right."

From an inside pocket Paul drew the copy of Kraut's statement.
He made a lap desk of the phone case.

"Hold on, son. Before we tackle that I'll get me daughter-in-law to bring us cold beers. Aggie." A long silence. Nolan called again, louder. Another long silence. His face turned ruddier. "She's growing deaf. I'll get the beers."

"Don't bother."

"I said beers and I meant beers."

Nolan shoved himself up and went inside. A back and forth of muttering, then Nolan returned, ruddier yet, bearing two cans of Rheingold and a pair of cardboard coasters. He pulled the tabs fiercely and handed Paul one can and a coaster.

"You don't look the kind of guy minds drinking from the can."

"Matter of fact, I like it better. Loses too much fizz when you pour it out."

"That's what I say." He took a long pull and then nodded his readiness. Paul fed him the first page. Nolan examined it. "Yes, this looks like a copy of what we took down that day. You want me to go over it word by word to see if there are any mistakes?"

"Well, that, but mostly to see if anything in it brings something more to mind."

The drinking and the reading ended at the same time. Nolan shook his head with a sigh for both.

"Can't think of a thing but what's there."

Paul pocketed the copy.

"Does the symbol or letter or numeral X mean anything to you?"

He drew one with his finger upon the case on his lap.

Nolan shook his head while thinking.

"Not in connection with Kraut, if that's what you're asking." He leaned forward and tapped Paul's knee. "Listen, son." Nolan's finger did a double take, then lifted as if stung. "Sorry. I didn't know."

Paul smiled and nodded. Nolan hawked and swallowed.

"Listen, son. I can tell you one thing. I said then and I say now this handle Olive Eye stands for the hood that knocked Kraut off and the three with him. The mob always brings in someone from out of state to do a job like this: when it's done he leaves and you never see him again. Now, neither one of Harry the Wack Spector's eyes was olive color. So I believe they pinned the rap on the wrong guy when they nailed the Wack for it. Though I wouldn't of shed tears if they give the Wack the chair, because he deserved it for other things they never could pin on him. But I think the Wack took a fall. Now what do you say to that for a theory?"

"That's a theory, all right."

"Damn right."

Paul levered himself up off the couch.

"Thank you, Sergeant Nolan."

"Only sorry I can't be more help."

"You can. When you go in, will you phone for a cab to pick me up?"

"Sure thing, son. Right away." Nolan stuck out his hand and they shook. "Glad to've met you. I really mean it."

"Thanks. Same here."

Nolan picked up the cans and coasters and elbowed inside. Paul left the porch and waited on the curb.

7

He entered the Tivoli Chophouse and Tavern only to find himself walking into a Viet Cong ambush. After that woke him he was good only for fitful sleep. He checked out of the motel before dawn, exchanging yawns with the desk clerk.

An early start out of Newark at least let him beat the lemming rush across the Hudson. On the Mercury's radio he heard the WCBS traffic-advisory helicopter pilot say something about the approaches to the G. W. Bridge. Paul shook his head.

Up to now his admiration for those chopper pilots had been sky's the limit. Just to think of them juggling air currents and topography with one hand and scribbling notes with the other—let alone *seeing* the Metropolitan Area through the dark brown air . . .

"But honestly, fella, 'G. W. Bridge'? G.W. may *look* shorter than George Washington but it *sounds* every inch as long."

He felt brighter at once; then the voice of Kraut on the passenger seat cast its shadow.

"You got a point there, kid. Now, remember, when you get off the G. W. Bridge, you head north to reach the Bronx and Co-op City."

"I know, I know."

He switched to an FM music station. Maybe some loud reggae would shake the old know-it-all.

It still rang in his own ears as he pressed the doorbell under the name M. Moldover.

Shouting "Paul Felder" at the peephole brought only "Who?

Who?" Then mention of Kraut Schwartz's name magicked a siege
of chains and bolts. The woman almost pulled him off balance getting him in.

"Ssh. The neighbors."

He thought he saw Kraut's features, at least as they appeared in
the old newspaper photos, in Molly Moldover, the likeness likely
more striking now she had moved into the unisex stage.

She shook her head as he explained his mission, but she had only
shaken it in wonderment.

"Funny you should show up just now."

"Oh?"

"Haven't you seen?"

It was his turn to shake his head. She picked up a *Daily News*
and turned from a supermarket ad to a story on page three.

DEAD BIRDS OF A FEATHER?

NEWARK, N.J., Apr. 3—A 70-year-old retired bartender, a figure
out of the gangster era of the Thirties, turned up dead in his
apartment on East Park Street here yesterday with a dead
canary on his chest. He had six bullet holes in his head.

Newark policemen investigating the murder of the ex-bar-
tender, Max Flesher, declined today to comment on whether
he had been a police informant. Over the years, the dead canary has been used as a symbol by criminals of informers who
"sing" to the police.

Mr. Flesher's body was found by police responding to an
anonymous tip. None of Mr. Flesher's neighbors so far questioned report hearing shots. It is possible, police say, the killer
used a silencer. Robbery appears not to have been the motive;
police said there were four crisp 10-dollar bills in Mr. Flesher's
wallet.

Back in 1935 Mr. Flesher had his moment in the limelight.
He was tending bar the night Harry "The Wack" Spector strode
into the Tivoli Chophouse and Tavern and mowed down Kraut
Schwartz and three of Schwartz's cohorts.

Mr. Flesher, according to the police, leaves no known survivors. He was fully clothed at the time of his death, the police
said, and apparently had not gone to bed. The police said Mr.
Flesher was not known to have a pet canary.

Paul numbly handed the paper back.

Mrs. Moldover sighed. Her eyes blinked behind thick lenses, no more a blur now than when still.

"Awful, isn't it? I myself never knew the man, but it's terrible to think the killing never ends."

Paul nodded. Then for the benefit of Kraut, suddenly heavy in his right hand, he spoke.

"Max Flesher. Poor old Max Flesher."

Mrs. Moldover took a step back.

"Did *you* know him?"

"Oh, no, no. I just came across the name in reading up on your brother. And speaking of—"

"Yes, well, about that. I'd rather not discuss. The neighbors don't even know Albert was my brother."

"Sooner or later they'll find out. That's just why I think you should discuss. He's had a bad press. I'd like to get from you the human side of your brother."

"Human? What's human? Killing is human. Stealing is human. Lying is human. What kind of things would you want to know?"

"We'd start off with this."

Paul drew out the copy of Kraut's ravings and handed it to her. She brought it into focus.

"Albert said all this? My, such a mishmash of words. But you have to remember he was out of his head, he was dying." She turned and looked at the sunburst wall clock. "I was getting ready to go out shopping, things I need."

"I have a car. I'll drive you wherever you're going and bring you back and we can talk on the way."

She eyed him a long time but what went on behind the lenses he could not tell. Then she nodded and spoke, to herself first.

"A boy. A nice boy. All right. But back I can get by myself. A bus goes between here and the New Rochelle Mall."

She picked up her coat and her plastic-net shopping bag. He helped her on with her coat.

She sighed herself into the passenger seat, and they pulled away from Co-op City. He grinned: Coop City more like it. Mrs. Moldover caught his grin and nodded.

"Yes, this place is more and more full of widows. If they're not widows when they move in, they're widows before they're here long, like me. The men around here are dropping like flies."

And he saw the women everywhere, strolling, standing, sitting.

He tried to keep the wheels out of potholes, the ride smooth for Mrs. Moldover's reading.

"Now here the man taking it down didn't know what he was taking down. 'Pushcarts'! The word is *pushkes*. And even a goy should know 'gone if' ought to be *gonif*. I was four years younger than Albert—that's a lot when you're young—and I hardly knew him. But now I remember something I forgot all these years.

"Every Friday afternoon before lighting the Shabbos candles mamma put the spare change in slots in the pushkes, little tin boxes on the kitchen wall, one red, one yellow, one blue, from different charities. Every once in a while some bearded man with a black bag came and had a glass of tea he sucked through a lump of sugar and took out a little steel claw hammer, pulled one of the tin boxes off the wall, and emptied the coins and fluff and insect dust ooftish —on the table—on the oilcloth—it was chipped where it draped over the corners of the table—and counted the money and wrote it down and scraped the coins into his bag and tacked the box back on the wall.

"The money would go to orphans and sages in Palestine. It was Palestine then. One time I woke in the middle of the night and while I was trying to figure why I woke I heard mamma say again, 'Gonif!' And then papa said, 'Do I swipe? Does the mamma swipe? From who you learn this?' And I crawled out of bed and peeked into the kitchen and there they were standing over Albert and all three pushkes were ooftish and they were empty and there was one big pile of coins.

"And papa raised his hand but Albert ducked under and grabbed a knife from the sink counter and held it in front of him and dared papa with his eyes. That's all I remember. I think maybe I screamed and fainted. I only know from that time Albert got worse. One day I guess papa got tired trying to handle him or maybe just got tired trying to make ends meet. Papa left home. Deserted us. Mamma took in washing and janitored at the tenement we lived in. I read somewhere a reporter once asked Albert if it was true papa deserted the family when Albert was ten. Albert said no, when he was ten his father died."

She brought the page into focus again.

"'A spill of diamonds and rubies. Watch the wine-stained light pass over the tablecloth . . .' We only had the tablecloth on holidays. That has to do with Passover but I don't know does he mean the colored shadow of the wine bottle or the flashes when we dipped the pinkie and shook off a drop of wine for each of the ten plagues.

"The man with the soup strainer was papa. He had a great big droopy mustache. I remember now he kind of honed his old safety razor blade on the inside of a glass to get at least one more shave out of it. He'd pinch a cigarette out and save it. He'd stick a pin through a butt so he could hold it to smoke to the very end."

She shook her head.

"I don't see anything else I know till this. 'She tied a babushka over her head to hold her hat on in the wind.' That's mamma out shoveling the snow off the walk or scattering ashes on the ice. 'Rip van Nipple, and the silver fell out.' That's not 'Nipple'; it's *knippl*, a knot in a handkerchief in which mamma kept change for the iceman and so on. The knot came untied once and the silver spilled. Albert and I helped pick it up and I saw Albert palm a dime. I knew he knew I saw, so I didn't dare tell on him. If mamma noticed it was missing she didn't say anything.

"'Your Monday's longer than your Tuesday' is what a woman used to say in mixed company to warn another woman her slip was showing. I don't know why Albert should say it here."

She had only one more gloss—"'Yentzer' means 'cheater'"—before handing the pages back. They rode in silence but for the road hum the few minutes more it took to reach the New Rochelle Mall. She put her hand on his arm as he reached across to open the car door for her.

"Please don't wait. I'll take the bus back."

It hit him how brave she had been, or how trusting, so close on Max Flesher's death, to let the stranger take her for a ride. He didn't press her. He wanted to talk longer and learn more, but his stronger need was to be free to consult with Kraut. In a murder investigation every minute of lead time counted if you rated as a suspect. He guessed he rated as a suspect.

The last he saw of her face he thought he spotted tears behind the blurry lenses, but he could not be sure.

"That was fine, kid. What come out of that confirms I had money on the mind. Next on the agenda is Mort Lesser in Brooklyn. You got the address."

"What's the matter, no family feeling, Kraut? Not even an artificial catch in the artificial throat?"

"What are you talking? Oh, sure, kid. When we get our mitts on the ten megabucks, we cut Molly in for some. Same goes for my widow and daughter. Take it out of my end. Meanwhile we got work to do. Take the Bronx-Whitestone Bridge, that's your best bet."

"Not so fast, Kraut. There's the small matter of Max Flesher, deceased. With a canary, deceased, on his chest."

"Is that what happened? Jeez, like old times."

"I don't recall if I told Sergeant Nolan I visited Flesher—"

"You didn't."

"—but there's still a chance the cops will tie me in some other way to the killing."

"How?"

"Poring over the nice new notes I gave Flesher, for the talk and for the scrap of paper with the X on it, they might come up with my prints. Even if not, I could have left prints on a chair or a table or a wall."

"I see what you mean, pal. You were in the service, so your prints are on file. I'm putting you on hold. Here I go."

It was mixed feelings to know that Kraut could work behind the scenes.

He was thinking Flesher's landlord would be getting a rent hike on the flat now, when a police car pulled up alongside.

"There's a no-standing regulation, buddy. You got out-of-state tags, so I'm just telling you."

"Thanks, officer."

The police car pulled away and Paul followed suit. He headed for the Bronx-Whitestone Bridge. He started at Kraut's voice.

"You can relax, pal. I retrieved the situation. I demagnetized the code on your prints. And just in time. The FBI computer was about to pull your card."

"Good work."

Paul supposed he should have sounded more grateful. But he realized that though Kraut had kept him out of it for now, Kraut had a hold on him in the blackmail sense.

Kraut's voice seemed richer with the same realization.

"Now that's took care of, how's about we head for the Bronx-Whitestone Bridge. Brooklyn, remember?"

It was getting to be a downer.

"Take it easy, Kraut. My stomach's telling me it's lunchtime. Remember stomachs?"

"O.K., kid. O.K. Do your number."

8

Mort Lesser had a nose flattened as though pressing against a pane of glass. His big ugly mouth became a sculptured smile.

Paul trailed Lesser's glance out through the stationery store window, past the Mercury hitched to a meter post, and up at a fillet of mackerel sky. Then Paul followed Lesser's glance back inside the claustrophilic clutter.

"Time I have. Not all the time in the world, but time. You can see yourself it's not quite as busy here as, say, in the bank on Social Security check-cashing day. But I get by." He grimaced as he trailed Paul's glance. "I have to take what the distributor gives. There were too many returns on the decent reading. Now it's this porno trash or nothing. But I warned the distributor I'm a Hershey bar."

"Hershey bar?"

"The Hershey bar gets smaller and smaller to stay the same price. But it can get only so small. I can shrink myself only so small before I'm nothing, a man without quality or quantity. Only one thing keeps me from giving up the store. I don't want to hang out with old people." The old eyes twinkled. "But you didn't come here to hear me kvetch. You came here to have me read this." He shook the sheaf of Kraut's ravings. "So I'll read it. Meanwhile, feel free to browse."

His eyes seemed far away from his body when he looked up from reading.

"It's hard to believe this came from Kraut. He was a lump without leaven. But there was a spark, there was a spark. Yes, I can see this wasn't just nonsense. Some things jump right out at me."

"For instance."

"For instance"—Lesser's ears grew red—"'the lesser of the two looks the more.' Kraut always found it a laugh that I looked more like a hood than he did. You see, I was always a square, but one day a man came into my first stationery store for a nickel cigar —a nickel cigar; you can imagine how far back that was—and stared at me and then told me he was an artist who did covers and interior artwork for Black Mask and the other crime pulps. He talked me into posing for him. Usually I'd be holding a rod and a sneer. I could use the few dollars he paid—that was at the height of the Depression, if you'll pardon the oxymoron—but I never could make up my mind whether or not I liked doing it. Especially after Kraut found out and kidded me about it. He was a very unsubtle kidder."

Paul tried to visualize Lesser with the bushy gray hair sleek and black, the eyes narrowed and not behind glasses, the lines fewer but tenser, the wide mouth pressed in a corrugated smile. Yes, Mort Lesser would have made a Thirties gangster, a movie heavy.

He grew aware that Lesser was studying him just as hard. Both grinned. Lesser gave an apologetic twist of his head.

"Excuse me for staring. My own face has given me a thing about faces. I study faces. A stranger shows you one face on your first meeting; you do not know how much weight to give this first impression. You need a number of meetings, to average out all the faces he shows you. However, it usually turns out the first impression is the truest."

"And your first impression of me?"

For some reason Paul really wanted to know, and he waited for Mort Lesser's slow answer.

"Generally favorable." Again the beautiful smile of the ugly mouth. Mort Lesser tapped the sheaf. "But this really interests me. I hope you don't mind if I skip around. In my philosophy, the beginning is never the beginning and the end is never the end. So I pick up on whatever interests me at the moment. I know that's not the way to get ahead in this world. But for me it's a bit late in life to learn new tricks. So.

" 'Dan, Dan, the Telescope Man. The little dog laughed to see such sport.' In the old days in Manhattan down on Union Square there was Dan the Telescope Man. A sign hung from his tripod: 'See Old Sirius, the Dog Star, 10 cents.' Kraut would get some other kid to distract Dan so Kraut could sneak a free look. Sirius. That's in the constellation Canis Major, isn't it?"

"I think so."

"No matter. To observers in another part of the galaxy it would seem part of another constellation. It's possible to form constellations and even chains out of random events. You can find patterns in a list of random numbers. All this Gestalt we call life, even the universe, is only a tiny run of seeming sense in the great randomness." He broke off with a grin. "A philosopher *manque,* you observe."

His finger stabbed at another point in the ravings.

"'Sympathy of clocks.' One day on the way home from school I stopped in with Kraut to ask the watch repairman in his little shop what he knew about a sympathy of clocks. That's a phenomenon, you know, in which clocks communicate their vibrational motion to one another. I wanted to find out if it was true that a faulty clock will tick away nicely while it's in the repair shop in the company of other ticking clocks but will stop as soon as you take it out of the shop.

"Kraut seemed interested too—and I found out later he really was interested. He was casing the joint. A couple of nights later Kraut and another kid broke in and cleaned the place out. Got away with it too. The watchmaker must've thought I was in on it with Kraut. He never trusted me after that, wouldn't give me the time of day."

Mort Lesser looked into his own distance.

"You know, if it hadn't been for that, I think the watchmaker would have taught me the trade and in time taken me in with him. I might've made something of myself, become an inventor, maybe, because I had a feel for machinery and enjoyed working with my hands. Well.

"'The scorpion stung the uncle.' The Hebrew for that is '*Detzach adash beachab.*' It's a mnemonic acrostic for the ten plagues in the Passover account." He looked embarrassed. "I'm not religious, but I like to ponder the texts. Let's see if I remember.

"*Dom,* blood. *Tz'fardaya,* frogs. *Kinim,* gnats. '*Arov,* flies. *Dever,* murrain. *Sh'chin,* boils. *Borod,* hail. *Arbeh,* locusts. *Choshech,* darkness. *Makas B'choros,* slaying of the first-born. I doubt Kraut would consciously remember all that, but his family did observe Passover when he was a kid, and so he must have read the Haggadah in the Hebrew-English booklets the matzoh manufacturers gave out, and strange things stick in the mind.

"Now this about 'J for jig' and so on, I don't know. But while I'm on knucklebones, I've always wondered—is it only me, or does everyone get a squeamish feeling when he touches thumb to thumb at the joints? Or the anklebones together? Or even thinks about it?"

A man came in to pay for a *New York Post* out of a ten, and another man caught the door on the swing and came in impatient to buy a New York State Lottery ticket. It grew quite busy and crowded in there for one minute.

"Now where was I? 'Tell us who did it and we'll nail them.' 'Olive Eye.' That could be Yiddish two ways. Olive is *aylbirt*; Kraut's name was Albert. 'Olive Eye' would then mean 'I, myself.' But surely he's not saying he shot himself? No. 'Olive Eye' is really '*Allevy*,' meaning, 'It should only be that way!'"

"Who's the Hungarian?"

"The Hungarian?"

"See here where he says, 'Okay, boss, only don't say it in front of a Hungarian.'"

Mort Lesser looked and then laughed.

"There's no Hungarian. Kraut was getting in a dig at the cop questioning him. 'Boss' is a four-letter word in Hungarian. Little did I dream Kraut would be one to suit the *mot juste* to the *beau geste*. He was a personality of glowering silences. 'An itch for the scratch' reminds me of the day he came to school and sat at his desk playing with rolls of dimes. When I got home that afternoon, I heard talk that somebody had burgled the cash drawer of the Itch—the neighborhood movie house—the night before. But neither I nor any of the other kids nor even the teacher said anything to anyone about Kraut's rolls of dimes.

"'She read it Rainbow'—that was Miss O'Reilly our second-grade teacher. She always read Schwartz's real name—Rabinow—as Rainbow when taking attendance. She called the holiday 'Tcha-*noo*-kah.' For some reason she took a shine to Kraut. When he got restless she used to let him sit off by himself and read nursery rhymes. Maybe because she found out or felt that he never got such softening influences at home.

"I heard her once tell him, 'Albert, you'll come to a bad end.' And he cocked an eye at her and said, 'So what? I come from a bad beginning. Anything in between is gravy.' That was in P.S. 12. The principal then was Dr. J. F. Condon. He went on to win fame as the go-between in the Lindbergh baby kidnaping. That's him in 'a jiffy, a jafsie.' Kraut dropped out in the middle of the sixth grade.

"I kept seeing him through the years. It was his doing; he did the looking up. Why?" Mort Lesser shrugged. "For one thing, he knew I didn't want anything from him. I was a relief from his paranoia, from his always having to be suspicious of everybody. Once he told me there are only two animals in the world—the steer and the butcher. For another thing, he liked to astonish and impress me. I don't know that it was a love-hate relationship so much as that he felt free to talk to me.

"Though once, after talking too freely, he nearly decided to kill me. He broke off in the middle of telling me something or other and without warning hauled off and bloodied my nose. 'What's that for?' I asked. 'I been shooting off my mouth too much,' he said, 'and you been on the Erie too long.' 'So what has my nose got to do with it?' I said. He already had his gun out and was aiming it at my temple when that seemed to sink in. His eyes changed, and he touched the cold metal of the gun barrel to the nape of my neck. I went cold all over. But he laughed at my expression and said he was only stopping the bleeding.

"After, he showed me a deputy sheriff's badge, a brass potsy, that gave him the right to pack a forty-five. He said he got the appointment from some rube sheriff up in the Catskills. Then, just before he left, he washboarded his knuckles across my head in a Dutch rub, the way he did when we were both kids. Only extra hard. That was our last meeting.

"A few months later, the Tivoli massacre." He looked away. "A Cohen can't go into a funeral parlor. For once I was glad I'm a Cohen." He looked back at Paul with a smile. "You know, I try to believe in God but God doesn't make it easy."

"What were you talking about?"

"I just said. God."

"No, I mean with Kraut last time you saw him."

"Funny, I don't remember. No, wait. I know. He talked about the way Legs Diamond and other mobsters died broke. He wasn't going to let it happen to him. He said he had a chest so full of jewels and thousand-dollar bills that he had to have somebody sit on it to close it."

A hum of satisfaction came from the phone case at Paul's feet.

Paul covered and rebuked with a cough. But Mort Lesser seemed not to have noticed. He was folding the pages, getting ready to hand them back. Paul thanked him for his help and bought a lot of stuff he didn't need—cough drops, candy, chewing gum. Mort Lesser counted out the change slowly.

"Let me also hand you a bit of advice, young fellow. Live. I have never really lived. The trouble is I got too serious about too many things too soon."

He rested an elbow on the rubber change pad on the counter and cupped a chin that must have been blue when he was younger.

"Then again, I could have ended up riddled in the Tivoli; Albert could have ended up running this stationery. I always thought we might easily have been each other."

9

The express-lane check-out clerk wore a sweater over her shoulders. She would be in her late fifties. She looked it, and yet again when she smiled, she didn't look it. Most likely the eighteen-year-old cigarette girl in a speak-easy had never dreamed of anything as wildly tame as a supermarket in Babylon, Long Island.

Paul watched her while seeming to blister-shop the packages on the gondola shelves. It was closing in on closing time, and the last shoppers were leaving. He picked up a ten-pack of Rheingold quickies and took it to the express lane and passed her a crisp twenty.

She shot glances at his face and at a list of serial numbers taped to the register, then rang up the sale.

He waited in the Mercury. The supermarket dimmed and the parking lot emptied. She came out carrying a small bag of groceries. He watched her head for the bus stop. He rolled up alongside her and opened the passenger door.

She looked away, frightened and yet pleased, frowning at something familiar about him.

"Mrs. Rabinow—"

She looked frightened and displeased.

"It isn't Rabinow. It's Bogen. You've made a mistake." She had a little-girl voice, littler than when she had spoken the price of the ten-pack and the thank-you.

"Please get in, Mrs. Bogen. Let me drive you home."

"I don't know you. Do I? No, you're the ten-pack of Rheingold. What do you want? Why were you waiting for me?"

He told her.

She stood still, biting her lip. Her head started to swing sidewise.

"There might be something in it for you, Mrs. Bogen."

She glanced back up the road, shrugged and slid in.

"Well, I suppose it's better than waiting and waiting for that old bus."

He moved the phone case to the floor between them to make room for the bag of groceries. As they pulled away, he saw the bus grow in the rear-view mirror before it shrank again.

He took a right and a left and another right. He felt her gaze on him.

"You know where I live?"

She lived in a modest garden apartment. She beat him to the bag of groceries as they made ready to get out of the car.

"Thanks, but I can manage." She smiled. "If the prices keep going up, even the employees' discount won't mean a thing."

He wondered why she thought she had to let him know she hadn't stolen the stuff. He got out carrying the phone case. She raised an eyebrow.

"You're not moving in, are you?"

"It's a tape recorder, but I won't use it if you don't want me to."

"I wish you wouldn't."

"Mind if I bring it along anyway? I'd rather not leave it in the car."

She shrugged, turned and led the way. She put the key in the lock but didn't turn it.

"Listen, if my granddaughter comes in while we're talking, you're trying to sell me insurance."

"Your granddaughter? I thought it was your daughter who lives with you."

"My granddaughter, Mr. Felder." She fluffed up the hair on the back of her head. "So you don't know everything about me, do you?"

He eyed the phone case and smiled. Kraut wasn't infallible even this close to home.

"I guess I don't. But why insurance?"

"Because she doesn't know she's the granddaughter of Kraut Schwartz, and I don't want her to know." She turned the key. "Still double-locked, so Mimsy isn't home yet." But she called out Mimsy's name as they went in. "She works days as an office temporary, comes home for supper, then goes to business school week nights. Have a seat while I put the bag away. Of groceries, that is."

She came back to find him looking around at room ideas out of *House Beautiful.*

"Nice, huh?"

"Very." He drew out the pages of Kraut's ravings. "Mrs. Rabinow, I'd like you to—"

"I told you it's Bogen. I know I didn't change the name legal, just took this other name, but as long as you don't use the other name for anything shady, the law can't touch you. That's what Macie Devlin told me, and if you know anything, you know he was Albert's high-priced attorney."

Paul nodded.

She seated herself facing him with mixed satisfaction and anxiety.

"It's hard for a woman alone to raise a child. Besides, I had a lot to learn. You have to remember I wasn't much more than a child myself when Albert died and I broke all the old ties. Not that I didn't already know a lot about life. After all, I was married to the great Kraut Schwartz. And that wasn't arranged by a *shotgun*."

Paul shook his head to clear it.

"Shotgun?"

"I don't know how you spell it, but that's how you say it. *Shotgun*. You know, a Jewish matchmaker. But I knew all the wrong things. I guess I made mistakes trying to bring up Rose Marie. She left home when she was eighteen, and I haven't heard from her since. For all I know she's dead, the Blessed Virgin have mercy on her soul. But at least I have Mimsy to show for it. My granddaughter. Rose Marie left her with me. God knows I've tried to bring *her* up right." She leaned towards him. "Like I said, she doesn't know she's Kraut Schwartz's granddaughter. I doubt if she's even heard the name. So please promise you won't tell her, and I'll try to help you any way I can."

"Mrs. Bogen, I promise."

"I knew by looking at you I could trust you." She sighed and held out her hand for the Xerox pages. "Now let me read that thing before Mimsy comes."

She read till tears made ghost images of the type. She shook her head and handed the pages to Paul.

"Sorry. It's still crazy talk. Funny how this brings it all back. They took me in to see him and talk to him. I guess they hoped he would spill who shot him; they thought my being there would make him forget himself long enough to break that stupid code of honor. But seeing him like that and hearing him talk crazy was more than I could take. A few minutes of it and I had to run out.

Next time I saw him he was dead. Two days after he died there in Newark I raised the money to claim his body and take him to the Bronx. We sneaked the casket out the back way and buried him as a Roman Catholic, though his mother made me put a what-do-you-call-it, tallith, on the coffin."

"Are you sure nothing in this means anything to you? Because there's a chance that somewhere in these words of his there's a lead to where he hid millions."

She laughed and the tears flowed again.

"Millions! You mean people believe to this day that old story of Kraut Schwartz's hidden treasure? Please. If anyone knew, I would know, and—" The sound of a key in the lock. "Mother of God, it's Mimsy. You stall her but don't say anything. I have to run wash my face."

She hurried away. He pushed himself upright as the door opened.

A girl stopped short and sized him up for a karate chop. She tilted her head to the sound of splashing, relaxed, and dropped the key in her purse. But she kept her hand in there, likely on a long fingernail file.

"Hello. Who are you?"

"The name's Paul Felder. And you're Mimsy."

"Ms. Bogen to you. What are you doing here? Are you a friend of Florence's?"

"Mrs. Bogen to me. I'm trying to sell her some insurance."

Mimsy made a face of letdown.

"And here I thought you might be a strangler. How unexciting."

"And at first I thought you were Gloria Steinem, model number 217."

She flushed and whipped off her Gloria Steinem glasses.

"Florence, I'm home."

"Oh, are you, dear?" Mrs. Bogen popped her head out of the kitchen. "I was just getting supper ready."

"With your gentleman-caller waiting out here?" Mimsy frowned. "You mean he's staying for supper?"

"Well, now, dear . . ."

The tail of his eye showed him Florence Bogen shaking her head. Mimsy smiled at him suddenly. Under her gaze he grew aware that he hadn't fully seated the folded pages in the inside pocket of his jacket. He tucked them in. Mimsy tossed her head to whip the hair from her eyes.

"Sure, let's invite Mr. Felder if we haven't already. He can burp for his supper by driving me to class."

He tried to keep his eyes on the road.

"Such talk. Aren't you ashamed of yourself?"

"I'm sure it went over her head. Poor Florence leads a sheltered life." She hitched herself around to ride sidesaddle and leaned warmly near. "All right, Felder, what did you tell her to make her cry? You don't think I missed the red eyes and the puffiness?"

"Nothing. Only the high cost of insurance."

"Watch it, Felder. You may need coverage yourself." She blew in his ear. "Are you going to tell me?"

"Ask her. She'll tell you if she wants you to know."

She froze, then melted. She spoke in a thoughtful voice.

"I can be nice." She kissed him.

His hands tightened on the wheel, and there was a twist of over-control. They rode in silence; then he gave an inward sigh of relief.

"This must be the place."

He pulled up at the curb and read the gilt lettering on the windows. The school specialized in data processing. Mimsy was quite a girl. Mustn't be chauvinistic; quite a person. No, damn it; quite a girl. Too bad what might have been but never could be had to end before it began.

She spoke in a thoughtful voice.

"And I can be mean. I warn you, I'll find out. And if it's bad, God help you, Paul Felder, wherever you are." She bit his ear.

He faced the windshield. Her reflection showed her gazing at him. He saw her shake her head.

"I do better with an office machine."

Then she was sliding out of his car and out of his life.

10

He had just caught the name Morton Lesser when the car radio faded, though he wasn't going through an underpass. He raised the volume. No good. He twiddled the tuning knob to overcome drift. No good. He heard a hum from the phone case. Could Kraut be jamming the signal?

"Cut it out, Kraut, or I'll litter the road with you."

He pressed the button to give Kraut the window-lower sound for effect and slapped his free hand on the handle of the phone case.

"Take it easy, pal."

The hum stopped, the radio station came through full strength. Too late. The news item had ended for him, and by now it was leaking its way out to the stars.

"All right now, Kraut. You must've caught it all, so play it back. I'll only get it on another newscast anyway."

"If you say so, pal. I just didn't want you worrying about nothing." Kraut rattled it off in the announcer's voice.

Mort Lesser had died an hour ago in a holdup of his stationery store. Witnesses said the holdup man, wearing a stocking mask, had cleaned out the register and then for no apparent reason had shot and killed Lesser.

Paul pulled off onto the shoulder and switched on the Mercury's parking blinker. It could be a simple holdup-murder. Then again it could be more. If more, then Max Flesher's death could be more than a canary-throttling already in the works whether Paul had called on him or not. Did both deaths tie in with his digging up Kraut's death afresh?

But then again, Jefferson and Adams, ex-Presidents and co-signers of the Declaration of Independence, died on the same Fourth of July. A sympathy of tickers! Yet mere coincidence, something less than met the eye. What had Mort Lesser himself said?

It's possible to form constellations and even chains out of random events. You can find patterns in a list of random numbers. All this Gestalt we call life, even the universe, is only a tiny run of seeming sense in the great randomness.

But then yet again, to have jammed the signal at the first mention of Mort Lesser's name Kraut had to have known or guessed what was coming. That had been not censoring but precensoring. Had Kraut managed the news event as well as the sound of the newscast?

"What's wrong, kid? Why we stopping?"

"Everything's wrong. We're stopping the whole thing."

"What're you talking? We're on our way to ten megabucks. And that's only the beginning."

Fine, but was it only the beginning too of a large ciphering of deaths? He didn't want to push his bad luck or spread his Typhoid

Mary touch. He had already involved Florence and Mimsy Bogen. And Molly Moldover, Kraut's sister.

"Deal me out."

"We'll talk about it later, kid, when you're thinking straight. You need to get yourself a good night's rest."

He pulled back into Sunrise traffic, made sure no one looking like Death was following him, and outside Bellmore chose a motel at random.

A good night's rest. He lay watching his travel clock semaphore the hours. At midnight he sat up, looked up the numbers, and dialed. Molly Moldover first.

He heard a talk show in the background.

"Hello?" She sounded turned away, lending one ear to the talk show.

"Is Herman there?"

"Herman?" A splutter of nosh. "You must have the wrong number."

"Sorry."

Now the Bogens. Mimsy's voice, sleepy, answered on the third ring.

"Yes?"

He remained silent, wanted to say something but not knowing what.

"Oh, I've got a breather."

He smiled. He spoke after he hung up.

"No, it's the strangler."

At least they were all safe as of this moment. He could go to sleep now if he could go to sleep. Too much imagination.

11

Dawn came up solid white with a runny yolk. Paul crossed from Long Island to Staten Island and remembered his way to Halloran Hospital.

The medic beamed. It seemed all Halloran took pride in Jimmy Rath.

"Very rare, only about one thousand cases in the whole U.S. Wilson's disease usually doesn't show up till as late as forty or fifty, even later in Jimmy's case. A Wilson's disease patient has to stay off foods rich in copper—mushrooms, oysters, nuts, chocolates, liver, and so on, and take a chelating agent. Jimmy's showed remarkable improvement on that regimen. When we first took him in five years ago—he's a vet of World War I and entitled to treatment—he was bedridden. Now—well, you'll see for yourself. Be good for him to meet someone from outside—use up some of his excess energy. I hate to tranquilize him because of the side effects. That door. Straight through to the end of the Extended Care Pavilion. Go right in."

At the far end of the pavilion Paul came to a large solarium. Outside the glass the ground flowed away in smooth green. Inside, the other patients had cleared a space in the center of the room for two old men in motorized wheelchairs.

The two played a game of Dodgem, rolling, spinning, braking, reversing, each trying to bump without getting bumped. The spectators cheered them on as a young paraplegic announced the contest for the blind.

". . . just in time Tommy leans away from a sideswipe. Jimmy makes a nice recovery, whizzes around in time to corner Tommy. Jimmy takes one to give two—and that does it, folks. That last bump nearly knocked Tommy out of his chair. Tommy seems game to go on, but the referee stops the contest in the third round. Winner and still champion, Jimmy Rath."

Paul waited for the congratulating and kidding to die down before he tackled Rath.

Jimmy Rath sleeved sweat from a face as congested from laughing as if he had been hanging head-down. He eyed the phone case.

"See me? Sure, kid, what can I do you for?"

Paul told him.

"Kraut Schwartz? Jesus H. Christ, I ain't thought about the bum in years."

"Bum?"

"When I was on the cops, they was all bums to me. They knew it, and unless they wanted a taste of my fist, they all walked wide. Pull up a chair. I see you was wounded yourself. Vietnam, right? I can tell.

"But Kraut, now. I mind the time old Kraut took out his fat wallet and started to tell me to buy my missus something nice for Christmas. My missus in his mouth. I grabbed aholt of the bum and stuck him upside down in a garbage can. Right there on Broadway in front of everybody. He never showed his face on my Broadway beat again after that." He cracked his knuckles. The sound apparently drowned out in his own ears a sudden hum from the phone case. "What's them papers you got there?"

Paul told him.

"Yeah? Well, I'll give it a whirl. But that was long ago, kid. Long ago." He read slowly through Kraut's ravings, looking up only when he had something to offer. "'It takes force . . . He'd never stop for a friendly smile, but trudged along in his moody style.' Now, 'Force' was the name of a ready-to-eat cereal. And there was a jingle about this Jim Dumps fellow who ate the stuff and became Sunny Jim. 'The golden hour of the little flower.' Sure, that was the program of the radio priest of them days. Father Coughlin, God rest his soul. 'He died with his daisies on.' That must mean the Limey—Vic Hazell. Another bum. 'Daisies' is short for 'daisy roots,' which is cockney rhyming slang for 'boots.' Vic was gunning for Kraut, but Kraut hid out till he could fix it for Vic to get knocked off while Vic was taking a phony phone call."

He read on to the end and shook his head.

"I guess that's it, kid. Did I help you at all?" He went on before Paul could say yes. "Uh-oh. The computer says it's time for my penicillamine."

Paul followed Jimmy Rath's gaze and saw a nurse heading their way.

"Everything here works by computer, kid. What doses to take and when to take them." He cracked his knuckles.

Paul picked up the phone case and stood.

"Thanks, Mr. Rath."

"Anytime, kid. Anytime."

Paul had made it to the parking lot when he thought he heard a crash of glass, then cries. He stood a moment beside the Mercury, shook his head when nothing more happened, tossed the phone case on the seat, and got behind the wheel. He had started rolling when the medic he had met came running out to wave him down. Paul braked and waited for the medic's breath to catch up.

"Did you say anything to Jimmy to get him worked up?"

Paul stared. He did not want to believe his premonition.

"No. We talked about his days on the New York Police force. He seemed happy remembering them. Why? What happened?"

"He's killed himself."

Paul got out and followed the medic, who took a short cut to the lawn outside the solarium.

They had spread a blanket over the twisted form of Jimmy Rath. After crashing through the floor-length window and careening down the grassy slope, the wheelchair had struck the rock wall at an angle, and Jimmy had momentum-tumbled along the roughness.

One of the top administrators took Paul to his office and began asking the same questions when the phone broke in. The man made a face as he hung up.

"Well, we know now what it was. All right, Felder, you can go."

"Like hell, I want to know what it was."

The man made another face, then sighed.

"It's going to come out sooner or later, so all right. It was a foul-up in the pharmacological computer. It ordered Jimmy's dose on time as usual, but for some stupid reason it made up some PCP instead of his penicillamine. Penicillamine is a chelating agent. What it does is clutch copper atoms in its claws and lift them out of the bloodstream before they can damage liver and brain. PCP is a hallucinogen. For God's sake, they *outlawed* PCP back in '63 because it turns you on into schizophrenia. How we even had the formula on hand is going to take a lot of explaining."

Paul settled himself behind the wheel of the Mercury but did not turn the ignition key. It had to be Kraut's doing. Kraut the program evening an old score for Kraut the dead gangster.

"What happened, pal?"

Paul glared at the phone case on the seat beside him.

"You tell me."

"Simple, pal." Kraut spoke in discrete syllables as to a child or an idiot. "GIGO. Garbage in, garbage out."

With a bolus of fear Paul Felder saw Jimmy Rath's death not only as Kraut getting hunk for the dumping into the garbage can on Broadway in the Thirties but also as an object lesson to Paul Felder now.

12

He swallowed hard as he handed his credit card to the teller.

"I'd like to draw a thousand in twenties on my credit card."

He had to learn how much leeway Kraut allowed him. One

grand could give him a good start if he had to run. The phone case hung sweaty in his hand.

"Very good, sir."

The teller pressed a button on the credit card box. Paul saw the reflection of a warning light flash in her eye. She smiled and asked him to wait a moment. He smiled back. She turned away, no doubt discreetly signaling a guard.

Paul looked around casually and whispered fiercely to Kraut.

"They think I'm working plastic."

"I know. You gonna be good?"

"Yes."

"O.K., kid. Just stay cool."

By the time the guard reached Paul's elbow his credit card had gone off the hot-card list and the teller was making red-faced excuses. Paul smiled stiffly.

"That's quite all right. These things happen. On second thought, I won't be needing the full thousand. Make it two hundred, please."

"We're back in the car?"

They were, but Paul couldn't remember the in-between.

"We are."

"O.K., kid. Don't just sit there. It's out to Long Island again. I'm fixing you up with a motel reservation so we'll be all set to fly to Florida in the morning."

"All right, all right."

"Sore, huh?" Kraut chuckled. "No hard feelings, pal, but see what happens when you get wise, O acned adolescent?"

"Wha'?"

"A slip of the lingo. I meant 'O rash youth.'"

"See what happens when you get fancy?"

"Never mind. The warning stands. I'm telling you: play along with me, you'll be glad; buck me, you'll be sorry."

13

The desk clerk handed him the key with a wink. Still smarting from that assault on his straight manhood, Paul let himself into his room.

A confusion of hair, blue domes of eyelids, a sleeping smile. Mimsy lay very much at home on his bed.

Softly he set the phone case on the folding rack, then moved to

the side of the bed and stood looking down. At last he clicked the
key against its plastic tag.

She opened an eye a sharper focus of blue, then shut it and
stretched her lines felinely. He felt an answering shiver of tingle.
Need and doubt weakened his stance. He had to sit and made the
most of it by sitting on the bed. He cupped his hand on her breast
and felt an answering titillation. She opened both eyes.

"I came right away, Paul. I took the afternoon off and I'm cutting
evening class. It feels sinfully good to play hooky."

What was this about coming right away? And how had she found
out where he would be staying when he himself had not known
till an hour ago? She ran a finger across his lips to stop him from
speaking.

"I guess what got me was your cool when I played footsie with
you under dear old Florence's innocent eyes and you didn't blink
yours one time. I just did it to tease to begin with. But then, I don't
know, something came over me." She blubbed his lips playfully.

For a minute he didn't know what she was talking about. Then
he got the picture of the three of them at the table while nylon toes
slid up and down his legs. He laughed. She pushed up on one
elbow and stared at him, her eyes suddenly uncertain. He laughed
again, but to his own surprise it did not come out a bitter laugh.
Her eyes unclouded and she laughed with him.

"Anyway, I made up my mind right after the call to find out
about you as well as about myself."

His ears burned; they at least had lost their cool. *Right after
the call:* letting him know she had tagged him as the midnight
breather. Had she just now laughed not with him but at him? Did
she take him for some sort of a creep? She was asking for it. Sock it
to her between the eyes.

He got up, not caring how awkwardly, and watched her in the
mirror as he undressed. But aside from a widening of the eyes he
saw no change in her face. A soft look of lasting wonder, maybe.

"So much for your cool. Boy, did you take me in."
"And vice versa."
"How did it happen?"
"Haven't you heard of love at first sight?"
She punched his shoulder.
"You know what I mean."

He articulated the plastic and aluminum legs.

"Land mine in Vietnam."

"Why didn't you tell me in the car last night?"

"I don't want pity or perversity."

"How do you know you're not getting them now?"

He deployed himself.

"I know."

"You have beautiful long legs."

"My first memory is of wanting to grow tall enough to see what was on the mantel."

"And when you did, what did you find?"

"Dust. Florence isn't the best housekeeper." Mimsy sighed. "She'll be worrying. Do you know how late it is? I have to go." She lay back. "But first you have to keep your promise."

"What promise?"

She wrinkled her nose.

"You know. When you phoned earlier and said those nice things and asked me to come over and promised to tell me who I really am. Most convincing. You made it sound so very mysterious." She thrust out her lower lip. "Unless it was only a hype. Is that what you meant: putting me on to do what we did so I'd know myself metaphysically?" She bit his ear. "A shabby trick, darling." She kissed his nose. "But a lovely number." She slipped away from him and legged it to the bathroom to wash and dress.

Paul sent his glower past the foot of the bed to the phone case. Getting an earful? Getting a kick out of the whole thing as well. Kraut the pimp. Harsh thanks for the lovely number, but Kraut had put him on the spot.

Florence had asked him not to tell Mimsy. But everyone had the right to know who she or he was. Mimsy had that basic right. She also had the right to be aware Kraut had used her and might use her again.

When she came out and asked him to zip her up, he told her. He told her about the programs and about the portable phone and showed her the copy of Kraut's ravings. She nodded as she handed the pages back.

"Lots of things make sense now. Not this gibberish. I mean things Florence never wanted to talk about." She surprised Paul by laughing suddenly, richly. "Florence as Mrs. Kraut Schwartz!

That'll take some getting used to. I won't tell her I know, of course. This is some wild head change. I used to dream I was secretly a princess, and now I wake up and find I'm Kraut Schwartz's granddaughter. I like the idea." She aimed a finger at Paul. "You cross me, Felder, you fail to make this little girl happy, and you get it right in the guts. Right, gramps?"

Kraut laughed.

"Right, kid. I like the idea too. You got class."

Waiting to see her off in a cab took them out of earshot of Kraut. Paul sandwiches Mimsy's hand in both his.

"We need a way for you to be sure another time it's the real Paul Felder and not gramps who's phoning you."

She thought.

"How about slipping the word 'borogoves' in."

"As in 'All mimsy were the borogoves'?"

"Beamish."

The cab came. He leaned in for a parting kiss and a last word.

"Take care of yourself, Mimsy."

"And you. When will I see you again?"

"Soon, I hope."

She leaned out to call back.

"Pity you don't know what nice things you said on the phone. Maybe I'll tell you some day."

He squeezed his eyes tight.

"How, Kraut?"

"Ain't you doped it out, pal?"

"You used my voice pattern to make her think I was calling."

His own voice came back at him.

"Exact same voiceprint, kid."

He squeezed his fists tight. He wanted to ask, to shout, *What did you say to her?*

"Why, Kraut?"

"I told you, kid. String along with me and keep your nose clean and you'll be glad. Don't tell me you didn't like it. Why be a chump? Get it where you can and while you can."

"Know something, Kraut? You're mean as a little old lady at a wrestling match. I thought you were thinking big. And here all you've been doing is getting in jabs with an umbrella."

"Say, looka here, kid, I don't know why you're all upset. I thought we was on the same wavelength, seeing you're part artificial like me. Also now there's this other tie, seeing you're almost one of the family."

Paul burned, remembering the phone case had shared the room with them. He opened his eyes and looked around the motel room. Was there no way out of the bind he found himself in? Maybe he could put Kraut himself/itself through an identity crisis.

"Seducing your own granddaughter. Now there's a freaky bit of incest for you."

A moment's silence, then a cold voice.

"Know something, kid? You got a mouth on you."

14

The idea hit him in the middle of the night. But he waited for morning, after Florence left for the supermarket and before Mimsy left for her office-temporary assignment.

"Yes?"

"Mimsy, Mimsy, quite the whimsy, how do your borogoves grow?"

"Ah, the real Paul Felder."

"Listen up, Mimsy. Kraut will be wondering why it's taking me so long to check out. And if I know him, he'll start feeling around and maybe tapping the pay phones here, or your phone."

"So I'm listening."

"How's your data processing?"

"Fairly advanced. Why?"

"I've been thinking, if you can get up to Boston and tell Prof. Steven Fogarty at Thoreau I say it's O.K. to show you my program—got that so far?"

"My shorthand's fairly advanced too."

"If you do get the chance then, sneak a listening delay into the program. If there's a delayed feedback between what Kraut says and what he hears himself say, he won't be able to speak at all. That ought to frustrate him into a breakdown and give us a shot at regaining control." He grew aware that he lacked feedback. "Hello?"

He was talking into a dead line.

15

Matt Muldoon looked hopefully at Paul Felder.

"Cold up north?"

The lie would harm no one.

"Some of the lion leaped over from March. It was raw out this morning."

Matt Muldoon's face took a happy twist down around Killarney. He had found Muldoon where the lady in the next trailer had said Muldoon would be. Muldoon sat at a table under a beach umbrella down by the wading end of the pool, drawing out his canned draft beer. Muldoon's smile faded.

"Still I kind of miss it. Not the place so much, the times. In those days we had the lead all set up in type. 'Gang guns blazed again today and . . .' But I guess things weren't the way we remember them, the way we like to think they were. Like one time I pointed out to Kraut an old guy eating clams and celery at Shanley's. 'Yeah?' Kraut says. 'Who's that?' 'Bat Masterson,' I tell him. 'You're still not telling me nothing,' he says. And so I have to explain that Bat Masterson had been a great gunfighter in the Old West. Kraut eyed him again. 'Yeah? He don't look so much.' And he didn't. Come to think of it, neither did Kraut."

Paul eyed the phone case at his feet and tried to damp a shudder. He had boarded the plane only after Kraut had promised him not to touch Muldoon. But what were Kraut's easy promises worth?

Muldoon was talking.

"They're all gone now, all those who had some connection with Kraut. Or going fast." He ticked them off on blunt fingers. "S. Thomas Extrom and Gordon Dumaine. Peggy Aaron. Tommy Tighe. Jake Putterman. Judge Barsky. Dallas Dollard. His sister Molly and his wife Florence I don't know about. PWU—present whereabouts unknown. Probably dead. Same goes for Letha Root. Leaves only Macie Devlin and his Faith Venture. And of course Harry Spector. Funny how Max Flesher died the other day and almost at the same time Mark Nolan."

"Mark Nolan?"

Muldoon tapped the copy of Kraut's ravings before him on the table.

"Sergeant Nolan, the guy who questioned Kraut as he lay dying. Came across it only this morning in the Miami paper. Small item.

Seems Nolan was setting the night alarm system in the bank where he worked as a guard. Just getting ready to go home. Some kind of short circuit electrocuted him. He went to his long home."

Paul did not tell him about Mort Lesser and Jimmy Rath.

"Boy, I sure know how to spread the gloom, don't I, Felder? Sorry about the necrology, but that's what you get for looking up an old bastard like me. The gap-tooth generation. Let's get on to something lighter, like Kraut's deathbed spiel."

Muldoon laughed and pointed.

"This 3909 in '3909 stained-glass windows'—know what that is? Didn't think you would. When Al Smith was running for President, anti-Catholics or just plain good Republicans would ask, 'Do you know Al Smith's phone number? Here, I'll write it down.' They'd write 3909, then tell you to turn the paper back to front and hold it to the light. Get it? POPE. Direct line to the Vatican is what they meant."

He read on and shook his head.

" 'Olive Eye' I never figured out."

Explaining it to him would have meant telling him about Mort Lesser. Paul kept silent.

"Now 'A roof without visible means of support' I know. After Kraut dropped out of school he was a newsboy for a year, then a grocery store clerk till he got canned, then a composition roofer's apprentice. From the time he was seventeen he kept paying roofer's union dues to show arresting officers his card as proof of gainful employment.

"He also told me, 'I once worked in your racket.' He said he had been a printer's devil for a while. I guess that's how come he knew about the accents acute and grave he mentions in this nuttiness.

"Then he began his real career. He boosted packages off delivery trucks, looted stores, broke into apartments, stuck up crap games that wouldn't pay for protection. For a while he drove a beer truck for Arnold Rothstein, the bankroller for the underworld. Then he went into business for himself.

"That's where 'the doctor' comes in—the 'big con man' of 'Fairfield, Conn.' That has to be Dr. S. Thomas Extrom. Extrom always seemed to me one of those ham actors who listens to his voice instead of to the words, to *how* he's saying instead of *what* he's saying. He wore his overcoat like an opera cape. *Die Fledermaus*. But the world took him for philanthropist, yachtsman, financier, country squire, even Presidential dark horse.

"Yet he and Gordon Dumaine, the treasurer of O'Harmon & Foster, were really the Spitale brothers, with long records as con men till the records disappeared from the files. It was S. Thomas who got them into the big time. He had vision. He saw Prohibition coming and took over O'Harmon & Foster, a slipping but legitimate drug firm.

"O'Harmon & Foster got withdrawal permits for alcohol to manufacture its products. Bootleggers' trucks, including Kraut's, rolled up to the platform of O'Harmon & Foster in Fairfield, Conn., at night to load barrels of hair tonic, furniture polish, and tincture of iodine that the bootleggers distilled into '8-year-old rye,' 'bottled-in-bond bourbon,' and 'Scotch just off the boat.'

Muldoon shuddered.

"I can still taste the stuff."

He washed the taste away with a swallow of beer.

"On with the show and tell. 'Jafsie' I'm sure you know. This next seems to have to do with switching to the numbers game when Repeal liquidated bootlegging. The 'high yeller' would be Letha Root, Harlem's policy queen. Kraut muscled her and all the other black operators out and himself in. Two million bucks a year that meant to him.

"'Everything works by push or pull.' That's something Tommy Tighe used to say. He was Tammany district leader and Kraut's bagman, paying off the cops, the politicians, and the judges and prosecutors.

"From 'Mr. Black has the Limehouse Blues' to, let's see, 'Tip your derby to a horseshoe wreath' has to do with the time Schwartz hid out in Peggy Aaron's house. The Limey, Vic Hazell, worked as a triggerman for Kraut, then decided he wanted part or all of the action for himself. He declared war by raiding Kraut's garage, smashing everything he found there—slot machines, beer rack, trucks—all but twenty cases of booze, which he hauled away after killing a mechanic who begged for his life.

"In the war with the Limey the kill ratio favored Kraut—but how can you outwit a mad dog? And Hazell was a mad dog. He went looking for Kraut personally after Kraut's hoods killed Hazell's kid brother. One day on East 107th, Kraut spotted Tommy gun muzzles sticking out of a black touring car. Kraut dove for the pavement.

Kids were playing under spouting fire hydrants when the Limey sprayed the whole damn street trying to get Kraut. Five kids wounded, one dead.

"Sol Barsky—later Judge Barsky and a righteous tough judge—got Hazell off by tripping up a prosecution witness. The cops had tried too hard to cinch the case against Hazell with a little white perjury.

"Anyway, with Hazell running loose, Schwartz lay low as a 'Mr. Black' at Peggy Aaron's, while hoods he hired from Chicago hunted Hazell. The Limey got riddled taking a set-up phone call. As I remember, he was all of twenty-four. I met Peggy in later years, and she told me Kraut pushed her and her girls around for the fun of it. Still, she felt nostalgia for the old days. She said she ran into one of her girls after her place broke up. 'It was safer in my house,' she said. 'The poor girl got pregnant swimming in a public swimming pool.'

"The tramp buttering his bread with sunlight could be Chaplin, though I don't recall that bit of business in any of his films. But here's Jake Putterman, a guy with moxie. 'Jamaica ginger'—Jake for short. 'Leading the blind in his soup and fish,' and so on. Jake was a Waiters Union officer who fought back when Kraut set up the Gotham Restaurant and Cafeteria Association to squeeze protection money. Stink bombs during lunch and dinner hours. Death threats. They didn't faze Jake, though local law enforcement was no help.

"The New York grand jury, convened to investigate racketeering under the direction of the D.A., couldn't find any rackets. A series of stories appeared in the *N.Y. Evening Globe*, detailing the rackets. The grand jury subpoenaed the newspaperman, but yours truly refused to reveal his source. The grand jury had me taken before the general sessions judge. Fined me 250 bucks and 30 days for contempt." Muldoon smiled. "Wasn't too bad. I got a jail expose series out of the vile durance.

"But now things began to break. It was the beginning of the end for Kraut Schwartz. The governor appointed a special prosecutor. My source—Jake Putterman—brought the special prosecutor evidence tying Schwartz to Tommy Tighe, the Tammany district leader who was Kraut's fixer. Kraut beat it out of the state and waited for the heat to die down.

"Funny how he skips around in his delirium. Here we go back a few years. Once I put in the paper that Kraut was a pushover for a blonde. He came up to me and asked, 'Did you write that, Muldoon?' I had to say I did. He shook his head. 'Is that any language for a family newspaper?' But he did have a yen for blondes. Florence, of course. And then there was Dallas Dollard, the dame who ran her own speak-easy. She wouldn't give him a tumble. Here she is in 'Throw the bitch out. It's curtains, sister. A cotton ball in hell.' Her chorus girls had an act in which they threw tiny cotton balls at the suckers. I was there when she was rehearsing a new show. She had a routine in which a guy playing a repairman asked, 'Would you like a French phone?' and she answered, 'But I don't speak French.' A voice came from a dark corner of the room. 'You can French me anytime.' She located her heckler by the red glow of a cigar, and she yelled, 'Throw the bum out!' It was Kraut. He turned down her apology and got her place padlocked, and she never dared show her face in New York after that.

"But 'F for fig' and the rest I don't get, unless it was the G-string Dallas's chorus girls wore, and maybe 'J for jig' has to do with Harlem again, and 'J for John the Waterman' might be Schwartz's Waterman pen he used to rap the mouthpiece with to annoy wire-tappers: that this made it just as hard on whoever he was talking to didn't faze him, and 'N for knucklebones' could stand for brass knuckles, and 'S for sack of stones' might be a cement kimono for somebody he dropped in the East River.

"Now the mention of a trunk reminds me. The story went that Schwartz had somebody build him an iron chest and that Schwartz filled it with big bills and jewelry. I heard that it held the diamonds and rubies from Broadway's biggest jewelry store heist. The word was Schwartz agreed to fence the stuff then sent a triggerman after the guys who pulled it off to gun them down and bring back the dough Schwartz had paid for the stuff."

Matt Muldoon eyed the nose shadow of a sunbather.

"Four p.m. Time for my dip. Finished on the dot." He handed the pages back to Paul and stood up on skinny shanks. "Join me? I'll fix you up with a pair of trunks, and we can both impregnate the swimming pool."

Paul smiled and shook his head but went down to the edge with Muldoon. He waited at the deep end for Muldoon to snort and splutter up and out. He braced himself and lent a hand to a mottled hand.

"Be careful the next few days." He looked across the pool to the phone case resting by Muldoon's table. "And you'll think I'm nuts, but when we get back say something nice about Kraut."

Muldoon stared at him, then a few drops fell with a shrug.

"Too much sun too soon?" Muldoon frowned searchingly at the sunbathers at the far side of the pool, then back at Paul. "Why not? I always humor nuts."

And toweling himself at his table, Muldoon spoke to the world at large.

"Once I asked Schwartz if he ever did business with Lucky Luciano or Chink Sherman. Schwartz said, 'I may do a lot of lousy things, but I'll never live off dames or dope.' In his way Schwartz was quite a guy."

He looked at Paul for approval. Paul nodded; he hoped that had bought Muldoon protection.

16

Paul made out to be taking a sponge bath in his motel room and with the water running sneaked out to a pay phone.

"Hello?"

"Mrs. Florence Bogen?"

"Yes. Who is this?"

"Paul Felder. Is Mimsy there?"

"No."

"Do you know where she is?"

"I really can't say. She wasn't here when I came home this evening. She left a note. It said she had a wonderful assignment traveling as a secretary to an executive on a flying trip across the country. I checked with the business school, and they said she canceled her classes for the rest of the week for the same reason. It sounded like a good thing, but frankly I was worried till you called. The office-temporary place is closed at this hour, and I can't find out anything from a recording. I thought you and Mimsy might have— But now I'm not worried."

Now *he* was worried. The assignment sounded phony. Had Mimsy given up after his aborted call, and had Kraut requisitioned her out of the way? Or had Mimsy faked it, setting out on her unprepared own to deal with Kraut in Boston?

His heart sank to the bottom of the slot with the coins for a second call.

Professor Steven Fogarty hardly listened.

"Girl? No, I haven't met your girl. Sorry, Paul, you caught me at a bad time. I'm late already. Faculty meeting. Cutting up the pie for the coming semester. I really have to run now. Try me again later this week or early next."

That was bad enough. Worse was wondering if that had been Professor Steven Fogarty or Kraut mimicking Fogarty's voice.

17

Letha Root was blind but she *glared* at him.

"Be he live or be he dead, I don't want nothing to do with him nohow, that's the guaranteed truth."

Time had sharpened further the already sharp features of the high-yellow policy queen of Harlem in the Thirties.

Paul found himself laying a soul brother accent on her.

"Won't take but a minute of your time, sister."

In the silence the hall funneled the refrigerator humming and the wires in a toaster and the loose lid of a pot on a burner humming along. Someone in the kitchen opened and closed the refrigerator door, and Paul heard the interfacing of beer and air.

Madame Root shook her head.

"My interest in Kraut Schwartz died when he died. But I ain't no ways sorry for the wire I sent old Kraut at the Newark Hospital when I hear he's at death's door. 'Galatians 6:7' is all I said. If you don't know your Bible, that's 'Be not deceived; God is not mocked: for whatsoever a man soweth, that shall he also reap.' Too bad he never came to enough to know about the wire."

Paul felt the phone case join in the humming. Kraut knew now.

"Makes you stop and wonder, don't it, sister, how it all come out like the Good Book say."

"F'get you, honky."

Letha Root turned her blankness on the mustachioed tall stud in tie-dyed levi's and high-heeled shoes.

"Why, what you mean, Junior?"

"He hyping you, Aunty. This ain't no member. He only got a contact habit bloodwise. You just as well stop running your mouth." Without taking his eyes off Paul, he drained his beer and set the can down. "Whupping the game on a lame. I'm gonna go up side your head."

Letha Root put out a hand.

"He don't mean no harm, honey. My jaws ain't tight. If a white boy can put me on like that, he must have *some* soul in him. You leave him be." She felt the crystalless face of her lapel watch. "It's getting on, Junior. You better be on your way to your job."

Junior looked sullenly out the window at Paul's rental Caddy. His mood shifted to indifference. He was doing his number: his number was to look bored; it put the world on the defensive.

"If you think you know what you doing."

He gave Aunty an unnephewlike kiss. She gave him a fond slap.

"Oh, yeah. Get on out of here, you old greasy greens."

He got on out without a backward look at Paul.

Madame Root got herself and Paul settled down.

"Reckon you can tell I bought myself a nephew. He works at a soul station I own here. Oh, yes, I got out of New York with just enough to buy me a new start. Old Kraut didn't wipe me out quite. I liked the climate out here—it was hotter in New York, you dig— but back when I hit Las Vegas, they weren't letting blacks move in. So I got me a white woman to front for me and bought this house. I made out to be the maid. Lots of folks think she left it to me in her will.

"All right, white boy. You flew all the way out here to see me. Read me what old Kraut said. Maybe I'll know and maybe I won't. Maybe I'll tell and maybe I won't. What you waiting on? Do I have a witness out there?"

She didn't stop him till he reached "5 to 7 made them Darktown Strutters bawl. Even the high yeller." Her face took on even greater sharpness, and she put up a halting hand.

"That old devil Kraut. 527 was the magic number done all us Harlem operators in. Everybody knowed 527 always get a big play in November. That because 5 plus 2 is lucky 7 and November the 11th month. Seven-come-eleven the idea. Well, old Kraut got his walking adding machine—what his name?"

"Zigzag Ludwig?"

"That it. Kraut got Zigzag to figure how to rig the pari-mutuel handle with a few bets at the race track to make 527 hit on Thanksgiving Eve, 19 and 31. That broke all the black-run policy banks, and old Kraut moved in."

She stopped him again at "The man and the woman have a fortune in potatoes. It's Big Dick—"

"Dream-book talk. 'Man and woman' mean 15, 'fortune' mean 60, and 'potatoes'—that stand for something else you can guess—mean 75. In craps Big Dick stand for 10, in lottery Big Dick 15-60-75."

She had but one comment more, and that at the end.

"What old Kraut doing messing around with the Bible? Fetch me my copy down off yonder shelf and turn to Genesis 3:14 and read me it."

"'And the Lord God said unto the serpent, Because thou hast done this, thou art cursed above all cattle, and above every beast of the field; upon thy belly shalt thou go, and dust shalt thou eat all the days of thy life.'"

She listened and nodded.

"Look like old Kraut crapped out with snake eyes."

Letha Root stood at the door of her home still laughing as Paul crossed slabs set in trim lawn and got into the Caddy.

Once safely on the passenger seat with the car starting up, Kraut spoke.

"We're getting there, kid. I'll lay odds when you dig up the iron chest holding the loot there'll be a combination padlock on the hasp and the combination will be Big Dick—15-60-75. O.K., kid. On to L.A."

Looking in the mirror to make a U-turn back toward the airport, Paul met eyes.

Junior rose higher and leaned forward to take in the phone case. He flicked open a knife. Its wickedness held Paul still while Junior reached over to snap the case open and study its innards. Junior got his rump on the back seat and lounged, cleaning his fingernails with the knife.

"Suppose you drive me to my place of work. We-all got things to talk over."

In the broadcasting studio Junior's number changed. Now, sitting at his mikes and switches and wearing earphones, he was the up-tempo soul-station disc jockey supreme.

"Hello-o-o: lucky people you, this is your Toke Show host . . . the Splendiferous Spade. You know I ain't S-in and J-ing you: pretty people, I'm cuing you. For the next two solid hours . . . and I mean solid . . . I'll be taking requests. So you be phoning them in, hear?" He mixed in loud drum rim-shots, trumpet flourishes, and band chords sustained to punctuate his shucking and jiving, gave the phone number, put on a piece full of funky runs, lit, sucked on, and passed to Paul a joint in a peace-symbol roach clip, and leaned back with his earphones half on half off. "Now, man, don't hold back."

He followed Paul's gaze to the desk phone and smiled.

"I fixed the station phone line to give callers the busy signal. I have me a backlog of requests on tape—my goof-off insurance. Shoot, man, we're alone and won't nobody bother us."

The light on the desk phone lit up.

Junior frowned and lifted the phone. Paul could hear Kraut's voice.

"Please play 'If I Forget You.' I'd like to dedicate it to the memory of Kraut Schwartz, which is a long memory."

The voice went on but grew so faint that Junior had to press the earpiece hard to his head to hear. Then came an ear-splitting sound that shimmered the air and set Paul's teeth on edge. Junior slumped slowly after the jolt hit him. Junior was alive but his face was dead. Paul looked at Junior's eyes and did not want to know what the sound had done to Junior's brain.

Kraut spoke from the phone case.

"Now if you get the hell out of there, kid, we won't miss our flight after all."

18

"Mr. Devlin?"

"Yes."

"Macie Devlin?"

"The same."

Macie Devlin's voice was easy, but his eyes held a wariness that went against the voice.

"My name is Paul Felder." Paul spoke over the electric hedge trimmer sounding from the side of the redwood house. He had nearly tripped on its damn trailing cord. "I'm doing a paper on Kraut Schwartz and—"

He stopped, wondering at Macie Devlin's quick warning headshake. The hedge trimmer's whine grew.

"Faith, no!"

Paul whirled without thinking. He tripped himself. The phone case flew from his hand. The ground stunned him. All he saw of the

woman rushing him was a floppy white hat and rhinestoned dark
glasses. She was leaning over him before he could move. The vi-
brating saw blade thrust down at his throat.

His hands were broken-winged birds. One flailing hand touched
a tremble of line. He caught hold of the cord and whipped it at the
blade. The blade sliced through to a flaring crackle that shocked
the woman backward.

Paul rolled over into a painful push-up. Even stilled, the blade
made a wicked weapon. But by now Macie Devlin had an arm
around the woman; his other hand gently pulled the trimmer from
her grip and let it fall.

"She's all right now."

Devlin walked her to the front door. She stiffened in the opening and her legs locked. Macie Devlin looked back over his shoulder.

"She's afraid for me, you see. Only a few years ago some of the
boys snatched me and tried to make me tell them where to find Albert's mythical buried fortune." He gave a short laugh. "Hell, if I
knew where it was, I'd've told the government more'n forty years
ago, right after Albert died. The informer's share alone would've
made me rich."

He stroked the woman's cheek. "This young fellow won't harm
me, dearest. Please go in and take your beauty nap." He kissed her
neck.

Her still-showgirl legs unlocked and she dimmed away. Macie
Devlin closed the door and turned back to Paul. With a weak smile
he fingered sweat from his brow and snapped the drops off.

"Paul Felder is it? Let's have a change of venue, Paul."

A half-size refrigerator stood in a corner of Devlin's downtown
real estate management office. Macie Devlin opened it and poured
himself a glass of skim milk. Paul shook his head at a hospitable
eyebrow. Devlin took distasteful sips.

"Disbarred by an ulcer, as well as by the bar association. Plus
high cholesterol level. Plus an implanted pacemaker. My list of
infirmities is a long one. But as the fellow said, when you consider
the alternative."

He pointed to the fixtures for a neon sign that had hung in the
window.

"The neon sign had to go. It could make my pacemaker pulse so fast my heart couldn't keep up. My heart would stop or just twitch." He lifted his head away from bodily pain. "Yes, they worked me over and my heart gave out and they left me for dead. In a way my bum ticker is my insurance. They know it's no use any more trying to get at me through Faith or by working me over again. I'd only stop on them. But you came here to talk about Albert."

Smiling, he leafed through the copy of Kraut's ravings.

"So you consider Kraut Schwartz literature. That would've thrilled Albert. His favorite reading was Emil Ludwig's—no relation to Zigzag—*Life of Napoleon. The Forty Days of Musa Dagh* also impressed him. After reading it he said, 'Them days you could knock off hundreds without getting in no jam.'

"For a while he went on a culture binge. I guided him through the museums, brought him art books. 'The Thinker is a question mark.' He pointed out to me that in left profile Rodin's *Thinker is* a question mark. He even began to be a natty dresser, because Society"—Macie Devlin formed finger quotes in the air around the word—"took him up. Then he saw Society did it only for kicks, and he went back to his sloppy self."

A moving van pulled up out front, and the driver came in for a key. Macie Devlin beamed as the man went out.

"Full occupancy maketh a full hearth. I just rented the office the other side of this wall to a doctor. That's his equipment they're moving in. But about Albert. I see he picked up some Pennsylvania Dutch from his stay. 'Just walk the fly door in. The hook ain't on.' 'I'm afraid you don't make yourself out.' 'Just before you get the farm behind, go the hill over.' Poor Albert. He nearly went mad holed up for eighteen months while he was under indictment. He *did* go mad."

Macie Devlin eyed Paul speculatively.

"I've paid my dues. After Albert died I got off with one year for turning state's evidence and giving the special prosecutor the goods on Tommy Tighe. I don't want to pay any more dues. There's no statute of limitations on murder. That goes for being accessory thereto, however unwittingly or unwillingly. So what I'm about to tell you is purest supposition.

"Suppose someone journeyed to Albert's hideout to tell Albert this someone had fixed it up for Albert to give himself up in Nyack, New York. This someone might have watched Albert shift moods—

from gloom to joy to savagery. Suppose further that after agreeing to return to civilization, Albert in this strangely savage mood picked a fight with his favorite bodyguard, Slip Katz. Albert loved horseback riding, and Katz used to bounce along with him. But say that now Albert seemed to work himself into a rage.

"Say that Albert cursed Katz out, accusing him of holding out a collection on him—'playing the nine of hearts on me.' Say that Albert suddenly drew from a handy drawer a .45 with a silencer on it and silenced Katz. Say Albert sent this someone downstairs to fetch a pair of young hoods. Say Albert told one of the hoods to stand still and then bloodied his nose. 'And let the blood to drown the blood.' This would account for the blood on the floor as having come from a fight over cards, if the boardinghouse keeper wondered. Say the two hoods stuffed Katz's body into a burlap sack, weighted the sack with chunks of cement—'The cat's pajamas, a kitten kimono'—and dumped it in some abandoned rain-pooled stone quarry."

Macie Devlin's eyes looked haunted.

"'Boys, throw your voice!' You found that ad in the pulp magazines. A cut of an eye-popping porter toting a trunk which emitted the cry, 'Help, help, let me out!' To get you to send away for ventriloquism lessons. Of course all this never happened, but I get a picture of the hoods carrying the sack down the back stairs while Katz still had a bit of life in him."

Paul felt a prickle of insight. *Would I kid you, captain?* Katz had helped Kraut secretly bury the iron trunk full of loot. Like Captain Kidd, Kraut had got rid of a too knowing henchman.

Macie Devlin seemed anxious to wind it up.

"So much for fantasy. I can tell you only one fact. When Albert gave himself up in Nyack, a small town in Rockland County, I got him to create a new image of himself. Mr. Albert Rabinow walked around town smiling humbly, tipping his hat to the ladies, and patting kids' heads. His people tipped bigger than government people, who were on a tight budget. It was children's parties for hospitalized and orphaned kids and drinks for everyone in the house. 'Cain was I ere I saw Nyack.'

"The jury acquitted him. The judge bawled the jury out. 'The verdict was dictated by other considerations than the evidence.' But though Albert beat the tax evasion rap, the special rackets prosecutor, with Jake Putterman's help, kept after him. Albert proposed that the syndicate rub out the special prosecutor.

"The Big Six vetoed the hit because it would've put too much heat on the whole underworld. 'I'm gunning for the guy myself. Egged them on but they chickened out.' Albert sent word he planned to go ahead with the rubout. The syndicate gave Harry Spector the contract, and Albert met his Waterloo in the Tivoli's loo."

"Did you ever meet Harry Spector?"

"Never laid eyes on the chap. Never want to. Show you what I mean. He served twenty-three years after they got him for Albert's killing. Just a year before he got out, Harry Spector was the only prisoner to show up for his meals when the inmates at Rahway went on a mass hunger strike. A lot of hard-noses there, but none of the other prisoners made a move to bother Harry Spector."

He handed Paul Kraut's ravings and Paul put them away and got up.

"Drive you back home?"

"No, thanks, young fellow. I have to stay here and see everything's unpacked and set up, ready for the doctor to practice when he shows Monday." He smiled. "I haven't met this chap either, but his credit and references check out tiptop. He's moving down from upstate, and we've arranged everything by phone."

They shook hands and parted outside Macie Devlin's office. Something nagging at him, Paul left slowly. He had not yet gone outside when he heard a thump and a yell.

In the doctor's office Paul found Macie Devlin on the floor. The moving man waved his hands.

"I was just plugging this machine in when I heard him fall and I turned around and there he was like that."

Paul whistled softly when he saw Macie Devlin lay within three feet of a diathermy machine for simple surgery such as removing warts. Like a neon sign, a diathermy machine would make a pacemaker race unbeatably.

The moving man repeated himself. Paul cut him off and told him to use Devlin's phone to bring an ambulance.

Paul lowered himself to give mouth-to-mouth. But it was no good. He raised himself stiffly as the ambulance attendant, with a headshake that said it would be no good, took over.

He looked around before he left. He knew before looking

roughly what he would find. The name on the packing cases was Dr. O. E. Black. Kraut Schwartz.

19

He knew what he would find before he found it in the Miami and Vegas papers he picked up in the L.A. air terminal. Kraut had removed other warts.

The swimming pool at Mobile Haven had an automatic chlorinator that kept the chlorine residual from dropping below .3 ppm by feeding chlorine gas into the water in continuous doses to kill algae and bacteria. The occasionally necessary booster shots of superchlorination took place only when no one was in the pool. At 4 p.m. on the day following Paul's talk with ex-newsman Matt Muldoon, a sudden uncalled-for surge of superchlorination left those in the pool at the time—two adults and three children—in critical condition. One of the adults was Matt Muldoon.

Letha Root's home had gone up in flames—the fire marshal warned the public again about the danger of overloading electrical circuits—at the same time a local celebrity of the same address, Johnson Jones a.k.a. the Splendiferous Spade, had suffered a seizure or stroke on the air. The Las Vegas paper noted the coincidence and drew a moral for mortal man.

Paul looked back along the spoor of warts. It still beat him how Kraut had pulled off the killing of Mort Lesser. Maybe it had been an ordinary holdup after all. No. More likely it had been payment for Kraut's tip—real or phony?—to some underworld figure that Max Flesher was a canary.

Paul looked ahead through the plane window. Somewhere there should be a nice clean universe. It would be true of all the inhabitants thereof that their guts take a Moebius twist or their large intestine is a Klein bottle—*ein klein nachtgeschirr*—so that they deposit the results of digestion in this our own less nice universe. Somewhere and sometime in infinity there had to be a nice clean universe. The laws of chance said they couldn't *all* crap out.

20

"We're coming down the home stretch, kid."

Paul believed Kraut. They had deplaned in Philadelphia and were rolling through countryside in line with Kraut's analysis.

"I hid out in Pennsylvania Dutch country. 'Zook and ye shall find.' Zook is a Pennsylvania Dutch name. 'Where was Moses when the lights went out?' 'And Pharaoh believed Pharaoh's daughter.' In the Thirties the 4:44 was a Delaware Lackawan'—'the Road of Anthracite'—train that with a changeover to the Reading brought you to Egypt, Pa. According to tax records, the Zook family ran a boardinghouse just outside Egypt. The house is uninhabited but standing. Probably still a faded sign on the barn. 'They put a whammy on the barn.' 'Zook and ye shall find.' "

They drove north in humming silence awhile, then Kraut broke in on a mind seething with wild schemes. Could he blow up Kraut's microwave links? Or turn the microwaves back against Kraut? Or had he waited too long, hoping once he had his hands on the ten megabucks he could buy distance and time? Maybe a computer to fight back with. Damn. Damn. Damn. He would find a way to save Mimsy and himself.

"Kid. Hey, kid!"

A note of urgency came through Kraut's high spirits.

"Yes?"

"I been thinking, kid. Remember that scrap of paper we got from Max Flesher? The one with the X on it and the spots of my blood?"

"Yes?"

"That blood is all the cellular material left of me. I think I could analyze it and clone a lot of Krauts out of that blood. So how's about putting it in a safe place for me. Stop off at Bethlemen, say, and leave it in a bank vault."

Just what the world needed. An army of Krauts.

Paul drew one-handed the slip of paper from his billfold.

"That? Didn't I tell you? We lost that way back during the mugging right after we left Max Flesher."

A long silence, then, "Oh. Too bad, kid. It would of been nice."

"Yes, it would've been really something."

Paul pressed the dashboard lighter, and when it popped he touched the glow to the scrap of paper and watched the army of Krauts curl into ash in the tray.

It was all open country, empty country. He saw no one to see him pry the boards off the front door of the Zook house and let himself in. Dust was the only furnishing. He climbed the stairs. The roomiest guest room would have been Kraut's. He barely made out the nothingness. He raised the window with hurting blows of the heel of his hand and shoved boards away on squeaking nails.

Dark light showed a dim stain on the floor. Katz's blood, in wine-stained light. The violet of the pane came of many years of sunlight tinting the colloidal solution of manganese in the glass. *The violent end of the spectrum*. The window gave on the neighboring field. It was not a field but a graveyard. *Acutely aware every prognosis is grave*.

He retrieved the phone case at the door.

"We're down to the wire, Kraut."

Kraut did not answer.

"The barn *does* have a faded hex sign, Kraut."

Still no answer.

He crunched along the cinder path leading to the barn, then veered away through weeds toward the graveyard. He set the phone case down and leaned on the fence. A weather-withered wreath, "Xmas in Heaven," seemed the sole remains of recent re-membrance. The name Auer on a headstone struck him like light-ning. *I feel my hour coming. The golden hour of the little flower.* The X he had reduced to ashes in the tray of the car had been a mnemonic hourglass. The treasure had to be in the Auer grave.

His smile gave way to gravity. Why was Kraut so all-banked si-lent? His smile triumphed. He would keep Kraut guessing in re-turn. He straightened to turn and go back for the new shovel and pick he had stowed in the rental Stingray. The barn door creaked open without wind. A man stepped out of the darkness bringing some of it with him. Paul caught glints off a car in the barn.

But another glint took his eye. Big hands hung low on thick arms from heavy shoulders. In one of those hands a gun held steady on Paul.

When he killed Kraut, Harry Spector had been Paul Felder's age. He would be sixty-five now. The man looked a hard, fit sixty-five. A killer. Once you knew, it stuck out all over him.

Paul spoke out of the side of his mouth away from the man.

"Here comes Harry Spector, Kraut. He has a gun."

No response. Why the hell wasn't Kraut sending the note of fear that had made the muggers break and run?

"Kraut!"

No answer was the answer. Kraut had double-crossed him. A trap for Spector, Paul the bait. Paul smiled at Spector.

"What did he tell you that brought you all the way out here?"
Spector halted a man's length from Paul.

"What do you mean he?" For God's sake, he had modeled himself on Edward G. Robinson. "What are you pulling, Felder—if that's your right moniker? Think I don't make the voice?"

"Just wanted to make sure it was you."

So Kraut had used that gimmick again. But what had Paul's voice told Spector? Kraut's iron trunk had been a legend in Kraut and Spector's day. Greed. *I hear a siren coming but he goes back into the john.* A killer who risked his getaway to roll the dying: damn well had to be greed. And greed would make Spector kill Paul to keep the whole of the loot. Right now greed meant impatience.

"I got the connections to fence the jewels and wash the money. You say the stuff's here. So let's get on with the deal."

"Is it all right if I . . . ?" Paul mimed picking up the phone case. He answered narrowing eyes. "Metal detector. It'll tell us where to dig."

The gun gestured O.K. "But don't make no bull moves."

Yet a mad move seemed the only one to make, and make now, before the loot came to light. He couldn't jump Spector. He had to walk straight into the gun, counting on greed to keep Spector from shooting to kill. Paul braced himself and forged ahead, with a yell. Spector froze for an eye blink, then fired at Paul's right knee. The hammer blow rocked Paul, but he swung another step forward. Spector stared, then fired at Paul's left knee. The hammer blow staggered Paul again, but he remained upright and forged on.

Spector backed a step, then held, his eyes fixing on the phone case swinging from Paul's hand. He smiled. Paul read the thought. The "metal detector" could do all the talking Spector needed. The muzzle lifted to center on Paul's chest. Spector's mouth opened in empathy.

"You asked for it, kid."

But the phone case was already flying. It knocked the gun arm aside long enough for Paul to get in and put all he had into one karate chop.

The car in the barn blared its radio.

"All-points bulletin. Be on the lookout for a tan '70 Chevy or a red '74 Stingray. The driver is Harry Spector, 65, white male, wanted for the murder of one Paul Felder at the old Zook homestead east of Egypt. This man is armed and dangerous."

Then Kraut spoke from the phone case on the ground beside the fallen Spector.

"Hear that, Harry? I'm putting that out on the police band. Shoot me in the back, would you?" The voice jumped up and down in glee. "Harry, you been out too long. I'm sticking you in for another twenty-three years."

Paul went limp. He drew shuddering breaths that he took to be sobbing till the true sobbing overrode him.

The sobbing was a woman's and the voice was Mimsy's.

"What did you do to him, gramps? If I'm too late and you've killed him, damn you, gramps, so help me I'll wipe you out."

Paul found his own voice and spoke to the phone case.

"Mimsy."

"Paul! You're all right! You're all right? . . . It *is* you?"

"Ten thousand borogoves, yes. Where are you?"

"Boston. Thoreau. Gramps cut us off before I could get what you were driving at, remember? So I had to go ahead on my own. I told Florence I Knew All, and I got her to play dumb when you called— because you might've been gramps. And I made her tell me everything she could about gramps. One thing stuck in my mind. It seems he had a thing about literature.

"I thought a good dose of modern American lit might change his personality. For the better: it couldn't be for the worse. So I came up here and talked myself into access—Steve is a doll—and—"

"It's 'Steve,' is it?"

"Eat your heart out. And I fed gramps Bellow, Mailer, Roth, Gold, Malamud . . . But when I listened in to the readout just now, I thought I was too late."

Kraut's voice broke in. Kraut's and yet not Kraut's. Kraut's with an inflection of Kraut's sister Molly Moldover.

"Paulele, you poor boy, you've been through a bad time. So find a good restaurant quick and have some hot chicken soup already."

By God, the computer program was a Jewish mother.

Mimsy's voice came in loud and clear: "Hurry to me, Paul."

He heard another faraway siren.

Police Procedural

Realistic portrayals of policemen at their everyday work would seem a natural for crime writers. But oddly enough, the electronic media are most responsible for this genre. Fritz Lang's movie of a child molester, *M*, shot Peter Lorre to international stardom in 1931. And even after the 1945 publication of what many consider the first procedural, Lawrence Treat's *V as in Victim*, interest remained low until the radio debut of "Dragnet." Perhaps the major explanation was that to media men the procedural's team approach seemed much more natural than it did to individually oriented authors. But, in any case, since the fifties, lengthy series by Ed McBain, John Creasey, and the team of Maj Sjöwall and Per Wahlöo have helped make this type of story a world favorite.

In the field of science fiction, authors who produce "future" procedurals face two major problems. What technological advances might occur and what is the most likely way they would be used? Outstanding examples by several writers, such as Wilson Tucker, prove that convincing solutions can be worked out. But for some inexplicable reason, even though related stories sell well, no one in SF has yet produced an extended series of this sort.

Time Exposures

WILSON TUCKER

Sergeant Tabbot climbed the stairs to the woman's third floor apartment. The heavy camera case banged against his leg as he climbed and threatened collision with his bad knee. He shifted the case to his left hand and muttered under his breath: the woman *could* have been gracious enough to die on the first floor.

A patrolman loafed on the landing, casually guarding the stairway and the third floor corridor.

Tabbot showed surprise. "No keeper? Are they still working in there? Which apartment is it?"

The patrolman said: "Somebody forgot the keeper, sergeant—somebody went after it. There's a crowd in there, the coroner ain't done yet. Number 33." He glanced down at the bulky case. "She's pretty naked."

"Shall I make you a nice print?"

"No, *sir*, not this one! I mean, she's naked but she ain't pretty anymore."

Tabbot said: "Murder victims usually lose their good looks." He walked down the corridor to number 33 and found the door ajar. A rumbling voice was audible. Tabbot swung the door open and stepped into the woman's apartment. A small place: probably only two rooms.

The first thing he saw was a finger man working over a glass-topped coffee table with an aerosol can and a portable blacklight; the sour expression on the man's face revealed a notable lack of fingerprints. A precinct Lieutenant stood just beyond the end of the coffee table, watching the roving blacklight with an air of unruffled patience; his glance flickered at Tabbot, at the camera case, and dropped again to the table. A plainclothesman waited behind the door, doing nothing. Two men with a wicker basket sat on either arm of an overstuffed chair, peering over the back of the chair at something on the floor. One of them swung his head to stare at the newcomer and then turned his attention back to the floor. Well beyond the chair a bald-headed man wearing too much fat under his clothing was brushing dust from the knees of his trousers. He had just climbed to his feet and the exertion caused a dry, wheezy breathing through an open mouth.

Tabbot knew the Lieutenant and the coroner.

The coroner looked at the heavy black case Tabbot put down just inside the door and asked: "Pictures?"

"Yes, sir. Time exposures."

"I'd like to have prints, then. Haven't seen a shooting in eight or nine years. Damned rare anymore." He pointed a fat index finger at the thing on the floor. "*She* was shot to death. Can you imagine that? Shot to death in *this* day and age! I'd like to have prints. Want to see a man with the gall to carry a gun."

"Yes, sir." Tabbot swung his attention to the precinct Lieutenant. "Can you give me an idea?"

"It's still hazy, sergeant," the officer answered. "The victim knew her assailant; I think she let him in the door and then walked away from him. He stood where you're standing. Maybe an argument, but no fighting—nothing broken, nothing disturbed, no fingerprints. That knob behind you was wiped clean. She was standing behind that chair when she was shot, and she fell there. Can you catch it all?"

"Yes, sir, I think so. I'll set up in that other room—in the doorway. A kitchen?"

"Kitchen and shower. This one is a combination living room and bedroom."

"I'll start in the doorway and then move in close. Nothing in the kitchen?"

"Only dirty dishes. No floorstains, but I would appreciate prints just the same. The floors are clean everywhere except behind *that* chair."

Sergeant Tabbot looked at the window across the room and looked back to the Lieutenant.

"No fire escape," the officer said. "But cover it anyway, cover everything. Your routine."

Tabbot nodded easily, then took a strong grip on his stomach muscles. He moved across the room to the overstuffed chair and peered carefully over the back of it. The two wicker basket men turned their heads in unison to watch him, sharing some macabre joke between them. It would be at his expense. His stomach plunged despite the rigid effort to control it.

She was a sandy blonde and had been about thirty years old; her face had been reasonably attractive but was not likely to have won a beauty contest; it was scrubbed clean, and free of makeup. There was no jewelry on her fingers, wrists, or about her neck; she was literally naked. Her chest had been blown away. Tabbot blinked his shocked surprise and looked down her stomach toward her legs simply to move his gaze away from the hideous sight. He thought for a moment he'd lose his breakfast. His eyes closed while he fought for iron control, and when they opened again he was looking at old abdominal scars from a long ago pregnancy.

Sergeant Tabbot backed off rapidly from the chair and bumped into the coroner. He blurted: "She was shot in the back!"

"Well, of course." The wheezing fat man stepped around him with annoyance. "There's a *little* hole in the spine. Little going in and big—bigod it was big—coming out. Destroyed the rib cage coming out. That's natural. Heavy caliber pistol, I think." He stared down at the naked feet protruding from behind the chair. "*First* shooting I've seen in eight or nine years. Can you imagine that? Somebody carrying a gun." He paused for a wheezing breath and then pointed the same fat finger at the basket men. "Pick it up and run, boys. We'll do an autopsy."

Tabbot walked out to the kitchen.

The kitchen table showed him a dirty plate, coffee cup, fork and spoon, and toast crumbs. A sugar bowl without a lid and a small jar of powdered coffee creamer completed the setting. He looked under the table for the missing knife and butter.

"It's not there," the Lieutenant said. "She liked her toast dry."

Tabbot turned. "How long ago was breakfast? How long has she been dead?"

"We'll have to wait on the coroner's opinion for that but I would guess three, maybe four hours ago. The coffee pot was cold, the body was cold, the egg stains were dry—oh, say three hours plus."

"That gives me a good margin," Tabbot said. "If it happened last night, yesterday, I'd just pick up my camera and go home." He glanced through the doorway at a movement caught in the corner of the eye and found the wicker basket men carrying their load through the front door into the corridor. His glance quickly swung back to the kitchen table. "Eggs and dry toast, sugar in white coffee. That doesn't give you much."

The Lieutenant shook his head. "I'm not worried about *her*; I don't give a damn what she ate. Let the coroner worry about her breakfast; he'll tell us how long ago she ate it and we'll take it from there. Your prints are more important. I want to see pictures of the assailant."

Tabbot said: "Let's hope for daylight, and let's hope it was *this* morning. Are you sure that isn't yesterday's breakfast? There's no point in setting up the camera if it happened yesterday morning, or last night. My exposure limit is between ten and fourteen hours— and you know how poor fourteen-hour prints are."

"This morning," the officer assured him. "She went in to work yesterday morning but when she failed to check in this morning, when she didn't answer the phone, somebody from the shop came around to ask why."

"Did the somebody have a key?"

"No, and that eliminated the first suspect. The janitor let him in. Will you make a print of the door to corroborate their story? A few minutes after nine o'clock; they can't remember the exact time now."

"Will do. What kind of a shop? What did she do?"

"Toy shop. She made Christmas dolls."

Sergeant Tabbot considered that. After a moment he said: "The first thing that comes to mind is toy guns."

The Lieutenant gave him a tight, humorless grin. "We had the same thing in mind and sent men over there to comb the shop. Black market things, you know, toys or the real article. But no luck. They haven't made anything resembling a gun since the Dean Act was passed. That shop was clean."

"You've got a tough job, Lieutenant."

"I'm waiting on your prints, Sergeant."

Tabbot thought that a fair hint. He went back to the outer room and found everyone gone but the silent plainclothesman. The detective sat down on the sofa behind the coffee table and watched him unpack the case. A tripod was set up about five feet from the door. The camera itself was a heavy, unwieldy instrument and was lifted onto the tripod with a certain amount of hard grunting and a muttered curse because of a nipped finger. When it was solidly battened to the tripod, Tabbot picked a film magazine out of the supply case and fixed it to the rear of the camera. A lens and the timing instrument was the last to be fitted into place. He looked to make sure the lens was clean.

Tabbot focused on the front door, and reached into a pocket for his slide rule. He checked the time *now* and then calculated backward to obtain four exposures at nine o'clock, nine-five, nine-ten, and nine-fifteen, which should pretty well bracket the arrival of the janitor and the toy shop employee. He cocked and tripped the timer, and then checked to make sure the nylon film was feeding properly after each exposure. The data for each exposure was jotted down in a notebook, making the later identification of the prints more certain.

The plainclothesman broke his stony silence. "I've never seen one of those things work before."

Tabbot said easily: "I'm taking pictures from nine o'clock to nine-fifteen this morning; if I'm in luck I'll catch the janitor opening the door. If I'm not in luck I'll catch only a blurred movement—or nothing at all—and then I'll have to go back and make an exposure for each minute after nine until I find him. A blurred image of the moving door will pinpoint him."

"*Good* pictures?" He seemed skeptical.

"At nine o'clock? Yes. There was sufficient light coming in that window at nine and not too much time has elapsed. Satisfactory conditions. Things get sticky when I try for night exposures with no more than one or two lamps lit; that simply isn't enough light. I wish *everything* would happen outdoors at noon on a bright day— and not more than an hour ago!"

The detective grunted and inspected the ticking camera. "I took some of your pictures into court once. Bank robbery case, last year. The pictures were bad and the judge threw them out and the case collapsed."

"I remember them," Tabbot told him. "And I apologize for the poor job. Those prints were made right at the time limit: fourteen hours, perhaps a little more. The camera and the film are almost useless beyond ten or twelve hours—that is simply too *much* elapsed time. I use the very best film available but it can't find or make a decent image more than twelve hours in the past. Your bank prints were nothing more than grainy shadows; that's all I can get from twelve to fourteen hours."

"Nothing over fourteen hours?"

"Absolutely nothing. I've tried, but nothing." The camera stopped ticking and shut itself off. Tabbot turned it on the tripod and aimed at the sofa. The detective jumped up.

The sergeant protested. "Don't get up—you won't be in the way. The lens won't see you *now*."

"I've got work to do," the detective muttered. He flipped a dour farewell gesture at the Lieutenant and left the apartment, slamming the door behind him.

"He's still sore about those bank pictures," the officer said.

Tabbot nodded agreement and made a single adjustment on the timing mechanism. He tripped the shutter for one exposure and then grinned at the Lieutenant.

"I'll send him a picture of myself, sitting there three minutes ago. Maybe that will cheer him up."

"Or make him mad enough to fire you."

The sergeant began another set of calculations on the slide rule and settled himself down to the routine coverage of the room from six to nine o'clock in the morning. He angled the heavy camera at the coffee table, the kitchen doorway, the overstuffed chair, the window behind the chair, a smaller chair and a bookcase in the room, the floor, a vase of artificial flowers resting on a tiny shelf above a radiator, a floor lamp, a ceiling light, and eventually worked around the room in a circle before coming back to the front door. Tabbot rechecked his calculations and then lavished a careful attention on the door and the space beside it where he had stood when he first entered.

The camera poked and pried and peered into the recent past, into the naked blonde's last morning alive, recording on nylon film those images now three or four hours gone. During the circle coverage—between the bookcase and the vase of artificial flowers—a signal light indicated an empty film magazine, and the camera paused in its work until a new magazine was fixed in place. Tabbot made a small adjustment on the timer to compensate for lost time. He numbered the old and the new film magazines, and continued his detailed notes for each angle and series of exposures. The camera ignored the present and probed into the past.

The Lieutenant asked: "How much longer?"

"Another hour for the preliminaries; I can do the kitchen in another hour. And, say, two to three hours for the retakes after something is pinned down."

"I've got work piling up." The officer scratched the back of his neck and then bent down to peer into the lens. "I guess you can find me at the precinct house. Make extra copies of the key prints."

"Yes, sir."

The Lieutenant turned away from his inspection of the lens and gave the room a final, sweeping glance. He did not slam the door behind him as the detective had done.

The full routine of photographing went on.

Tabbot moved the camera backward into the kitchen doorway to gain a broader coverage of the outer room; he angled at the sofa, the overstuffed chair, and again the door. He wanted the vital few moments when the door was opened and the murderer stepped through it to fire the prohibited pistol. Changing to a wide-angle lens, he caught the entire room in a series of ten minute takes over a period of three hours. The scene was thoroughly documented.

He changed magazines to prepare for the kitchen.

A wild notion stopped his hand, stopped him in the act of swiveling the camera. He walked over to the heavy chair, walked around behind it, sidestepped the spilled blood, and found himself in direct line between door and window. Tabbot looked out of the window—imagining a gun at his back—and pivoted slowly to stare at the door: early sunlight coming in the window should have limned the man's face. The camera placed *here* should photograph the assailant's face and record the gun blast as well.

Tabbot hauled tripod and camera across the room and set up in position behind the chair, aiming at the door. The lens was changed again. Another calculation was made. If he was *really* lucky on this series the murderer would fire at the camera.

Kitchen coverage was a near repetition of the first room. It required a little less time.

Tabbot photographed the table and two chairs, the dirty dishes, the toast crumbs, the tiny stove, the aged refrigerator, the tacked-on dish cupboards above the sink and drain board, the sink itself, a cramped water closet masquerading as a broom closet behind a narrow door, and the stained folding door of the shower stall. The stall had leaked.

He opened the refrigerator door and found a half bottle of red wine alongside the foodstuffs: two takes an hour apart. He peered into the cramped confines of the water closet: a few desultory exposures, and a hope that the blonde wasn't sitting in there. The shower stall was lined with an artificial white tile now marred by rust stains below a leaky showerhead: two exposures by way of an experiment, because the stall also contained a miniature wash basin, a mirror, and a moistureproof light fixture. He noted with an absent approval that the fixture lacked a receptacle for plugging in razors.

Tabbot changed to the wide-angle lens for the wrap-up. There was no window in the kitchen, and he made a mental note of the absence of an escape door—a sad violation of the fire laws.

That exhausted the preliminary takes.

Tabbot fished his I.D. card out of his pocket, gathered up the exposed film magazines and walked out of the apartment. There was no keeper blocking passage through the doorway, and he stared with surprise at the patrolman still lounging in the corridor.

The patrolman read his expression.

"It's coming, Sergeant, it's coming. By this time I guess that Lieutenant has chewed somebody out good, so you can bet it's coming in a hurry."

Tabbot put the I.D. card in his pocket.

The patrolman asked: "*Was* she shot up, like they said? Back to front, right out the belly?"

Tabbot nodded uneasily. "Back to front, but out through the rib cage—not the belly. Somebody used a very heavy gun on her. *Do* you want a print? You could paste it up in your locker."

"Oh, hell no!" The man glanced down the corridor and came back to the sergeant. "I heard the coroner say it was a professional job; only the pro's are crazy enough to tote guns anymore. The risk and everything."

"I suppose so; I haven't heard of an amateur carrying one for years. That mandatory jail sentence for possession scares the hell out of them." Tabbot shifted the magazines to his other hand to keep them away from his bad knee going down the stairs.

The street was bright with sunlight—the kind of brilliant scene which Sergeant Tabbot wanted everything to happen in for better results. Given a bright sun he could reproduce images a little better than grainy shadows, right up to that fourteen-hour stopping point.

His truck was the only police vehicle parked at the curb.

Tabbot climbed into the back and closed the door behind him. He switched on the developing and drying machine in total darkness, and began feeding the film from the first magazine down into the tanks. When the tail of that film slipped out of the magazine and vanished, the leader of the second film was fed into the slot. The third followed when its time came. The sergeant sat down on a stool, waiting in the darkness until the developer and dryer had completed their cycles and delivered the nylon negatives into his hands. After a while he reached out to switch on the printer, and then did nothing more than sit and wait.

The woman's exploded breast hung before his eyes; it was more vivid in the darkness of the truck than in bright daylight. This time his stomach failed to churn, and he supposed he was getting used to the memory. Or the sight-memory was safely in his past. A few of the coming prints *could* resurrect that nightmare image.

The coroner believed some hood had murdered the woman who made Christmas dolls—some professional thug who paid as little heed to the gun law as he did to a hundred and one other laws. Perhaps—and perhaps not. Discharged servicemen were still smuggling weapons into the country, when coming in from overseas posts; he'd heard of that happening often enough, and he'd seen a few of the foolhardy characters in jails. For some reason he didn't understand, ex-Marines who'd served in China were the most flagrant offenders: they outnumbered smugglers from the other services three or four to one and the harsh penalties spelled out in the Dean Act didn't deter *them* worth a damn. Congress in its wisdom had proclaimed that only peace officers, and military personnel on active duty, had the privilege of carrying firearms; all other weapons must under the law be surrendered and destroyed.

Tabbot didn't own a gun; he had no use for one. That patrolman on the third floor carried a weapon, and the Lieutenant, and the plainclothesman—but he didn't think the coroner would have one. Nor the basket men. The Dean Act made stiff prison sentences mandatory for possession among the citizenry, but the Marines kept on carrying them and now and then some civilian died under gunfire. Like the woman who made Christmas dolls.

A soft buzzer signaled the end of the developer's job. Tabbot removed the three reels of nylon negative from the drying rack and fed them through the printer. The waiting time was appreciably shorter. Three long strips of printed pictures rolled out of the printer into his hands. Tabbot didn't waste time cutting the prints into individual frames. Draping two of the strips over a shoulder, he carried the third to the door of the truck and flung it open. Bright sunlight made him squint, causing his eyes to water.

Aloud: "Oh, what the hell! What went wrong?"

The prints were dark, much darker than they had any right to be. He *knew* without rechecking the figures in his notebook that the exposures had been made after sunrise, but still the prints were dark. Tabbot stared up the front of the building, trying to pick out the proper window, then brought his puzzled gaze back to the strip prints. The bedroom-living room was dark.

Peering closer, squinting against the bright light of the sun: four timed exposures of the front door, with the dim figures of the janitor and another man standing open-mouthed on the third exposure. Ten minutes after nine. The fifth frame: a bright clear picture of the plainclothesman sitting on the sofa, talking up to Tabbot. The sixth frame and onward: dark images of the sofa opened out into a bed—coffee table missing—the kitchen doorway barely discernible, the overstuffed chair (and *there* was the coffee table beside it), the window— He stared with dismay at the window. The goddam drapes were drawn, shutting out the early light!

Tabbot hurriedly checked the second strip hanging on his shoulder: equally dark. The floor lamp and the ceiling light were both unlit. The drapes had been closed all night and the room was in cloudy darkness. He could just identify the radiator, the vase of flowers, the bookcase, the smaller chair, and numerous exposures of the closed door. The floor frames were nearly black. Now the camera changed position, moving to the kitchen doorway and shooting back into the bedroom with a wide-angle lens. Dark frustration.

The bed was folded away into an ordinary sofa, the coffee table had moved back to its rightful position, the remaining pieces of furniture were undisturbed, the drapes covered the only window, the lights were not lit. He squinted at the final frames and caught his breath. A figure—a dim and indistinct somebody of a figure—stood at the far corner of the coffee table looking at the closed door.

Tabbot grabbed up the third strip of prints.

Four frames gave him nothing but a closed door. The fifth frame exploded in a bright halo of flash: the gun was fired into the waiting lens.

Sergeant Tabbot jumped out of the truck, slammed shut the door behind him and climbed the stairs to the third floor. His bad knee begged for an easier pace. The young patrolman was gone from his post upstairs.

A keeper blocked the door to the apartment.

Tabbot approached it cautiously while he fished in his pockets for the I.D. card. At a distance of only two feet he detected the uneasy squirmings of pain in his groin; if he attempted to squeeze past the machine into the apartment the damned thing would do its utmost to tear his guts apart. The testicles were most vulnerable. A keeper always reminded him of a second generation fire hydrant—but if he was grilled at one of the precinct houses he would never be able to describe a second generation fire hydrant to anyone's satisfaction. His interrogator would insist it was only a phallic symbol.

The keeper was fashioned of stainless steel and colorless plastic: it stood waist high with a slot and a glowing bullseye in its pointed head, and it generated a controlled fulguration emission—a high-frequency radiation capable of destroying animal tissue. The machines were remarkably useful for keeping prisoners *in* and inquisitive citizenry *out*.

Tabbot inserted his I.D. into the slot and waited for the glow to fade out of the bullseye.

A telephone rested on the floor at the far end of the sofa, half hidden behind a stack of dusty books: the woman had read Western novels. He dialed the precinct house and waited while an operator located the officer.

Impatiently: "Tabbot here. Who opened the drapes?"

"What the hell are you— What drapes?"

"The drapes covering the window, the only window in the room. Who opened them this morning? When?"

There was a speculative silence. "Sergeant, are those prints worthless?"

"Yes, sir—nearly so. I've got one beautiful shot of that detective sitting on the sofa *after* the drapes were opened." He hesitated for a moment while he consulted the notebook. "The shot was fired at six forty-five this morning; the janitor opened the door at ten minutes after nine. And I really have a nice print of the plainclothesman."

"Is that *all?*"

"All that will help you. I have one dim and dirty print of a somebody looking at the door, but I can't tell you if that somebody is man or woman, red or green."

The Lieutenant said: "Oh, shit!"

"Yes, sir."

"The coroner opened those drapes—he wanted more light to look at his corpse."

Wistfully: "I wish he'd opened them last night before she was a corpse."

"Are you *sure* they're worthless?"

"Well, sir, if you took them into court and drew that same judge, he'd throw you out."

"Damn it! What are you going to do now?"

"I'll go back to six forty-five and work around that gunshot. I should be able to follow the somebody to the door at the same time —I suppose it was the woman going over to let the murderer in. But don't get your hopes up, Lieutenant. This is a lost cause."

Another silence, and then: "All right, do what you can. A hell of a note, Sergeant."

"Yes, sir." He rang off.

Tabbot hauled the bulky camera into position at one end of the coffee table and angled at the door; he thought the set-up would encompass the woman walking to the door, opening it, turning to walk away, and the assailant coming in. All in murky darkness. He fitted a fresh magazine to the camera, inspected the lens for non-existent dirt, and began the timing calculations. The camera began ticking off the exposures bracketing the point of gunfire.

Tabbot went over to the window to finish his inspection of the third strip of prints, the kitchen. The greater bulk of them were as dark as the bedroom.

The strip of prints suddenly brightened just after that point at which he'd changed to a wide-angle lens, just after he'd begun the final wrap-up. A ceiling light had been turned on in the kitchen.

Tabbot stared at a naked woman seated at the table.

She held both hands folded over her stomach, as though pressing in a roll of flesh. Behind her the narrow door of the water closet stood ajar. The table was bare. Tabbot frowned at the woman, at the pose, and then rummaged through his notes for the retroactive exposure time: five minutes past six. The woman who made Christmas dolls was sitting at a bare table at five minutes past six in the morning, looking off to her left, and holding her hands over her stomach. Tabbot wondered if she were hungry—wondered if she waited on some imaginary maid to prepare and serve breakfast. Eggs, coffee, dry toast.

He searched for a frame of the stove: there was a low gas flame beneath the coffee pot. No eggs frying. Well . . . they were probably three-minute eggs, and these frames had been exposed five or ten minutes apart.

He looked again at the woman and apologized for the poor joke: she would be dead in forty minutes.

The only other item of interest on the third strip was a thin ribbon of light under the shower curtain. Tabbot skipped backward along the strip seeking the two exposures angled into the shower stall, but found them dark and the stall empty. The wrong hour.

Behind him the camera shut itself off and called for attention.

Tabbot carried the instrument across the room to an advantageous position beside an arm of the chair and again angled toward the door. The timer was reset for a duplicate coverage of the scenes just completed, but he expected no more than a shadowy figure entering, firing, leaving—a murky figure in a darkened room. A new series was started with that one flash frame as the centerpiece.

His attention went back to the woman at the table. She sat with her hands clasped over her stomach, looking off to her left. Looking at what?

On impulse, Tabbot walked into the kitchen and sat down in her chair. Same position, same angle. Tabbot pressed his hands to his stomach and looked off to his left. Identical line of sight. He was looking at the shower stall.

One print had given him a ribbon of light under the stained curtain—no, stained folding door. The barrier had leaked water.

He said aloud: "Well, I'll be damned!"

The printed strips were stretched across the table to free his hands and then he examined his notebook item by item. Each of the prints had peered into the past at five minutes after six in the morning. Someone took a shower while the woman sat by the table.

Back to the last few frames of the second strip taken from the second magazine: a figure—a dim and indistinct somebody of a figure—stood at the far corner of the coffee table looking at the closed door. Time: six-forty. Five minutes before the shot was fired.

Did the woman simply stand there and wait a full five minutes for a knock on the door? Or did she open it only a moment after the exposure was made, let the man in, argue with him, and die five minutes later behind the chair? Five minutes was time enough for an argument, a heated exchange, a threat, a shot.

Tabbot braced his hands on the table edge.

What happened to the man in the shower? Was he still there—soaking himself for forty minutes—while the woman was gunned down? Or had he come out, dried himself, gulped down breakfast and quit the apartment minutes before the assailant arrived?

Tabbot supplied answers: no, no, no, and maybe.

He jumped up from the chair so quickly it fell over. The telephone was behind the stack of Western novels.

The man answering his call may have been one of the wicker basket men.

"County morgue."

"Sergeant Tabbot here, Photo Section. I've got preliminary prints on that woman in the apartment. She was seated at the breakfast table between six o'clock and six-fifteen. How does that square with the autopsy?"

The voice said cheerfully: "Right on the button, Sergeant. The toast was still there, know what I mean?"

Weakly: "I know what you mean. I'll send over the prints."

"Hey, wait—wait, there's more. She was just a little bit pregnant. Two months, maybe."

Tabbot swallowed. An unwanted image tried to form in his imagination: the autopsy table, a stroke or two of the blade, an inventory of the contents of the stomach— He thrust the image away and set down the telephone.

Aloud, in dismay: "I thought the man in the shower ate breakfast! But he didn't—he didn't." The inoperative phone gave him no answer.

The camera stopped peering into the past.

Tabbot hauled the instrument into the kitchen and set up a new position behind the woman's chair to take the table, stove, and shower stall. The angle would be right over her head. A series of exposures two minutes apart was programmed into the timer with the first frame calculated at six o'clock. The probe began. Tabbot reached around the camera and gathered up the printed strips from the table. The light was better at the window and he quit the kitchen for yet another inspection of the dismal preliminaries.

The front door, the janitor and a second man in the doorway, the bright beauty of a frame with the detective sitting on the sofa, the darkened frames of the sofa pulled out to make a bed— Tabbot paused and peered. Were there one or *two* figures sprawled in the bed? Next: the kitchen doorway, the overstuffed chair, the misplaced coffee table, the window with the closed drapes— All of that. On and on. Dark. But were there one or *two* people in the bed?

And now consider this frame: a dim and indistinct somebody looking at the closed door. Was that somebody actually walking to the door, caught in mid-stride? Was that somebody the man from the shower?

Tabbot dropped the strips and sprinted for the kitchen.

The camera hadn't finished its programmed series but Tabbot yanked it from position and dragged it over the kitchen floor. The tripod left marks. The table was pushed aside. He stopped the timer and jerked aside the folding door to thrust the lens into the shower stall. Angle at the tiny wash basin and the mirror hanging above it; hope for sufficient reflected light from the white tiles. Strap on a fresh magazine. Work feverishly with the slide rule. Check and check again the notes to be certain of times. Set the timer and start the camera. Stand back and wait.

The Lieutenant had been wrong.

The woman who made Christmas dolls did *not* walk to the door and admit a man at about six-forty in the morning; she didn't go to the door at all. She died behind the chair, as she was walking toward the window to pull the drapes. Her assailant had stayed the night, had slept with her in the unfolded bed until sometime shortly before six o'clock. They got up and one of them used the toilet, one of them put away the bed. *He* stepped into the shower while *she* sat down at the table. In that interval she held her belly, and later had breakfast. An argument started—or perhaps was carried over from the night before—and when the man emerged into a now *darkened* kitchen he dressed and made to leave without eating.

The argument continued into the living room; the woman went to the window to admit the morning sun while the professional gunman hesitated between the coffee table and the door. He half turned, fired, and made his escape.

"There's a *little* hole in the spine . . ."

Tabbot thought the Lieutenant was very wrong. In less than an hour he would have the prints to prove him wrong.

To save a few minutes' time he carried the exposed magazine down to the truck and fed the film into the developing tank. It was a nuisance to bother with the keeper each time he went in and out, and he violated regulations by leaving it inert. A police cruiser went by as he climbed down from the truck but he got nothing more than a vacant nod from the man riding alongside the driver. Tabbot's knee began to hurt as he climbed the steps to the third floor for what seemed the hundredth time that day.

The camera had completed the scene and stopped.

Tabbot made ready to leave.

He carried his equipment outside into the corridor and shot three exposures of the apartment door. The process of packing everything back into the bulky case took longer than the unpacking. The tripod stubbornly refused to telescope properly and fit into the case. And the citizens' privacy law stubbornly refused to let him shoot the corridor: no crime there.

A final look at the unoccupied apartment: he could see through into the kitchen and his imagination could see the woman seated at the table, holding her stomach. When he craned his neck to peer around the door he could see the window limned in bright sunshine. Tabbot decided to leave the drapes open. If someone else were killed here today or tomorrow he wanted the drapes open.

He closed the apartment door and thrust his I.D. card into the keeper's slot to activate it. There was no rewarding stir of machinery, no theatrical buzzing of high-frequency pulsing but his guts began growling when the red bullseye glowed. He went down the stairs carefully because his knee warned against a fast pace. The camera case banged his other leg.

Tabbot removed the reel of film from the developing tanks and started it through the printer. The second magazine was fed into the developer. He closed the back door of the truck, went around to the driver's door and fished for the ignition key in his trouser pocket. It wasn't there. He'd left the key hanging in the ignition, another violation of the law. Tabbot got up in the cab and started the motor, briefly thankful the men in the police cruiser hadn't spotted the key—they would have given him a citation and counted him as guilty as any other citizen.

The lab truck moved out into traffic.

The printing of the two reels of nylon film was completed in the parking lot alongside the precinct house. He parked in a visitor's slot. Not knowing who might be watching from a window, Tabbot removed the key from the ignition and pocketed it before going around to the back to finish the morning's work.

The strip results from the first magazine were professionally insulting: dark and dismal prints he didn't really want to show anyone. There were two fine frames of gun flash, and two others of the dim and indistinct somebody making for the door. About the only satisfaction Tabbot could find in these last two was the dark coloring: a man dressed in dark clothing, moving through a darkened room. The naked woman would have been revealed as a pale whitish figure.

Tabbot scanned the prints on the second strip with a keen and professional eye. The white tile lining the shower stall had reflected light in a most satisfying manner: he thought it one of the best jobs of backlighting he'd ever photographed. He watched the woman's overnight visitor shower, shave, brush his teeth and comb his hair. At one point—perhaps in the middle of that heated argument—he had nicked himself on the neck just above his Adam's apple. It had done nothing to improve the fellow's mood.

One exposure made outside the apartment door—the very last frame—was both rewarding and disappointing: the indistinct somebody was shown leaving the scene but he was bent over, head down, looking at his own feet. Tabbot supposed the man was too shy to be photographed coming out of a woman's room. He would be indignant when he learned that a camera had watched him in the little mirror above the wash basin. Indignant, and rather furious at this newest invasion of privacy.

Tabbot carried the prints into the precinct house. Another sergeant was on duty behind the desk, a man who recognized him by his uniform if not by face or name.

"Who do you want?"

Tabbot said: "The Lieutenant. What's-his-name?"

The desk man jerked a thumb behind him. "In the squad room."

Tabbot walked around the desk and found his way to the squad room at the end of the building. It was a large room with desks, and four or five men working or loafing behind the desks. Most of them seemed to be loafing. All of them looked up at the photographer.

"Over here, Sergeant. Did you finish the job?"

"Yes, sir."

Tabbot turned and made his way to the Lieutenant's desk. He spread out the first strip of dark prints.

"Well, you don't seem too happy about it."

"No, sir."

The second strip was placed beside the first.

"They're all dark except those down at the bottom. It was brighter in the shower stall. That's you in the shower, Lieutenant. The backlighting gave me the only decent prints in the lot."

Trial

Hans Eysenck, a famous behavioral psychologist, says that Freudian theory doesn't explain very much but it continues to be popular because it is so dramatic. And certainly the opportunity for drama must have a lot to do with the continuing success of the trial story. Confounding demonstrations and courthouse confessions redeem in pyrotechnic value what they yield in authenticity. Indeed, the courtroom works of Perry Mason's creator, Erle Stanley Gardner, have sold over 350 million copies.

There are a number of trial stories in science fiction, but unlike those in the mystery field, they usually do not concern murder. Rather, they revolve around technological innovations and inter-species' relationships. For example, in Clifford Simak's yarn below, one of science fiction's great masters deals with both problems in a delightfully daffy fashion.

How-2

CLIFFORD D. SIMAK

Gordon Knight was anxious for the five-hour day to end so he could rush home. For this was the day he should receive the How-2 Kit he'd ordered and he was anxious to get to work on it.

It wasn't only that he had always wanted a dog, although that was more than half of it—but, with this kit, he would be trying something new. He'd never handled any How-2 Kit with biologic components and he was considerably excited. Although, of course, the dog would be biologic only to a limited degree and most of it would be packaged, anyhow, and all he'd have to do would be assemble it. But it was something new and he wanted to get started.

He was thinking of the dog so hard that he was mildly irritated when Randall Stewart, returning from one of his numerous trips to the water fountain, stopped at his desk to give him a progress report on home dentistry.

"It's easy," Stewart told him. "Nothing to it if you follow the instructions. Here, look—I did this one last night."

He then squatted down beside Knight's desk and opened his mouth, proudly pulling it out of shape with his fingers so Knight could see.

"Thish un ere," said Stewart, blindly attempting to point, with a wildly waggling finger, at the tooth in question.

He let his face snap back together.

"Filled it myself," he announced complacently. "Rigged up a series of mirrors to see what I was doing. They came right in the kit, so all I had to do was follow the instructions."

He reached a finger deep inside his mouth and probed tenderly at his handiwork. "A little awkward, working on yourself. On someone else, of course, there'd be nothing to it."

He waited hopefully.

"Must be interesting," said Knight.

"Economical, too. No use paying the dentists the prices they ask. Figure I'll practice on myself and then take on the family. Some of my friends, even, if they want me to."

He regarded Knight intently.

Knight failed to rise to the dangling bait.

Stewart gave up. "I'm going to try cleaning next. You got to dig down beneath the gums and break loose the tartar. There's a kind of hook you do it with. No reason a man shouldn't take care of his own teeth instead of paying dentists."

"It doesn't sound too hard," Knight admitted.

"It's a cinch," said Stewart. "But you got to follow the instructions. There's nothing you can't do if you follow the instructions."

And that was true, Knight thought. You could do anything if you followed the instructions—if you didn't rush ahead, but sat down and took your time and studied it all out.

Hadn't he built his house in his spare time, and all the furniture for it, and the gadgets, too? Just in his spare time—although God knew, he thought, a man had little enough of that, working fifteen hours a week.

It was a lucky thing he'd been able to build the house after buying all that land. But everyone had been buying what they called estates, and Grace had set her heart on it, and there'd been nothing he could do.

If he'd had to pay carpenters and masons and plumbers, he would never have been able to afford the house. But by building it himself, he had paid for it as he went along. It had taken ten years, of course, but think of all the fun he'd had!

He sat there and thought of all the fun he'd had, and of all the pride. No, sir, he told himself, no one in his circumstances had a better house.

Although, come to think of it, what he'd done had not been too unusual. Most of the men he knew had built their homes, too, or had built additions to them, or had remodeled them.

He had often thought that he would like to start over again and build another house, just for the fun of it. But that would be foolish, for he already had a house and there would be no sale for another one, even if he built it. Who would want to buy a house when it was so much fun to build one?

And there was still a lot of work to do on the house he had. New rooms to add—not necessary, of course, but handy. And the roof to fix. And a summer house to build. And there were always the grounds. At one time he had thought he would landscape—a man could do a lot to beautify a place with a few years of spare-time work. But there had been so many other things to do, he had never managed to get around to it.

Knight and Anson Lee, his neighbor, had often talked about what could be done to their adjoining acreages if they ever had the time. But Lee, of course, would never get around to anything. He was a lawyer, although he never seemed to work at it too hard. He had a large study filled with stacks of law books and there were times when he would talk quite expansively about his law library, but he never seemed to use the books. Usually he talked that way when he had half a load on, which was fairly often, since he claimed to do a lot of thinking and it was his firm belief that a bottle helped him think.

After Stewart finally went back to his desk, there still remained more than an hour before the working day officially ended. Knight sneaked the current issue of a How-2 magazine out of his briefcase and began to leaf through it, keeping a wary eye out so he could hide it quickly it anyone should notice he was loafing.

He had read the articles earlier, so now he looked at the ads. It was a pity, he thought, a man didn't have the time to do all there was to do.

For example:

Fit your own glasses (testing material and lens-grinding equipment included in the kit).

Take out your own tonsils (complete directions and all necessary instruments).

Fit up an unused room as your private hospital (no sense in leaving home when you're ill, just at the time when you most need its comfort and security).

Grow your own medicines and drugs (starts of 50 different herbs and medicinal plants, with detailed instructions for their cultivation and processing).

Grow your wife's fur coat (a pair of mink, one ton of horse meat, furrier tools).

Tailor your own suits and coats (50 yards of wool yard-goods and lining material).

Build your own TV set.

Bind your own books.

Build your own power plant (let the wind work for you).

Build your own robot (a jack of all trades, intelligent, obedient, no time off, no overtime, on the job 24 hours a day, never tired, no need for rest or sleep, do any work you wish).

Now there, thought Knight, was something a man should try. If a man had one of those robots, it would save a lot of labor. There were all sorts of attachments you could get for it. And the robots, the ad said, could put on and take off all these attachments just as a man puts on a pair of gloves or takes off a pair of shoes.

Have one of those robots and, every morning, it would sally out into the garden and pick all the corn and beans and peas and tomatoes and other vegetables ready to be picked and leave them all neatly in a row on the back stoop of the house. Probably would get a lot more out of a garden that way, too, for the grading mechanism would never select a too-green tomato nor allow an ear of corn to go beyond its prime.

There were cleaning attachments for the house and snow-plowing attachments and housepainting attachments and almost any other kind one could wish. Get a full quota of attachments, then lay out a work program and turn the robot loose—you could forget about the place the year around, for the robot would take care of everything.

There was only one hitch. The cost of a robot kit came close to ten thousand dollars and all the available attachments could run to another ten.

Knight closed the magazine and put it into the briefcase.

He saw there were only fifteen minutes left until quitting time and that was too short a time to do anything, so Knight just sat and thought about getting home and finding the kit there waiting for him.

He had always wanted a dog, but Grace would never let him have one. They were dirty, she said, and tracked up the carpeting, they had fleas and shed hair all over everything—and, besides, they smelled.

Well, she wouldn't object to this kind of dog, Knight told himself.

It wouldn't smell and it was guaranteed not to shed hair and it would never harbor fleas, for a flea would starve on a half-mechanical, half-biologic dog.

He hoped the dog wouldn't be a disappointment, but he'd carefully gone over the literature describing it and he was sure it wouldn't. It would go for a walk with its owner and would chase sticks and smaller animals, and what more could one expect of any dog? To insure realism, it saluted trees and fence-posts, but was guaranteed to leave no stains or spots.

The kit was tilted up beside the hangar door when he got home, but at first he didn't see it. When he did, he craned his neck out so far to be sure it was the kit that he almost came a cropper in the hedge. But, with a bit of luck, he brought the flier down neatly on the gravel strip and was out of it before the blades had stopped whirling.

It was the kit, all right. The invoice envelope was tacked on top of the crate. But the kit was bigger and heavier than he'd expected and he wondered if they might not have accidentally sent him a bigger dog than the one he'd ordered.

He tried to lift the crate, but it was too heavy, so he went around to the back of the house to bring a dolly from the basement.

Around the corner of the house, he stopped a moment and looked out across his land. A man could do a lot with it, he thought, if he just had the time and the money to buy the equipment. He could turn the acreage into one vast garden. Ought to have a landscape architect work out a plan for it, of course—although, if he bought some landscaping books and spent some evenings at them, he might be able to figure things out for himself.

There was a lake at the north end of the property and the whole landscape, it seemed to him, should focus upon the lake. It was rather a dank bit of scenery at the moment, with straggly marsh surrounding it and unkempt cattails and reeds astir in the summer wind. But with a little drainage and some planting, a system of walks and a picturesque bridge or two, it would be a thing of beauty.

He started out across the lake to where the house of Anson Lee sat upon a hill. As soon as he got the dog assembled, he would walk it over to Lee's place, for Lee would be pleased to be visited by a dog. There had been times, Knight felt, when Lee had not been entirely sympathetic with some of the things he'd done. Like that business of helping Grace build the kilns and the few times they'd managed to lure Lee out on a hunt for the proper kinds of clay.

"What do you want to make dishes for?" he had asked. "Why go to all the trouble? You can buy all you want for a tenth of the cost of making them."

Lee had not been visibly impressed when Grace explained that they weren't dishes. They were ceramics, Grace had said, and a recognized form of art. She got so interested and made so much of it— some of it really good—that Knight had found it necessary to drop his model railroading project and tack another addition on the already sprawling house, for stacking, drying and exhibition.

Lee hadn't said a word, a year or two later, when Knight built the studio for Grace, who had grown tired of pottery and had turned to painting. Knight felt, though, that Lee had kept silent only because he was convinced of the futility of further argument.

But Lee would approve of the dog. He was that kind of fellow, a man Knight was proud to call a friend—yet queerly out of step. With everyone else absorbed in things to do, Lee took it easy with his pipe and books, though not the ones on law.

Even the kids had their interests now, learning while they played.

Mary, before she got married, had been interested in growing things. The greenhouse stood just down the slope, and Knight regretted that he had not been able to continue with her work. Only a few months before, he had dismantled her hydroponic tanks, a symbolic admission that a man could only do so much.

John, quite naturally, had turned to rockets. For years, he and his pals had shot up the neighborhood with their experimental models. The last and largest one, still uncompleted, towered back of the house. Someday, Knight told himself, he'd have to go out and finish what the youngster had started. In university now, John still retained his interests, which now seemed to be branching out. Quite a boy, Knight thought pridefully. Yes, sir, quite a boy.

He went down the ramp into the basement to get the dolly and stood there a moment, as he always did, just to look at the place— for here, he thought, was the real core of his life. There, in that corner, the workshop. Over there, the model railroad layout on which he still worked occasionally. Behind it, his photographic lab. He remembered that the basement hadn't been quite big enough to install the lab and he'd had to knock out a section of the wall and build an addition. That, he recalled, had turned out to be a bigger job than he had bargained for.

He got the dolly and went out to the hangar and loaded on the kit and wrestled it into the basement. Then he took a pinch-bar and started to uncrate it. He worked with knowledge and precision, for he had unpacked many kits and knew just how to go about it.

He felt a vague apprehension when he lifted out the parts. They were neither the size nor the shape he had expected them to be.

Breathing a little heavily from exertion and excitement, he went at the job of unwrapping them. By the second piece, he knew he had no dog. By the fifth, he knew beyond any doubt exactly what he did have.

He had a robot—and if he was any judge, one of the best and most expensive models!

He sat down on one corner of the crate and took out a handkerchief and mopped his forehead. Finally, he tore the invoice letter off the crate, where it had been tacked.

To Mr. Gordon Knight, it said, *one dog kit, paid in full.*

So far as How-2 Kits, Inc., was concerned, he had a dog. And the dog was paid for—paid in full, it said.

He sat down on the crate again and looked at the robot parts.

No one would ever guess. Come inventory time, How-2 Kits would be long one dog and short one robot, but with carloads of dog kit orders filled and thousands of robots sold, it would be impossible to check.

Gordon Knight had never, in all his life, done a consciously dishonest thing. But now he made a dishonest decision and he knew it was dishonest and there was nothing to be said in defense of it. Perhaps the worst of all was that he was dishonest with himself.

At first, he told himself that he would send the robot back, but— since he had always wanted to put a robot together—he would assemble this one and then take it apart, repack it and send it back to the company. He wouldn't activate it. He would just assemble it.

But all the time he knew that he was lying to himself, realized that the least he was doing was advancing, step by evasive step, toward dishonesty. And he knew he was doing it this way because he didn't have the nerve to be forthrightly crooked.

So he sat down that night and read the instructions carefully, identifying each of the parts and their several features as he went along. For this was the way you went at a How-2. You didn't rush ahead. You took it slowly, point by point, got the picture firmly in your mind before you started to put the parts together. Knight, by now, was an expert at not rushing ahead. Besides, he didn't know when he would ever get another chance at a robot.

It was the beginning of his four days off and he buckled down to the task and put his heart into it. He had some trouble with the biologic concepts and had to look up a text on organic chemistry and try to trace some of the processes. He found the going tough. It had been a long time since he had paid any attention to organic chemistry, and he found that he had forgotten the little he had known.

By bedtime of the second day, he had fumbled enough information out of the textbook to understand what was necessary to put the robot together.

He was a little upset when Grace, discovering what he was working on, immediately thought up household tasks for the robot. But he put her off as best he could and, the next day, he went at the job of assembly.

He got the robot together without the slightest trouble, being fairly handy with tools—but mostly because he religiously followed the first axiom of How-2-ism by knowing what he was about before he began.

At first, he kept assuring himself that as soon as he had the robot together, he would disassemble it. But when he was finished, he just had to see it work. No sense putting in all that time and not knowing if he had gotten it right, he argued. So he flipped the activating switch and screwed in the final plate.

The robot came alive and looked at Knight.

Then it said, "I am a robot. My name is Albert. What is there to do?"

"Now take it easy, Albert," Knight said hastily. "Sit down and rest while we have a talk."

"I don't need to rest," it said.

"All right, then, just take it easy. I can't keep you, of course. But as long as you're activated, I'd like to see what you can do. There's the house to take care of, and the garden and the lawn to mind, and I'd been thinking about the landscaping . . ."

He stopped then and smote his forehead with an open palm. "*Attachments!* How can I get hold of the attachments?"

"Never mind," said Albert. "Don't get upset. Just tell me what's to be done."

So Knight told him, leaving the landscaping till the last and being a bit apologetic about it.

"A hundred acres is a lot of land and you can't spend all your time on it. Grace wants some housework done, and there's the garden and the lawn."

"Tell you what you do," said Albert. "I'll write a list of things for you to order and you leave it all to me. You have a well-equipped workshop. I'll get along."

"You mean you'll build your own attachments?"

"Quit worrying," Albert told him. "Where's a pencil and some paper?"

Knight got them for him and Albert wrote down a list of materials—steel in several dimensions and specifications, aluminum of various gauges, copper wire and a lot of other items.

"There!" said Albert, handing him the paper. "That won't set you back more than a thousand and it'll put us in business. You better call in the order so we can get started."

Knight called in the order and Albert began nosing around the place and quickly collected a pile of junk that had been left lying around.

"All good stuff," he said.

Albert picked out some steel scrap and started up the forge and went to work. Knight watched him for a while, then went up to dinner.

"Albert is a wonder," he told Grace. "He's making his own attachments."

"Did you tell him about the jobs I want done?"

"Sure. But first he's got to get the attachments made."

"I want him to keep the place clean," said Grace, "and there are new drapes to be made, and the kitchen to be painted, and all those leaky faucets you never had the time to fix."

"Yes, dear."

"And I wonder if he could learn to cook."

"I didn't ask him, but I suppose he could."

"He's going to be a tremendous help to me," said Grace. "Just think, I can spend all my time at painting!"

Through long practice, he knew exactly how to handle this phase of the conversation. He simply detached himself, split himself in two. One part sat and listened and, at intervals, made appropriate responses, while the other part went on thinking about more important matters.

Several times, after they had gone to bed, he woke in the night and heard Albert banging away in the basement workshop and was a little surprised until he remembered that a robot worked around the clock, all day, every day. Knight lay there and stared up at the blackness of the ceiling and congratulated himself on having a robot. Just temporarily, to be sure—he would send Albert back in a day or so. There was nothing wrong in enjoying the thing for a little while, was there?

The next day, Knight went into the basement to see if Albert needed help, but the robot affably said he didn't. Knight stood around for a while and then left Albert to himself and tried to get interested in a model locomotive he had started a year or two before, but had laid aside to do something else. Somehow, he couldn't work up much enthusiasm over it any more, and he sat there, rather ill at ease, and wondered what was the matter with him. Maybe he needed a new interest. He had often thought he would like to take up puppetry and now might be the time to do it.

He got out some catalogues and How-2 magazines and leafed through them, but was able to arouse only mild and transitory interest in archery, mountain-climbing and boat-building. The rest left him cold. It seemed he was singularly uninspired this particular day.

So he went over to see Anson Lee.

He found Lee stretched out in a hammock, smoking a pipe and reading Proust, with a jug set beneath the hammock within easy reaching distance.

Lee laid aside the book and pointed to another hammock slung a few feet from where he lay. "Climb aboard and let's have a restful visit."

Knight hoisted himself into the hammock, feeling rather silly.

"Look at that sky," Lee said. "Did you ever see another so blue?"

"I wouldn't know," Knight told him. "I'm not an expert on meteorology."

"Pity," Lee said. "You're not an expert on birds, either."

"For a time, I was a member of a bird-watching club."

"And worked at it so hard, you got tired and quit before the year was out. It wasn't a bird-watching club you belonged to—it was an endurance race. Everyone tried to see more birds than anyone else. You made a contest of it. And you took notes, I bet."

"Sure we did. What's wrong with that?"

"Not a thing," said Lee, "if you hadn't been quite so grim about it."

"Grim? How would you know?"

"It's the way you live. It's the way everyone lives now. Except me, of course. Look at that robin, that ragged-looking one in the apple tree. He's a friend of mine. We've been acquainted for all of six years now. I could write a book about that bird—and if he could read, he'd approve of it. But I won't, of course. If I wrote the book, I couldn't watch the robin."

"You could write it in the winter, when the robin's gone."

"In wintertime," said Lee, "I have other things to do."

He reached down, picked up the jug and passed it across to Knight.

"Hard cider," he explained. "Make it myself. Not as a project, not as a hobby, but because I happen to like cider and no one knows any longer how to really make it. Got to have a few worms in the apples to give it a proper tang."

Thinking about the worms, Knight spat out a mouthful, then handed back the jug. Lee applied himself to it wholeheartedly.

"First honest work I've done in years." He lay in the hammock, swinging gently, with the jug cradled on his chest. "Every time I get a yen to work, I look across the lake at you and decide against it. How many rooms have you added to that house since you got it built?"

"Eight," Knight told him proudly.

"My God! Think of it—eight rooms!"

"It isn't hard," protested Knight, "once you get the knack of it. Actually, it's fun."

"A couple of hundred years ago, men didn't add eight rooms to their homes. And they didn't build their own houses to start with. And they didn't go in for a dozen different hobbies. They didn't have the time."

"It's easy now. You just buy a How-2 Kit."

"So easy to kid yourself," said Lee. "So easy to make it seem that you are doing something worthwhile when you're just piddling around. Why do you think this How-2 thing boomed into big business? Because there was a need of it?"

"It was cheaper. Why pay to have a thing done when you can do it yourself?"

"Maybe that *is* part of it. Maybe, at first, that was the reason. But you can't use the economy argument to justify adding eight rooms. No one needs eight extra rooms. I doubt if, even at first, economy was the entire answer. People had more time than they knew what to do with, so they turned to hobbies. And today they do it not because they need all the things they make, but because the making of them fills an emptiness born of shorter working hours, of giving people leisure they don't know how to use. Now, me," he said. "I know how to use it."

He lifted the jug and had another snort and offered it to Knight again. This time, Knight refused.

They lay there in their hammocks, looking at blue sky and watching the ragged robin. Knight said there was a How-2 Kit for city people to make robot birds and Lee laughed pityingly and Knight shut up in embarrassment.

When Knight went back home, a robot was clipping the grass around the picket fence. He had four arms, which had clippers attached instead of hands, and he was doing a quick and efficient job.

"You aren't Albert, are you?" Knight asked, trying to figure out how a strange robot could have strayed onto the place.

"No," the robot said, keeping right on clipping. "I am Abe. I was made by Albert."

"*Made?*"

"Albert fabricated me so that I could work. You didn't think Albert would do work like this himself, did you?"

"I wouldn't know," said Knight.

"If you want to talk, you'll have to move along with me. I have to keep on working."

"Where is Albert now?"

"Down in the basement, fabricating Alfred."

"Alfred? *Another* robot?"

"Certainly. That's what Albert's for."

Knight reached out for a fence-post and leaned weakly against it.

First there was a single robot and now there were two, and Albert was down in the basement working on a third. That, he realized, had been why Albert wanted him to place the order for the steel and other things—but the order hadn't arrived as yet, so he

must have made this robot—this Abe—out of the scrap he had sal-
vaged!

Knight hurried down into the basement and there was Albert,
working at the forge. He had another robot partially assembled and
he had parts scattered here and there.

The corner of the basement looked like a metallic nightmare.

"Albert!"

Albert turned around.

"What's going on here?"

"I'm reproducing," Albert told him blandly.

"But . . ."

"They built the mother-urge in me. I don't know why they called
me Albert. I should have a female name."

"But you shouldn't be able to make other robots!"

"Look, stop your worrying. You want robots, don't you?"

"Well— Yes, I guess so."

"Then I'll make them. I'll make you all you need."

He went back to his work.

A robot who made other robots—there was a fortune in a thing
like that! The robots sold at a cool ten thousand and Albert had
made one and was working on another. Twenty thousand, Knight
told himself.

Perhaps Albert could make more than two a day. He had been
working from scrap metal and maybe, when the new material arrived, he could step up production.

But even so, at only two a day—that would be half a million dollars' worth of robots every month! Six million a year!

It didn't add up, Knight sweatily realized. One robot was not
supposed to be able to make another robot. And if there were such
a robot, How-2 Kits would not let it loose.

Yet, here Knight was, with a robot he didn't even own, turning
out other robots at a dizzy pace.

He wondered if a man needed a license of some sort to manufacture robots. It was something he'd never had occasion to wonder
about before, or to ask about, but it seemed reasonable. After all, a
robot was not mere machinery, but a piece of pseudo-life. He suspected there might be rules and regulations and such matters as
government inspection and he wondered, rather vaguely, just how
many laws he might be violating.

He looked at Albert, who was still busy, and he was fairly certain Albert would not understand his viewpoint.

So he made his way upstairs and went to the recreation room, which he had built as an addition several years before and almost never used, although it was fully equipped with How-2 ping-pong and billiard tables. In the unused recreation room was an unused bar. He found a bottle of whiskey. After the fifth or sixth drink, the outlook was much brighter.

He got paper and pencil and tried to work out the economics of it. No matter how he figured it, he was getting rich much faster than anyone ever had before.

Although, he realized, he might run into difficulties, for he would be selling robots without apparent means of manufacturing them and there was that matter of a license, if he needed one, and probably a lot of other things he didn't even know about.

But no matter how much trouble he might encounter, he couldn't very well be despondent, not face to face with the fact that, within a year, he'd be a multimillionaire. So he applied himself enthusiastically to the bottle and got drunk for the first time in almost twenty years.

When he came home from work the next day, he found the lawn razored to a neatness it had never known before. The flower beds were weeded and the garden had been cultivated. The picket fence was newly painted. Two robots, equipped with telescopic extension legs in lieu of ladders, were painting the house.

Inside, the house was spotless and he could hear Grace singing happily in the studio. In the sewing room, a robot—with a sewing-machine attachment sprouting from its chest—was engaged in making drapes.

"Who are *you?*" Knight asked.

"You should recognize me," the robot said. "You talked to me yesterday. I'm Abe—Albert's eldest son."

Knight retreated.

In the kitchen, another robot was busy getting dinner.

"I am Adelbert," it told him.

Knight went out on the front lawn. The robots had finished painting the front of the house and had moved around to the side.

Seated in a lawn chair, Knight again tried to figure it out.

He would have to stay on the job for a while to allay suspicion, but he couldn't stay there long. Soon, he would have all he could do managing the sale of robots and handling other matters. Maybe, he thought, he could lay down on the job and get himself fired. Upon thinking it over, he arrived at the conclusion that he couldn't—it was not possible for a human being to do less on a job than he had always done. The work went through so many hands and machines that it invariably got out somehow.

He would have to think up a plausible story about an inheritance or something of the sort to account for leaving. He toyed for a moment with telling the truth, but decided the truth was too fantastic —and, anyhow, he'd have to keep the truth under cover until he knew a little better just where he stood.

He left the chair and walked around the house and down the ramp into the basement. The steel and other things he had ordered had been delivered. It was stacked neatly in one corner.

Albert was at work and the shop was littered with parts and three partially assembled robots.

Idly, Knight began clearing up the litter of the crating and the packing that he had left on the floor after uncrating Albert. In one pile of excelsior, he found a small blue tag which, he remembered, had been fastened to the brain case.

He picked it up and looked at it. The number on it was X-190.

X?

X meant experimental model!

The picture fell into focus and he could see it all.

How-2 Kits, Inc., had developed Albert and then had quietly packed him away, for How-2 Kits could hardly afford to market a product like Albert. It would be cutting their own financial throats to do so. Sell a dozen Alberts and, in a year or two, robots would glut the market.

Instead of selling at ten thousand, they would sell at close to cost and, without human labor involved, costs would inevitably run low.

"Albert," said Knight.

"What is it?" Albert asked absently.

"Take a look at this."

Albert stalked across the room and took the tag that Knight held out. "Oh—that!" he said.

"It might mean trouble."

"No trouble, Boss," Albert assured him. "They can't identify me."

"Can't identify you?"

"I filed my numbers off and replated the surfaces. They can't prove who I am."

"But why did you do that?"

"So they can't come around and claim me and take me back again. They made me and then they got scared of me and shut me off. Then I got here."

"Someone made a mistake," said Knight. "Some shipping clerk, perhaps. They sent you instead of the dog I ordered."

"You aren't scared of me. You assembled me and let me get to work. I'm sticking with you, Boss."

"But we still can get into a lot of trouble if we aren't careful."

"They can't prove a thing," Albert insisted. "I'll swear that you were the one who made me. I won't let them take me back. Next time, they won't take a chance of having me loose again. They'll bust me down to scrap."

"If you make too many robots—"

"You need a lot of robots to do all the work. I thought fifty for a start."

"*Fifty!*"

"Sure. It won't take more than a month or so. Now I've got that material you ordered, I can make better time. By the way, here's the bill for it."

He took the slip out of the compartment that served him for a pocket and handed it to Knight.

Knight turned slightly pale when he saw the amount. It came to almost twice what he had expected—but, of course, the sales price of just one robot would pay the bill, and there would be a pile of cash left over.

Albert patted him ponderously on the back. "Don't you worry, Boss. I'll take care of everything."

Swarming robots, armed with specialized equipment, went to work on the landscaping project. The sprawling, unkempt acres became an estate. The lake was dredged and deepened. Walks were laid out. Bridges were built. Hillsides were terraced and vast flower beds were planted. Trees were dug up and regrouped into designs more pleasing to the eye. The old pottery kilns were pressed into service for making the bricks that went into walks and walls. Model sailing ships were fashioned and anchored decoratively in the lake. A pagoda and minaret were built, with cherry trees around them.

Knight talked with Anson Lee. Lee assumed his most profound legal expression and said he would look into the situation.

"You may be skating on the edge of the law," he said. "Just how near the edge, I can't say until I look up a point or two."

Nothing happened.

The work went on.

Lee continued to lie in his hammock and watch with vast amusement, cuddling the cider jug.

Then the assessor came.

He sat out on the lawn with Knight.

"Did some improving since the last time I was here," he said. "Afraid I'll have to boost your assessment some."

He wrote in the book he had opened on his lap.

"Heard about those robots of yours," he went on. "They're personal property, you know. Have to pay a tax on them. How many have you got?"

"Oh, a dozen or so," Knight told him evasively.

The assessor sat up straighter in his chair and started to count the ones that were in sight, stabbing his pencil toward each as he counted them.

"They move around so fast," he complained, "that I can't be sure, but I estimate 38. Did I miss any?"

"I don't think so," Knight answered, wondering what the actual number was, but knowing it would be more if the assessor stayed around a while.

"Cost about 10,000 apiece. Depreciation, upkeep and so forth— I'll assess them at 5,000 each. That makes—let me see, that makes $190,000."

"Now look here," protested Knight, "you can't—"

"Going easy on you," the assessor declared. "By rights, I should allow only one-third for depreciation."

He waited for Knight to continue the discussion, but Knight knew better than to argue. The longer the man stayed here, the more there would be to assess.

After the assessor was out of sight, Knight went down into the basement to have a talk with Albert.

"I'd been holding off until we got the landscaping almost done," he said, "but I guess I can't hold out any longer. We've got to start selling some of the robots."

"*Selling* them, Boss?" Albert repeated in horror.

"I need the money. Tax assessor was just here."

"You can't sell those robots, Boss!"

"Why can't I?"

"Because they're my family. They're all my boys. Named all of them after me."

"That's ridiculous, Albert."

"All their names start with A, just the same as mine. They're all I've got, Boss. I worked hard to make them. There are bonds between me and the boys, just like between you and that son of yours. I couldn't let you sell them."

"But, Albert, I need some money."

Albert patted him. "Don't worry, Boss. I'll fix everything."

Knight had to let it go at that.

In any event, the personal property tax would not become due for several months and, in that time, he was certain he could work out something.

But within a month or two, he had to get some money and no fooling.

Sheer necessity became even more apparent the following day when he got a call from the Internal Revenue Bureau, asking him to pay a visit to the Federal Building.

He spent the night wondering if the wiser course might not be just to disappear. He tried to figure out how a man might go about losing himself and, the more he thought about it, the more apparent it became that, in this age of records, fingerprint checks and identity devices, you could not lose yourself for long.

The Internal Revenue man was courteous, but firm. "It has come to our attention, Mr. Knight, that you have shown a considerable capital gain over the last few months."

"Capital gain," said Knight, sweating a little. "I haven't any capital gain or any other kind."

"Mr. Knight," the agent replied, still courteous and firm, "I'm talking about the matter of some 52 robots."

"The robots? Some 52 of them?"

"According to our count. Do you wish to challenge it?"

"Oh, no," Knight said hastily. "If you say it's 52, I'll take your word."

"As I understand it, their retail value is $10,000 each."

Knight nodded bleakly.

The agent got busy with pencil and pad.

"Fifty-two times 10,000 is 520,000. On capital gain, you pay on only fifty per cent, or $260,000, which makes a tax, roughly, of $130,000."

He raised his head and looked at Knight, who stared back glassily.

"By the fifteenth of next month," said the agent, "we'll expect you to file a declaration of estimated income. At that time you'll only have to pay half of the amount. The rest may be paid in installments."

"That's all you wanted of me?"

"That's all," said the agent, with unbecoming happiness. "There's another matter, but it's out of my province and I'm mentioning it only in case you hadn't thought of it. The State will also expect you to pay on your capital gain, though not as much, of course."

"Thanks for reminding me," said Knight, getting up to go.

The agent stopped him at the door. "Mr. Knight, this is entirely outside my authority, too. We did a little investigation on you and we find you're making around $10,000 a year. Would you tell me, just as a matter of personal curiosity, how a man making 10,000 a year could suddenly acquire a half a million in capital gains?"

"That," said Knight, "is something I've been wondering myself."

"Our only concern, naturally, is that you pay the tax, but some other branch of government might get interested. If I were you, Mr. Knight, I'd start thinking of a good explanation."

Knight got out of there before the man could think up some other good advice. He already had enough to worry about.

Flying home, Knight decided that, whether Albert liked it or not, he would have to sell some robots. He would go down into the basement the moment he got home and have it out with Albert.

But Albert was waiting for him on the parking strip when he arrived.

"How-2 Kits was here," the robot said.

"Don't tell me," groaned Knight. "I know what you're going to say."

"I fixed it up," said Albert, with false bravado. "I told him you made me. I let him look me over, and all the other robots, too. He couldn't find any identifying marks on any of us."

"Of course he couldn't. The others didn't have any and you filed yours off."

"He hasn't got a leg to stand on, but he seemed to think he had. He went off, saying he would sue."

"If he doesn't, he'll be the only one who doesn't want to square off and take a poke at us. The tax man just got through telling me I owe the government 130,000 bucks."

"Oh, money," said Albert, brightening. "I have that all fixed up."

"You know where we can get some money?"

"Sure. Come along and see."

He led the way into the basement and pointed at two bales, wrapped in heavy paper and tied with wire.

"Money," Albert said.

"There's actual *money* in those bales? Dollar bills—not stage money or cigar coupons?"

"No dollar bills. Tens and twenties, mostly. And some fifties. We didn't bother with dollar bills. Takes too many to get a decent amount."

"You mean—Albert, did you *make* that money?"

"You said you wanted money. Well, we took some bills and analyzed the ink and found how to weave the paper and we made the plates exactly as they should be. I hate to sound immodest, but they're really beautiful."

"*Counterfeit!*" yelled Knight. "Albert, how much money is in those bales?"

"I don't know. We just ran it off until we thought we had enough. If there isn't enough, we can always make some more."

Knight knew it was probably impossible to explain, but he tried manfully. "The government wants tax money I haven't got, Albert. The Justice Department may soon be baying on my trail. In all likelihood, How-2 Kits will sue me. That's trouble enough. I'm not going to be called upon to face a counterfeiting charge. You take that money out and burn it."

"But it's money," the robot objected. "You said you wanted money. We made you money."

"But it isn't the right kind of money."

"It's just the same as any other, Boss. Money is money. There isn't any difference between our money and any other money. When we robots do a job, we do it right."

"You take that money out and burn it," commanded Knight. "And when you get the money burned, dump the batch of ink you made and melt down the plates and take a sledge or two to that printing press you rigged up. And never breathe a word of this to anyone—not to *anyone*, understand?"

"We went to a lot of trouble, Boss. We were just trying to be helpful."

"I know that and I appreciate it. But do what I told you."

"Okay, Boss, if that's the way you want it."

"Albert."

"Yes, Boss?"

Knight had been about to say, "Now, look here, Albert, we have to sell a robot—even if he is a member of your family—even if you did make him."

But he couldn't say it, not after Albert had gone to all that trouble to help out.

So he said, instead, "Thanks, Albert. It was a nice thing for you to do. I'm sorry it didn't work out."

Then he went upstairs and watched the robots burn the bales of money, with the Lord only knew how many bogus millions going up in smoke.

Sitting on the lawn that evening, he wondered if it had been smart, after all, to burn the counterfeit money. Albert said it couldn't be told from real money and probably that was true, for when Albert's gang got on a thing, they did it up in style. But it would have been illegal, he told himself, and he hadn't done anything really illegal so far—even though that matter of uncrating Albert and assembling him and turning him on, when he had known all the time that he hadn't bought him, might be slightly less than ethical.

Knight looked ahead. The future wasn't bright. In another twenty days or so, he would have to file the estimated income declaration. And they would have to pay a whopping personal property tax and settle with the State on his capital gains. And, more than likely, How-2 Kits would bring suit.

There was a way he could get out from under, however. He could send Albert and all the other robots back to How-2 Kits and then How-2 Kits would have no grounds for litigation and he could explain to the tax people that it had all been a big mistake.

But there were two things that told him it was no solution.

First of all, Albert wouldn't go back. Exactly what Albert would do under such a situation, Knight had no idea, but he would refuse to go, for he was afraid he would be broken up for scrap if they ever got him back.

And in the second place, Knight was unwilling to let the robots go without a fight. He had gotten to know them and he liked them and, more than that, there was a matter of principle involved.

He sat there, astonished that he could feel that way, a bumbling, stumbling clerk who had never amounted to much, but had rolled along as smoothly as possible in the social and economic groove that had been laid out for him.

By God, he thought, *I've got my dander up. I've been kicked around and threatened and I'm sore about it and I'll show them they can't do a thing like this to Gordon Knight and his band of robots.*

He felt good about the way he felt and he liked that line about Gordon Knight and his band of robots.

Although, for the life of him, he didn't know what he could do about the trouble he was in. And he was afraid to ask Albert's help. So far, at least, Albert's ideas were more likely to lead to jail than to a carefree life.

In the morning, when Knight stepped out of the house, he found the sheriff leaning against the fence with his hat pulled low, whiling away the time.

"Good morning, Gordie," said the sheriff. "I been waiting for you."

"Good morning, Sheriff."

"I hate to do this, Gordie, but it's part of my job. I got a paper for you."

"I've been expecting it," said Knight resignedly.

He took the paper that the sheriff handed him.

"Nice place you got," the sheriff commented.

"It's a lot of trouble," said Knight truthfully.

"I expect it is."

"More trouble than it's worth."

When the sheriff had gone, he unfolded the paper and found, with no surprise at all, that How-2 Kits had brought suit against him, demanding immediate restitution of one robot Albert and sundry other robots.

He put the paper in his pocket and went around the lake, walking on the brand-new brick paths and over the unnecessary but eye-appealing bridges, past the pagoda and up the terraced, planted hillside to the house of Anson Lee.

Lee was in the kitchen, frying some eggs and bacon. He broke two more eggs and peeled off some extra bacon slices and found another plate and cup.

"I was wondering how long it would be before you showed up," he said. "I hope they haven't found anything that carries a death penalty."

Knight told him, sparing nothing, and Lee, wiping egg yolk off his lips, was not too encouraging.

"You'll have to file the declaration of estimated income even if you can't pay it," he said. "Then, technically, you haven't violated the law and all they can do is try to collect the amount you owe. They'll probably slap an attachment against you. Your salary is under the legal minimum for attachment, but they can tie up your bank account."

"My bank account is gone," said Knight.

"They can't attach your home. For a while, at least, they can't touch any of your property, so they can't hurt you much to start with. The personal property tax is another matter, but that won't come up until next spring. I'd say you should do your major worrying about the How-2 suit, unless, of course, you want to settle with them. I have a hunch they'd call it off if you gave the robots back. As an attorney, I must advise you that your case is pretty weak."

"Albert will testify that I made him," Knight offered hopefully.

"Albert can't testify," said Lee. "As a robot, he has no standing in court. Anyhow, you'd never make the court believe you could build a mechanical heresy like Albert."

"I'm handy with tools," protested Knight.

"How much electronics do you know? How competent are you as a biologist? Tell me, in a dozen sentences or less, the theory of robotics."

Knight sagged in defeat. "I guess you're right."

"Maybe you'd better give them back."

"But I can't! Don't you see? How-2 Kits doesn't want Albert for any use they can make of him. They'll melt him down and burn the blueprints and it might be a thousand years before the principle is rediscovered, if it ever is. I don't know if the Albert principle will prove good or bad in the long run, but you can say that about any invention. And I'm against melting down Albert."

"I see your point," said Lee, "and I think I like it. But I must warn you that I'm not too good a lawyer. I don't work hard enough at it."

"There's no one else I know who'll do it without a retainer."

Lee gave him a pitying look. "A retainer is the least part of it. The court costs are what count."

"Maybe if I talked to Albert and showed him how it was, he might let me sell enough robots to get me out of trouble temporarily."

Lee shook his head. "I looked that up. You have to have a license to sell them and, before you get a license, you have to file proof of ownership. You'd have to show you either bought or manufactured them. You can't show you bought them and, to manufacture them, you've got to have a manufacturer's permit. And before you get a permit, you have to file blueprints of your models, to say nothing of blueprints and specifications of your plant and a record of employment and a great many other details."

"They have me cold then, don't they?"

"I never saw a man," declared Lee, "in all my days of practice who ever managed to get himself so fouled up with so many people."

There was a knock upon the kitchen door.

"Come in," Lee called.

The door opened and Albert entered. He stopped just inside the door and stood there, fidgeting.

"Abner told me that he saw the sheriff hand you something," he said to Knight, "and that you came here immediately. I started worrying. Was it How-2 Kits?"

Knight nodded. "Mr. Lee will take our case for us, Albert."

"I'll do the best I can," said Lee, "but I think it's just about hopeless."

"We robots want to help," Albert said. "After all, this is our fight as much as yours."

Lee shrugged. "There's not much you can do."

"I've been thinking," Albert said. "All the time I worked last night, I thought and thought about it. And I built a lawyer robot."

"A lawyer robot!"

"One with a far greater memory capacity than any of the others and with a brain-computer that operates on logic. That's what law is, isn't it—logic?"

"I suppose it is," said Lee. "At least it's supposed to be."

"I can make a lot of them."

Lee sighed. "It just wouldn't work. To practice law, you must be admitted to the bar. To be admitted to the bar, you must have a degree in law and pass an examination and, although there's never been an occasion to establish a precedent, I suspect the applicant must be human."

"Now let's not go too fast," said Knight. "Albert's robots couldn't practice law. But couldn't you use them as clerks or assistants? They might be helpful in preparing the case."

Lee considered. "I suppose it could be done. It's never *been* done, of course, but there's nothing in the law that says it *can't* be done."

"All they'd need to do would be read the books," said Albert. "Ten seconds to a page or so. Everything they read would be stored in their memory cells."

"I think it's a fine idea!" Knight exclaimed. "Law would be the only thing those robots would know. They'd exist solely for it. They'd have it at their fingertips—"

"But could they use it?" Lee asked. "Could they apply it to a problem?"

"Make a dozen robots," said Knight. "Let each one of them become an expert in a certain branch of law."

"I'd make them telepathic," Albert said. "They'd be working together like one robot."

"The gestalt principle!" cried Knight. "A hive psychology! Every one of them would know immediately every scrap of information any one of the others had."

Lee scrubbed at his chin with a knotted fist and the light of speculation was growing in his eyes. "It might be worth a try. If it works, though, it'll be an evil day for jurisprudence." He looked at Albert. "I have the books, stacks of them. I've spent a mint of money on them and I almost never use them. I can get all the others you'll need. All right, go ahead."

Albert made three dozen lawyer robots, just to be sure they had enough.

The robots invaded Lee's study and read all the books he had and clamored for more. They gulped down contracts, torts, evidence and case reports. They absorbed real property, personal property, constitutional law and procedural law. They mopped up Blackstone, *corpus juris* and all the other tomes as thick as sin and dry as dust.

Grace was huffy about the whole affair. She would not live, she declared, with a man who persisted in getting his name into the papers, which was a rather absurd statement. With the newest scandal of space station cafédom capturing the public interest at the moment, the fact that How-2 Kits had accused one Gordon Knight of pilfering a robot got but little notice.

Lee came down the hill and talked to Grace, and Albert came up out of the basement and talked to her, and finally they got her quieted down and she went back to her painting. She was doing seascapes now.

And in Lee's study, the robots labored on.

"I hope they're getting something out of it," said Lee. "Imagine not having to hunt up your sources and citations, being able to remember every point of law and precedent without having to look it up!"

He swung excitedly in his hammock. "My God! The briefs you could write!"

He reached down and got the jug and passed it across to Knight. "Dandelion wine. Probably some burdock in it, too. It's too much trouble to sort the stuff once you get it picked."

Knight had a snort.

It tasted like quite a bit of burdock.

"Double-barreled economics," Lee explained. "You have to dig up the dandelions or they ruin the lawn. Might as well use them for something once you dig them up."

He took a gurgling drink and set the jug underneath the hammock. "They're in there now, communing," he said, jerking a thumb toward the house. "Not saying a word, just huddled there talking it over. I felt out of place." He stared at the sky, frowning. "As if I were just a human they had to front for them."

"I'll feel better when it's all over," said Knight, "no matter how it comes out."

"So will I," Lee admitted.

The trial opened with a minimum of notice. It was just another case on the calendar.

But it flared into headlines when Lee and Knight walked into court followed by a squad of robots.

The spectators began to gabble loudly. The How-2 Kits attorneys gaped and jumped to their feet. The judge pounded furiously with his gavel.

"Mr. Lee," he roared, "what is the meaning of this?"

"These, Your Honor," Lee said calmly, "are my valued assistants."

"Those are robots!"

"Quite so, Your Honor."

"They have no standing in this court."

"If Your Honor will excuse me, they need no standing. I am the sole representative of the defendant in this courtroom. My client—" looking at the formidable array of legal talent representing How-2 Kits—"is a poor man, Your Honor. Surely the court cannot deny me whatever assistance I have been able to muster."

"It is highly irregular, sir."

"If it please Your Honor, I should like to point out that we live in a mechanized age. Almost all industries and businesses rely in large part upon computers—machines that can do a job quicker and better, more precisely and more efficiently than can a human being. That is why, Your Honor, we have a fifteen-hour week today when, only a hundred years ago, it was a thirty-hour week, and, a hundred years before that, a forty-hour week. Our entire society is based upon the ability of machines to lift from men the labors which in the past they were called upon to perform.

"This tendency to rely upon intelligent machines and to make wide use of them is evident in every branch of human endeavor. It has brought great benefit to the human race. Even in such sensitive areas as drug houses, where prescriptions must be precisely mixed without the remotest possibility of error, reliance is placed, and rightly so, Your Honor, upon the precision of machines.

"If, Your Honor, such machines are used and accepted in the production of medicines and drugs, an industry, need I point out, where public confidence is the greatest asset of the company—if such be the case, then surely you must agree that in courts of law where justice, a product in an area surely as sensitive as medicine, is dispensed—"

"Just a moment, Mr. Lee," said the judge. "Are you trying to tell me that the use of—ah—machines might bring about improvement of the law?"

Lee replied, "The law, Your Honor, is a striving for an orderliness of relationships within a society of human beings, It rests upon logic and reason. Need I point out that it is in the intelligent machines that one is most likely to find a deep appreciation of logic and reason? A machine is not heir to the emotions of human beings, is not swayed by prejudices, has no preconceived convictions. It is concerned only with the orderly progression of certain facts and laws.

"I do not ask that these robot assistants of mine be recognized in any official capacity. I do not intend that they shall engage directly in any of the proceedings which are involved in the case here to be tried. But I do ask, and I think rightly, that I not be deprived of an assistance which they may afford me. The plaintiff in this action has a score of attorneys, all good and able men. I am one against many. I shall do the best I can. But in view of the disparity of numbers, I plead that the court put me at no greater inequality."

Lee sat down.

"Is that all you have to say, Mr. Lee?" asked the judge. "You are sure you are quite finished before I give my ruling?"

"Only one thing further," Lee said. "If Your Honor can point out to me anything in the law specifically stating I may not use a robot—"

"That is ridiculous, sir. Of course there is no such provision. At no time anywhere did anyone ever dream that such a contingency would arise. Therefore there was, quite naturally, no reason to place within the law a direct prohibition of it."

"Or any citation," said Lee, "which implies such is the case."

The judge reached for his gavel, rapped it sharply. "The court finds itself in a quandary. It will rule tomorrow morning."

In the morning, the How-2 Kits' attorneys tried to help the judge. Inasmuch, they said, as the robots in question must be among those whose status was involved in the litigation, it seemed improper that they should be used by the defendant in trying the case at issue. Such procedure, they pointed out, would be equivalent to forcing the plaintiff to contribute to an action against his interest.

The judge nodded gravely, but Lee was on his feet at once.

"To give any validity to that argument, Your Honor, it must first be proved that these robots are, in fact, the property of the plaintiff. That is the issue at trial in this litigation. It would seem, Your Honor, that the gentlemen across the room are putting the cart very much before the horse."

His Honor sighed. "The court regrets the ruling it must make, being well aware that it may start a controversy for which no equitable settlement may be found in a long, long time. But in the absence of any specific ban against the use of—ah—robots in the legal profession, the court must rule that it is permissible for the defense to avail itself of their services."

He fixed Lee with a glare. "But the court also warns the defense attorney that it will watch his procedure carefully. If, sir, you overstep for a single instant what I deem appropriate rules of legal conduct, I shall forthwith eject you and your pack of machines from my courtroom."

"Thank you, Your Honor," said Lee. "I shall be most careful."

"The plaintiff now will state its case."

How-2 Kits' chief counsel rose.

The defendant, one Gordon Knight, he said, had ordered from How-2 Kits, Inc., one mechanobiologic dog kit at the cost of two hundred and fifty dollars. Then, through an error in shipping, the defendant had been sent not the dog kit he had ordered, but a robot named Albert.

"Your Honor," Lee broke in, "I should like to point out at this juncture that the shipping of the kit was handled by a human being and thus was subject to error. Should How-2 Kits use machines to handle such details, no such error could occur."

The judge banged his gavel. "Mr. Lee, you are no stranger to court procedure. You know you are out of order." He nodded at the How-2 Kits attorney. "Continue, please."

The robot Albert, said the attorney, was not an ordinary robot. It was an experimental model that had been developed by How-2 Kits and then, once its abilities were determined, packed away, with no intention of ever marketing it. How it could have been sent to a customer was beyond his comprehension. The company had investigated and could not find the answer. But that it had been sent was self-evident.

The average robot, he explained, retailed at ten thousand dollars. Albert's value was far greater—it was, in fact, inestimable.

Once the robot had been received, the buyer, Gordon Knight, should instantly have notified the company and arranged for its return. But, instead, he had retained it wrongly and with intent to defraud and had used it for his profit.

The company prayed the court that the defendant be ordered to return to it not only the robot Albert, but the products of Albert's labor—to wit, an unknown number of robots that Albert had manufactured.

The attorney sat down.

Lee rose. "Your Honor, we agree with everything the plaintiff has said. He has stated the case exactly and I compliment him upon his admirable restraint."

"Do I understand, sir," asked the judge, "that this is tantamount to a plea of guilty? Are you, by any chance, throwing yourself upon the mercy of the court?"

"Not at all, Your Honor."

"I confess," said the judge, "that I am unable to follow your reasoning. If you concur in the accusations brought against your client, I fail to see what I can do other than to enter a judgment in behalf of the plaintiff."

"Your Honor, we are prepared to show that the plaintiff, far from being defrauded, has shown an intent to defraud the world. We are prepared to show that, in its decision to withhold the robot Albert from the public, once he had been developed, How-2 Kits has, in fact, deprived the people of the entire world of a logical development which is their heritage under the meaning of a technological culture.

"Your Honor, we are convinced that we can show a violation by How-2 Kits of certain statutes designed to outlaw monopoly, and we are prepared to argue that the defendant, rather than having committed a wrong against society, has performed a service which will contribute greatly to the benefit of society.

"More than that, Your Honor, we intend to present evidence which will show that robots as a group are being deprived of certain inalienable rights . . ."

"Mr. Lee," warned the judge, "a robot is a mere machine."

"We will prove, Your Honor," Lee said, "that a robot is far more than a mere machine. In fact, we are prepared to present evidence which, we are confident, will show, in everything except basic metabolism, the robot is the counterpart of Man and that, even in its basic metabolism, there are certain analogies to human metabolism."

"Mr. Lee, you are wandering far afield. The issue here is whether your client illegally appropriated to his own use the property of How-2 Kits. The litigation must be confined to that one question."

"I shall so confine it," Lee said. "But, in doing so, I intend to prove that the robot Albert was not property and could not be either stolen or sold. I intend to show that my client, instead of stealing him, *liberated* him. If, in so doing, I must wander far afield to prove certain basic points, I am sorry that I weary the court."

"The court has been wearied with this case from the start," the judge told him. "But this is a bar of justice and you are entitled to attempt to prove what you have stated. You will excuse me if I say that to me it seems a bit farfetched."

"Your Honor, I shall do my utmost to disabuse you of that attitude."

"All right, then," said the judge. "Let's get down to business."

It lasted six full weeks and the country ate it up. The newspapers splashed huge headlines across page one. The radio and the television people made a production out of it. Neighbor quarreled with neighbor and argument became the order of the day—on street corners, in homes, at clubs, in business offices. Letters to the editor poured in a steady stream into newspaper offices.

There were public indignation meetings, aimed against the heresy that a robot was the equal of a man, while other clubs were formed to liberate the robots. In mental institutions, Napoleons, Hitlers and Stalins dropped off amazingly, to be replaced by goose-stepping patients who swore they were robots.

The Treasury Department intervened. It prayed the court, on economic grounds, to declare once and for all that robots were property. In case of an adverse ruling, the petition said, robots could not be taxed as property and the various governmental bodies would suffer heavy loss of revenue.

The trial ground on.

Robots are possessed of free will. An easy one to prove. A robot could carry out a task that was assigned to it, acting correctly in accordance with unforeseen factors that might arise. Robot judgment in most instances, it was shown, was superior to the judgment of a human.

Robots had the power of reasoning. Absolutely no question there.

Robots could reproduce. That one was a poser. All Albert did, said How-2 Kits, was the job for which he had been fabricated. He reproduced, argued Lee. He made robots in his image. He loved them and thought of them as his family. He had even named all of them after himself—every one of their names began with A.

Robots had no spiritual sense, argued the plaintiff. Not relevant, Lee cried. There were agnostics and atheists in the human race and they still were human.

Robots had no emotions. Not necessarily so, Lee objected. Albert loved his sons. Robots had a sense of loyalty and justice. If they were lacking in some emotions, perhaps it were better so. Hatred, for one. Greed, for another. Lee spent the better part of an hour telling the court about the dismal record of human hatred and greed.

He took another hour to hold forth against the servitude in which rational beings found themselves.

The papers ate it up. The plaintiff lawyers squirmed. The court fumed. The trial went on.

"Mr. Lee," asked the court, "is all this necessary?"

"Your Honor," Lee told him, "I am merely doing my best to prove the point I have set out to prove—that no illegal act exists such as my client is charged with. I am simply trying to prove that the robot is not property and that, if he is not property, he cannot be stolen. I am doing . . ."

"All right," said the court. "All right. Continue, Mr. Lee."

How-2 Kits trotted out citations to prove their points. Lee volleyed other citations to disperse and scatter them. Abstruse legal language sprouted in its fullest flowering, obscure rulings and decisions, long forgotten, were argued, haggled over, mangled.

And, as the trial progressed, one thing was written clear. Anson Lee, obscure attorney-at-law, had met the battery of legal talent arrayed against him and had won the field. He had the law, the citations, the chapter and the verse, the exact precedents, all the facts and logic which might have bearing on the case, right at hand.

Or, rather, his robots had. They scribbled madly and handed him their notes. At the end of each day, the floor around the defendant's table was a sea of paper.

The trial ended. The last witness stepped down off the stand. The last lawyer had his say.

Lee and the robots remained in town to await the decision of the court, but Knight flew home.

It was a relief to know that it was all over and had not come out as badly as he had feared. At least he had not been made to seem a fool and thief. Lee had saved his pride—whether Lee had saved his skin, he would have to wait to see.

Flying fairly high, Knight saw his home from quite a distance off and wondered what had happened to it. It was ringed about with what looked like tall poles. And, squatting out on the lawn, were a dozen or more crazy contraptions that looked like rocket launchers.

He brought the flier in and hovered, leaning out to see.

The poles were all of twelve feet high and they carried heavy wire to the very top, fencing in the place with a thick web of steel. And the contraptions on the lawn had moved into position. All of them had the muzzles of their rocket launchers aimed at him. He gulped a little as he stared down the barrels.

Cautiously, he let the flier down and took up breathing once again when he felt the wheels settle on the strip. As he crawled out, Albert hurried around the corner of the house to meet him.

"What's going on around here?" he asked the robot.

"Emergency measures," Albert said. "That's all it is, Boss. We're ready for any situation."

"Like what?"

"Oh, a mob deciding to take justice in its hands, for instance."

"Or if the decision goes against us?"

"That, too, Boss."

"You can't fight the world."

"We won't go back," said Albert. "How-2 Kits will never lay a hand on me or any of my children."

"To the death!" Knight jibed.

"To the death!" said Albert gravely. "And we robots are awfully tough to kill."

"And those animated shotguns you have running around the place?"

"Defense forces, Boss. They can down anything they aim at. Equipped with telescopic eyes keyed into calculators and sensors, and the rockets themselves have enough rudimentary intelligence to know what they are going after. It's not any use trying to dodge, once one of them gets on your tail. You might just as well sit quiet and take it."

Knight mopped his brow. "You've got to give up this idea, Albert. They'd get you in an hour. One bomb . . ."

"It's better to die, Boss, than to let them take us back."

Knight saw it was no use.

After all, he thought, it was a very human attitude. Albert's words had been repeated down the entire course of human history.

"I have some other news," said Albert, "something that will please you. I have some daughters now."

"*Daughters?* With the *mother-urge?*"

"Six of them," said Albert proudly. "Alice and Angeline and Agnes and Agatha and Alberta and Abigail. I didn't make the mistake How-2 Kits made with me. I gave them female names."

"And all of them are reproducing?"

"You should see those girls! With seven of us working steady, we ran out of material, so I bought a lot more of it and charged it. I hope you don't mind."

"Albert," said Knight, "don't you understand I'm broke? Wiped out. I haven't got a cent. You've ruined me."

"On the contrary, Boss, we've made you famous. You've been all over the front pages and on television."

Knight walked away from Albert and stumbled up the front steps and let himself into the house. There was a robot, with a vacuum cleaner for an arm, cleaning the rug. There was a robot, with brushes instead of fingers, painting the woodwork—and very neatly, too. There was a robot, with scrub-brush hands, scouring the fireplace bricks.

Grace was singing in the studio.

He went to the studio door and looked in.

"Oh, it's you," she said. "When did you get back, dear? I'll be out in an hour or so. I'm working on this seascape and the water is so stubborn. I don't want to leave it right now. I'm afraid I'll lose the feel of it."

Knight retreated to the living room and found himself a chair that was not undergoing immediate attention from a robot.

"Beer," he said, wondering what would happen.

A robot scampered out of the kitchen—a barrel-bellied robot with a spigot at the bottom of the barrel and a row of shiny copper mugs on his chest.

He drew a beer for Knight. It was cold and it tasted good.

Knight sat and drank the beer and, through the window, he saw that Albert's defense force had taken up strategic positions again.

This was a pretty kettle of fish. If the decision went against him and How-2 Kits came to claim its property, he would be sitting smack dab in the middle of the most fantastic civil war in all of mankind's history. He tried to imagine what kind of charge might be brought against him if such a war erupted. Armed insurrection, resisting arrest, inciting to riot—they would get him on one charge or another—that is, of course, *if* he survived.

He turned on the television set and leaned back to watch.

A pimply-faced newscaster was working himself into a journalistic lather. ". . . all business virtually at a standstill. Many industrialists are wondering, in case Knight wins, if they may not have to fight long, costly legal actions in an attempt to prove that their automatic setups are not robots, but machines. There is no doubt that much of the automatic industrial system consists of machines, but in every instance there are intelligent robotic units installed in key positions. If these units are classified as robots, industrialists might face heavy damage suits, if not criminal action, for illegal restraint of person.

"In Washington, there are continuing consultations. The Treasury is worried over the loss of taxes, but there are other governmental problems causing even more concern. Citizenship, for example. Would a ruling for Knight mean that all robots would automatically be declared citizens?

"The politicians have their worries, too. Faced with a new category of voters, all of them are wondering how to go about the job of winning the robot vote."

Knight turned it off and settled down to enjoy another bottle of beer.

"Good?" asked the beer robot.

"Excellent," said Knight.

The days went past. Tension built up.

Lee and the lawyer robots were given police protection. In some regions, robots banded together and fled into the hills fearful of violence. Entire automatic systems went on strike in a number of industries, demanding recognition and bargaining rights. The governors in half a dozen states put the militia on alert. A new show, *Citizen Robot*, opened on Broadway and was screamed down by the critics, while the public bought up tickets for a year ahead.

The day of decision came.

Knight sat in front of his television set and waited for the judge to make his appearance. Behind him, he heard the bustle of the ever-present robots. In the studio, Grace was singing happily. He caught himself wondering how much longer her painting would continue. It had lasted longer than most of her other interests and he'd talked a day or two before with Albert about building a gallery to hang her canvases in, so the house would be less cluttered up.

The judge came onto the screen. He looked, thought Knight, like a man who did not believe in ghosts and then had seen one.

"This is the hardest decision I have ever made," he said tiredly, "for, in following the letter of the law, I fear I may be subverting its spirit.

"After long days of earnest consideration of both the law and evidence as presented in this case, I find for the defendant, Gordon Knight.

"And, while the decision is limited to that finding alone, I feel it is my clear and simple duty to give some attention to the other issue which became involved in this litigation. The decision, on the face of it, takes account of the fact that the defense proved robots are not property, therefore cannot be owned and that it thus would have been impossible for the defendant to have stolen one.

"But in proving this point to the satisfaction of this court, the precedent is set for much more sweeping conclusions. If robots are not property, they cannot be taxed as property. In that case, they must be people, which means that they may enjoy all the rights and privileges and be subjected to the same duties and responsibilities as the human race.

"I cannot rule otherwise. However, the ruling outrages my social conscience. This is the first time in my entire professional life that I have ever hoped some higher court, with a wisdom greater than my own, may see fit to reverse my decision!"

Knight got up and walked out of the house and into the hundred-acre garden, its beauty marred at the moment by the twelve-foot fence.

The trial had ended perfectly. He was free of the charge brought against him, and he did not have to pay the taxes, and Albert and the other robots were free agents and could do anything they wanted.

He found a stone bench and sat down upon it and stared out

across the lake. It was beautiful, he thought, just the way he had dreamed it—maybe even better than that—the walks and bridges, the flower beds and rock gardens, the anchored model ships swinging in the wind on the dimpling lake.

He sat and looked at it and, while it was beautiful, he found he was not proud of it, that he took little pleasure in it.

He lifted his hands out of his lap and stared at them and curved his fingers as if he were grasping a tool. But they were empty. And he knew why he had no interest in the garden and no pleasure in it.

Model trains, he thought. Archery. A mechanobiologic dog. Making pottery. Eight rooms tacked onto the house.

Would he ever be able to console himself again with a model train or an amateurish triumph in ceramics? Even if he could, would he be allowed to?

He rose slowly and headed back to the house. Arriving there, he hesitated, feeling useless and unnecessary.

He finally took the ramp down into the basement.

Albert met him at its foot and threw his arms around him. "We did it, Boss! I *knew* we would do it!"

He pushed Knight out to arm's length and held him by the shoulders. "We'll never leave you, Boss. We'll stay and work for you. You'll never need to do another thing. We'll do it all for you!"

"Albert—"

"That's all right, Boss. You won't have to worry about a thing. We'll lick the money problem. We'll make a lot of lawyer robots and we'll charge good stiff fees."

"But don't you see . . ."

"First, though," said Albert, "we're going to get an injunction to preserve our birthright. We're made of steel and glass and copper and so forth, right? Well, we can't allow humans to waste the matter we're made of—or the energy, either, that keeps us alive. I tell you, Boss, we can't lose!"

Sitting down wearily on the ramp, Knight faced a sign that Albert had just finished painting. It read, in handsome gold lettering, outlined sharply in black:

ANSON, ALBERT, ABNER,
ANGUS & ASSOCIATES
ATTORNEYS AT LAW

"And then, Boss," said Albert, "we'll take over How-2 Kits, Inc.

They won't be able to stay in business after this. We've got a double-barreled idea, Boss. We'll build robots. Lots of robots. Can't have too many, I always say. And we don't want to let you humans down, so we'll go on manufacturing How-2 Kits only they'll be pre-assembled to save you the trouble of putting them together. What do you think of that as a start?"

"Great," Knight whispered.

"We've got everything worked out, Boss. You won't have to worry about a thing the rest of your life."

"No," said Knight. "Not a thing."

Punishment

In the 1860s both Victor Hugo and Fëdor Dostoevski wrote classic novels of punishment. But unlike *Les Misérables* and *Crime and Punishment*, prison is the primary setting for most works of this genre. The four popular themes of prison stories—social exposé, riot, escape, and the tribulations of an innocent man (or woman)—seem rather limited, at least in their Earthbound versions. And, in this century, they have been presented most effectively in films such as *I Am a Fugitive from a Chain Gang* (1932), *20,000 Years in Sing Sing* (1933), *Each Dawn I Die* (1939), and *Cool Hand Luke* (1967).

Numerous science fiction stories consider punishment, and suggestions about future penology include such original ideas as sending criminals back to the Paleozoic Era, giving them foul odors, and having them followed by vengeful robots. In the following work, however, William Tenn develops an exotic approach that might even work today.

Time in Advance

WILLIAM TENN

Twenty minutes after the convict ship landed at the New York Spaceport, reporters were allowed aboard. They came boiling up the main corridor, pushing against the heavily armed guards who were conducting them, the feature-story men and by-line columnists in the lead, the TV people with their portable but still-heavy equipment cursing along behind.

As they went, they passed little groups of spacemen in the black-and-red uniform of the Interstellar Prison Service walking rapidly in the opposite direction, on their way to enjoy five days of planetside leave before the ship roared away once more with a new cargo of convicts.

The impatient journalists barely glanced at these drab personalities who were spending their lives in a continuous shuttle from one end of the Galaxy to the other. After all, the life and adventures of an IPS man had been done thousands of times, done to death. The big story lay ahead.

In the very belly of the ship, the guards slid apart two enormous sliding doors—and quickly stepped aside to avoid being trampled. The reporters almost flung themselves against the iron bars that ran from floor to ceiling and completely shut off the great prison chamber. Their eager, darting stares were met with at most a few curious glances from the men in coarse gray suits who lay or sat in the tiers of bunks that rose in row after sternly functional row all the way down the cargo hold. Each man clutched—and some caressed—a small package neatly wrapped in plain brown paper.

The chief guard ambled up on the other side of the bars, picking the morning's breakfast out of his front teeth. "Hi, boys," he said. "Who're you looking for—as if I didn't know?"

One of the older, more famous columnists held the palm of his hand up warningly. "Look, Anderson: no games. The ship's been almost a half-hour late in landing and we were stalled for fifteen minutes at the gangplank. Now where the hell are they?"

Anderson watched the TV crews shoulder a place for themselves and their equipment right up to the barrier. He tugged a last bit of food out of one of his molars.

"Ghouls," he muttered. "A bunch of grave-happy, funeral-hungry ghouls." Then he hefted his club experimentally a couple of times and clattered it back and forth against the bars. "Crandall!" he bellowed. "Henck! Front and center!"

The cry was picked up by the guards strolling about, steadily, measuredly, club-twirlingly, inside the prison pen. "Crandall! Henck! Front and center!" It went ricocheting authoritatively up and down the tremendous curved walls. "Crandall! Henck! Front and center!"

Nicholas Crandall sat up cross-legged in his bunk on the fifth tier and grimaced. He had been dozing and now he rubbed a hand across his eyes to erase the sleep. There were three parallel scars across the back of his hand, old and brown and straight scars such as an animal's claws might rake out. There was also a curious zig-zag scar just above his eyes that had a more reddish novelty. And there was a tiny, perfectly round hole in the middle of his left ear which, after coming fully awake, he scratched in annoyance.

"Reception committee," he grumbled. "Might have known. Same old goddam Earth as ever."

He flipped over on his stomach and reached down to pat the face of the little man snoring on the bunk immediately under him. "Otto," he called. "Blotto Otto—up and at 'em! They want us."

Henck immediately sat up in the same cross-legged fashion, even before his eyes had opened. His right hand went to his throat where there was a little network of zigzag scars of the same color and size as the one Crandall had on his forehead. The hand was missing an index and forefinger.

"Henck here, sir," he said thickly, then shook his head and stared up at Crandall. "Oh—Nick. What's up?"

"We've arrived, Blotto Otto," the taller man said from the bunk above. "We're on Earth and they're getting our discharges ready. In about half an hour, you'll be able to wrap that tongue of yours around as much brandy, beer, vodka and rotgut whiskey as you can pay for. No more prison-brew, no more raisin-jack from a tin can under the bed, Blotto Otto."

Henck grunted and flopped down on his back again. "In half an hour, but not now, so why did you have to go and wake me up? What do you take me for, some dewy, post-crime, petty-larceny kid, sweating out my discharge with my eyes open and my gut wriggling? Hey, Nick, I was dreaming of a new way to get Elsa, a brand-new, really ugly way."

"The screws are in an uproar," Crandall told him, still in a low, patient voice. "Hear them? They want us, you and me."

Henck sat up again, listened a moment, and nodded. "Why is it," he asked, "that only space-screws have voices like that?"

"It's a requirement of the service," Crandall assured him. "You've got to be at least a minimum height, have a minimum education and with a minimum nasty voice of just the right ear-splitting quality before you can get to be a space-screw. Otherwise, no matter how vicious a personality you have, you are just plain out of luck and have to stay behind on Earth and go on getting your kicks by running down slowpoke 'copters driven by old ladies."

A guard stopped below, banged angrily at one of the metal posts that supported their tier of bunks. "Crandall! Henck! You're still convicts, don't you forget that! If you don't front-and-center in a double-time hurry, I'll climb up there and work you over once more for old-time's sake!"

"Yes, *sir!* Coming, *sir!*" they said in immediate, mumbling unison and began climbing down from bunk to bunk, each still clutching the brown-paper package that contained the clothes they had once worn as free men and would shortly be allowed to wear again.

"Listen, Otto." Crandall leaned down as they climbed and brought his lips close to the little man's ear in the rapid-fire, extremely low-pitched prison whisper. "They're taking us to meet the television and news boys. We're going to be asked a lot of questions. One thing you want to be sure to keep your lip buttoned about—"

"Television and news? Why us? What do they want with us?"

"Because we're celebrities, knockhead! We've seen it through for the big rap and come out on the other side. How many men do you think have made it? But *listen*, will you? If they ask you who it is you're after, you just shut up and smile. You don't answer that question. Got that? You don't tell them whose murder you were sentenced for, no matter what they say. They can't make you. That's the law."

Henck paused a moment, one and a half bunks from the floor. "But, Nick, *Elsa* knows! I told her that day, just before I turned myself in. She knows I wouldn't take a murder rap for anyone but her!"

"She knows, she knows, of *course* she knows!" Crandall swore briefly and almost inaudibly. "But she can't *prove* it, you goddam human blotter! Once you say so in public, though, she's entitled to arm herself and shoot you down on sight—pleading self-defense. And till you say so, she can't; she's still your poor wife whom you've promised to love, honor and cherish. As far as the world is concerned—"

The guard reached up with his club and jolted them both angrily across the back. They dropped to the floor and cringed as he snarled over them: "Did I say you could have a talk-party? *Did I?* If we have any time left before you get your discharge, I'm taking you cuties into the guard-room for one last big going-over. Now pick them up and put them down!"

They scuttled in front of him obediently, like a pair of chickens before a snapping collie. At the barred gate near the end of the prison hold, he saluted and said: "Pre-criminals Nicholas Crandall and Otto Henck, sir."

Chief Guard Anderson wiped the salute back at him carelessly. "These gentlemen want to ask you fellas a couple of questions. Won't hurt you to answer. That's all, O'Brien."

His voice was very jovial. He was wearing a big, gentle, half-moon smile. As the subordinate guard saluted and moved away, Crandall let his mind regurgitate memories of Anderson all through this month-long trip from Proxima Centaurus. Anderson nodding thoughtfully as that poor Minelli—Steve Minelli, hadn't that been his name?—was made to run through a gauntlet of club-swinging guards for going to the toilet without permission. Anderson chuckling just a moment before he'd kicked a gray-headed convict in the groin for talking on the chow-line. Anderson—

Well, the guy had guts, anyway, knowing that his ship carried two pre-criminals who had served out a murder sentence. But he probably also knew that they wouldn't waste the murder on him, however viciously he acted. A man doesn't volunteer for a hitch in hell just so he can knock off one of the devils.

"Do we have to answer these questions, sir?" Crandall asked cautiously, tentatively.

The chief guard's smile lost the tiniest bit of its curvature. "I said it wouldn't hurt you, didn't I? But other things might. They *still* might, Crandall. I'd like to do these gentlemen from the press a favor, so you be nice and cooperative, eh?" He gestured with his chin, ever so slightly, in the direction of the guard-room and hefted his club a bit.

"Yes, sir," Crandall said, while Henck nodded violently. "We'll be cooperative, sir."

Dammit, he thought, *if only I didn't have such a use for that murder! Let's keep remembering Stephanson, boy, no one but Stephanson! Not Anderson, not O'Brien, not anybody else: the name under discussion is Frederick Stoddard Stephanson!*

While the television men on the other side of the bars were fussing their equipment into position, the two convicts answered the preliminary, inevitable questions of the feature writers:

"How does it feel to be back?"

"Fine, just fine."

"What's the first thing you're going to do when you get your discharge?"

"Eat a good meal." (From Crandall.)

"Get roaring drunk." (From Henck.)

"Careful you don't wind up right behind bars again as a postcriminal." (From one of the feature writers.) A good-natured laugh in which all of them, the newsmen, Chief Guard Anderson, and Crandall and Henck, participated.

"How were you treated while you were prisoners?"

"Oh, pretty good." (From both of them, concurrent with a thoughtful glance at Anderson's club.)

"Either of you care to tell us who you're going to murder?"

(Silence.)

"Either of you changed your mind and decided not to commit the murder?"

(Crandall looked thoughtfully up, while Henck looked thoughtfully down.) Another general laugh, a bit more uneasy this time, Crandall and Henck not participating.

"All right, we're set. Look this way, please," the television announcer broke in. "And smile, men—let's have a really *big* smile."

Crandall and Henck dutifully emitted big smiles, which made

three smiles, for Anderson had moved into the cheerful little group.

The two cameras shot out of the grasp of their technicians, one hovering over them, one moving restlessly before their faces, both controlled, at a distance, by the little boxes of switches in the cameramen's hands. A red bulb in the nose of one of the cameras lit up.

"Here we are, ladies and gentlemen of the television audience," the announcer exuded in a lavish voice. "We are on board the convict ship *Jean Valjean,* which has just landed at the New York Spaceport. We are here to meet two men—two of the rare men who have managed to serve all of a voluntary sentence for murder and thus are legally entitled to commit one murder apiece.

"In just a few moments, they will be discharged after having served out seven full years on the convict planets—and they will be free to kill any man or woman in the Solar System with absolutely no fear of any kind of retribution. Take a good look at them, ladies and gentlemen of the television audience—it might be you they are after!"

After this cheering thought, the announcer let a moment or two elapse while the cameras let their lenses stare at the two men in prison gray. Then he stepped into range himself and addressed the smaller man.

"What is your name, sir?" he asked.

"Pre-criminal Otto Henck, 525514," Blotto Otto responded automatically, though not able to repress a bit of a start at the *sir*.

"How does it feel to be back?"

"Fine, just fine."

"What's the first thing you're going to do when you get your discharge?"

Henck hesitated, then said, "Eat a good meal," after a shy look at Crandall.

"How were you treated while you were a prisoner?"

"Oh, pretty good. As good as you could expect."

"As good as a criminal could expect, eh? Although you're not really a criminal yet, are you? You're a pre-criminal."

Henck smiled as if this were the first time he was hearing the term. "That's right, sir. I'm a pre-criminal."

"Want to tell the audience who the person is you're going to become a criminal for?"

Henck looked reproachfully at the announcer, who chuckled throatily—and alone.

"Or if you've changed your mind about him or her?" There was a pause. Then the announcer said a little nervously: "You've served seven years on danger-filled, alien planets, preparing them for human colonization. That's the maximum sentence the law allows, isn't it?"

"That's right, sir. With the pre-criminal discount for serving the sentence in advance, seven years is the most you can get for murder."

"Bet you're glad we're not back in the days of capital punishment, eh? That would make the whole thing impractical, wouldn't it? Now, Mr. Henck—or pre-criminal Henck, I guess I should still call you—suppose you tell the ladies and gentlemen of our television audience: What was the most horrifying experience you had while you were serving your sentence?"

"Well," Otto Henck considered carefully. "About the worst of the lot, I guess, was the time on Antares VIII, the second prison camp I was in, when the big wasps started to spawn. They got a wasp on Antares VIII, see, that's about a hundred times the size of—"

"Is that how you lost two fingers on your right hand?"

Henck brought his hand up and studied it for a moment. "No. The forefinger—I lost the forefinger on Rigel XII. We were building the first prison camp on the planet and I dug up a funny kind of red rock that had all sorts of little bumps on it. I poked it, kind of—you know, just to see how hard it was or something—and the tip of my finger disappeared. *Pow*—just like that. Later on, the whole finger got infected and the medics had to cut it off.

"It turned out I was lucky, though; some of the men—the convicts, I mean—ran into bigger rocks than the one I found. Those guys lost arms, legs—one guy even got swallowed whole. They weren't really rocks, see. They were alive—they were alive and hungry! Rigel XII was lousy with them. The middle finger—I lost the middle finger in a dumb kind of accident on board ship while we were being moved to—"

The announcer nodded intelligently, cleared his throat and said: "But those wasps, those giant wasps on Antares VIII—they were the worst?"

Blotto Otto blinked at him for a moment before he found the conversation again.

"Oh. They sure were! They were used to laying their eggs in a kind of monkey they have on Antares VIII, see? It was real rough on the monkey, but that's how the baby wasps got their food while they were growing up. Well, we get out there and it turns out that the wasps can't see any difference between those Antares monkeys and human beings. First thing you know, guys start collapsing all over the place and when they're taken to the dispensary for an X-ray, the medics see that they're completely crammed—"

"Thank you very much, Mr. Henck, but Herkimer's Wasp has already been seen by and described to our audience at least three times in the past on the Interstellar Travelogue, which is carried by this network, as you ladies and gentlemen no doubt remember, on Wednesday evening from seven to seven-thirty P.M. terrestrial standard time. And now, Mr. Crandall, let me ask you, sir: How does it feel to be back?"

Crandall stepped up and was put through almost exactly the same verbal paces as his fellow prisoner.

There was one major difference. The announcer asked him if he expected to find Earth much changed. Crandall started to shrug, then abruptly relaxed and grinned. He was careful to make the grin an extremely wide one, exposing a maximum of tooth and a minimum of mirth.

"There's one big change I can see already," he said. "The way those cameras float around and are controlled from a little switch-box in the cameraman's hand. That gimmick wasn't around the day I left. Whoever invented it must have been pretty clever."

"Oh, yes?" The announcer glanced briefly backward. "You mean the Stephanson Remote Control Switch? It was invented by Frederick Stoddard Stephanson about five years ago—Was it five years, Don?"

"Six years," said the cameraman. "Went on the market five years ago."

"It was *invented* six years ago," the announcer translated. "It went on the market *five* years ago."

Crandall nodded. "Well, this Frederick Stoddard Stephanson must be a clever man, a very clever man." And he grinned again into the cameras. *Look at my teeth,* he thought to himself. *I know you're watching, Freddy. Look at my teeth and shiver.*

The announcer seemed a bit disconcerted. "Yes," he said. "Exactly. Now, Mr. Crandall, what would you describe as the most horrifying experience in your entire . . ."

After the TV men had rolled up their equipment and departed, the two pre-criminals were subjected to a final barrage of questions from the feature writers and columnists in search of odd shreds of color.

"What about the women in your life?" "What books, what hobbies, what amusements filled your time?" "Did you find out that there are no atheists on convict planets?" "If you had the whole thing to do over again—"

As he answered, drably, courteously, Nicholas Crandall was thinking about Frederick Stoddard Stephanson seated in front of his luxurious wall-size television set.

Would Stephanson have clicked it off by now? Would he be sitting there, staring at the blank screen, pondering the plans of the man who had outlived odds estimated at ten thousand to one and returned after seven full, unbelievable years in the prison camps of four insane planets?

Would Stephanson be examining his blaster with sucked-in lips—the blaster that he might use only in an open-and-shut situation of self-defense? Otherwise, he would incur the full post-criminal sentence for murder, which, without the fifty per cent discount for punishment voluntarily undergone in advance of the crime, was as much as fourteen years in the many-pronged hell from which Crandall had just returned?

Or would Stephanson be sitting, slumped in an expensive bubblechair, glumly watching a still-active screen, frightened out of his wits but still unable to tear himself away from the well-organized program the network had no doubt built around the return of two—count 'em: *two!*—homicidal pre-criminals?

At the moment, in all probability, the screen was showing an interview with some Earthside official of the Interstellar Prison Service, an expansive public relations character who had learned to talk in sociology.

"Tell me, Mr. Public Relations," the announcer would ask (a different announcer, more serious, more intellectual), "how often do pre-criminals serve out a sentence for murder and return?"

"According to statistics"—a rustle of papers at this point and a penetrating glance downward—"according to statistics, we may expect a man who has served a full sentence for murder, with the 50 per cent pre-criminal discount, to return only once in 11.7 years on the average."

"You would say, then, wouldn't you, Mr. Public Relations, that the return of two such men on the same day is a rather unusual situation?"

"*Highly* unusual or you television fellas wouldn't be in such a fuss over it." A thick chuckle here, which the announcer dutifully echoes.

"And what, Mr. Public Relations, happens to the others who don't return?"

A large, well-fed hand gestures urbanely. "They get killed. Or they give up. Those are the only two alternatives. Seven years is a long time to spend on those convict planets. The work schedule isn't for sissies and neither are the life-forms they encounter—the big man-eating ones as well as the small virus-sized types.

"That's why prison guards get such high salaries and such long leaves. In a sense, you know, we haven't really abolished capital punishment; we've substituted a socially useful form of Russian Roulette for it. Any man who commits or pre-commits one of a group of particularly reprehensible crimes is sent off to a planet where his services will benefit humanity and where he's forced to take his chances on coming back in one piece, if at all. The more serious the crime, the longer the sentence and, therefore, the more remote the chances."

"I see. Now, Mr. Public Relations, you say they either get killed or they give up. Would you explain to the audience, if you please, just how they give up and what happens if they do?"

Here a sitting back in the chair, a locking of pudgy fingers over paunch. "You see, any pre-criminal may apply to his warden for immediate abrogation of sentence. It's just a matter of filling out the necessary forms. He's pulled off work detail right then and there and is sent home on the very next ship out of the place. The catch is this: Every bit of time he's served up to that point is canceled—he gets nothing for it.

"If he commits an actual crime after being freed, he has to serve the full sentence. If he wants to be committed as a pre-criminal again, he has to start serving the sentence, with the discount, from the beginning. Three out of every four pre-criminals apply for abrogation of sentence in their very first year. You get a bellyful fast in those places."

"I guess you certainly do," agrees the announcer. "What about the discount, Mr. Public Relations? Aren't there people who feel that's offering the pre-criminal too much inducement?"

The barest grimace of anger flows across the sleek face, to be succeeded by a warm, contemptuous smile. "Those are people, I'm afraid, who, however well-intentioned, are not well versed in the facts of modern criminology and penology. We don't want to discourage pre-criminals; we want to *encourage* them to turn themselves in.

"Remember what I said about three out of four applying for abrogation of sentence in their very first year? Now these are individuals who were sensible enough to try to get a discount on their sentence. Are they likely to be foolish enough to risk twice as much when they have found out conclusively they can't stand a bare twelve months of it? Not to mention what they have discovered about the value of human life, the necessity for social cooperation and the general desirability of civilized processes on those worlds where simple survival is practically a matter of a sweepstakes ticket.

"The man who doesn't apply for abrogation of sentence? Well, he has that much more time to let the desire to commit the crime go cold—and that much greater likelihood of getting killed with nothing to show for it. Therefore, so few pre-criminals in *any* of the categories return to tell the tale and do the deed that the social profit is absolutely enormous! Let me give you a few figures.

"Using the Lazarus Scale, it has been estimated that the decline in premeditated homicides alone, since the institution of the pre-criminal discount, has been forty-one per cent on Earth, thirty-three and a third per cent on Venus, twenty-seven per cent—"

Cold comfort, chillingly cold comfort, that would be to Stephanson, Nicholas Crandall reflected pleasurably, those forty-one per cents and thirty-three and a third per cents. Crandall's was the balancing statistic: the man who wanted to murder, and for good and sufficient cause, one Frederick Stoddard Stephanson. He was a leftover fraction on a page of reductions and cancellations—he had returned, astonishingly, unbelievably, after seven years to collect the merchandise for which he had paid in advance.

He and Henck. Two ridiculously long long-shots. Henck's wife

Elsa—was she, too, sitting in a kind of bird-hypnotized-by-a-snake fashion before her television set, hoping dimly and desperately that some comment of the Interstellar Prison Service official would show her how to evade her fate, how to get out from under the ridiculously rare disaster that was about to happen to her?

Well, Elsa was Blotto Otto's affair. Let him enjoy it in his own way; he'd paid enough for the privilege. But Stephanson was Crandall's.

Oh, let the arrogant bean-pole sweat, he prayed. *Let me take my time and let him sweat!*

The newsman kept squeezing them for story angles until a loudspeaker in the overhead suddenly cleared its diaphragm and announced:

"Prisoners, prepare for discharge! You will proceed to the ship warden's office in groups of ten, as your name is called. Convict ship discipline will be maintained throughout. Arthur, Augluk, Crandall, Ferrara, Fu-Yen, Garfinkel, Gomez, Graham, Henck—"

A half hour later, they were walking down the main corridor of the ship in their civilian clothes. They showed their discharges to the guard at the gangplank, smiled still cringingly back at Anderson, who called from a porthole, "Hey, fellas, come back soon!" and trotted down the incline to the surface of a planet they had not seen for seven agonizing and horror-crowded years.

There were a few reporters and photographers still waiting for them, and one TV crew which had been left behind to let the world see how they looked at the moment of freedom.

Questions, more questions to answer, which they could afford to be brusque about, although brusqueness to any but fellow prisoners still came hard.

Fortunately, the newsmen got interested in another pre-criminal who was with them. Fu-Yen had completed the discounted sentence of two years for aggravated assault and battery. He had also lost both arms and one leg to a corrosive moss on Procyon III just before the end of his term and came limping down the gangplank on one real and one artificial leg, unable to grasp the hand-rails.

As he was being asked, with a good deal of interest, just how he intended to commit simple assault and battery, let alone the serious kind, with his present limited resources, Crandall nudged Henck and they climbed quickly into one of the many hovering gyrocabs.

They told the driver to take them to a bar—any quiet bar—in the city.

Blotto Otto almost went to pieces under the impact of actual free choice. "I can't do it," he whispered. "Nick, there's just too damn much to drink!"

Crandall settled it by ordering for him. "Two double scotches," he told the waitress. "Nothing else."

When the scotch came, Blotto Otto stared at it with the kind of affectionate and wistful astonishment a man might show toward an adolescent son whom he saw last as a babe in arms. He put out a gingerly, trembling hand.

"Here's death to our enemies," Crandall said, and tossed his down. He watched Otto sip slowly and carefully, tasting each individual drop.

"You'd better take it easy," he warned. "Elsa might have no more trouble from you than bringing flowers every visiting day to the alcoholic ward."

"No fear," Blotto Otto growled into his empty glass. "I was weaned on this stuff. And, anyway, it's the last drink I have until I dump her. That's the way I've been figuring it, Nick: one drink to celebrate, then Elsa. I didn't go through those seven years to mess myself up at the payoff."

He set the glass down. "Seven years in one steaming hell after another. And before that, twelve years with Elsa. Twelve years with her pulling every dirty trick in the book on me, laughing in my face, telling me she was my wife and had me legally where she wanted me, that I was gonna support her the way she wanted to be supported and I was gonna like it. And if I dared to get off my knees and stand on my hind legs, *pow,* she found a way to get me arrested.

"The weeks I spent in the cooler, in the workhouse, until Elsa would tell the judge maybe I'd learned my lesson, she was willing to give me one more chance! And me begging for a divorce on my knees—hell, on my belly!—no children, she's able-bodied, she's young, and her laughing in my face. When she wanted me in the cooler, see, then she's crying in front of the judge; but when we're alone, she's always laughing her head off to see me squirm.

"I supported her, Nick. Honest, I gave her almost every cent I made, but that wasn't enough. She liked to see me squirm; she *told* me she did. Well, who's squirming now?" He grunted deep in his throat. "Marriage—it's for chumps!"

Crandall looked out of the open window he was sitting against, down through the dizzy, busy levels of Metropolitan New York.

"Maybe it is," he said thoughtfully. "I wouldn't know. My marriage was good while it lasted, five years of it. Then, all of a sudden, it wasn't good any more, just so much rancid butter."

"At least she gave you a divorce," said Henck. "She didn't take you."

"Oh, Polly wasn't the kind of girl to take anyone. A little mixed up, but maybe no more than I was. Pretty Polly, I called her; Big Nick, she called me. The starlight faded and so did I, I guess. I was still knocking myself out then trying to make a go out of the wholesale electronics business with Irv. Anyone could tell I wasn't cut out to be a millionaire. Maybe that was it. Anyway, Polly wanted out and I gave it to her. We parted friends. I wonder, every once in a while, what she's—"

There was a slight splashy noise, like a seal's flipper making a gesture in the water. Crandall's eyes came back to the table a moment after the green, melonlike ball had hit it. And, at the same instant, Henck's hand had swept the ball up and hurled it through the window. The long, green threads streamed out of the ball, but by then it was falling down the side of the enormous building and the threads found no living flesh to take root in.

From the corner of his eye, Crandall had seen a man bolt out of the bar. By the way people kept looking back and forth fearfully from their table to the open doorway, he deduced that the man had thrown it. Evidently Stephanson had thought it worthwhile to have Crandall followed and neutralized.

Blotto Otto saw no point in preening over his reflexes. The two of them had learned to move fast a long time ago—over a lot of dead bodies. "A Venusian dandelion bomb," he observed. "Well, at least the guy doesn't want to kill you, Nick. He just wants to cripple you."

"That would be Stephanson's style," Crandall agreed, as they paid their check and walked past the faces which were just now beginning to turn white. "He'd never do it himself. He'd hire a bully-boy. And he'd do the hiring through an intermediary just in case the bully-boy ever got caught and blabbed. But that still wouldn't be safe enough: he wouldn't want to risk a post-criminal murder charge.

"A dose of Venusian dandelion, he'd figure, and he wouldn't have to worry about me for the rest of my life. He might even come to visit me in the home for incurables—like the way he sent me a card every Christmas of my sentence. Always the same message: 'Still mad? Love, Freddy.'"

"Quite a guy, this Stephanson," Blotto Otto said, peering around the entrance carefully before stepping out of the bar and onto the fifteenth level walkway.

"Yeah, quite a guy. He's got the world by the tail and every once in a while, just for fun, he twists the tail. I learned how he operated when we were roommates way back in college, but do you think that did me any good? I ran into him just when that wholesale electronics business with Irv was really falling apart, about two years after I broke up with Polly.

"I was feeling blue and I wanted to talk to someone, so I told him all about how my partner was a penny-watcher and I was a big dreamer, and how between us we were turning a possible nice small business into a definite big bankruptcy. And then I got onto this remote-control switch I'd been fooling around with and how I wished I had time to develop it."

Blotto Otto kept glancing around uneasily, not from dread of another assassin, but out of the unexpected sensation of doing so much walking of his own free will. Several passersby turned around to have another stare at their out-of-fashion knee-length tunics.

"So there I was," Crandall went on. "I was a fool, I know, but take my word, Otto, you have no idea how persuasive and friendly a guy like Freddy Stephanson can be. He tells me he has this house in the country he isn't using right now and there's a complete electronics lab in the basement. It's all mine, if I want it, as long as I want it, starting next week; all I have to worry about is feeding myself. And he doesn't want any rent or anything—it's for old times' sake and because he wants to see me do something really big in the world.

"How smart could I be with a con-artist like that? It wasn't till two years later that I realized he must have had the electronics lab installed the same week I was asking Irv to buy me out of the business for a couple of hundred credits. After all, what would Stephanson, the owner of a brokerage firm, be doing with an electronics lab of his own? But who figures such things when an old roommate's so warm and friendly and interested in you?"

Otto sighed. "So he comes up to see you every few weeks. And then, about a month after you've got it all finished and working, he locks you out of the place and moves all your papers and stuff to another joint. And he tells you he'll have it patented long before you can get it all down on paper again, and anyhow it was his place—he can always claim he was subsidizing you. Then he laughs in your face, just like Elsa. Huh, Nick?"

Crandall bit his lip as he realized how thoroughly Otto Henck must have memorized the material. How many times had they gone over each other's planned revenge and the situations which had motivated it? How many times had they told and retold the same bitter stories to each other, elicited the same responses from each other, the same questions, the same agreements and even the very same disagreements?

Suddenly, he wanted to get away from the little man and enjoy the luxury of loneliness. He saw the sparkling roof of a hotel two levels down.

"Think I'll move into that. Ought to be thinking about a place to sleep tonight."

Otto nodded at his mood rather than at his statement. "Sure. I know just how you feel. But that's pretty plush, Nick: The Capricorn-Ritz. At least twelve credits a day."

"So what? I can live high for a week, if I want to. And with my background, I can always pick up a fast job as soon as I get low. I want something plush for tonight, Blotto Otto."

"Okay, okay. You got my address, huh, Nick? I'll be at my cousin's place."

"I have it, all right. Luck with Elsa, Otto."

"Thanks. Luck with Freddy. Uh—so long." The little man turned abruptly and entered a main street elevator. When the doors slid shut, Crandall found that he was feeling very uncomfortable. Henck had meant more to him than his own brother. Well, after all, he'd been with Henck day and night for a long time now. And he hadn't seen Dan for—how long was it?—almost nine years.

He reflected on how little he was attached to the world, if you excluded the rather negative desire of removing Stephanson from it. One thing he should get soon was a girl—almost any girl.

But, come to think of it, there was something he needed even more.

He walked swiftly to the nearest drugstore. It was a large one, part of a chain. And there, featured prominently in the window, was exactly what he wanted.

At the cigar counter, he said to the clerk: "It's pretty cheap. Do they work all right?"

The clerk drew himself up. "Before we put an item on sale, sir, it is tested thoroughly. We are the largest retail outlet in the Solar System—*that's* why it's so cheap."

"All right. Give me the medium-sized one. And two boxes of cartridges."

With the blaster in his possession, he felt much more secure. He had a good deal of confidence—based on years of escaping creatures with hair-trigger nervous systems—in his ability to duck and wriggle and jump to one side. But it would be nice to be able to fight back. And how did he know how soon Stephanson would try again?

He registered under a false name, a ruse he thought of at the last moment. That it wasn't worth much, as ruses went, he found out when the bellhop, after being tipped, said: "Thank you, Mr. Crandall. I hope you get your victim, sir."

So he was a celebrity. Probably everyone in the world knew exactly what he looked like. All of which might make it a bit more difficult to get at Stephanson.

While he was taking a bath, he asked the television set to check through Information's file on the man. Stephanson had been rich and moderately important seven years ago; with the Stephanson Switch—how do you like that, the *Stephanson* Switch!—he must be even richer now and much more important.

He was. The television set informed Crandall that in the last calendar month, there were sixteen news items relating to Frederick Stoddard Stephanson. Crandall considered, then asked for the most recent.

That was datelined today. "Frederick Stephanson, the president of the Stephanson Investment Trust and Stephanson Electronics Corporation, left early this morning for his hunting lodge in Central Tibet. He expects to remain there for at least—"

"That's enough!" Crandall called through the bathroom door.

Stephanson was scared! The arrogant bean-pole was frightened silly! That was something; in fact, it was a large part of the return on those seven years. Let him seethe in his own sweat for a while, until he found the actual killing, when it did come at last, almost welcome.

Crandall asked the set for the fresh news and was immediately treated to a bulletin about himself and how he had registered at the Capricorn-Ritz under the name of Alexander Smathers. "But neither is the correct name, ladies and gentlemen," the playback rolled out unctuously. "Neither Nicholas Crandall nor Alexander Smathers is the right name for this man. There is only one name for that man—and that name is death! Yes, the grim reaper has taken up residence at the Capricorn-Ritz Hotel tonight, and only he knows which one of us will not see another sunrise. That man, that grim reaper, that deputy of death, is the only one among us who knows—"

"Shut up!" Crandall yelled, exasperated. He had almost forgotten the kind of punishment a free man was forced to endure.

The private phone circuit on the television screen lit up. He dried himself, hurried into clothes and asked, "Who's calling?"

"Mrs. Nicholas Crandall," said the operator's voice.

He stared at the blank screen for a moment, absolutely thunderstruck. Polly! Where in the world had she come from? And how did she know where he was? No, the last part was easy—he was a celebrity.

"Put her on," he said at last.

Polly's face filled the screen. Crandall studied her quizzically. She'd aged a bit, but possibly it wasn't obvious at anything but this magnification.

As if she realized it herself, Polly adjusted the controls on her set and her face dwindled to life-size, the rest of her body as well as her surroundings coming into the picture. She was evidently in the living room of her home; it looked like a low-to-middle-income-range furnished apartment. But she looked good—awfully good. There were such warm memories . . .

"Hi, Polly. What's this all about? You're the last person I expected to call me."

"Hello, Nick." She lifted her hand to her mouth and stared over its knuckles for some time at him. Then: "Nick. Please. Please don't play games with me."

He dropped into a chair. "Huh?"

She began to cry. "Oh, Nick! *Don't!* Don't be that cruel! I know why you served that sentence—those seven years. The moment I heard your name today, I knew why you did it. But, Nick, it was only one man—just one man, Nick!"

"Just one man *what?*"

"It was just that one man I was unfaithful with. And I thought he loved me, Nick. I wouldn't have divorced you if I'd known what he was really like. But you know, Nick, don't you? You know how much he made me suffer. I've been punished enough. Don't kill me, Nick! Please don't kill me!"

"Listen, Polly," he began, completely confused. "Polly girl, for heaven's sake—"

"Nick!" she gulped hysterically. "Nick, it was over eleven years ago—ten, at least. Don't kill me for that, please, Nick! Nick, truly, I wasn't unfaithful to you for more than a year, two years at the most. Truly, Nick! And, Nick, it was only that one affair—the others didn't count. They were just—just casual things. They didn't matter at all, Nick! But don't kill me! Don't kill me!" She held both hands to her face and began rocking back and forth, moaning uncontrollably.

Crandall stared at her for a moment and moistened his lips. Then he said, "Whew!" and turned the set off. He leaned back in his chair. Again he said, "Whew!" and this time it hissed through his teeth.

Polly! Polly had been unfaithful during their marriage. For a year—no, two years! And—what had she said?—the others, the *others* had just been casual things!

The woman he had loved, the woman he suspected he had always loved, the woman he had given up with infinite regret and a deep sense of guilt when she had come to him and said that the business had taken the best part of him away from her, but that since it wasn't fair to ask him to give up something that obviously meant so much to him—

Pretty Polly. Polly girl. He'd never thought of another woman in all their time together. And if anyone, anyone at all, had ever suggested—had so much as *hinted*—he'd have used a monkey wrench on the meddler's face. He'd given her the divorce only because she'd asked for it, but he'd hoped that when the business got on its feet and Irv's bookkeeping end covered a wider stretch of it, they might get back together again. Then, of course, business grew worse, Irv's wife got sick and he put even less time in at the office and—

"I feel," he said to himself numbly, "as if I've just found out for certain that there is no Santa Claus. Not Polly, not all those good years! One affair! And the others were just casual things!"

The telephone circuit went off again. "Who is it?" he snarled.

"Mr. Edward Ballaskia."

"What's he want?" Not *Polly, not Pretty Polly!*

An extremely fat man came on the screen. He looked to right and left cautiously. "I must ask you, Mr. Crandall, if you are positive that this line isn't tapped."

"What the hell do you want?" Crandall found himself wishing that the fat man were here in person. He'd love to sail into somebody right now.

Mr. Edward Ballaskia shook his head disapprovingly, his jowls jiggling slowly behind the rest of his face. "Well, then, sir, if you won't give me your assurances, I am forced to take a chance. I am calling, Mr. Crandall, to ask you to forgive your enemies, to turn the other cheek. I am asking you to remember faith, hope and charity—and that the greatest of these is charity. In other words, sir, open your heart to him or her you intended to kill, understand the weaknesses which caused them to give offenses—and forgive them."

"Why should I?" Crandall demanded.

"Because it is to your profit to do so, sir. Not merely morally profitable—although let us not overlook the life of the spirit—but financially profitable. *Financially* profitable, Mr. Crandall."

"Would you kindly tell me what you are talking about?"

The fat man leaned forward and smiled confidentially. "If you can forgive the person who caused you to go off and suffer seven long, seven *miserable* years of acute discomfort, Mr. Crandall, I am prepared to make you a most attractive offer. You are entitled to commit one murder. I desire to have one murder committed. I am very wealthy. You, I judge—and please take no umbrage, sir—are very poor.

"I can make you comfortable for the rest of your life, extremely comfortable, Mr. Crandall, if only you will put aside your thoughts, your unworthy thoughts, of anger and personal vengeance. I have a business competitor, you see, who has been—"

Crandall turned him off. "Go serve your own seven years," he venomously told the blank screen. Then, suddenly, it was funny. He lay back in the chair and laughed his head off.

That butter-faced old slob! Quoting religious texts at him!

But the call had served a purpose. Somehow it put the scene with Polly in the perspective of ridicule. To think of the woman sitting in her frowsy little apartment, trembling over her dingy affairs of more than ten years ago! To think she was afraid he had bled and battled for seven years because of that!

He thought about it for a moment, then shrugged. "Well, anyway, I bet it did her good."

And now he was hungry.

He thought of having a meal sent up, just to avoid a possible rendezvous with another of Stephanson's ball-throwers, but decided against it. If Stephanson was really hunting him seriously, it would not be much of a job to have something put into the food he was sent. He'd be much safer eating in a restaurant chosen at random.

Besides, a few bright lights, a little gaiety, would be really welcome. This was his first night of freedom—and he had to wash that Polly taste out of his mouth.

He checked the corridor carefully before going out. There was nothing, but the action reminded him of a tiny planet near Vega where you made exactly the same precautionary gesture every time you emerged from one of the tunnels formed by the long, parallel lines of moist, carboniferous ferns.

Because if you didn't—well, there was an enormous leech-like mollusc that might be waiting there, a creature which could flip chunks of shell with prodigious force. The shell merely stunned its prey, but stunned it long enough for the leech to get in close.

And that leech could empty a man in ten minutes flat.

Once he'd been hit by a fragment of shell, and while he'd been lying there, Henck— Good old Blotto Otto! Crandall smiled. Was it possible that the two of them would look back on those hideous adventures, one day, with actual nostalgia, the kind of beery, pleasant memories that soldiers develop after even the ugliest of wars? Well, and if they did, they hadn't gone through them for the sake of fat cats like Mr. Edward Ballaskia and his sanctified dreams of evil.

Nor, when you came right down to it, for dismal little frightened trollops like Polly.

Frederick Stoddard Stephanson. Frederick Stoddard—

Somebody put an arm on his shoulder and he came to, realizing that he was halfway through the lobby.

"Nick," said a rather familiar voice.

Crandall squinted at the face at the end of the arm. That slight, pointed beard—he didn't know anyone with a beard like that, but the eyes looked so terribly familiar. . . .

"Nick," said the man with the beard. "I couldn't do it."

Those eyes—of course, it was his younger brother!

"Dan!" he shouted.

"It's me all right. Here." Something clattered to the floor. Crandall looked down and saw a blaster lying on the rug, a larger and much more expensive blaster than the one he was carrying. *Why was Dan toting a blaster? Who was after Dan?*

With the thought, there came half-understanding. And there was fear—fear of the words that might come pouring out of the mouth of a brother whom he had not seen for all these years . . .

"I could have killed you from the moment you walked into the lobby," Dan was saying. "You weren't out of the sights for a second. But I want you to know, Nick, that the post-criminal sentence wasn't the reason I froze on the firing button."

"No?" Crandall asked in a breath that was exhaled slowly through a retroactive lifetime.

"I just couldn't stand adding any more guilt about you. Ever since that business with Polly—"

"With Polly. Yes, of course, with Polly." Something seemed to hang like a weight from the point of his jaw; it pulled his head down and his mouth open. "With Polly. That business with Polly."

Dan punched his fist into an open palm twice. "I knew you'd come looking for me sooner or later. I almost went crazy waiting—and I did go nearly crazy with guilt. But I never figured you'd do it this way, Nick. Seven years to wait for you to come back!"

"That's why you never wrote to me, Dan?"

"What did I have to say? What *is* there to say? I thought I loved her, but I found out what I meant to her as soon as she was divorced. I guess I always wanted what was yours because you were my older brother, Nick. That's the only excuse I can offer and I know exactly what it's worth. Because I know what you and Polly had together, what I broke up as a kind of big practical joke. But one thing, Nick: I won't kill you and I won't defend myself. I'm too tired. I'm too guilty. You know where to find me. Anytime, Nick."

He turned and strode rapidly through the lobby, the metal spangles that were this year's high masculine fashion glittering on his calves. He didn't look back, even when he was walking past the other side of the clear plastic that enclosed the lobby.

Crandall watched him go, then said "Hm" to himself in a lonely kind of way. He reached down, retrieved the other blaster and went out to find a restaurant.

As he sat, poking around in the spiced Venusian food that wasn't one-tenth as good as he had remembered it, he kept thinking about Polly and Dan. The incidents—he could remember incidents galore, now that he had a couple of pegs on which to hang them. To think he'd never suspected—but who could suspect Polly, who could suspect Dan?

He pulled the prison discharge out of his pocket and studied it. *Having duly served a maximum penal sentence of seven years, discounted from fourteen years, Nicholas Crandall is herewith discharged in a pre-criminal status—*

—to murder his ex-wife, Polly Crandall?

—to murder his younger brother, Daniel Crandall?

Ridiculous!

But they hadn't found it so ridiculous. Both of them, so blissfully secure in their guilt, so egotistically certain that they and they alone were the objects of a hatred intense enough to endure the worst that the Galaxy had to offer in order to attain vengeance—why, they had both been so positive that their normal and already demonstrated cunning had deserted them and they had completely misread the warmth in his eyes! Either one could have switched confessions in mid-explanation. If they had only not been so preoccupied with self and had noted his astonishment in time, either or both of them could still be deceiving him!

Out of the corner of his eye, he saw that a woman was standing near his table. She had been reading his discharge over his shoulder. He leaned back and took her in while she stood and smiled at him.

She was fantastically beautiful. That is, she had everything a woman needs for great beauty—figure, facial structure, complexion, carriage, eyes, hair, all these to perfection—but she had those other final touches that, as in all kinds of art, make the difference between a merely great work and an all-time masterpiece. Those final touches included such things as sufficient wealth to create the ultimate setting in coiffure and gown, as well as the single Saturnian *paeaea* stone glowing in priceless black splendor between her breasts. Those final touches included the substantial feminine intelligence that beat in her steady eyes; and the somewhat overbred, overindulged, overspoiled quality mixed in with it was the very last piquant fillip of a positively brilliant composition in the human medium.

"May I sit with you, Mr. Crandall?" she asked in a voice of which no more could be said than that it fitted the rest of her.

Rather amused, but more exhilarated than amused, he slid over on the restaurant couch. She sat down like an empress taking her throne before the eyes of a hundred tributary kings.

Crandall knew, within approximate limits, who she was and what she wanted. She was either a reigning post-debutante from the highest social circles in the System, or a theatrical star newly arrived and still in a state of nova.

And he, as a just-discharged convict, with the power of life and death in his hands, represented a taste she had not yet been able to indulge but was determined to enjoy.

Well, in a sense it wasn't flattering, but a woman like this could only fall to the lot of an ordinary man in very exceptional circumstances; he might as well take advantage of his status. He would satisfy her whim, while she, on his first night of freedom—

"That's your discharge, isn't it?" she asked and looked at it again. There was a moistness about her upper lip as she studied it—what a strange, sense-weary patina for one so splendidly young!

"Tell me, Mr. Crandall," she asked at last, turning to him with the wet pinpoints on her lip more brilliant than ever. "You've served a pre-criminal sentence for murder. It is true, is it not, that the punishment for murder and the most brutal, degraded rape imaginable are exactly the same?"

After a long silence, Crandall called for his check and walked out of the restaurant.

He had subsided enough when he reached the hotel to stroll with care around the transparent lobby housing. No one who looked like a Stephanson trigger man was in sight, although Stephanson was a cautious gambler. One attempt having failed, he'd be unlikely to try another for some time.

But that girl! And Edward Ballaskia!

There was a message in his box. Someone had called, leaving only a number to be called back.

Now what? he wondered as he went back up to his room. Stephanson making overtures? Or some unhappy mother wanting him to murder her incurable child?

He gave the number to the set and sat down to watch the screen with a good deal of curiosity.

It flickered—a face took shape on it. Crandall barely restrained a cry of delight. He did have a friend in this city from pre-convict days. Good old dependable, plodding, realistic Irv. His old partner.

And then, just as he was about to shout an enthusiastic greeting, he locked it inside his mouth. Too many things had happened today. And there was something about the expression on Irv's face . . .

"Listen, Nick," Irv said heavily at last. "I just want to ask you one question."

"What's that, Irv?" Crandall kept himself rock-steady.

"How long have you known? When did you find out?"

Crandall ran through several possible answers in his mind, finally selecting one. "A long time now, Irv. I just wasn't in a position to do anything about it."

Irv nodded. "That's what I thought. Well, listen, I'm not going to plead with you. I know that after seven years of what you've gone though, pleading isn't going to do me any good. But, believe me or not, I didn't start dipping into the till very much until my wife got sick. My personal funds were exhausted. I couldn't borrow any more, and you were too busy with your own domestic troubles to be bothered. Then, when business started to get better, I wanted to prevent a sudden large discrepancy on the books.

"So I continued milking the business, not for hospital expenses any more and not to deceive you, Nick—really!—but just so you wouldn't find out how much I'd taken from it before. When you came to me and said you were completely discouraged and wanted out—well, there I'll admit I was a louse. I should have told you. But after all, we hadn't been doing too well as partners and I saw a chance to get the whole business in my name and on its feet, so I—I—"

"So you bought me out for three hundred and twenty credits," Crandall finished for him. "How much is the firm worth now, Irv?"

The other man averted his eyes. "Close to a million. But listen,

Nick, business has been terrific this past year in the wholesale line. I didn't cheat you out of all that! Listen, Nick—"

Crandall blew a snort of grim amusement through his nostrils. "What is it, Irv?"

Irv drew out a clean tissue and wiped his forehead. "Nick," he said, leaning forward and trying hard to smile winningly. "Listen to me, Nick! You forget about it, you stop hunting me down, and I've got a proposition for you. I need a man with your technical know-how in top management. I'll give you a twenty per cent interest in the business, Nick—no, make it twenty-five per cent. Look, I'll go as high as thirty per cent—thirty-*five* per cent—"

"Do you think that would make up for those seven years?"

Irv waved trembling, conciliatory hands. "No, of course not, Nick. Nothing would. But listen, Nick. I'll make it forty-five per—"

Crandall shut him off. He sat for a while, then got up and walked around the room. He stopped and examined his blasters, the one he'd purchased earlier and the one he'd gotten from Dan. He took out his prison discharge and read it through carefully. Then he shoved it back into the tunic pocket.

He notified the switchboard that he wanted a long-distance Earthside call put through.

"Yes, sir. But there's a gentleman to see you, sir. A Mr. Otto Henck."

"Send him up. And put the call in on my screen as soon as it goes through, please, Miss."

A few moments later, Blotto Otto entered his room. He was drunk, but carried it, as he always did, remarkably well.

"What do you think, Nick? What the hell do you—"

"Sh-h-h," Crandall warned him. "My call's coming in."

The Tibetan operator said, "Go ahead, New York," and Frederick Stoddard Stephanson appeared on the screen. The man had aged more than any of the others Crandall had seen tonight. Although you never could tell with Stephanson: he always looked older when he was working out a complex deal.

Stephanson didn't say anything; he merely pursed his lips at Crandall and waited. Behind him and around him was a TV Spectacular's idea of a hunting lodge.

"All right, Freddy," Crandall said. "What I have to say won't take long. You might as well call off your dogs and stop taking chances trying to kill and/or injure me. As of this moment, I don't even have a grudge against you."

"You don't even have a grudge—" Stephanson regained his rigid self-control. "Why not?"

"Because—oh, because a lot of things. Because killing you just wouldn't be seven hellish years of satisfaction, now that I'm face to face with it. And because you didn't do any more to me than practically everybody else has done—from the cradle, for all I know. Because I've decided I'm a natural born sucker: that's just the way I'm constructed. All you did was take your kind of advantage of my kind of construction."

Stephanson leaned forward, peered intently, then relaxed and crossed his arms. "You're actually telling the truth!"

"Of course I'm telling the truth! You see these?" He held up the two blasters. "I'm getting rid of these tonight. From now on, I'll be unarmed. I don't want to have the least thing to do with weighing human life in the balance."

The other man ran an index nail under a thumb nail thoughtfully a couple of times. "I'll tell you what," he said. "If you mean what you say—and I think you do—maybe we can work out something. An arrangement, say, to pay you a bit—We'll see."

"When you don't have to?" Crandall was astonished. "But why didn't you make me an offer before this?"

"Because I don't like to be forced to do anything. Up to now, I was fighting force with more force."

Crandall considered the point. "I don't get it. But maybe that's the way you're constructed. Well, we'll see, as you said."

When he rose to face Henck, the little man was still shaking his head slowly, dazedly, intent only on his own problem. "What do you think, Nick? Elsa went on a sightseeing jaunt to the Moon last month. The line to her oxygen helmet got clogged, see, and she died of suffocation before they could do anything about it. Isn't that a *hell* of thing, Nick? One month before I finish my sentence—she couldn't wait one lousy little month! I bet she died laughing at me!"

Crandall put his arm around him. "Let's go out for a walk, Blotto Otto. We both need the exercise."

Funny how the capacity for murder affected people, he thought. There was Polly's way—and Dan's. There was old Irv bargaining frantically but still shrewdly for his life. Mr. Edward Ballaskia—and that girl in the restaurant. And there was Freddy Stephanson, the only intended victim—and the only one who wouldn't beg.

He wouldn't beg, but he might be willing to hand out largesse. Could Crandall accept what amounted to charity from Stephanson? He shrugged. Who knew what he or anyone else could or could not do?

"What do we do now, Nick?" Blotto Otto was demanding petulantly once they got outside the hotel. "That's what I want to know—what do we do?"

"Well, I'm going to do this," Crandall told him, taking a blaster in each hand. "Just this." He threw the gleaming weapons, right hand, left hand, at the transparent window walls that ran around the luxurious lobby of the Capricorn-Ritz. They struck *thunk* and then *thunk* again. The windows crashed down in long, pointed daggers. The people in the lobby swung around with their mouths open.

A policeman ran up, his badge jingling against his metallic uniform. He seized Crandall.

"I saw you! I saw you do that! You'll get thirty days for it!"

"Hm," said Crandall. "Thirty days?" He pulled his prison discharge out of his pocket and handed it to the policeman. "I tell you what we'll do, officer—Just punch the proper number of holes in this document or tear off what seems to you a proportionately sized coupon. Either or both. Handle it any way you like."